Also by Malcolm Macdonald

The WORLD FROM ROUGH STONES
The RICH ARE WITH YOU ALWAYS
SONS OF FORTUNE

These are Borzoi Books, published in New York by Alfred A. Knopf.

ABIGAIL

The life and love

Abigail

Malcolm Macdonald

a Victorian girl

Alfred A. Knopf　New York 1979

THIS IS A BORZOI BOOK
PUBLISHED BY ALFRED A. KNOPF, INC.

Copyright © 1979 by Malcolm Macdonald
All rights reserved under International and Pan-American Copyright Conventions. Published in the
United States by Alfred A. Knopf, Inc., New York, and simultaneously in Canada by Random
House of Canada Limited, Toronto. Distributed by Random House, Inc., New York.

Library of Congress Cataloging in Publication Data
Macdonald, Malcolm, [1932]
Abigail.   I. Title.
PZ4.M13485Ab   1979   [PR6063.A1692]   823'.9'14   79'–392
ISBN 0–394–50492–5

Manufactured in the United States of America
First American Edition

For Candida
Thursday's child
a Leo from Virgo

PART ONE

The Old Fountain, 1868

Chapter 1

There was a secret—something to do with men and women. Grown-ups knew it; and servants knew it, too. At least, Annie certainly did. And since servants were more vulnerable than other adults, Abigail decided that Annie was going to yield this secret.

It happened one winter day in London when Abigail went out to pay a call in the carriage. The horse cast a shoe, and she sent the coachman, Dilks, to have it reshod while she paid her call. Knowing Dilks' fondness for a drop, she sent Annie along to keep him out of mischief.

In the coachman's case the trick had worked—he had taken drink all right, but not enough to show any effect. But poor Annie, who had matched him glass for glass, and who lacked his practised capacity, had well and truly lost the edge of her sobriety.

At first, Abigail did not realize that this was her chance. The Secret was far from her thoughts. The whiff of gin shocked her. She turned on the maid: "Annie, you've been drinking!"

The girl giggled, but Abigail could see that she was terrified. That terror halted her; she was caught between the righteousness of her anger and what she imagined was a tolerant worldliness.

She had been angry with servants before, of course, but always as a child of the house. Here the situation was hers to be mistress of—but what sort of mistress? Stern, pious, unbending? Aloof and condescending? She had never been either of those. Tolerant worldliness—a weary worldliness—seemed the most inviting, and the most like her.

"Why on earth do you drink gin?" she said. "It's such a tipple."

Annie smiled weakly with relief. "I didn't want to," she said. "But I thought I'd stand a better chance o' gettin' who's'sname, Dilks, out the public if I went in with him like, my lady."

The thought of such forbidden behaviour made Abigail wistful. "Isn't it funny, Annie—you can be so free and yet I'm like a prisoner."

The maid giggled again. "It's 'cos you got to keep your jewels, isn't it!"

"But I haven't come out with any jewels."

Annie clapped her hands and screamed with laughter. Abigail, feeling acutely shut out, wished she had played the stern, unbending mistress when she had the chance.

That was when she remembered The Secret. Suddenly she knew that Annie's laughter was about The Secret. Here was her chance to find out. She smiled in a way that she knew would provoke the girl first to silence and then to curiosity: a smile of pleasure relived.

"Oh, Annie," she asked, "did you ever let a man kiss you?"

"Did I!" Annie chuckled. "I should just say so." Then, remembering why she was there, she asked with tipsy sternness: "And who, may I ask, has been a-kissing of you, my lady?"

Abigail smiled complicitly. "Oh come, where's the harm?"

"Harm! Where's the harm! Don't you know the harm?"

"A little kiss? A few kisses? A few tender embraces? I can see no harm in that."

"Hah!" Annie exploded. "That's how it begins. But we all know where it may lead, your ladyship."

"I'm sure *I* don't, Annie. A few more kisses, and a few more?"

"Ah—and *then!*"

"Yes, Annie? And *then?*"

"Then they've got you."

"Where?"

"Right where they want you."

"What nonsense!" Abigail was disappointed. The Secret evaporated as fast as they uncovered it.

Annie looked at her uncertainly. "You mean you really don't know? No one never told you?"

"They might have, and I might have forgotten."

Annie laughed. "Not that, you wouldn't. Well, here's a pickle, I must say."

"What?"

"Well, I don't think it's right, being in ignorance. Dangerous, I'd call it." She looked at Abigail again. "Straight? You really don't know?"

"I don't believe you know either, Annie. You're just pretending."

Annie grinned wickedly. "If I was to say, 'He worked the hairy oracle' . . . If I was to say, 'He put Nebuchadnezzar out to graze' . . . If I was to say, 'She's seen the elephant . . . got jack-in-the-bush . . . been shot twixt wind and water' . . ." At each circumlocution she looked at Abigail for some spark of recognition. But Abigail's bafflement merely revived the comedy in the words—a comedy that usage had long since staled. Annie laughed. "Why, you ain't got no idea what I'm on about, have you!"

Abigail seethed with resentment. Most annoying of all, the words seemed so rich in meaning, making her feel that she hovered at the very rim of enlightenment. Something within her—something below or beyond the reach of conscious thought—actually understood what Annie was driving at. That unreachable part of her would not be surprised at whatever new truths were about to emerge.

Annie was suddenly glum. "Strike me! I don't know as if I should tell you."

"I'll never tell anyone of it if you do."

"God's honour? If Lady Wharfedale was to hear . . ."

"I'll never breathe a word." Abigail leaned forward, smiling eagerly to encourage the girl.

"Well . . ." Annie sniggered. "It's what men and women best like doing together. And boys and gels. And lords and ladies, I don't doubt. It's your national indoor game, the four-leg frolic, taking on beef. . . . You sure you don't know, my lady?"

"Not these words. Do get on, Annie. Why d'you beat about the bush so!"

Annie laughed uproariously. "You could say that," she added. "Beat about the bush! Oh yes! You could say that all right." Then seeing Abigail's anger, she went on hastily: "It's when men and women get off their clothes and lie together. *Now* d'you know?"

Abigail stared at her, openmouthed. She *did* know! Or part of her did know. Part of her was surfacing with that knowledge, leaving the rest of her aghast.

"You know how we're different from them? Well—put that difference together. There now—I can't say it nicer."

"Difference?" Abigail said—though, of course, she knew the difference. On their holidays in Connemara she and her eight brothers and sisters had always swum au naturel. She knew the difference very well.

"Where we go in, they . . . stick out. Put it together."

"But why?"

Annie smiled, not at her young mistress but at something a hundred miles away. "I daresay it's the greatest fun we ever have."

"But you said it was dangerous."

The word brought Annie back to the here and now. She clutched at Abigail's arm. "And so it is, my lady. For that's how we make new feet for baby stockings. What passes then from them to us at such times is what quickens us."

Abigail gulped audibly. "Like *animals!*"

"Yes, of course." Annie looked affronted. "You said you never knew."

"Well, I knew about animals, naturally." She gazed out at the passing houses—those houses her mother's property firm had built, the houses she despised so heartily—and a new element of horror was suddenly added to them.

For now she saw those thin, fallen-chested clerks and their pasty, adenoidal wives lying naked side by side in all those mean upstairs rooms, doing what bulls and cows did, doing what stallions and mares did, and daring to say—like Annie—that it was the greatest fun they ever had. It was . . . loathsome, noisome . . . noxious. It was vile.

She looked back at Annie, bearer of these dreadful tidings. "Have you—did you—ever?" she asked, blushing hotly.

Annie licked her lower lip uncertainly. "Is it truth you want, my lady? Or a servant's answer?"

"A servant should always be truthful."

Annie laughed bitterly. "And there's many a servant gel now walking the streets for no more than a telling of the simple truth."

Walking the streets! The full meaning of that phrase now struck Abigail. One saw the girls everywhere, of course—or rather, one saw them and did not see them. They were never discussed, yet were constantly written about in the newspapers. The Social Evil. The Great Evil. So that's who they were! Dismissed servant girls who, having nothing to lose, had abandoned themselves to "the greatest fun we ever have"!

"Well, I shall never dismiss you for telling the truth, Annie," she said.

Annie considered the promise before she continued. "I was born in Hackney, my lady. Our dad was a billposter, which pays about half a farthing above portering. We were in and out the workhouse all our lives and when we were out, like as not we'd have a room, just one room, for all ten of us—and we'd have to keep a lodger, or starve. Sometimes we starved even with a lodger."

"But my mother said you came from an orphanage."

"That's right, my lady. When a family goes into a workhouse, the father goes to the men's, the mother to the women's, and the young 'uns to the orphanage. Last time we was in was ten months. I never seen our dad, nor—"

"But how dreadful! Your parents simply abandoned you? They made no attempt to see you?"

"Course they didn't! It would've been death to them."

"Death!"

"They'd've been slung out, wouldn't they? And never no more let back."

"Just for trying to *see* you?"

"Or each other. I've heard tell of a soft work'us over the river where men and wives may speak through iron gratings six foot apart, that they may not touch, but I never did see it."

"Oh, Annie!" Abigail involuntarily clutched the girl's hand and squeezed it. "I had no idea."

"Huh!" Annie was bragging now. "We were like kings compared to some. But to answer your question, my lady, when ten shares a room they cannot keep secret what has been kept secret from you until now. Nor may they preserve the jewels such as you have preserved."

Luckily for Abigail it was several days before Annie's meaning broke through the still-considerable mists of bafflement and semiunderstanding. She was thoughtful and silent for so long that Annie eventually had to say, "I hope but what I did right, my lady. Speaking as I did."

Abigail fixed her with the most earnest gaze and said, "I want you always to tell me the truth, Annie. I intend to be a writer, as you know. And there are so many things to find out that I cannot find out in books. Like these things you have told me. I need to know them all."

Annie smiled and relaxed, promising she would always tell the unvarnished truth when it was demanded of her.

At that moment they happened to be passing down Piccadilly, near the end of their journey home. To test this new resolve, Abigail pointed at all the gaudy women who are seen and not seen. "These—creatures," she said. "They are what you're talking about, too."

Annie looked out at them with something in her eye that was neither contempt nor envy but a bit of both. "That's the money side of it," she said.

"Money?"

"They go with gentlemen, they do what the gentlemen like, and the gentlemen pay them. That's the way of it."

"Oh." Abigail was feeling weak at this surfeit of revelation.

"Half hour from now," Annie said, pointing at a girl who had just taken on a man, "that gel—that blowsabella, as we call them—will be richer by as much as I earn in a week—maybe two weeks."

"But *why!*"

"Makes you think, don't it!"

"I don't understand it."

"Men go mad to lift a gel's skirts. There's times when they'd do anything to get across us. Why, in my last place . . ." She glanced nervously at Abigail, wondering if perhaps honesty might already have reached its bounds for today.

But Abigail was looking out of the carriage window in disgust. "You mean that—that girl doesn't know that man? Has never seen him before?"

"Probably not."

"Oh, but how dreadful! How *can* she?"

"As long as there's gentlemen prowling like the wolves they are, she can."

"Gentlemen? What gentlemen? What do *you* know of gentlemen? I have been to many dances with gentlemen and have talked for hours with gentlemen of every kind at my mother's salons, and never have I received so much as a hint of any of this. I begin to doubt all you have told me now."

Annie smiled tolerantly. "Not to *you*. Of course they wouldn't show it. But where d'you think they work it off! They try to get about us servants in dark corners. And they come down here to the West End. And the East End. And North and South Ends, too, if there are such places. For there's gay women and gay houses everywhere."

"Stop it!" Abigail commanded. "I don't want to hear any more of this."

She was trembling and unaccountably near to tears as she ran up the front steps of Hamilton Place to the secure and, she fancied, innocent warmth of her mother's drawing room.

Chapter 2

Her mother was busy, as always. She was either at her property company, or at her banker's, or sitting on the committee for this or the committee for that—or sometimes, on a whim, she would even take the train down to Maran Hill, their country place near Hertford, and surprise the servants there. Abigail, alone in the drawing room at teatime, ate a little cinnamon toast, drank a small cup of China tea, and then went up to her room.

There she read the entire manuscript—all one hundred and thirty pages—of a children's story she was writing; and as she finished each page she crumpled it and threw it in the wastepaper basket. This was by no means the first such orgy of destruction; indeed, she had lost count of the number of times the manuscript had swelled to a respectable, serious thickness only to dwindle again to a mere sheet or two.

But there was a difference between this and previous orgies: On those earlier occasions she was destroying evidence (as it had seemed to her) of her own incompetence or lack of inspiration; this time she was acknowledging something far greater—the passing of her own innocence, or naïvety, as she now saw it to be. Her life, her perception of life, would certainly never be the same from this day on; so her writing had better make a new start, too.

At heart, though, it was the same perfectionism that drove her, then and earlier, to destroy; for Abigail was a perfectionist of the very worst kind—the pessimistic kind. For all that she was only eighteen, she had no illusions about the world and people. The world, she knew (had always known), was mean and shoddy; people would always let you down—in the end, *everyone* would let you down. Her search for perfection was thus a kind of terror; when small things went wrong she read their failure as an omen that the ultimate disappointments were about to descend upon her. So by eradicating those small imperfections she kept the larger ones at bay.

No one understood it. The received wisdom in the family was that Abbie behaved as she did out of a kind of inferiority: If she demanded only the best, she imagined the world would overlook her own imperfections. Only Winifred, the eldest, sensed that the true reasons lay deeper, that Abigail was in some way merely justifying herself to herself; the world's opinion did not come into it.

When Abigail had begun writing her story, the previous year, Winifred had been her most admiring and encouraging reader. And Abigail, for her part, had been so astonished at such praise—for Winifred was by nature most sparing of praise (as any girl in her school, or any teacher on her staff, would vouch)—that she became absurdly dependent on Winifred's visits and Winifred's encouragement. But the praise was heartfelt. Winifred truly (and, as later events showed, rightly) believed her sister's tale was the product of a delightful and original talent.

But not all the praise nor all the encouragement she could lavish would prevent Abigail from destroying a page that was not—to her mind—perfect.

"*Why?*" Winifred would ask furiously when she discovered that some passage she had admired was now no more.

Usually it was because something—a phrase, or even a single word—had displeased Abigail.

"Then cross it out. Write over the top. Use a different colour ink."

"No!"

"You don't have to scrap the whole page."

"I do."

"I'm sure you'd find Dickens' manuscripts, or *any* writer's manuscripts, a mass of crossings out and misspellings and corrections."

"But not *mine*."

"No! Not *yours!*" Winifred's scorn—so effective on everyone else—rarely worked on Abigail. "At this rate you'll never finish," she said once.

"Life is long," Abigail answered.

"No dear. That's Art. *Ars longa, vita brevis*. Life is the short one."

"Vita Brevis! What a splendid name for a character! She'd be a fizzy, bubbling girl, wouldn't she! She'd depart from every scene trailing gorgeous cataracts of fire and laughter, leaving everyone else a bit flat . . . giving them the feeling that the real fun will be wherever she's going next—don't you think?" And she laughed.

Privately Winifred thought that was just the sort of girl Abigail would love to be.

Fortunately Abigail was not at all perfectionist in her destructions. She did not tear her rejected pages into little shreds but merely crumpled and discarded them, leaving them for the maids to pick up.

It was toward the end of the summer of 1864, when Winifred was first setting up her school, The Girls' College, Highgate, that she entered a conspiracy with the maids to salvage these crumpled sheets and give them to her whenever she called in at home. But for that subterfuge, Abigail's book would never have been finished, much less published.

And the course of their lives would have been quite different.

Chapter 3

In 1863 Highgate was a remote village, as far out of London as Hampstead. In fact, both villages, Hampstead and Highgate, stood at opposite ends of that long, high ridge which defined every Londoner's northern skyline. Healthy and bracing, it reared above the dreadful pea-soup fogs that could clamp down around the smoke of a million coal fires and choke even the chirpiest cockney spirit. And when summer filled the bowl of the city with the stink of sewage (and with the fear of its pale horseman, cholera), the village of Highgate rode in the fresh country air that topped the miasma. "As healthy," Winifred told the girls' parents, "as the Yorkshire dales."

In that first summer of 1864 there were a lot more parents than there were, finally, girls. When people heard that Lady Winifred Stevenson was about to start a new boarding school for girls, they flocked to enrol their daughters. True, Lady Winifred was only twenty-three years old; but she was by all accounts a remarkable young woman. Her mother, the Countess of Wharfedale, was one of the leaders of London Society—or rather, since London has dozens of societies, a leading patron of artists, musicians, and men of science. She was forever in the papers and the ladies' journals.

Her father, too, was an extraordinary man. Now the Earl of Wharfedale, he had started life as plain John Stevenson, a railway navvy, from which level he had risen to become the most notable civil-engineering contractor in the country before he had entered public life. He was always sitting on commissions or running the most delicate and secret errands for the government. The ideal nonparty man, he had the ear of every prime minister. The Prince Consort, they said, used to listen more to him than to anyone. They also said (excusing themselves for venturing on a topic so vulgar) that the Earl was one of the richest men in the world—and that the Countess, Nora, was even richer, though she, too, had started from very humble origins.

And on the academic side (which, of course, one must not entirely forget—even in the education of girls), Lady Winifred had taken all the honours in the Cambridge public exams. Moreover, she had taught for a while at Cheltenham Ladies' College under no less a person than Miss Beale. All in all, Lady Winifred had everything in her—and her new college's—favour.

To be sure, there *was* an ugly whisper about a rather protracted visit to France the previous year—no one knew why . . . and she certainly had not been seen in French Society at that time. But then you know how people's tongues love to wag, especially to devise a scandal where there is none.

And her fees, at £15 a year, were surprisingly modest.

So people flocked to enrol their daughters. But to their annoyance, they found a school that, in every particular, either failed to meet, or ran absolutely (one would almost say wilfully) counter to, their expectations.

"But you do teach the accomplishments?" one exasperated father was moved to ask after Winifred had outlined the Highgate curriculum.

She suppressed a sigh, knowing she had already lost this parent. Nothing short of the complete reversal of all she believed in would bring his daughter to Highgate.

"Accomplishments?" she asked.

"Yes. Needlework, you know. Watercolours. Flowers. Foreign lingos. That sort of thing."

"We certainly teach foreign languages. Up to six hours a week, in fact. And most girls will do an hour's needlework and an hour at art study."

"An hour! I had expected, Lady Winifred, that you would say a *day*. If not two days."

"No, Mr. Dale, an hour. There is no time for more."

Dale looked at the printed curriculum in his hand. "Forgive me, Lady Winifred, forgive me for saying this, but it does very strongly resemble the curriculum for a boys' school, don't you know."

"Better, I hope, Mr. Dale. I doubt a boys' school would devote six hours to French and German. Or seven to mathematics. Or five to natural history. Or only three to classical studies."

Dale sighed. "It is a very . . . *modern* . . . er—I—"

"It was Edmund Burke," Winifred intervened, "who said 'a great empire and little minds go ill together.' " She held him pinned with her stare. "The girls of Highgate will be the wives and mothers of the leaders of our empire, Mr. Dale. To fill their heads with stitchery and coloured daubs would be ill-preparation indeed for such a role. . . ."

"I almost had him then," she told her mother that evening. "He distinctly wavered."

"Of course he did," Nora answered. "It is a very good point."

"I have won several parents with it—you know, people who come looking for a cheap way to turn out and finish off their middle-class missies, and who presume—"

"But not Mr. Dale?"

"No. I could see a sort of terror in his eye as he realized there might actually be something in the argument. He didn't know what to do then. Should he bring on this girl to be fit for an imperial match . . . or would that be to risk being left with a pert, assertive, forward hussy whom no man in his right mind would marry?"

"And of course he is right, dear," Nora said solemnly. "A spinster daughter past marrying age is a terrible burden for many parents."

Winifred laughed. "You speak from experience!"

Nora grinned smugly, half closing her eyes.

"May I have a peach?" Winifred asked.

"You still have room? After all you ate at dinner?"

Winifred weighed the peach undecidedly, as if she had not considered whether she was actually hungry.

"Don't let yourself run to fat, dear," Nora said, serious again. "You used to be so beautiful and slender."

"You mean"—Winifred would not join in her seriousness—"if I eat as I like, then I never will marry!"

"No. Do it just for your own sake. I hate all these indolent, *spreading* women. They're only half alive, most of them. They leave me exhausted just to look at them."

Winifred sighed, but she put back the peach. "You have the best chef in London, they say. How do you stay so *thin?*"

"But that is the whole point of having a good chef. If one is to eat only morsels, each one must tell."

"I think Steamer has plans to entice Anton from you."

"Caspar! He'd never dare." But the suggestion alarmed her. Caspar, her young son, now master of half the family business, usually got what he wanted. "Besides, he and Linny already have an excellent cook."

"But not for this absurd palace they are planning. The latest count is two hundred and eighty rooms, you know. With a whole suite for a chef. That's not going to be for their present cook, however excellent she may be."

"Anton would never leave." She didn't want to talk about it any more. And Winifred, who was driven enough by her own ambitions to be quite insensitive to those of others—insensitive enough to mention the possible loss of London's finest chef as a topic of mere passing interest—unconsciously obliged her. "Would you say," she asked, "that I am pert, or assertive, or forward?"

"Yes."

"Oh."

"But you're a headmistress. And a member of the aristocracy. You'd be failing if you were *not* the dreadful person you are."

Winifred laughed and shook her mother's arm. "I meant it as a serious question."

"Oh? Are you wondering then why you're not married?"

"You know why. Until women may have property independently of their husbands, I could not risk . . ."

"I know, dear. I will try to be serious. Why did you ask?"

"I mean, even the most honourable and best-intentioned husband could be bankrupted through no fault of his own, and then my school would . . ."

"I know." Nora did not repeat her long-standing offer to set up the school as a trust so as to remove this barrier to Winifred's possible marriage. She knew that from the moment the girl had decided to give her life to teaching, she had put aside all thought of marriage. This business about married women's property, though true enough, was a justification she kept, so to speak, at the front of her mind, to stifle any deeper questioning of her motives. "Why did you ask if you were forward?"

Winifred did not at once answer. The street noises began to intrude—the clip-clop of horse hooves, the ring of iron tyres on cobblestones. Someone at Apsley House was ill and the servants had put out straw and rushes to deaden the racket. With your ear, and your mind's eye, you could follow a vehicle up from Hyde Park Corner, then lose it as it fell into that sound-limbo of straw, then pick it up again as it dwindled away along Piccadilly.

"Oh dear," Winifred said ruefully. "Here we are, barely begun, and already I'm beginning to doubt the wisdom of what I'm doing."

"Be thankful for that. It's when you cease to doubt that you should—"

"Thank you, Mama dear. Very proper and correct. But I mean real doubt. Not a casual sort of 'I wonder—hum-hum.' "

"Why? In what way?"

"It's my argument with Father all over again—you remember when I first went to teach at Cheltenham? He hated the very idea of my teaching, but if I had to, then he wanted the work at least to be honorary. And of course I didn't *need* the money, so it was very hard to put a convincing argument against him. And I think even Miss Beale was a little contemptuous of me for taking a salary. But I *had* to. You understand, don't you?"

Nora smiled, like one who avoids a trap. "I understand why *you* felt you had to take a salary."

"And you agreed!"

"Since you felt so passionately, I agreed it was right for you. But I would not have condemned any other girl for taking a different course."

Winifred's laugh conceded the unprofitability of this line. "You'll never come down off that fence, I suppose."

"Not until it's rewarding to do so. Or expedient. I'm not much moved by the moral argument. But I know you felt that if you turned the work of teaching into a sort of honorary hobby, you'd be taking bread out of—"

"The point is," Winifred cut in eagerly, "that three out of every four teachers are women. Most of them are daughters of tradesmen and artisans. They need the money. No! It isn't money. Money isn't that important—it's only a barometer. What I mean is that teaching is one of the few honourable ways a woman has to an independent life."

"Lots of women keep shops."

"One shopkeeper in five, if you want to be precise. And they start with capital, or an inheritance or something. I'm talking about *women*. Womankind. Not a lucky few. Teaching—the teaching *profession*, if that doesn't make you laugh—is our Trojan horse. It's going to be the way up for countless women. Up onto a plateau from where we'll spread outwards into other jobs. There are ninety-five thousand office clerks in this country—d'you know how many are women? Three hundred! Yet there's over three and a half million women at work up and down the land—and you know where most of them are: wherever there's muck and no money!"

"And in some obscure way," Nora challenged, "this impressive display of statistical research has led you to have second thoughts about your curriculum?" She let her tongue linger on her lip. Secretly Winifred the Campaigner always excited her. All her life Winifred had been a solemn, studious, earnest girl—frequently childish in the way that only highly intellectual people can be childish; but she always took care to master a subject before she spoke of it to others. And on any subject she had mastered she was always impressive—in that unanswerable way which frightened off potential husbands by the sackful.

"Yes—no! Well, in a way. What I mean is that more and more women of the artisan and tradesmen's classes are going to get education and independence. It can't be long now before we have universal and compulsory schooling for all children. My God! We'll be the last civilized country to do so. Already the schooling given to girls of the lower classes is vastly superior to the useless mixture of mindless accomplishments and trivia drilled into middle-class girls at vast expense. What I'm saying is that this country will soon face the paradox of having a discontented and angry regiment of well-educated women of the poorer classes—and where may they look for a lead, eh? To the ignorant, fatuous, empty-headed hoydens who are allegedly their social superiors?"

The point of Winifred's argument suddenly struck Nora. "But," she said, aghast, "what you wish to do, then, is to educate girls of good class into that same state of anger and discontent!"

"Exactly!" Winifred said excitedly. Then she sank her head into her hands and repeated, in despair, the selfsame word: "Exactly!"

"You tell the parents this? *Before* you take their fees?"

"Some."

"You mean, I suppose, that you tell the ones who you know already agree with you!"

"I tell everyone exactly what sort of daughter they may expect to get back. They must draw their own conclusions."

"But is that fair? You have given the subject a great deal more thought than they. It's a kind of intellectual bullying."

"If they're too stupid, or too lazy, or too impressionable to see where the choice may lead, is it *my* duty to guide them?" Winifred broke into laughter even before she had finished speaking, for she knew she had picked exactly the argument her mother would find unanswerable. To make the point doubly certain, she added, "Caveat emptor—let the buyer beware—surely. In education as in everything else."

"Well . . ." Nora dipped her head, conceding. "We seem to have resolved your ethical doubts at least."

Winifred's face fell. "Not at all. It's the *girls*, don't you see. I have no qualms about the parents. But the girls . . . Here is young Jane, who could be taught embroidery, dancing, music, and sketching, and grow up frivolous and empty-headed, and marry a gay hussar, and lead a life of mindless domestic tranquility. Or I can teach her, first that she *has* a mind (which most girls find hard to believe of themselves), then how to use it, and she will grow up to be contemptuous of most other women (or pitying—which is as bad). She will suffer them badly, and frighten the men and dogs and horses, and in general be a thorough misfit."

Nora would have had no such qualms. To her the happiness of Winifred was worth ten thousand other blighted lives. "It is not your concern," she said with vast assurance. "They are their parents' responsibility as far as that choice goes."

"I haven't told you the nub of it yet. The real point is that if women—women as a *class*—are ever going to change their station—our station—we are going to need thousands of such misfits. Need their intellect, their money, their social position, their contempt or pity for their sisters—and, not least, their ability to frighten men and other animals. Their discontent will be the steam to drive our engine forward. From station to station." She laughed at her own pun, but with little humour.

"Not a school, but a hotbed of discontent," Nora said.

"A seedbed of Womanism!"

"Whatever that may be."

"Yes. I often wonder what it's going to be." This time her laugh was genuine.

At that moment Abigail came in, so innocently that Winifred's eyes narrowed at once. "Have you been eavesdropping?"

"You bray like Stentor. It's hard to avoid." She took the peach Winifred had earlier toyed with. "Anyway, I see no dilemma."

"Oh?" Winifred was torn between a desire to have someone—anyone—lay out an answer to her ethical doubts, and a lifelong unwillingness to accord any wisdom whatever to her younger sister.

"Yes. Who says the average ill-educated girl is happy with her gay hussar? Only three-decker novelists. And what's wrong with discontent? Especially if it leads you to *do* something. You've swallowed the very notion of happiness you reject as the proper goal for a modern woman!"

Nora laughed and clapped her hands. Abigail had not one-tenth of Winifred's persistence or intellectual rigor; she could never master a subject with that utter thoroughness of Winifred's. But every now and then she had these flashes of insight that were worth a year of plodding inquiry. Even now, as she spoke the words that would surely banish all of Winifred's qualms, she seemed much more interested in skinning the peach without getting its juice all over her.

Winifred stared at Abigail, mouth open, testing her words for flaws and finding none.

"Cause and effect," Abigail said absently, still working fastidiously at the peach skin. "If the cause is right, we must pursue it with all our heart, and leave the effects to God."

Winifred stood and ran across the room to her sister. "Abbie! You angel! You are so very, very right, of course!" And she hugged her.

Abigail looked at the spilled peach juice on her arms and Winifred's hands. "*Some* of the effects, anyway," she said solemnly.

Chapter 4

The heavy rain was a mere squall at the leading edge of the shower. Abigail stood beneath the cedar, halfway up the driveway to Winifred's school, and watched it pass, a filmy sheet of gray falling with a tender slowness on slate roofs and among bare branches. It unfurled wetness on Parliament Hill, over Gospel Oak, Tufnell Park, Kentish Town . . . on into London. The names, not the cold, made her shudder: those ghastly suburbs, filled with ghastly houses, all built and rented by her mother. Worth eight million one day soon, she said. Abigail wouldn't have given a penny for them, those awful furnished tombs where lives were whiled away in furtive cheeseparing and carefully graded public show.

A few nights ago, when Winnie had spoken of those foolish qualms to their mother, the vision of domestic bliss that had presented itself to eavesdropping Abigail was the loathsome one-percent life in those pinched, meanly grand houses of her mother's where men and women behaved like bulls and cows. It seemed absurd that anyone could have qualms about rescuing girls from such a destiny. She had wanted to say as much, but thought it would hurt their mother, and so had made her point another way.

The light shower followed the rain down the hill to London. Patches of blue showed between the clouds, but of the sun there was no sign. In that cold, blue light everything seemed to be made of pewter or lead. Abigail looked around before lifting her skirts ever so slightly to step out over a patch of mud at the edge of the drive. But at that moment she became aware of someone else, also sheltering under a branch. The tree was a large, spreading cedar and the other person, a girl of about her own age, was at the farther end of its shade. She came smiling toward Abigail.

"You could paint it all with chalk and soot," the girl said. "But I wouldn't advise it. Not here. Don't let them catch you painting here!" She laughed and took Abigail's arm, walking her toward the school. "You're new, aren't you? Well, of course, we all are. But you are very new. I am Celia Addison."

"I am Lady Winifred's younger sister Abigail."

Celia dropped her arm at once.

Abigail smiled. "But that doesn't mean I'm her spy. I'd treasure anything scurrilous you may have to say about her. Have you an older sister, Celia?"

"Yes." Celia smiled too.

"Then you'll understand, I'm sure."

Celia laughed and took Abigail's arm again. "Don't say you've come here voluntarily! Was she always such a gorgon, at home I mean?"

"Gorgon?"

"Oh yes, everyone here goes in dread of her, you know. Aren't you all terrified of her?"

"Well, that's interesting, but hardly scurrilous."

Celia shrugged. "I suppose that means she isn't. It's so hard to imagine her as anyone's sister. Or daughter either. I've always thought of Lady Winifred as having come into the world already fully grown. Do you go to school? How old are you, Abigail?"

"I was eighteen at Christmas."

"I'm going to be eighteen this summer."

"We had a tutor. He was drunk most of the time, but he was also a very brilliant man. Winnie and he used to talk Latin and Greek—conversations, you know—when she was twelve."

"Winnie!" Celia dared only to whisper the name. Then she giggled. "It's devastatingly unimaginable!"

"He doesn't teach *me* now. Only the younger children. I just read all the time. Read and read and read. I adore it, don't you? I read anything. I want to read the whole of English Literature before I'm twenty. I do three books a week. In summer I can do five when there's more light."

Still arm in arm they walked past the old house—once a private asylum—that formed the nucleus of the Girls' College. The path stopped abruptly at a river of clay mud, the demarcation line between building workers and girls.

"We're allowed to come as far as this, but we have to turn back at once," Celia said.

Abigail appeared not to hear her. "These are our own workers building this, I suppose you know. My mother calls it my father's 'penance.' He's paying all the wages and costs."

Celia looked in agitation at the old house, at Lady Winifred's window. "Why 'penance'?" she asked, tugging Abigail's arm.

But Abigail did not move. "There, now I've told you something disreputable about her. You owe me that."

"Come on!" Celia said. And only when Abigail, at last, began to move back toward the house, did she relax herself sufficiently to add: "What's disreputable? I don't understand that at all."

"Our father wanted her to marry. A foul, detestable young man, too. And when she refused, he kidnapped her and sent—"

"The awful young man?" Celia asked.

"No! The Earl. Her father. He kidnapped her from my mother's house—because the Countess took her part, of course—and he sent her away to an odious private prison in France, an *école corrective et tempérante*. But in the end he had to relent, because all Winnie ever wanted to do was teach. Now he's building the school for her. It's like a sort of penance, isn't it?"

Celia stopped in the middle of this story and stared openmouthed; then her eyes narrowed: "Are you making it up?"

"Of course not." Abigail was annoyed. "If I was, d'you think I couldn't do a lot better than that?"

Celia, afraid of that anger, took Abigail's arm again and squeezed it. "Of course I believe you. How exciting it must be to have such stormy lives. You are lucky. My mother's greatest dramas are about when to go from black to purple mourning or who took a quarter pound of cheese from the pantry!"

"And your father?"

"Papa doesn't have dramas. His lips go white and he takes his hat, his coat, his leave, and a cab." They both laughed. "That's what my brother Peter always says. I'd adore you to meet him, he's such great fun!"

Abigail, who had stiffened at this trespass on their slight intimacy, forced herself to relax. *You have to meet lots of people*, she told herself. *Every writer has to.*

"But fancy Lady Winifred refusing an offer of marriage!" Celia went on. "I'm sure I'll never have such a chance. I'll have to take whoever offers."

Now it was Abigail who stared openmouthed. "But why?"

"Because both Papa and Mama say it is so. There's a great surplus of females, they say. The men have the pick now, and we shan't get two chances—we may not even get one."

Abigail pulled her arm from Celia's grasp. "You fool," she shouted, stamping her foot in anger. "You stupid fool!"

Celia looked back at her in horror at this sudden reversal of mood; then she burst into tears and ran away.

A sash window screeched up. It left a black space in the red brick. And there, framed in that black, was Winifred. "Abigail. Will you come in here, please," she commanded. She hauled the protesting window down again without waiting for an answer.

Abigail smiled at the wizened rose hips and rusty heads of shrivelled hydrangea that bordered her way to the private front door.

"Where is your chaperone?" Winifred asked at once.

"I made them wait by the gate."

"They should first have delivered you to the door. That is quite unforgiveable."

"I wanted to walk."

Winifred made an angry face. "*Want?* What you want has nothing to do with it. You just mustn't get into the habit of sending whoever is chaperoning you away—however justified the errand. You mustn't get the reputation for doing that sort of thing."

"Sorry, Winnie." Abigail smiled disarmingly. "I felt the chances of being socially compromised on the front drive of the Highgate Girls' College were fairly slender."

"It has nothing to do with being socially compromised."

"With what, then?"

Winifred coloured. "If you don't know, just take it on trust."

That blush and the heightened pitch of Winifred's voice alerted Abigail: This was part of The Secret! My God, that's what they were afraid of! That's what all this chaperoning was for! To stop her and some man from "putting the difference together," or "letting Nebuchadnezzar out to graze" (whatever that meant). How little they knew her!

Winifred went on: "What did you say to upset young Celia Addison like that?"

Abigail sat on a stiffly upholstered and very upright chair. "How can you live in this fireless cell! Miss Celia Addison upset me, as a matter of fact."

"So you struck back as only you know how."

"It is her view that every girl is obliged to marry the first man who asks her, because women are in a surplus. Is that true?"

"Yes. There are between half and three-quarters of a million more of us. That's another reason why it's so important not to compromise your reputation."

Abigail closed her eyes and shook her head; but it was a gesture of pity, not of defiance. "I could have the pick of two dozen," she said. "And I'll turn them all down. And silly little Celia would take *anyone*." She laughed bitterly. "Life may be hard, but some people don't do much to soften it for themselves, do they!"

Winifred smiled, trying to keep any hint of patronage out of her voice. "How can you possibly know that! You could be swept up tomorrow."

"I know I won't be. The same way I know if I like strawberries or not. Or if I really believe in God. Or if a page is worth keeping or crumpling. It's only *your* kind of knowledge one acquires. All the really important knowledge one is born with."

Winifred glared at her, trying to be angry; but in the end she burst into unwilling laughter, looking guiltily over her own shoulder as she did so.

"Oh, Abbie, Steamer always says how easy it is to *become* angry with you, and how difficult to *stay* angry."

"I can't think why." Abigail shrugged, unable to handle the compliment—indeed, uncertain that it was a compliment.

The carriage drew up outside.

"For the same reason that one cannot sustain one's anger at a child. What are you going to do when you grow up?"

"Grow up some more, I hope."

Winifred sighed with half-despairing humour and then grew serious once more. "When you say you won't marry—I hope that has nothing to do with *my* decision not to marry?"

Abigail puckered her face in a would-be wicked grin. "To be sure, it has not. We are like Mr. Dangle and Shakespeare—two minds hit upon the same thought, and Shakespeare made use of it first, that's all."

"Because it would be extremely silly if that were the case. I have every good reason for staying unattached."

"So have I. Excellent reasons, if you must know."

"Yes," Winifred said firmly. "I would very much like to know."

Abigail was suddenly flustered. She had not meant to open up the subject at all. "The book," she said. "Lord knows when I'll finish that."

Normally it would have deflected Winifred; any mention of the book made her eager. But not this time; now she sensed something bigger and more important behind Abigail's assertion—and her confusion. She stared Abigail out, making her speak again.

"I don't want to have anything to do with *men*," Abigail said defiantly.

"Oh? Why not? This misanthropy is something new. What are you reading at the moment?"

Abigail tossed her head. "That has nothing to do with it. It's simply that I've found out—something."

"What?"

"I've found out—that I just don't want to marry. That's all."

Winifred smiled, greatly relieved. "Oh! Well if that's all!"

This direct devaluation of what Abigail considered the most profound and permanent decision of her life stung her into saying what she would otherwise never have said: "I've found out why men and women are—as they are. Why they are different. And I think it's appalling."

Winifred's smile vanished, replaced by a great pity, deep and tender. She rose and came quickly to her sister, taking her by the hand. Later she thought of all the things she ought to have asked—like, "How did you find out . . . ?" "Who told you . . . ?" "In what circumstances . . . ?" and so on. But Abigail's appealing eyes and the thinly masked terror in her words put such practical thoughts from her. All she could think to say was, "You mustn't let it affect you like that, darling. Don't think of it like that."

Abigail was astounded. The possibility of any other response had not even occurred to her—even though Annie had called it "the greatest fun." Annie was working class; her opinions and judgements counted for less than nothing.

"How else *can* I think of it!"

Winifred shook her head, still in pity. "Is there no one?" she asked. "Do you feel no—especial—I mean, at a ball for instance, is there no young man for whom . . . "

"I prefer older men. Their conversation is more intelligent."

Winifred laughed, trying to wean Abigail from her wide-eyed solemnity. "And older men prefer you?"

"Yes! They do."

"For the same reason? Your conversation?"

To give time for the notion to sink in, Winifred went to the door, opened it, and looked up and down the corridor. It was an empty gesture; no one, girl or teacher, would dare even to loiter there, much less to eavesdrop.

Abigail was speechless.

"Surely," Winifred said, "even you never supposed it was for the profundity and breadth of your conversation?"

Abigail was too dry in the mouth to answer.

"It's the way people are, darling," Winifred said gently. "Wait until you're a bit older."

"People?" Abigail croaked. She swallowed, and licked her lips. "You mean people like us?"

Winifred nodded.

"You?"

"Only in thought, of course. Anything else is out of the question. But if a scullery maid may dream of Cinderella—and probably be a better scullery maid for it—I suppose an old maid of a head-mistress, or even a *young* maid, come to that, may dream of—of a Great Otherwise. And be the better for it, too. You'll see. When you're older."

Abigail retreated from her. "I'll never feel other than I do now," she said. "I'm sick just thinking of it."

Winifred smiled a wistful concession. "Well, my life would be a great deal easier if I could feel as you do."

But then the importance of the thing would not permit her to leave it at this easy half truth. She had to add: "Yet I doubt I'd be a better *person* for all that. Because what we are talking about, darling, is love."

Abigail turned toward the door. "I must go," she said.

Winifred, not wanting to part on so abrupt a note, nor so solemn a subject, said, "In any case, I don't suppose you came here to talk about this."

And Abigail, having been made to feel small and very much the little sister, said, "No. In fact, Mother asked me to come. She wants to know about your new building and about how many men Father has working here."

A curious look came over Winifred's face, more of resignation than annoyance. "Tell her she needn't send you spying. If Father goes back on his word—or even falters in keeping it—I'll let her know soon enough."

Abigail, glad of the change of subject, said, "That wouldn't suit our mother, and you know it. She trusts nothing she learns indirectly. The other day she asked me the time, but when I told her, she had to get out her binoculars and see what the clock on Lord Astley's mantelpiece over in Park Lane was saying. *Then* she believed me. Steamer is just the same."

Winifred gaped at her. "Really?" she asked. "Did she really do that?"

Abigail threw up her arms in mock despair and turned on her heels. "Of course she didn't," she said as she went out to the carriage. "Till next week then."

Halfway down the drive they passed the cedar tree under which she had sheltered; Celia Addison was there again. Abigail stopped her carriage and leaned out.

"Not crying?" she asked cheerfully. "Why when I was your age, Miss Celia, I could cry for three days without ceasing."

Celia, uncertain at first, broke into laughter. "Will you come here again?" she asked. "Shall I see you?"

"Next week."

* * *

But they did not meet the following week. The things Winifred hinted at so disturbed Abigail that she began to wake up in the small hours with the feeling of a great dark weight upon her, a sense of unremembered nightmare. The muscles of her body tensed as if to flee some unseen, unheard, unknown pursuer; yet all she could hear was the night silence; all she could touch was the familiar bric-a-brac of her room. She would lie there shivering, and she wondered what oppressed her so.

At the end of the week she did what she had always done in a time of crisis: she went to her brother Caspar.

Dear Steamer!

Only dear Steamer was no longer comfortably near, in his room down the corridor. Dear Steamer was building a vast palace in the Cotswolds, eighty miles away.

Chapter 5

Falcon Wood is a mainly Georgian house, built in the northern Cotswolds by the same John Wood who, with his son, built the grand houses and crescents of the city of Bath. Its severely classical lines, rising to a completely undecorated pediment straddling the eight Ionic columns of the entrance portico, did not please Caspar. The whole building was wrong. Its public rooms were too many and too huge; its private rooms too cramped and awkward. Vast and draughty stone staircases swept grandly up to a point where they vanished from the visitor's sight, whereupon they immediately dwindled to something mean—marble balusters were supplanted by limestone of the same design and hue; alabaster panels turned to painted stucco; real pillars soared to an entablature and then continued as cast pilasters. Even in the painted vertical frieze that flanked the monumental Adam fireplace in the ballroom the same principle of economy was employed, for the vines teemed with butterflies and scarabs to exactly eight feet above the floor, but the remaining twelve feet of vegetation displayed not a single insect.

"A dishonest bit of building from an age of barbarism and sham," Caspar had said even before he and Caroline had bought the place. "We'll pull it down and build afresh."

But Caroline (remembering that her father was not expected to live and that her mother would almost certainly leave Caer Gwent, her family's monstrous and depressing home in South Wales, as soon as she could) had persuaded Caspar that Falcon Wood might yet serve a purpose.

"We may need a dower house," she said. "And for a dower house Falcon Wood is quite fair. In any case, this valley is too small for a really grand house. Why not build our new place in that valley we rode through yesterday? It's much broader." And when Caspar still looked dubious, she dug him in the ribs and said, "Surely in eight and a half thousand acres we can find some suitably large valley?"

"But what shall we call it then?" Caspar objected. "If this house still exists, everyone will go on calling it Falcon Wood. I like that name."

"We'll call the new place Falconwood," she said simply; and then she watched Caspar's face as the idea took hold—watched his bewilderment give way to a smile, and the smile turn to laughter.

"Linny! You're a marvel! It's superb."

"It will sort out the sheep from the goats, anyway," she said contentedly. "The world will divide into people who know Falconwood is not Falcon Wood"—she favoured this group with her right hand, as if her thumb and finger felt fine silk cloth—"and people who don't." With her left hand, she dismissed this group into the dark.

Caspar hugged her and laughed again. "Only you could have thought of it," he said, without much exaggeration.

*   *   *

Abigail and her maid Annie came by train as far as Stroud, where Caspar's carriage was waiting.

"Is my brother at home or at the new building?" she asked the coachman.

"At the new building, my lady."

"Take me there then." She was annoyed at having forgotten the man's name.

The first part of the journey—about five miles—lay along the valley bottom, all the way to Nailsworth. In summer it was closed about in deep green shade; a hot silence seemed always to pervade these leaf-hung lanes. But today, with winter only just beginning to loosen its grip, all was the colour of stone and bark and bright gray sky—bathed in a cold, pellucid light that fell evenly from every quarter, illuminating everything but taking from it all sense of weight and solidity. It might have been a landscape of painted drapes and thin mist.

She said nothing of Annie's recent tipsy revelations. The shock of them had gone too deep within her for any of its ripples to reach the surface. Outwardly she was unchanged; but inwardly *all* was changed—the world and all the people in it. They had gained a new dimension. Before, people had been simply different from one another: this one fat, that one slender, another jolly, another sour . . . commanding respect . . . worthy of pity . . . provoking annoyance . . . enlisting friendship . . . all different. But a new gloss had come to unite them, and in some way to narrow that wide diversity. They *all* did that thing Annie had told her about.

Since then she had looked at people and tried to imagine it. The mechanics of the action were not clear. She thought they must stand motionless as people stand when they kiss. (Lord—would she ever be able to kiss again!) She did not realize that they needed to move.

In the end it was not the images of others that disturbed her, but the image of *herself* in that situation. It was an unthinkable violation to allow that—that *maleness* to possess her. Worse—it was actually frightening. At least, she took the tremors induced by the thought as the tremors of fear. Maleness was rough, like sandpaper; hard like boxers' fists and footballers' knees; strong, like navvies' arms; and arrogant, like her father, like Steamer, like all men.

She would never let it possess her. Or so she vowed. Yet the evidence of the world was entirely against her. People did this thing. Even archbishops and their wives, even the Queen before the Prince Consort's death. How could she hope to escape? That was why she had come to Caspar; he would know what's what.

Beyond Nailsworth stretched the part she had come to think of as "The Ends"—Tickmorend, Downend, Nupend, Barton End, Tiltups End. "Well, Steamer," she had told Caspar when he first brought her this way, "at least no one can complain that the journey to Falcon Wood is endless."

"Steamer" was a school nickname that had stuck into adulthood because it seemed so much more apt than the baptismal "Caspar." He *was* a steamer—busy, noisy, thrusting, unstoppable. Yet when he did stop (of his own accord, naturally) he seemed as immobile, as dead, as an engine off the boil. The bustle of activity was so normal to him that any pause seemed like torpor itself.

Her first view of him on this afternoon, up on the tops of the Cotswolds, where the cold winds tugged at hair and clothing, showed him with his back to her, framed between a piledriver and a temporary site hut, trying to clutch at plans, fighting for them with the wind, while he gestured away down the valley, spotting-in the covert and copses, the rides and lakes, that would one day embellish its sheep-cropped sides.

"What?" she called. "The house not up yet? For shame, Steamer!"

The wind and his own absorption had kept the sound of the approaching carriage from him. He turned with a wide, welcoming smile and ran to help her down. His architect, Nick Thornton, snatched the plans into safekeeping.

Side by side, partly in the lee of the site hut, brother and sister ran satisfied eyes up and down the landscape.

"It's the only valley on the whole estate whose northern side faces the sun at exactly half past two of an afternoon," he said.

"You told me that last time."

"But we shall have to plant twelve thousand trees a year for the next ten years to get anything halfway decent in the way of a view."

She almost whistled but the wind had dried her lips.

"That's forty trees every working day," he went on. "Do you know how many different kinds of tree there are?"

"No." She loved it when Steamer was out to impress her with facts.

"Nor do I. It would greatly help us if, when you return to London, you could pop over to Kew and find out."

She groaned aloud at the idea—but even more at the knowledge that she would, indeed, do as he asked. She never refused him. It was part of the unspoken pact between them.

"Hello, Nick," she said at last. Her delay had been a deliberate tease.

"Good afternoon, Lady Abigail," he said, not seeming to mind her afterthought greeting.

All her life she had been plain "Abbie" to him—until she came out, and until he had begun to work for Caspar on Falconwood. She did not like the change, but she was beginning to see why childhood friendships could not persist unaltered into maturity.

At that moment a thought came that almost felled her on the spot. More of a picture than a thought. A picture of herself and Nick "putting the difference together," in Annie's delicate phrase. But it was different from all the other pictures, for Nick was moving . . . *rutting*, like a boar.

Even now, here on the windswept hilltop, his eyes gleamed, boarlike, as he shook her hand.

The gleam was replaced by concern. "Are you all right?" he asked.

She recovered swiftly. "I must have been sitting too long." She grabbed Steamer's arm. "Take me around and show me how it's all changed since I was last here," she commanded.

He showed her how they had decided to double the size of the fountain and bring two grand marble steps around each side, "like Versailles," he said.

"What are they digging?" she asked, pointing to where she knew the kitchens would one day be.

"The wine cellar and, below part of it, the hydraulic cellar, deeper still."

"Oh, good," she said. "I meant to ask about that last time. I saw no provision on your map for a hydraulic cellar and I'm sure every decent house should have at least one, don't you?"

He sniffed coldly, not rising to it. "A map of a house is called a 'plan,' " he said.

She laughed. "Steamer! For goodness' sake, what *is* a hydraulic cellar?"

"It will power a big platform—lift it to any floor. Hydraulically. All the luggage and furniture and laundry and hot water and food trolleys will go up and down by it. But if we build it first, we can even use it to help in the building—carry all the materials we need."

She was delighted at the idea. "Oh, pike I!" she begged.

"What?"

"Pike I be first to ride up on it."

He shook his head. "If I know our pater, he'll be first. It was his idea. We're casting the cylinders ourselves—building the whole engine, in fact."

But she had already transferred her interest. "Is that where you're going to put all these trees?" she asked, pointing down the valley. "There's quite a lot there already."

"But they're all in the bottom. I want lakes along the bottom. And I want to see them from here; so I want the trees higher up the slopes and on top."

"But nature put them at the bottom. Don't you think there may be a reason? Mayn't it have something to do with shelter from the wind?"

Caspar laughed pityingly. "The whole point of being human, my love, is to teach Mother Nature tricks she never dreamed of. It was Nature who made ponies; *we* turned them into horses. My latest thing is electricity. I'm going to bury two-inch-diameter copper bars under all the floorboards. We'll pension off the night."

"Electricity?"

"One of these days, and soon, someone is going to invent a practical kind of electric light, and it will be much cheaper and cleaner than gas. A fine mess it would make to rip up all the floorboards then! Oh, Abbie, there's so *much* to think of."

She saw that he was trying to look harassed, and she laughed. "You love it!" she said.

"I can only spend two days a week at it, you see: Fridays and Saturdays. That's the trouble."

"You *love* it."

"Why did you come, Abbie? Is anything the matter at home?"

"Should there be?"

"Is Father pestering Mother?"

"He knows better than that. Why should you think something's wrong?"

They strolled among marker pegs labelled BALLROOM . . . GUN ROOM . . . BILLIARD ROOM . . . BACHELORS' STAIR . . . SCULPTURE GALLERY . . . VALET-DU-JOUR, seeing only Cotswold turf and Cotswold mud.

"I've found out," she said at last.

"Found out what?"

Their rambling had brought them close to the site hut and the carriage. Even though no one was in view, it was too close for comfort.

"Something," she said.

"Oh *good!* I can't tell you how glad that makes me." He laughed.

"After dinner I'll beat you at billiards," she said. "If we may be alone, I'll tell you then."

*   *   *

At dinner Caroline was very scathing on the subject of electricity.

"Dr. Collins says it will be most injurious to have these currents swilling to and fro beneath us and overhead as we sleep," she told Caspar.

"Oh?" Caspar pretended to take it seriously.

"It'll create magnetism that will interfere with our own magnetism."

"My dear, we already live and breathe, and sleep, in a magnetic field several thousand times stronger than anything our conductors will produce."

"You may. I'm sure I don't. I would feel it."

"So would I," Abigail said. "I'm *very* sensitive to magnetism."

Caspar smiled at Nick and shrugged. The gesture annoyed Caroline, not only for its implied patronage of her ideas, but also because she considered that Nick, being an architect, should eat in the servants' hall, not at her table—never mind his being an old family friend.

Abigail noted these undercurrents and relished them, for they helped restore an ancient conviction that she was above and outside the passions which moved the rest of mankind. Her own rages and delights were of an altogether different order.

Toward the end of dinner, when conversation turned yet again to the plans for Falconwood, she even risked a little dart of her own.

"By the way," she said casually, "I saw no provision on your plan for a newspaper-ironing room. Such a pity."

"Newspaper-ironing room?" Caroline asked.

"Yes. Louise Beaumont was telling me. Apparently it all started with the Prince Consort—in the year before he died, he took a strong objection to having folded newspapers delivered to the breakfast table. He insisted the footman should iron them first. And now all the royal residences have newspaper-ironing rooms. I thought Falconwood could be the first private house with the same accommodation."

"Oh, Abbie, you *treasure!*" Caroline was delighted as she turned inquiringly to Nick.

"The menservants' bootroom," he said, "could go out into the corridor, leaving that room at the foot of the menservants' staircase free. I don't suppose it takes much space to iron a newspaper."

Thus Abigail became the founder of an entirely spurious fashion. But it served Steamer right—the way he went on about Falconwood and all its wonders.

Later, in the billiard room when she was one frame up and well into a break of forty, "despite these ridiculously hampering clothes," as she pointed out, Caspar again asked her what was wrong.

She smiled and sank the red ball in the far pocket with a convincing thwack! "I feel a bit of a fool, Steamer. When I wired you, I was in a somewhat state. But I seem to have weathered it."

"Was it important?" He put the red back on its spot.

"Not really. Well . . . yes. Yes, it was. I found out about men and women—and, you know, babies."

The red shuddered between the cushions guarding a pocket and failed to sink. But Caspar did not give his usual cry of mockery. He did not move from where he was.

"Your ball," she said. And when he continued to stare at her she asked, "What?" For his look was almost that of a prosecutor.

"D'you remember the Christmas before last we were all at Maran Hill? And you came and told me you'd found out about the pater's mistress? That girl called Charity? And you said he had children by her?"

"I didn't."

"Pardon me, Abbie, but you did. You said the children were 'only Stevensons by charity'!"

"It was only a way of speaking. Good heavens—did you think I knew how such things happened *then?*"

Her vehemence and obvious sincerity shook him, for he had been sure, then and since, that Abbie knew.

"You really didn't?" he asked.

She ran and threw her arms about him. "Oh, Steamer! I had no idea what you would say. Or even how I could bring myself to tell you. And it's so easy, isn't it?"

"How did you find out? Who told you?"

"Never mind. That's not important. A girl at a dance. She had a headache and I played the Miss Nightingale. It was quite dark. And confidences always come more easily then, don't you find?"

This piling up of irrelevant circumstantial detail sounded convincing, she hoped.

"Well!" He broke free and addressed the cue ball again. "So now you know . . . everything!"

"And she told me such quaint phrases, too, Steamer! 'Putting Nebuchadnezzar out to graze' . . . 'seeing the elephant' . . . 'the four-leg frolic'!"

She laughed, hoping he would laugh too, both as a relief and as a welcome into the grown-up world. But he paused in mid-shot and fixed her with a piercing stare. "I see!" was all he would say.

Twenty points further into his break he said, "You read a deuce of a lot, Abbie. What—for instance—did you think *Othello* was all about?"

Abigail pondered a while. How strange that until this moment she had related her new-found knowledge only to the actual world. As if the world of literature were hermetic and guided by different laws of behaviour and motive.

"To tell the truth," she said, laughing at herself (for it was the truth), "I always thought it much too much ado about nothing. To go and strangle your wife merely for lending your handkerchief to a friend!''

When their laughter died she said, "Steamer, is it really the best fun ever?"

To her dismay she saw that the question embarrassed him acutely. "You really shouldn't ask," he said. Too coolly. "It will be time enough for such knowledge when you marry."

"I shall never marry."

He smiled provokingly. "Then it need never concern you."

Suddenly she hated him. He was marvellous when he talked to her as equal to equal; but when he became superior like this he was . . . offensive. Like Winnie when she played big sister.

"Don't think I shan't try to find out," she warned.

He slammed the cue down upon the table. The tip leapt from it in an explosion of chalk dust. She had not seen him so angry in a long time. "You would," he choked, fighting to master himself.

She would do anything to placate him now, to stop this terrifying anger. "I was only hitting out," she said, "because you keep such secrets. I wouldn't really try."

He became a little calmer. But when he grasped her shoulders she could still feel him trembling. "Oh, but you would," he said, as much rueful as angry. "*You* would. Out of curiosity—or to spite someone—or simply through being swept away. You, of all people, my love, you would." He looked around as if for aid or comfort. "What to do?" Annie had looked about her in just that way before letting out The Secret.

She wanted to say, "Spike my curiosity," but she knew that if the suggestion came from her, he would never act on it. Instead, in a breathless voice, full of hollow sincerity—well-meant enough but hollow—she said, "I wouldn't, Steamer. Truly now, I just *know* I wouldn't."

The empty frailty of her vow persuaded him. Still he held her shoulders. "Listen, love. You're going to have to grow up rather early, for a girl of your class. I'm going to have to trust you with information that is normally kept only for married ladies, or ladies of a certain maturity. But it is to save you from any experiment that might damn you forever."

She squirmed in his grip and looked back at the table, implying she would far rather be going on with the game. But of course—and as she had intended—the gesture only made Caspar the more determined to speak out.

"It is, as you call it, 'the best fun ever.' For women, too, whatever learned doctors may say to the contrary. More than fun. A kind of intoxication. A delirium. All the high-flown love poetry you've ever read is a pale echo of—a mere hint." He smiled and the tremble left his voice; now that the ice was breached, the unthinkable could be thought, the unsayable said, quite easily and calmly. "Difficult to believe? I have known it since I was thirteen. Not because I am in any way cleverer, but because men grow up differently—men *are* different. With men, our passions are all on our sleeve. Simple. Even a bit mechanical. It prevents us from ever really becoming noble, of ourselves, of our own accord. It's as if we must always look for a light ahead to guide us, a pattern to copy, a better example. In other words: women. So a woman, both in her upbringing and in her very nature, is different, is purer, is nobler—of herself and of her own accord. That is why this knowledge is not for her, at least until she marries. For she has a darker, more earthy, less noble side to her nature—every woman, I mean. You have it, though I'm sure you aren't remotely aware of it yet."

She noticed that his eyes strayed from her face during these last few words. Did he fear to see a denial there? she wondered. She wanted to assure him it was true: She had no such side to her nature. Yet, paradoxically, his utter assurance affronted her—so much so that she felt like shouting aloud: "It's not true! I feel it just as you do!"

"Funnily enough," Caspar went on, "it was Nick's father—Uncle Walter, I mean—who made it clear to me. He caught us, Nick and me, gawping at the fallen women outside the station in York." Caspar edited and bowdlerized the memory for her; Walter had actually caught them doing more than merely gawping. "I'll never forget it. He told us how a woman's nobility, her purity, was like a lighthouse to a man in the storms and tempests of life; and so it is something doubly precious—to her, and to him. Only the very worst kind of man trifles with it and sullies it. Because it is a very short step from being pure to being polluted; it can be five minutes' work. But once it's done, it can never be undone. The polluted woman can never find her way back to purity."

"What about Mary Magdalene?"

Caspar was puzzled. "Well, she was *saved*, I suppose. Yes, of course she was. But she was never made pure again." And when Abigail frowned, as if about to argue, he added, "In a religious sense I'm sure she was patched up as good as a saint. But I'm talking about Society. Forgiveness is God's business, not Society's, or it would all fall to bits, wouldn't it? No. Believe me—once a woman has crossed that narrow line, there's no way back."

"And men?"

He smiled. "Sinners all, I fear." He took a new cue and began to assess the lie of the table. "But it don't signify, Abbie, dear love. It don't signify. We bear no children. Our father's bastards, as you so wittily said—and before you even understood what you meant—our father's wayside oats are 'only Stevensons by charity.' They'll never assume any legal relationship to us."

Next morning, while Abigail was out riding, he sent Annie home to London, carrying a letter to his mother, Lady Wharfedale.

Chapter 6

Not until the day after her return to London did Abigail notice Annie's absence.

"Where's Annie?" she asked her mother.

Nora met it head on. "I'm afraid there was no question of her continuing in our service," she said.

For a moment Abigail did not understand. "She gave notice?"

"I dismissed her."

"But why?"

"You know very well why."

Abigail stared at her, numb at the shock of her dawning understanding. "She told you?"

"In the end. There was no point in her trying to deny it."

"You threw her out?" Abigail asked, and then answered herself with the same words, now accusatorial: "You threw her out." A third time, now with anger, she repeated the words: "You threw her out!"

For one frightened moment Nora thought the girl would hit her; but she stood her ground. "Of course I threw her out. And of course she expected to be thrown out. She made less of it than you are now—"

"When?" Abigail interrupted.

"The moment she returned."

"Steamer's letter!" she exploded. "He made her carry her own death warrant!"

Nora laughed, not feeling the least humorous but wanting to show Abigail how absurdly she was magnifying things. "Death warrant!"

"Yes! A death warrant. To cast a young servant girl out on the street without a character is a death warrant. What do *you* know of poverty!" she sneered, forgetting that her mother had grown up in circumstances every bit as low as those Annie had described (or, rather, not exactly forgetting, but *choosing* to forget).

Nora knew that even Abigail, even in the grip of this anguish, would realize that her last taunt was too wide of its mark to measure; so, instead of venting the anger she felt, she put her head on one side and smiled tolerantly, letting time do its work for her. She hoped some of the fight would then go out of the girl.

But it did not. If anything, she grew even more pugnacious. "How did Steamer know?" she shouted. "I didn't tell him. What did I say? It must have been something I said. I gave her away. It's my fault. It's *my* fault!"

With a weary anger born of ten thousand such clashes, Nora stifled an impulse to grasp her daughter by the shoulders and shake her until the brain rattled, to stop that brew of venom and self-disgust from reaching the boil. The girl was so pretty, so talented—she could have such a marvellous life if only she would let go, drift a little, be more accepting of things.

It was too late. Nothing could stop that boiling over. Nothing had ever been able to stop it. Abigail ran, white-faced and tight-lipped, from the room, seeking the anodyne of activity to crowd out the accusations that pressed upon her mind from every angle. Nora's cry to the footmen followed her down the marble stair. Flutelike echoes of it swept the galleries as a footman, also too late, ran to bar the door. Abigail, hatless and gloveless, was already striding up Piccadilly.

Half a mile she went, beyond Burlington Arcade, before she could admit the futility of it. Her hopes turned every girl along the street into Annie—from a distance; close to, they became caricatures, not of Annie, but of the *thing* to which Annie had been reduced. Portraits in henna, powder, and rouge. Her disgusted spirit shrank from all contact with them; it turned within, banking up the accusations: *your fault . . . your fault . . . your fault.*

How had Steamer learned? What had she said to make it so clear to him? A few unguarded words—even one unguarded word—would be enough, for he was quick to grasp such hints. No one kept secrets long near him.

And what would she not give now to unsay their whole conversation, to unvisit Falconwood. Why had she gone there anyway? What good had it really done? It was the action of a child. When would she grow up and learn some sense?

She became aware that she was attracting attention; a young gentlewoman out in a busy and fashionable part of London without hat, gloves, or chaperone—it was enough excitement to make the day for most of those who saw her and to wind up their tongues for a week. She looked around at that sea of inquisitive, uncaring city faces and felt something close to panic. She stepped backwards off the pavement.

A man, a gentleman, more kindly than the rest, came toward her, opening his mouth and squaring himself to speak. But the voice came from somewhere above her head: "Why, Miss A!"

The day darkened. Things were no longer quite real. The advancing gentleman looked up and beyond her. "You know this young lady, sir?" he asked.

She turned to face the gleaming, varnished cliffside of a phaeton. The coat of arms was familiar. And the voice.

"I do, sir. Thank you for your interest."

Lord Culffe, a family friend—or, rather, since it was years since they had been anything you could call a family, a friend of her father's.

"Well, here's a coincidence," Lord Culffe said. "I'm on my way to meet your father. Step in."

His two grand white muttonchop whiskers hung toward her like the prongs of a pitchfork. Years ago, she remembered, when her father had still been plain John Stevenson, they had seemed even larger and grander; his lordship had dandled her on his knee and let her tug at them gently. And she had disgraced herself and almost ruined the family by tugging at one and imitating the flushing of a water closet. It had seemed exquisitely funny to her eight-year-old mind—until she had glanced up into those terrifying eyes. Then she had curled up in an embarrassment that still had the power to make her cringe. Did he remember any of it now? She was sure he did. Sometimes all you could ever remember about a person was one searing, shocking thing. Usually an insult.

While she hesitated, one of her mother's footmen came breathlessly up with her hat, cloak, and gloves. Now she had a choice—to walk straight home, or to accept Lord Culffe's invitation. Her freedom not to do so made it easy to accept.

"I'm to meet Lord Wharfedale at the Admiralty and take him on to Westminster," Lord Culffe said. "The coach can take you home from there." And when she was settled opposite him, he said, "Well here's a young lady who has grown!"

Their talk, all the way to the Admiralty, barely strayed above that level of banality. He was well mannered enough not to ask why she had been in Piccadilly in that state; it was the same instinctive good manners that had made him, despite his surprise, identify her as "Miss A." Not even "Lady A."

Her father was in good spirits. She could tell it even when he and Lord Culffe were still a hundred yards off, for he trod with a lightness that belied both his fifty-odd years of age and his giant frame. At one point he stopped, said something to Lord Culffe, clapped him on the shoulders, and the pair of them gave a laugh that put up every pigeon in Charing Cross.

"Lady Abigail, your servant." Her father was laughing as he got in. It was a quotation from a charade they had done last Christmas.

" 'La, sir, do I know you?' " she quoted back, also laughing.

He sat facing her, drinking her in, delighting in all he saw. "Well, I hardly know you," he said at last. "My! Since you came out last autumn you've become quite the woman." He nudged his companion. "Say? Culffe?"

Culffe joined in. "Time she married, Wharfedale. No point in waiting."

They laughed, and so did Abigail, but she could see something serious and calculating in her father's scrutiny of her. He did not ask how she came to be alone in Piccadilly; Lord Culffe had probably managed to imply that she had been out shopping with a servant, who had been sent on home.

And she, for her part, managed to conceal from him the anguish she still felt at Annie's dismissal. His good humour made it easy; he was marvellous company when he was like that—the sort of man you'd trust your life to, for he seemed to carry life itself around with him. Things suddenly heightened when he appeared; zest became more zestful, joy more joyful, light brighter, reality more aware. The very air around him seemed different—somehow more valuable. Certainly when he and Lord Culffe got out at the Palace of Westminster the drabness they left behind, which was the drabness within herself, seemed ten times more desolate.

His parting words to her were, "Who's At Home next Tuesday?"

"Mrs. Pelham," she told him. "If I'm wrong, I'll get word to you."

"I'll see you there."

And he was gone.

The "you" was plural; it included her mother. The whole exchange had been a kind of code, meaning, "Make sure your mother is there." The pair of them still appeared in Society together, gave the required number of entertainments together, fulfilled slightly more than a grudging minimum of their joint obligations, determined to show Society that, though on a private level they could no longer live together, on a public level they knew their Duty. And Society, on the whole, Approved.

The bleakness of it all merely added to the dreariness that filled the carriage the moment she was left alone.

At once her thoughts returned to poor Annie. She remembered the time the girl had spoken of her childhood. There, in the safe, gloomy warmth of the carriage, she had told of the poverty and squalor she had known. How easy it must have been for Annie to look back from the comfort and security of her job in Hamilton Place—the grand house, the spacious rooms, the carpeted floors, the good and plentiful food—how easy to look back from all that, Abigail thought (forgetting how peripheral a share Annie had taken of all these good things, and how tenuous a grip upon them hers had been), and shiver safely at such past horrors. And now the poor girl had been cast back into that pit. For in Abigail's mind—indeed, as in everybody's mind—vice, poverty, and squalor were three words with one meaning. More than that, you needed only to link them together, in any order, and each became a sufficient explanation and cause of its next-in-line: a perfect circular argument that no external force (such as truth or evidence) was likely to breach.

But guilt is a slow burner; and once its flame had consumed the immediate tinder—these bright and easy images of pitiful Annie—its more permanent glow, being much dimmer, seemed a kind of death. And the carriage was not yet halfway home! To revive its hurtful sparkle she sought new images.

She tried to imagine herself inside Annie's head, standing there in Piccadilly, looking at the men—at the hundred men who would pass before even one would approach her. Not nice men, either. Not good men. Not men of the stamp of her father and brothers. Not any man of any sort she might know. But grubby men. The men disgorged by second-class railway carriages. Clean-shirt-once-a-week men. Tipsy men. Tobacco-toothed men with dewlaps. Men from mean houses in Kentish Town. Men with the remnants of jellied eels, oysters, and a cowheel pie between their teeth and gums. Aimless and truculent, sniffing chancers and stray dogs, they accosted her, paid their rent, stripped her, and got her marvellous, her unique, her only, person for their own. Her shame and guilt were back on the boil by the time she returned to Hamilton Place. Full circle.

Nora, guessing what sort of mood her daughter would be in and knowing she would need an audience, let the girl come to her; but she did not let her speak first.

"Listen, popsie," she began (a childhood endearment of hers).

"I'm not a child," Abigail was stung to reply.

"So you say. Listen! If you want to make a fool of yourself over the dismissal of one servant girl, I cannot stop you. God, I should know that!

No earthly power can stop you. But you might at least acquaint yourself with the facts."

Abigail was not going to let Nora dictate the course of the discussion like that. "What was wrong, I want to know. What did Annie do that was so wrong?"

"There's no point in going back over all that. The girl herself certainly didn't question it."

"Didn't question it! I'll swear she didn't even remember it."

"Oh but she—"

"How could she? She was drunk."

"Drunk?" Nora's confidence was dented; she had caught a particular glint in Abigail's eyes.

"I got her drunk and *made* her tell me. Now d'you understand why I—"

"Abigail! You are just saying this."

"I'm telling you the truth. I got her drunk before she'd tell me."

Nora sat down, winded. "But that is terrible."

"Yes. Now imagine how I feel."

"No. I mean terrible that you would think of doing such a thing. And almost boast of it. What could have possessed you?"

Abigail shrugged. "I didn't know what she was going to say. How could I? Though ever since I've been wondering I was so blind. But all I knew was that there was a secret that Winnie hinted at and Steamer hinted at and all the world knew except me. Tell me one thing—honestly: If Annie hadn't told me, who would have? You?"

"I expect so."

"And when?"

"At the proper time."

"The eve of my wedding, I suppose? When it would be too late."

Nora smiled a knowing smile. "You would have—ah—reconciled yourself to it, I promise."

"Never!" Abigail shouted in panic, feeling all her grand, simple guilt being undermined. "And never shall I marry. Never!" She stormed from the room.

Nora gave her twenty minutes and then followed. She found Abigail at her writing desk. The sheet of paper beneath her fingers was covered, perhaps, three hundred times, with the one word: *Never*. In the first examples of it the pen had almost pierced the paper; ink spattered from where the angry nib had stuck. But the latest examples were decorated with curlicues, and the one she had just finished was made of tearful little mannikins contorting themselves into the shape of the letters:

She was so immersed in these absurd little creatures that she failed to hear her mother until she was only a pace or two away. Then, half-heartedly, she covered the drawing; but all the passion seemed to have gone out of her, and when her mother delicately lifted her hands from the page she did not resist.

Nora smiled. "The saddest thing about passion," she said, "is that it never lasts."

Abigail, to her own surprise, was touched—and a little fearful that her mother was about to confess some secrets of her own marriage.

But Nora said, "Don't fret about Annie. She wasn't nearly as upset about her dismissal as you might imagine."

Abigail shrugged.

"But," Nora went on, "I came here to talk about the Manly girl, Effie Manly."

"Mrs. Caldecott as she is now, you mean?"

"Yes." For a moment Nora appraised her daughter. "Tell me. Did it ever strike you as an *odd* match? The Honourable Effie and a major in the Royal Engineers?"

"I thought she was very much in love with him."

"Indeed she had every cause to be. And grateful. Did you know that her dowry was not far short of fifty thousand pounds?"

"But why? I would have thought—"

"And d'you know why they were married so quickly?"

"Because he was posted to India, surely."

"But do you know the *real* reason?"

And when Abigail still looked blank, Nora's hands sculpted a pregnancy in the air in front of her.

Abigail was dumbfounded.

"Think of it, darling," Nora went on evenly. "Imagine yourself in that situation. Think of a little wriggling, squirming thing growing there inside you. Growing and growing and growing. And nothing you can do to stop it. And all the while you know that it will soon become impossible to hide your guilt and your shame. And then you will never be able to marry. You will never have any position in Society. All your friends will cease to know you, even to recognize you. You pass them in the street and they do not bother to turn away, as they would if they were snubbing you. They don't even recognize you to that degree. They simply stare right through you. No one even talks about you. You never were. Your existence has been blotted out of everyone's register. And all of that for one brief act of folly that was probably inept, humiliating, and painful."

Abigail sat tensely, her eyes shut, shivering. She wanted to run from the room. She wanted to stay and listen to every word. She wanted her mother to tell it to her again and again. She didn't want to hear it.

Nora went on: "And, in my view, this happened to poor Effie all because dear Lady Jane believes—or *believed*—in telling her daughters what you made poor Annie tell you. And Effie, being rather like another young lady not a million miles from here, has to see for herself if it's true. And that's what frightens me, because I *know* you. I know you will be quite incapable of letting such knowledge—"

"Me!" Abigail cried, both horrified and angry. "You think I could do that? Let any man do that?"

"If I gave you the key to paradise and said—"

"Paradise? You said it was painful. And humiliating."

"Only the first time or so. No, it is clear to me that you must—"

"Before Annie told me, I remember now, before she told me, she had a little private argument with herself. And she decided it was too dangerous not to know such things. And I agree."

"So do I!" Nora laughed tendentiously. "So does everyone. Good heavens above—why do you think you are chaperoned everywhere and never given even thirty *seconds* of opportunity! But as I was saying: You must be engaged as soon as possible and married as soon as is decent. There's no other course now."

Abigail felt suddenly as if she were at the edge of a whirlpool. Invincible forces would soon clutch at her—already, in her father's words, and now in her mother's, she felt their first tugging. They would drag her down. Somewhere out there was an unknown man who, for the exchange of a few vows and the gift of a name, would acquire the right to *her*.

"I'd rather be—" she began to blurt out.

And then she went very silent.

Chapter 7

I'd rather be a nun, she had been going to say—meaning it to be such a ridiculous overreaching of the possible that her mother would be shocked into understanding how she truly felt. But even in the heat of that intended outburst some little element of persuasion had bitten off the sentence and tucked the unspoken half away for calmer reflection. It was not, after all, impossible.

Her reading then took a new and, to her parents, alarming turn. She read the whole of *The Imitation of Christ* at one sitting, and then reread it many times. St. Augustine's *Confessions* followed. Then Renan's *La Vie de Jésus*, which confirmed rather than diminished her faith. Volumes of sermons, most from the previous century, began to fill her bookshelves, until she knew as much of Socinianism ("Light without heat") as of Methodism (or "Heat without light"—as she dismissed both, pretending the phrases were hers). She scanned the pages of *The Times* and *The Morning Post* until she knew every nuance of the current ecclesiastical controversy and could talk of Puseyites and Vestments and Ritual with the best.

Could talk—and did. For at weekends, when the family went down to their country house at Maran Hill in Hertfordshire, Abigail soon became the village's most fervent Sunday school teacher, and this gave her licence to invite the curate to tea each Saturday, where they determined the lessons, the texts, and all the other business for the morrow. Within a year she had him into wooden sandals and a haircloth habit, cowl and all, living off bread and water, as miserably ecstatic as St. Jerome himself—and guiltily seeking escape into another curacy (a comfortable one on some remote, windswept Hebridean island, beyond the Friday-to-Monday reach of this intense and strangely compelling girl).

It was a dangerous game but it bought her two years during which no one dared press her too seriously on the subject of marriage, for fear of driving her yet deeper into this present mania. It was dangerous because the forces she was playing with, the forces of Faith, held particular perils for a maiden girl at the end of her teens, especially one who had no real occupation in life. And so it proved with her.

What had begun in panic, as the only possible (because the only respectable) reason for opposing her parents' determination to see her married, soon consumed every waking moment and even pursued her into her dreams. The rector counselled the family that religious manias of this kind were not uncommon among girls of Abigail's age and that they rarely lasted long enough to be worrisome. The family were not comforted. They knew Abigail as the rector did not. Even Winifred, who to start with (and rightly) suspected her sister's sincerity, soon grew as worried as the rest. She tried to steer Abigail's thinking toward the classical virtues of moderation and skepticism, but to no avail; reason and burning faith have no meeting ground—as Caspar, soon afterwards, discovered.

On a visit to Falcon Wood, while they were watching one of the lakes being dug (she would not go near the new house—she wanted that to be a surprise when it was finished), he suddenly asked her, "D'you think it's wise to put so much trust in God, Abbie?"

She was too astounded to do more than repeat his word. "Wise?"

"Yes, it seems to me, looking back through history with an unbiased eye, that about the only thing you can say with certainty is that if God has any profession at all, it consists entirely in letting His followers down."

He was prepared for her to run away; his hands were ready to grab at her arm as she gathered her skirts. Abigail of old would have run. But the new Abigail, secure in the fortress of her faith, merely smiled knowingly—forgivingly—and told him he was wasting his breath, like every other member of the family.

" 'My God, my God, why has thou forsaken me?' " he quoted. "They've all said it, you know, in their different ways."

Again that smile. "When you test a piece of steel and it breaks, Steamer, d'you give up the business of steelmaking? D'you send out the town crier to ring his bell and tell the world that 'Stevenson's steel breaks'? Because that's what you're saying about God, you know."

"The only ones who didn't get their fingers burned are those who obviously had no faith at all. The hunting, wenching popes of the Renaissance, who gave us Raphael and Michelangelo and Leonardo and Bramante and Vasari and the glory that is Rome. No grumbles about being forsaken there!"

"They also gave us the Protestant faith. Surely that was no small monument."

Caspar laughed incredulously. "And that was God's *purpose?*"

"Of course. How simpleminded you are sometimes, Steamer. Henry the Eighth was hardly any better when it came to hunting and wenching. Yet he was the vessel through whom God managed to keep burning the light of our one, true Catholic Church. I may be young and silly but if there's anything I've learned this last year or so, it's that you get nowhere by trying to fathom divine purpose."

"Hmm!" It was all Caspar could say; he had been sure the argument would be much easier than this.

"Anyway," Abigail went on, "this is fine talk from the man who reads the lessons in such tones of ringing sincerity each Sunday!"

"Oh, I don't underestimate the value of religion—socially, I mean. But everything in its place, you know."

"You don't believe at all."

"I do."

"What, Steamer? Tell me what you believe."

Caspar scratched his scalp with all ten fingernails, raising his hat on the spider of his knuckles. He gave a half-embarrassed laugh. "D'you really want to know?" he asked. "You won't like it. I believe that religion—whether or not there's any truth in it—is absolutely necessary. If we look back over all the different sorts of civilizations that ever were, the only two things they had in common were a ruling class and a servant class. They may or may not have had lots of other classes, but they all had those two. And the rulers' aim has always been to get the servants to work as hard as they could for the smallest possible share."

Abigail was shocked. "D'you think that's right?"

"Dearest Abbie—I'm not now talking about right or wrong. I'm talking about what is. And what always has been. And always will be."

"But why? It won't always be so."

"It will. For the simple reason that there isn't enough to go round. And never will be." He pointed at the navvies before them, digging out the lakes and carrying the spoil to form new, artificial hills. "It would be impossible for all these men to have as much as we have, for instance. So our purpose is to persuade them to do what they are doing for as little a share as possible of what we have."

"Our purpose, maybe," Abigail began hotly. "But not God's purpose."

Caspar smiled wickedly. " 'I may be young and silly but if I have learned anything this last year or so—' " he quoted.

"All right!" she interrupted, still angry. "But when I said that I did not mean to imply—"

"No!" he cut across her. "You asked, and now you shall hear. I said we must persuade them to do the greatest amount of work for the smallest possible reward. That is and always has been the aim of all rulers. One way we could do it is by simple slavery. In theory that would be the most effective way of all. Slaves work till they drop and they get no more than bare subsistence. But there are two objections to slavery. In the first place it is now morally repugnant—to *us*, the rulers. And in the second place, it stultifies progress. For if a slave has no money, what part can he take in promoting trade and commerce?

"The slave's reward is negative: a mere respite from the master's whip. But once a civilization has progressed beyond the stage of slavery, as ours has, it needs an entirely different set of rewards. And that's where religion comes in. Most of these men are Methodists or Baptists. But whatever they are—Anglicans, papists, whatever—they all go to church every Sunday, and they all hear 'blessed are the poor . . . blessed are the meek . . . blessed are the humble . . . it is harder for a rich man to get to heaven than for a camel to go through the eye of a needle . . . sell all that thou hast and give it to the poor' and so on and so on and so on. And here we all are on Monday morning, them and me, happy to know that poverty and meekness and humility are building them a heavenly mansion, while earthly mansions like Falconwood will crumble and their owners, like me, will rot in hell."

At last he looked at her to see the effect of his words. He was puzzled, for he had expected an explosion long before this.

"You will, too," she said bleakly, as much to herself as to him.

"When the bishops come begging for bread at my back door, I'll begin to worry."

She sighed. "Oh, Steamer! I know you mean to shock me. You're like everyone else in the family—you want to argue me out of religion. There's a lot of truth in what you say. But if I thought it was the entire truth, I'd rather the whole business of organized religion were torn down and—"

"Hah!" His laugh was surprisingly bitter. "D'you think that would change anything? Just suppose it were possible (which I don't think it would be, but suppose it were possible) to devise a civilization entirely without religion. A purely secular state. It wouldn't change anything. There would still be a few rulers and a vast mass of servants. And there would still be not nearly enough to go round. The ruling class would simply have to invent a different kind of reward. One that they could invoice without ever actually delivering. A Golden Tomorrow—a New Age of Mankind—something like that. They'd have to make the servants see how noble it is to sacrifice the here-and-now rewards for the sake of the Golden Future."

"At least it would be more honest."

"Would it? Any secular ruler who could believe such nonsense would have to be remarkably stupid. He wouldn't last long. At least one can believe in some small part of *our* nonsense. How else d'you think I keep going?"

Suddenly Abigail found herself on the point of weeping for him. "Oh, darling Steamer!" she cried. "What has made you so bitter?"

He forced a laugh then. "I grew up, I suppose. I put away childish things—like meekness, and humility, and simple faith."

"Then I hope I never grow up."

"Life will cheat you into it in the end."

His tone was so lugubrious it lent to their conversation an air of melodrama that embarrassed even Caspar.

To cover her own confusion—or her unwillingness to pursue his particular line of thought any deeper—she asked him why he had told her all this. "I mean, apart from the fact that Mama or Papa probably asked you to set me straight. Why?"

He shrugged. "I haven't enjoyed it, you know. I didn't do it for my own good." And he walked away hastily and began telling one of the foremen that he wanted the work done in a different way.

She watched him with great tenderness. There were few things in his life that Steamer had ever bungled. She hated to have had so close a part in one of them.

*　　*　　*

Abigail did not maintain her rather aggressive faith with unblinking ferocity throughout the years that followed the incident of Annie and that first threat to marry her off. She (or something within her) was already too mature and too smart for that. To be sure, the light of her belief never failed to shine, but it would flicker. Enough to let her at least contemplate, with every outward sign of compliance, the fate her parents had in mind for her.

For long months she appeared at first resigned to and then glad at the prospect of marriage to this or that candidate—always a candidate chosen by her parents. But each came to grief. To end every courtship she contrived a blistering row that sent the fellow off, gasping with relief at the luck of his escape. No one could then be more heartbroken, more vulnerable, more clinging to her mother than Abigail. Nor more certain of her vocation as a religious.

Of course Nora saw through it; yet she felt powerless to act in any very positive way. In the first place she was not sure just how conscious Abigail was of all she was doing. From the moment the girl could talk she had been able to mesmerize herself, so that attitudes, wishes, tantrums, angers—any wilful thought or act (though it began quite deliberately and consciously)—very soon possessed her to a degree that was far beyond her own power to unsay or unthink or unfeel. Then any attempt to argue or laugh or punish her out of that possession was futile—indeed worse, for Abigail seemed only to gain strength from such resistance.

Moreover Abigail was no underendowed middle-class miss who had to take whatever husband offered first. With her income and connections, she could still marry well at thirty.

"God forbid it should come to that!" Nora said when she made the point to John. "But she could stay single till then. And no harm done. She's not an extravagant girl to keep. Far from it! But if we continue pushing her into these unwilling matches, with these same results, she'll get a nasty name as a filly for refusals—and that *could* hurt her chances."

John saw the truth of it. "Not only that," he said, for he knew Abigail every bit as well as Nora, "if she gets the idea people are talking about her that way, she could set herself to trump us all by taking this nun business absolutely seriously."

And so they agreed between them to push her gently, if at all. And Abigail responded by going alternately to the brink of marriage and to the brink of a vocation, but never taking either plunge. And so, imperceptibly, it passed over. The nearer she came to her twenty-first birthday, the more she felt herself to be mistress of her own destiny and the closer she returned to being what those nearest her thought of as her true self.

Ironically enough Abigail's faith was finally tempered with skepticism through the efforts of a fellow believer who aimed to reassure her—the Reverend Paine, rector of Tewin parish, at whose Sunday school Abigail had taught so assiduously for the best part of two years.

One Saturday when young Mr. Melpomenus, the curate, was down with a heavy cold, the Reverend Paine had called in his place to take tea and discuss tomorrow's Sunday school. They met in her father's business room, since a clergyman, not being in Society, would be ill at ease in the Countess' drawing room. When their discussion was finished and the tea nearly gone, he relaxed, looked around as if refreshing his memory, and said, "It is rare indeed that I am called to this house."

For a wild moment she fancied he was fishing for an invitation; but it was merely his somewhat clumsy preamble to his next remark: "Yet there is one occasion I shall never forget. Can you, Lady Abigail, guess when that was?"

"I'm afraid I cannot, Reverend."

"You of all people should be able to guess. It was one terrible night, the Christmas of 1846."

"When I was born!"

"Yes."

"And *you* were sent for?"

"Yes. They despaired of Mrs. Stevenson (as she was then) . . . they despaired of her life, you see. Bless me! That's nearly twenty-one years ago. And now here you are, the very pillar of our church. And young Nicholas was only seven then. Or six? I forget. And now here he is designing such a great house for your brother. Dear me! Such changes!"

"You have every right to be proud of your grandson, Reverend. My brother says he will be one of the great architects of the age." (But, she thought, if Steamer had a goose, he'd call it a swan. He'd automatically promote any architect he employed. It would be unthinkable for the man to be less than "the greatest of the age.")

"I feel proud of you all, my dear. Especially of you."

She cringed at his confidence. "Oh, Reverend Paine," she blurted out, "if you could only see within, you would see how insecure my faith truly is."

He sat up and looked around him—at her, at the windows—in jerks that reminded her of a turkey, or of some automaton set going at the push of a button. "Really?" he said. "There is no need for that. It is true we live in a skeptical age, but everything can be explained, you know. I expect it's the miracles, what? It usually is."

He peered intently at her, and she was too astonished to say that, no, it was not the miracles.

"Don't you think," he went on, "that if you were eating and simultaneously listening to a very distinguished speaker, and were utterly absorbed in what he was saying, don't you think you might chew on one mouthful for many minutes—and end up believing you had taken a whole meal?"

She stared at him in bewilderment, not yet having caught his drift at all. And he, mistaking her gaze, plunged on: "Or take Galilee. I've been there, you know. I have fished in the same waters where Our Lord and his disciples went fishing. And I assure you, the wind and the light play the strangest tricks. The winds can descend out of the hills with a fury that is astounding in its suddenness—and the storm can be stilled just as swiftly. A man who knew the signs could say 'Peace, be still' at just the right moment, and the elements would give every appearance of obeying him.''

Now she wanted to cry out in dismay. Here was her pastor explaining how her Saviour was really just some kind of mountebank who had a gift for words.

"And there are parts of Galilee, you know," he was saying, "where the sandbanks lie only inches below the surface. Yet if the light falls on them in a certain way, it looks for all the world like deep water. I have seen, with these very eyes, I have seen men walking on the water, but it was merely—"

She thanked him for setting her thinking straight on the matter of miracles and made obvious preparations to rise.

He was startled out of his monologue. "Ah . . . one more thing, Lady Abigail. One more matter." He breathed heavily a few times, gathering his wits. "It is, ah, something I have meant to say for quite some time, ah. It concerns young Mr. Melpomenus. Ah, Mr. Melpomenus is very dear to us all. A good curate. Ah. The best. The very best. But, ah, I fear he is—a—a—a—a—*born* curate, d'ye see? Yes."

"You mean his calling is most sincere, Reverend?"

"Yes. And—and—and more. Of course, sincere, but—ah. I mean, he is unlikely to rise. Yes. To rise, d'ye see? Unlikely. I mean he is not a born *bishop*. He is in the same case as myself: no family connections."

"I doubt that worries him."

"No. No. To be sure, of course not. But—ah—it worries your mother. And your father," he finally blurted out.

At last Abigail saw where he was leading. The notion was so comic that she burst into laughter. "You mean they are afraid that Melpomenus and I . . ." She laughed again. "Oh, Reverend, I assure you, no such attachment has even crossed my mind. Nor his, I am sure."

The relief in his face was huge. *Surely*, she thought, *he is exaggerating*. But suppose he were not! Melpomenus was such a compliant, biddable little puppy, his natural manner could easily keep *gallons* of adoration concealed from her. But the Reverend Paine would have noticed. He would have seen how eagerly the curate went off to Maran Hill for his Saturday teas with Lady Abigail; he would have observed how readily Melpomenus adopted his sandals and his monklike habit at Lady Abigail's suggestion—and it had been no more than the merest suggestion on her part. Suddenly even she saw, in this light, how ridiculous it was. Oh, the poor creature! She was moved for him without being the slightest bit more inclined toward him. The Reverend Paine's next words jolted her out of this somewhat abstract compassion.

"But young Reverend Cater at Essendon, now—the Honourable and Reverend Ralph Cater—has the very best—ah—as of course you know—ah."

She knew. The Hon. and Rev. Ralph never missed a hunt. A jolly, hearty, mindless snob who had passed plain Mrs. Stevenson, nose in air, for years and who now fawned like a spaniel over the Countess of Wharfedale. Yes! A match with one of the Earl's younger daughters would suit that ninny (only someone as old as Reverend Paine would call him "young") very well.

She rose and rang the bell. "Indeed I do know," she said. "Ralph Cater has squired me, I should think, over every hedge in Lord Salisbury's country. He is a pleasant enough gentleman and a good companion to hunt with. But you may tell—er, anyone who you think may be interested that I am most unlikely to form any deeper attachment or desire any closer acquaintance than is at present the case."

The moment the Reverend Paine had gone, Abigail ran to her mother and told her, most vehemently, that she had no inclination to marry Ralph Cater—or any other clergyman.

The moment Abigail had gone, Nora gave three light skips of joy, heaved one great sigh of relief, then went down on her knees and thanked God that her prayers were being answered.

Chapter 8

Though Nora had sensed the end of Abigail's "religious phase" that summer after the meeting with the Reverend Paine, no one could be sure of it until Christmas, when the whole family went down to the great opening of Falconwood. It was also Abigail's twenty-first birthday and there was to be a grand double-celebration ball on Boxing Day, when the whole county and half London Society were invited.

Caspar and Linny had moved in from the old house in October, and Linny had needed every intervening minute to prepare for this first grand occasion. Even so, the last of the workmen, a team of French polishers, were paid off only the week before Christmas. It barely left time for the photographer from Stroud to take his pictures—shaking his head at the dim lighting and fretting anxiously through ten- and fifteen-minute exposures. The following day the Stevensons and Sherringhams began to arrive.

Winifred and Abigail were first, at Abigail's insistence. She wanted to catch the house poised, as it were, between its private and its public life. All she had seen of it until then were the foundations, the piles of stone, sand, and gravel, the site huts, the lime burners' pits, and the hole for the hydraulic cellar.

The two girls travelled down to Stroud together and then out to the new house in Caspar's coach. The day sparkled with the cold. On every twig a rime of hoar frost mimicked the white Christmas that weather sages had promised for weeks. No wind disturbed its frozen stillness; no cloud marred the cerulean sky. At several places they made the coachman halt while they admired some especially fine and frosted view. From here and there in the valley came the irregular thwack of the woodsplitter's axe; it was a time to look to the woodstore and to remember how swift a cheery blaze devours the logs.

From the hillcrest they looked back into the glacial pool of the shaded valley and watched the blue smoke rise in smooth, unbroken shafts, as if in glass tubes, until stray eddies far above stirred them into lazy dispersion. Upon the tops of the Cotswolds a light, powdery snow had drifted against the weather side of the hedgerows and ridges. It was no place to linger; the two carriage horses trotted briskly over the gravelled lanes, making the iron tyres sing almost as sweet as the metal-on-metal of the railway. Soon they breasted the rise on whose southern slopes stood Falconwood.

"Gothic!" Abigail cried in surprise. Only the belltower broke the skyline as yet.

"Of course," Winifred said. "I thought you knew at least that."

"No. I heard them discussing it." She laughed. "I thought it so funny, you know. There was this vast palace, planned to the very last closet, and—"

"Not to mention newspaper-ironing room."

"Oh?" Abigail asked innocently. "Have they one of those?"

Winifred smiled with thin-lipped sarcasm. "Nick told me. You almost gave him an apoplexy; he doesn't know how you managed it with such a straight face."

Abigail was pleased at the tribute but annoyed that anyone had seen through her joke. "Well, they deserved it," she said. "I know we Stevensons are supposed to be the *nouveaux riches* and the Sherringhams have all the blue blood in Wales, but Caroline seems much more of a tuft-hunter than any of us. If anyone deserves a newspaper-ironing room, it's her. And Steamer's as bad." She resumed her former brightness. "Anyway, I was saying—here was this *palace*, planned to the last little window, and there was Nick, saying 'we really must make up our minds soon what style we're going to build in.' And then all the arguments. Graeco-Roman was more solid and reliable. It suggested an ancient and patrician lineage. Gothic was more spiritual, nobler, more respectable. . . . It went on a whole Friday-to-Monday." She looked again at the house, now visible from the first floor upward, and becoming almost frighteningly large. "So the final vote was for spirituality. Well—if the purpose of opposites is to show off each other, gothic spirituality will show off Steamer and Linny to perfection!"

"In that case," Winifred said, "I look forward to visiting you in your own home—which will be built, no doubt, entirely of sugar and humble pie."

But Abigail, for once, was too overawed to reply. Her description "palace," intended as sarcasm, was the only word for the place.

The public approach was from the north, where a long and high brick wall denied the visitor any view of the house as a whole until the carriage drove beneath a quaintly romantic gatelodge and burst in upon two acres of gravel and formal garden. The house itself was L-shaped; the longer wing ran east-west and comprised the main building. Its western end was encased in a miniature Crystal Palace, so that the winter drawing room (on the ground floor) and the balconies of the principal guest rooms (on the upper floors) opened out, not to the elements, but to the tropical and perfumed confines of a palm-filled winter garden. The shorter wing, which ran north-south, held the kitchens, stores, furnaces, servants' hall, wine cellars, and female servants' rooms. (The male servants were dormitoried in the attics of the main house, reached by a four-storey spiral stair with access only to the ground and attic floors. The females' staircase was near the housekeeper's quarters. There were thus 362 mostly vertical paces between the nearest beds of the two sexes.)

Wedged at the junction of the two wings were all the rooms of inter-mediate status—the day and night nurseries, the chef's suite, the butler's pantry, the under butler's room (with silver safe let into one of its walls), quarters for the nursemaids and the visiting ladies' maids, the sanitarium, and—to be sure—the newspaper-ironing room.

Subtle differences of architectural style—a meanness of window glass, a narrowness in the stone banding, a steepness of slope in the staircase lights—made the difference between the two wings instantly apparent even to the least observant visitor. The servants' wing could be admired for its unobtrusive quietness and then could be forgotten. But the main wing could be appraised with profit for hours. It was grand without opulence, majestic without hauteur, sublime without the least ostentation. It looked centuries old; it could not have been built even ten years earlier.

The carriage drew into a covered court, lined on most of three sides by a red-brick arcade in the Venetian style. Destined eventually to house Caspar's future collection of sculpture, it presently displayed casts in ciment-fondu of the Venus de Milo, the Discus Thrower, and the Elgin Marbles (works that would later be distributed on plinths and in little pavilions and gazebos about the grounds).

Caspar, to Caroline's annoyance, welcomed his sisters in person. "Oh, come," he chided. "We are *en famille* until the nonfamily people come. I'll give them a warmer hello than any valet-du-jour." And he did.

While they were still hugging each other their luggage was being whisked aloft in hydraulic silence on the platform of the lift.

"Was it worth the waiting?" he asked Abigail.

And she, still overawed, said, "Oh, Steamer, it's breathtaking."

"It's a machine." He laughed, waving his hands around and gesturing them up the steps. "A machine for living in."

The entrance hall was a great picture gallery, rising three floors through the heart of the house to a roof of glass. A glazed arcade on each side gave light to the passages on the next two floors above. Cathedral-like columns of granite and Purbeck marble rose two floors to flattened gothic arches. The top floor was arcaded in massive piers of carved oak that bent over, the fluting unbroken, to form shallow collarbeams. The infill was of plain and coloured glass.

"Still no pictures," Winifred said.

"There's a Rubens down there. And a Canaletto. But we decided in the end to leave the paintings-by-the-yard business to Sir Georgius Midas and his kind. Every time you come there will be some new treasure to look forward to."

We decided! Abigail thought. *That would be Linny.* "What's that great wrought-iron bridge for?" she asked.

The grand stone stairway swept from the centre of the far end of the hall to a broad half-landing that housed a display of armour and medieval weapons; from there, still preserving the unbroken sweep of the balustrade, two stairs continued, one each side, to arrive at an open gallery spanning the end of the hall at first-floor level. From the middle of this gallery, down the centre of the hall, soared an elegant wrought-iron bridge, supported only at its ends.

Caspar chuckled. "It is the neatest solution to our greatest puzzle," he said. "You will see."

He showed them first the rooms to the north of the great hall: the all-male rooms—business and deed rooms, gun room, smoking and billiard rooms. Solid, chunky rooms, full of oak panelling and muscular stone. "And here, you see, is the bachelors' stair. So convenient. Come on up."

The girls looked indecisively at each other. "Is that proper?" Winifred asked.

"Until the nonfamily guests come, I should say so. But go up the main stair if you wish."

They went up the main stair. He met them up on the first floor and showed them the north-side rooms there—the governess' room, schoolrooms, and chapel, and a spare room where the yet-to-be-born children could make their own museum.

"Hard to know where to stow a governess, Winnie," Caspar said. "They belong to the family yet you can hardly put them among people in Society. An awkward class—teachers."

Winifred pretended to see a hint in this play-insult that Caspar had certainly not intended. "Never fear, Steamer," she promised, "I'll send you a gel who'll fill your daughters' heads with emptiness, turn your sons into budding Newtons, and be only too glad *not* to suffocate herself in the boredom that will reign on the south side of the house!"

And Caspar had to grin and pretend he took Winifred's barely playful insult as a joke, too. "The bachelors," he said, waving a hand above his head, "have nine bedrooms: on the second floor, over these rooms you've just seen."

He led them to the western end of the house, to admire the principal visitors' rooms, with their balconies that opened onto the fragrant warmth of the winter gardens.

"Seven tons of coke a day," Caspar said. "And when every room in the house is occupied, we'll take ten tons of anthracite a day, too."

"So now you know," Caroline said from the door, "why he married the heiress to a dozen coal mines."

There was much laughing and kissing.

"And the coking plant and gasworks," Caspar said.

Caroline took them through the remaining bedrooms on the south side, showing the ingenious double corridor that separated the guests from the family. The bedrooms alternately projected and receded so that, though each had a balcony, it was impossible to get from one to another without risking a twenty-foot drop to the terrace below.

"How ingenious," Abigail said. "Morality is built into the very stones!"

"It was my idea," Caroline said, taking Abigail's words as a compliment.

"As I said," Caspar added. "A machine for living in. We can move around here, informally, without disturbing our guests or they us."

"We do not occupy the grandest room," Caroline said. "So, when Important Persons visit we are not obliged to yield them our beds and dressing rooms."

"Upper servants can move without meeting the lower servants or persons, except when required. The lower servants can clean-sweep-and-polish without disturbing the family or visitors. Bachelors can reach their rooms without mingling with married people; and menservants can reach them without mingling with any other servants."

Caroline took over the litany. "Young ladies have their own stair from this floor"—she pointed to it—"and their maids can reach them without mingling with the visitors' menservants, who are on the floor above."

"And the children, you see"—Caspar wafted an imaginary river of them through the passageway ahead—"can go from nursery to schoolroom without sight of family or visitors. But here was our problem, you see: the young ladies."

They had come the full half circle and were now at the minstrel gallery, immediately above the door by which they had first entered the house, looking along the wrought-iron bridge to the armour gallery at the far end of the hall.

"The young bachelors go up out of sight in that corner. Everyone else retires up the main stair. But how do we get the young ladies from that end to their own staircase at this end? Eh? Hardly through the schoolroom! And hardly through the family corridor on this side. Hence—" He slapped the balustrade of the wrought-iron bridge; the metal sang in the echoing hall. "The only way to the foot of the young ladies' stair is along that fifty-three-foot length of clanging conspicuousness. Now! Is Nick not a truly great architect!"

"Eleven different circulations of people, who need never meet unless required to do so," Caroline added.

"A machine," Caspar said. "A machine for living in. Come and see the servant girls' rooms."

There were eleven of them; four for eight visitors' maids, two for five ladies' maids, two for four housemaids, one for two kitchenmaids, one for two scullery maids, and the servants' cook had a room to herself, next to the housekeeper. "Most of the female servants live out, of course," Caroline said.

The rooms were as neat and cheerful as barrack quarters.

"Come and see the future!" Caspar cried from outside the housekeeper's apartment. He led them through a workroom full of maids sewing Christmas bunting. They rose when they saw who their visitors were, but Caroline smoothed them back into their seats with one waft of her gloved hand.

Winifred was impressed. "They are extraordinarily quiet and industrious for such young girls," she said.

"Yes," Caroline agreed as they walked into the next room—the female ablutions. "But you have to remember that we are the only substantial givers of work for miles."

Caspar, smiling like a magician at the climax of his act, gestured at a row of gleaming porcelain basins and brass taps. He turned one of the taps. Within moments he was seemingly enveloped in great gouts of steam.

"Hot water!" Abigail said in astonishment. She scalded her fingers as the price of half belief.

"For the servants?" Winifred asked Caroline.

Caroline smiled. "Of course, that was how I felt. I thought it absurd. But darling Caspar"—she smiled indulgently at him— "came at me with pencil and paper and proved that the time they *didn't* spend carrying their own hot water and slops they could spend in serving us."

"No sense in paying servants to wait upon themselves," Caspar said.

"Have all *our* rooms got hot water, too?" Abigail asked excitedly.

"Certainly not!" Caroline said. But Caspar smiled at her as if her scorn were only half the tale. "People would think," she went on, "that we could not afford the servants to bring hot water in the proper way."

Still Caspar smiled.

"What is it, Steamer?" Winifred asked.

"When I was in America," he said, "I remember a bath with a little charcoal stove at one end. You could fill it with water, light the stove, and in forty-five minutes it was piping hot. You could sit in it up to your neck."

"Oooh!" Abigail luxuriated in the very thought of it.

"See!" Caspar waved at her as if she proved a point. "The voice of tomorrow. I'm convinced that within twenty years even the English may begin to feel that a bath should consist of more than four jugs of tepid water lugged along half a mile of frigid corridor by a frail domestic with 'the rheumaticks.' "

"Therefore?"

"Therefore I have laid down over a mile of piping in the fabric of this house, ready to carry cold water and steam-heated hot water to its every corner. And waste pipes to carry off the slops."

"Your dear brother cannot distinguish between what is practical and what is sensible," Caroline said. There was an edge of asperity in her voice, as if she had heard the argument once too often.

They began to walk back to the main wing.

"But does it all just come bubbling up out of the bedroom floor?" Abigail asked. "Like a hot spring?"

"No. The bath is fixed. That means it needs a room of its own. A bath room."

"Do I have such a room?" Abigail was excited again.

"Of course not," Caroline said crossly. "No one does."

"Except the chef, the butler, and the nurseries."

"I mean *people* don't," Caroline corrected, as if Caspar's qualification had been ultra-pedantic. "But the result is that we are left with fourteen small, windowless rooms with empty pipes beneath their boards, waiting for this bath-time revolution Caspar is so confident of. I shall tell people they may put their servants to sleep there if they want them nearby."

"I've cooled toward the idea already," Abigail said. "The whole fun of taking a bath is stepping out in front of the fire and watching the towel steam as it toasts. And being inside it."

The sybaritic qualities of this vision, however innocent, embarrassed the other three.

"Well, Steamer," Winifred said quickly. "You have copper bars waiting for the electric revolution, and iron pipes waiting for the revolution in bathing. What other wonders are yet slumbering around us, ready to spring from their concealment as science dictates, and"—she nodded at Caroline—"as Society permits?"

Caspar drew breath to answer but Caroline cut in: "Oh, do not be surprised to find contraptions of feathers and sealing wax among the rafters—ready against the day when *all* houses fly!"

*   *   *

Later Caspar offered to take his sisters for a brief drive around the park before the daylight fled. Winifred, who had letters and speeches to write, papers to mark, timetables to prepare, and professional jealousies to settle, declined; but Abigail was delighted to accept. Wrapped for Siberia, they sat in the governess' cart and trotted at a brisk clip down into the valley and up the other side.

"Poor Linny," Caspar said, feeling that some explanation of her acerbity was due. "These last three years can't have been easy. To live in a crumbling old place like Falcon Wood, knowing that so much needed doing to it—and knowing also how wasteful that would be. And to see nothing but the hugger-mugger of a building site here. To have to entertain and make her mark on the county in the old place—all the time knowing what a splash she could be making if only this place had been ready. It must have been very hard."

"Perhaps you shouldn't have lived so close."

"From her point of view, that's true. But since I could devote only two days a week to the building, if we had taken a house elsewhere, I'd never have seen her. Work! It's our curse."

"You are happy, aren't you, Steamer?"

"Indeed!" He laughed. "Why d'you ask?"

"When you mentioned America I nearly dropped. I never heard you . . . I thought you'd obliterated that memory."

"America." His voice was curiously flat, neither questioning nor musing.

"D'you ever think of *her?*"

He stared at his sister a long time. "Of course," he said at last. "Every day."

"Oh, Steamer. I'm so sorry."

He smiled. "Every day I imagine her trying to manage Falconwood. And how she'd fail. And how miserable that failure would make her. And how superbly Linny copes with it all. You know we shall be sleeping forty-six, apart from ourselves, on Boxing Day? And the ball is for over five hundred. Poor Laney could never have managed anything on that scale. She's better off in New York. She is a queen there, just as Linny is here."

"Even so . . ."

"Even so! Even so!" he mocked. "You Stevenson women will never understand. I think you and Winnie would actually prefer me to die of a broken heart. Well, I'm sorry but I shan't oblige. When I took on the responsibility for the firm, it automatically became necessary for me to marry someone like Linny. I'm lucky enough to love her, too. So spare me your easeful deaths, if you please."

She smiled and hugged his arm, not quite believing him but content to let matters rest.

"Also," Caspar went on, "I'd be grateful if you'd do all you can—you and Winnie—to help her make a success of this first big occasion. You are both very self-assured young ladies and very at ease with people. You could do a great deal, you know—more perhaps than even you think."

"Of course!" Abigail almost shouted the assurance. Her brother seemed so vulnerable in his appeal, she would have done anything to restore his usual ebullience.

"I know we Stevensons are supposed to be the new arrivals and the Sherringhams are the old guard, but in some curious way Linny craves to be accepted by us. And especially by you and Winnie."

Abigail was astounded at this news; the thought had never occurred to her. Linny was such a patrician sort of person most of the time.

"I'd be more than grateful, Abbie," Caspar said.

The sun, hugely red yet heatless, flattened as it sank toward the mists above the skyline. The valley was already dark. The frozen lakes along its bottom gleamed like vast, dull stones. As the cart followed the winding driveway up the far side, it seemed they climbed into a second dawning.

Abigail deliberately did not look at Falconwood until the cart drew up near a small pavilion and Caspar said, "Now."

They had timed it perfectly. The sun laid a majestic fire across the red brick of the house. It caught each projection and moulding and lined it with gold. The still untarnished copper spire on the clock tower burned against the violet of advancing night. The orange glow of gaslights flickered through the black windows. And in front of the house gleamed the pale marble of the terrace and steps, colder than the frosted lawns or the ice-sheeted waters.

It was so exactly what Caspar had wanted that she laughed. She wanted to stand up and jump and clap her hands, like a child. "Oh, Steamer!" she said rapturously. "Just think, if God had been as rich as us, He could have done the whole world like that!"

When the blasphemy of her words—an utterly unintended blasphemy—struck her, she turned to him and gripped his arm. "I mean—"

But Caspar was already laughing hugely—a laughter that seemed to carry more relief than humour. "Oh," he said as he grew calm again, "I told the mater not to worry. Wait till I tell her this!"

"No. Please! I didn't mean it in that way."

He looked at her, disbelieving, then a little worried. "Really?"

She thought back. *Had* she meant it? Had some part of her, just behind her immediate thoughts, actually meant it? She smiled. "Perhaps just a little bit," she said. "I meant to be funny—say something absurd. But not blasphemous."

Life was getting so complicated lately. Until very recently she would never have questioned what lay beyond her immediate consciousness; *that* would have seemed a kind of blasphemy.

Then, for the first time in two years, she felt an urge to be writing. Her long-abandoned children's tale surfaced in her mind just as, in childhood days, thoughts of iced orangeade and pantomimes had surfaced. *Pop!*

Caspar, grinning again, stretched an arm about her and squeezed. "Let's go home," he said.

She looked back at Falconwood, knowing that however many times she would see it in years to come, from whatever angles and in whatever moods, it would never again look as lovely as it did now, newborn and waiting to begin its life.

On their way down into the dark of the vale he turned to her. "That—what you said. I wouldn't repeat it to Linny. She is very conventional that way."

As they breasted the farther slope and emerged again into the last of the twilight he stopped and headed the pony across the drive so that they could look once more at the valley. As night slipped up from the east the brightest stars were already twinkling out of the purple. The colours of the park and woodland had sunk to the darkest resonance of their daylight splendour—a dull mightiness of jostling patchwork at the very limits of vision. Somewhere far off a vixen yapped, a sharp, plaintive call that seemed to double the intensity of the frost.

Caspar clucked the pony into movement once again. "What a difference a few dozen degrees make," he said. "Last July I was standing here wondering how to endure the heat—and the insects. And *now!*"

Abigail smiled. "Think of Boy in India." Boy—whose real name was John—was their eldest brother.

"I suppose so. Funny thing about those insects. Mostly little midges. They were thick enough, you know, to form actual clouds. It was like a mist. A drifting mist in quite a stiff, steady breeze. There must have been hundreds of millions of them to make clouds like that. And that was just the output of this one valley. Think of all the valleys, all the land, in

England. And they're quite at the mercy of the breeze, you know. A lot of them, millions and millions, just get carried out to sea and die."

As his words formed an image in her mind's eye a sharp sadness caught her up. The waste of it all . . . the sheer profligacy! She remembered something one of the learned men in her mother's salon had said to her: "If you think in mere numbers, then the most typical living thing is a creature actually in its death throes or within moments of them." In a curious way he had intended it as a sign of hope. "To survive one day in the kingdom of plants and animals," he had concluded, "is a small miracle. And a great mercy to us." When she thought of those millions of insects being wafted to their collective death from this one valley—this one lovely peaceful haven—it was hard to find comfort in her own survival.

"D'you think they chatter to each other as they go, Steamer?" she asked. "About life? And God? And happiness?"

He laughed. "What strange ideas you do get!"

As they clattered over the new cobbles of the stable yard he remembered something. "Whom has Winnie invited down, d'you know? She wasn't sure last week."

"A man called Laon, I think. Percy Laon. Or is it Peter?"

"Does he do anything?"

"Everyone Winnie knows *does* something. She wouldn't tolerate an idler. I think he's something to do with ladies' magazines."

"A scribbler?"

"I don't know."

"It's a queer name, Laon. Sounds foreign."

"Tut tut!" Abigail mocked as she skipped ahead of him toward the house.

They were late. Tea was already served, and their parents, John and Nora—looking very much the Earl and Countess amid the gothic splendour of the morning room—were thawing gratefully by the fire.

"I haven't shown them around," Caroline said quickly to Caspar, as soon as the welcomes were over. She turned to Nora. "It would be more than my life is worth."

Nora laughed. "He was like that with all his toys. Anyway, I'm sure John already knows every stone."

Abigail sat on John's lap and began to tell him how superb the house had looked from across the valley. Caspar asked where all the children were—though the only children left in the family were his youngest sister and brother: Rosalind, who would be sixteen come March, and Sefton, now getting on for eight. Mather, now seventeen, and Hester, almost twenty, were of the grownups. (At least until the more formal, post-Christmas festivities began.)

"In your nurseries, I hope," his mother told him. "And having the time of their lives, I expect."

"By the way," John said, "marvellous news. Young John may be coming. I had a telegram from the India Office just this morning."

Everyone was delighted at the news. Abigail glanced at Winifred; usually the word "telegram" brought on an attack of classical Greek and a lecture on the preferability of "telegrapheme." But not today, it seemed.

"I say, Winnie," Caspar called to her. "Who's this Laon person you're bringing?"

"Oh, a friend. A guardian of one of my girls, in fact. But a friend as well."

"Abbie says he's a scribbler."

"I did not," Abigail began, looking at Caroline in alarm.

"He is a publisher," Winifred said evenly, knowing how Caspar loved to provoke an overreaction. "He publishes *My Lady's Companion, The Drawing Room, At Home* and—I don't know . . . Several other ladies' journals."

Caroline relaxed again. "He sounds most interesting," she said.

"Funny name though," Caspar persisted. "Is he foreign?"

"His father was. A Dutchman called Porzelijn. But Mr. Laon has anglicized it to Percy Laon."

Both Abigail and Caroline saw the sudden change in Caspar's face; the name meant something to him. It meant something to Nora, too, for she immediately drew breath and looked at Caspar.

"What did the father do?" Caspar asked. His tone was harsh. There was no suggestion that this was idle curiosity.

Winifred was momentarily taken aback. "I have no idea," she said. "Mr. Laon has had a violent quarrel with his father and has severed all connection with him. That's why he changed his name."

"No idea?" Caspar pressed. "You really have no idea?"

"Caspar!" Nora warned.

Winifred, goaded, feeling all eyes upon her, said, "I believe I heard once that he was some kind of dealer in antiques."

Caspar drew breath, nodding and smiling savagely, as if that was exactly what he had expected to hear. "I must ask you," he said, "to telegraph this person and put him off."

"I beg your pardon?" Winifred bridled. Her eyes filled with that awesome black intensity before which many a young girl had quailed. Even Caspar had to master an urge to retreat.

"I think you heard me, Winnie," he said. To anyone else he would have repeated his original words even more forcefully.

"Caspar," Nora said. "Be wise now."

He turned to her. "How can I have this man here, Mother?"

Nora stood, looking at Caroline. "Be a dear," she said, "and take us to another room where we may discuss this."

"I shall agree with Caspar," Caroline warned, "whatever his decision."

"But you also have a very cool head. And I'm sure Caspar will welcome your advice." She was already moving to the door; Winifred rose to join her. "Not just yet, popsie," Nora told her. Caspar and Caroline had no choice but to follow her out of the door, leaving Winifred standing a little lost in the middle of the carpet.

Abigail sprang from her father's lap. "Come on," she said, taking her sister by the arm. "Let's see how they've unpacked." She turned and shrugged an apology to her father.

Winifred, whose instinct was to rush after the others and demand to be a party to any discussion involving her guest, let herself be led only so far in the opposite direction. Abigail, feeling her arm stiffen, said, "Poor Papa. He has no idea what is happening here. He resents being cut out, you know."

"He has no one but himself to blame," Winifred said coldly. "If he hadn't tried to rule all of us, and Mama, with such a heavy hand . . . Anyway"—her tone changed—"you talk as if *you* know."

"I do."

The butler, hearing them pass, stepped out into the passage. "Can I be of assistance, my ladies? There's only the kitchens that way."

"Thank you, Lucas," Abigail said. "We shall travel up in the hydraulic lift."

"The master frowns on that, ma'am."

"We shan't make a habit of it," Abigail told him.

"It emerges by the visiting menservants' rooms, my lady."

"Then we certainly shan't make a habit of it, Lucas," Winifred said.

When they were in the lift and the door was shut, she added, "That was naughty of us. Now—what d'you know about this? Why is Steamer behaving in this monstrous way?" She wished she could see Abigail's face but it was pitch dark in there.

They had not been in so many lifts that the sensation of rising vertically had ceased to thrill. Abigail giggled until her stomach settled. "You remember Mary Coen?" she asked. "That servant girl we had in—"

"Of course I remember Mary Coen!"

"Steamer was once in love with her."

They arrived at the second floor and pushed open the door, glad of the light again. Winifred, with a condescending smile, said, "For once you are wrong, Abbie dear. It was Boy who fell for Mary Coen."

Abigail grinned triumphantly. "That was before. First Boy, then Steamer."

"Steamer would never have let himself be smitten by a maidservant."

"Steamer would have married her," Abigail said very firmly.

Winifred's eyes narrowed. "You read his diaries!"

"Every chance I got," Abigail said, without a trace of shame. "He deserved it. I used to tell him everything and he'd never tell me a thing. Anyway, he knew I did. He expected it. It was the only way he could . . . you'll never understand."

They passed their bedroom door without going in, thus tacitly acknowledging that the whole journey here had been a mere ruse of Abigail's.

"What secrets could you have that would interest Steamer, anyway?" Winifred taunted. Inwardly she wondered what was happening to her—to cheek the butler like that, like a naughty girl, and then to argue with Abbie in this small-minded way.

"I told him why Mama and Papa separated," Abigail said. "The real reason."

She sounded very confident, and Winifred, not wanting to hand her further triumph, changed her attack. "It has nothing to do with Steamer's present extraordinary behaviour."

They began to descend the young ladies' stair. Halfway down Abigail paused, forcing Winifred to halt, too. "The man who kidnapped Mary Coen was an antique dealer by the name of Porzelijn."

"Kidnapped?" Winifred repeated. She wished Abbie did not sound so horribly certain. "Surely Mary Coen just absconded?"

Abigail continued the descent of the stairs. She reached the bottom and looked along all three passages before she added: "You remember that summer we were on our way to Connemara and Steamer jumped off the ship in Liverpool?"

"When he went to Paris? Four or five years ago? That was to do with business."

Abigail smiled. "His only business in Paris was to find Mary Coen, who had been taken there by this Ignaz Porzelijn."

Winifred held her sister's sleeve. "This is too extraordinary altogether for you to invent. You aren't inventing it, are you?"

"Try to understand why Steamer behaved as he did. After all, he was only sixteen when he fell in love with Mary."

Winifred tried to imagine it. Mary Coen, one half of whose face had been burned to a pulp in childhood. True, she was the kindest, gentlest, sweetest of girls—but she was *hideous*. How could they? Both Boy and Steamer! She shuddered and Abigail felt the tremor. "I know it's hard," she said.

They started along the wrought-iron bridge that led across the main hall to the armour gallery and main stair. Winifred was bewildered by her sudden switch of roles with Abigail. All her life she had been very much the elder sister—there was, after all, nearly six years between them; and now, in a few moments, Abbie seemed to have cancelled out the difference. "Try to understand," she had said! As if to a child. And "I know it's hard." Those had always been *her* lines.

The change did not altogether displease her. She had a particular reason for wanting Abigail to put the spoiled little girl (and, lately, the pious spoiled little girl) behind her; and Mr. Laon—or P.P. as she called him—was here to help.

As they neared the armour gallery she looked down into the gloom of the hall and saw Caspar, watching them. When he knew she had spotted him he smiled and held up his arms.

He came bounding up the stairs to meet them. "I'm sorry," he told Winifred. "What may I say? I was wrong."

She hugged him. "No, Steamer. Not really."

He drew back in astonishment, looking first at Winifred, then at Abigail. "I see," he said.

"She told me."

"Told you what?" Caspar asked with tendentious innocence. "I'm sure there's nothing to tell."

Smiling a see-what-I-mean smile at Winifred, Abigail took Caspar's arm and began to steer him down and back to the morning room. "Nonetheless, Steamer dear," she said smugly, "I told it beautifully."

*   *   *

P. P. Laon came before noon on Christmas Eve. To everyone's surprise he proved to be quite young; somehow no one had thought a *publisher* could be a young man. But Laon was just twenty-six, almost a year younger than Winifred.

Nora was disappointed. She had sensed an excitement in Winifred whenever the subject of Mr. Laon had come up; indeed, she had almost imagined that the girl was in love with him. And Nora, alone of all the family, still had hopes of Winifred's marrying. But the moment she saw the two of them together she knew the idea, at least in this instance, was forlorn. Laon was altogether too pleasant, too easy, too friendly with Winifred; they were like old colleagues. And though Winifred had spoken of him in such bright-eyed tones, she now took her cue from him and behaved with the warm reserve of long-standing friends.

After lunch the pair of them and Abigail went for a walk around the winter garden. The palms were small as yet, so the sense of being in a jungle was lacking; but the air was as scented as that of any jungle, heavy with the fragrance of freesias, eucalyptus, and myrtles. Here and there a new perfume—a lemon-scented verbena or an oriental hyacinth—would intrude. Merely to walk there was a kind of intoxication. Nor was colour lacking. From rich-leaved coleus and shrimp plants, through mallows and spurges, to great banks of roses, the two women needed their finest dresses and ribbons merely to be seen.

"We live, surely, in the midst of a new rebirth," Laon said. "A second Renaissance, more profound and more eternal than the first."

Winifred looked at him in amazement. "Last month it was a new age of barbarism. What has happened?"

"What has happened is that I have seen Falconwood. It's a pinnacle of this century's achievement. Your servant girls—d'you realize this, I wonder—even your servant girls live in greater comfort than a monarch of Tudor days."

"How can you say that, Mr. Laon?" Abigail asked. "Surely the style of Henry the—"

"Ah, style! I did not say style, but comfort, Lady Abigail. Can you picture what life must have been like in those draughty, dark, smoke-filled halls, amid people who rarely washed, much less had a bath, trying to eat meat whose putrefaction was masked by heavy spices? And yourself with a head full of bad teeth?"

It was, to say the least, not a conventional line in conversation. Abigail was pleased. It certainly made a refreshing change from talk of the weather and the Season and Sport, which was the usual grist of young men's conversation.

"P. P.!" Winifred cried.

His face fell. "Sorry," he said. "Carried away. Hobbyhorse of mine—don't like the Pre-Raphaelites." He looked at Abigail. "Please accept—"

Her broad smile halted his words. "I have never met anyone," she said, "whose hobbyhorse was to dwell on the more repellent aspects of medieval society." Suddenly she became earnest, as if the topic were quite vital to her. "Is it a new Movement?" she asked. "Does it publish a journal? May one join?"

For a moment this breakneck change of mood left him nonplussed. He stopped and gazed at her. He had a leonine head with sleek black hair. His profile was spoiled by a heavy ridge of bone across his brow, but seen full face he was quite handsome; that same ridge shaded his eyes and gave them a darkly luminous quality that compelled attention.

She betrayed herself with a flicker of a smile. He smiled too, with relief, and his eyes dwelled in hers a moment longer in full-scale revaluation.

"Look," Winifred said. "Hibiscus. Now, isn't that a gorgeous pink?"

They agreed it was.

"You are antiromantic then, Mr. Laon?" Abigail asked.

"I am highly in favour of romance, Lady Abigail."

"But not of the romantic movement?"

"Nor of the classical movement, either," Winifred added.

"Nor," Laon said, "of *any* backward-looking movement. The Pre-Raphaelites are an English disaster. Ruskin is a one-man blight. We grow desperate for a new voice."

Abigail laughed in delight. If she had feared any tedium this Christmas, Mr. Laon was the man to dispel it. "Well," she said, as if it were a quotation, "'That's *my* humble opinion, doctor. What's *yours?*'"

Again Laon was puzzled. But he, too, caught up quickly with her humour and laughed, though not quite so wholeheartedly as before. "You have far too brilliant and mercurial a mind for me, Lady Abigail," he said. "I feel quite pedestrian."

"I somehow doubt that, Mr. Laon," Abigail said, feeling not the least rebuked. "I certainly detect no dullness."

Winifred looked at her young sister in amazement. Abigail, though aware of the implied flattery—and aware, too, that she was being more forthcoming, not to say downright forward, than she had ever been before with a man—was not altogether surprised. After all, during these last years she had passed many hours in her mother's salon, talking with witty and learned men; the only difference now was that she was saying aloud the things she had earlier thought and suppressed. Indeed she would still be suppressing them if Laon hadn't proved so engaging and unconventional.

"Tell us about this 'new voice,' " she prompted.

"Oh, please don't," Winifred said. "Tell her instead about her book."

"Now?" Laon asked in astonishment. "You think it wise?"

"My book? What book?"

"The one you abandoned two years ago."

Abigail felt her heart hammering sharply in her throat. An unreasoning panic rose within her. "What does he know about my book?"

Winifred smiled at Laon. "Shall we tell her?"

Laon smiled at Abigail, desperate to calm her and win back her good humour. "After all, she is twenty-one."

"I destroyed it," Abigail said. "It was wretched."

Winifred, now realizing that she had bungled this revelation badly, nevertheless kept up a brave smile. "And I—with the help of the maids—rescued it. Page by page."

Abigail began to shiver; it made her voice piping and querulous. "And showed them to *him?*" The last word was almost a shriek.

She turned to run, but Laon, to her utter amazement, reached out and grabbed her by the arm. "Listen!" he said fiercely.

It was so unpardonable that she was shocked into a false and momentary calm.

"I have read your—"

"Mr. Laon!" she said vehemently, looking at his hand.

"I'm sorry," he said, not sounding the least sorry—indeed looking at his own hand as if it were quite beyond his control, "but in view of the importance of this occasion I have already decided to forgive myself entirely. And so"—again his dark eyes held her, filling her with a confidence that was almost hypnotic—"if you will only hear me out—will you?"

She wanted to go on being angry; it was still a luxury she found it hard to deny herself. But the ghost of a smile about his lips prodded her the wrong way at just the wrong moment. Trying not to smile in response, she said, "I think it is your third finger that is causing me the greatest pain." Her voice still carried a shiver.

He opened his hand but left its palm deliberately on her arm, as if to say, "I may grab you again at any moment." There was something electrifying in his touch.

"I shall not run," she said, wondering why she said it so calmly and what this odd rapport was that now seemed to exist between them. It alarmed her. "I thought you were going to strike me," she said.

"I?"

"Yes, it is amazing how total *strangers* assume a godlike right to strike anyone they imagine to be hysterical."

"I detect the voice of experience," he said, ignoring this frank attempt to put a distance between them. And to underline the point he grasped her arm again, but this time with a friendly strength. In that way he steered her along the paved walks of the winter garden with Winifred hurrying along beside them, and began talking in the most avuncular tone. "You're quite right to despise your work. It's full of faults. Parts of it are ridiculously childish. Every page is marred in some way. It's a veritable primer of infelicitous writing, want of subtlety, and overblown emotion."

Abigail felt hollow, as if Laon had taken a knife too sharp to feel and had eviscerated her.

Winifred was outraged. "P. P.!" she cried.

But one look from him quelled her. He let a small silence grow to the limit of tolerability. Then, just as Abigail realized she had not breathed since he began his attack, he continued. "And yet I tell you that despite all those faults (and don't let what I am now going to say minimize them), yet despite those faults I found a quality of quite magical delight that carried me triumphantly through all my annoyance at your shallowness and ineptitude. You have, in short, the only quality that really matters: I could not put your story down. You are, I regret to say, every bit as bad as Dickens."

Abigail, at the edge of hysteria, now began to laugh. "But—" she stammered, "the story is not even a quarter written."

"On the contrary, I think it is within one chapter of its conclusion. I do not believe it should be a long book."

"Mr. Laon wants to publish it," Winifred blurted out.

"Not as it is," Laon said hastily. "But as it will be."

Abigail felt the cold on her cheeks and fingers as the blood drained from them. Until now she had imagined, insofar as she had thought at all, that Laon and Winnie were offering her a very generalized encouragement—an extended pat on the head and a "good girl." The notion that Laon was talking professionally and seriously had not even nudged the outermost edge of her consciousness. She halted in her tracks. "Publish?" she asked. "Oh, no."

Laon shrugged. "It would be a great loss if you did not agree. I truly believe that, with the right sort of editorial help, your story could mark a new beginning in this one small corner of English literature. I have certainly never read anything quite like it."

Abigail burst into tears and ran blindly for the door that led back into the winter drawing room. This time Laon made no move to prevent her.

"What a mess we made of that," Winifred said bleakly.

But he was all smiles. "Not a bit! True—it's not how I would have planned it, but I couldn't have planned it better."

"How can you say that?"

He looked at her in amusement. "You forget. Almost all my contributors are females. I probably have more experience of lady writers than any man in England. We'll publish your sister's book before another Christmas is upon us."

Winifred shook her head sadly. "How little you know her."

But Laon was not to be shaken. "In this respect," he said, "I believe I already know her a great deal better than you."

The assertion filled Winifred with sadness, as if something had been stolen from her and she could not say what.

*   *   *

Abigail did not appear at teatime, but by half past seven, when everyone assembled for a glass of sherry or a "cocktail" (a custom Caspar had brought back from New York), she was there, talking to Laon, bright as ever, just as if no word of any kind had passed between them.

"Tell me, Mr. Laon," she asked at one point. "When you anglicized your name, why did you not choose 'Lane'? It is certainly more English than Laon."

"Ah, Lady Abigail, but by then I was already certain I was to be a publisher. 'Lane' would not have sounded at all right."

"Why not?" Nora asked.

"Too rural, Countess," Laon said. "Too back-streety, don't you know. Not dignified enough for a publisher. *Lane*. It doesn't sound right."

Caroline thought it ridiculous to hear a tradesman giving himself such airs; she had a hard time of it to keep a solemn face.

"But Laon sounds foreign," Caspar objected. "If you'll pardon me."

"Not at all." Laon smiled. "It is deliberate, don't you see? The ladies like it—the readers, I mean. They see: *The Drawing Room*, which sounds dependable and comfortable and very English. And then they see this foreign-sounding fellow as publisher and it adds a little dash of spice. Just the right combination."

"Did you really think all that out first?" Nora asked, full of admiration.

"It's very important," Laon said. "Every word on the page has an effect. If I were to publish an *Iron & Steel Journal*, say, I'd call myself P.P. Stevenson without hesitation." He bowed toward John, who smiled and bowed back.

Abigail picked up the game at once. "Or the *Fishmonger's Telegraph*, published by P. P. Walton," she said.

Then everyone laughed and joined in—*The India Teamerchant's Gazette*, by P. P. Clive . . . *The Public Schools Cane Finishers' Times* by P. P. Arnold . . . *The Slave Trader and Mart* by P. P. Livingstone, and so on.

The game died as casually as it had started.

"Well," Nora said over the last of their laughter, "I'm sure it makes you a very clever young man to think of such details."

"Oh, but he's even cleverer than that," Abigail said brightly. "Didn't you know? He's going to publish my children's story and make my fortune!"

Chapter 9

Boy arrived on Boxing Day morning just when everyone had given him up. He found the house deserted, of course, for the one hunt of the year that no one missed was the Boxing Day meet; even the most indifferent horseman would feel obliged to turn out on Boxing Day—especially in the northern Cotswolds, where the least enthusiastic had a choice of three hunts, and the really keen man could take his pick of no fewer than seven. It was said of one sportsman that he came to Cheltenham—only a dozen miles away—with a stud of ten horses and a wife, and that he left it with ten children and his stud down to one. "But the devil of a rider still!"

Boy wasted no time before he changed into hunting clothes. With the Puckeridge and Lord Middleton's he hunted in pink, but here, having no idea which hunt his people would be out with nor what their sensibilities might be, he thought it wiser to hunt in black. The stable lad who prepared his horse told him the others were probably with the North Cotswold, "over Beverstone"—no more than a couple of hills away to the east.

No fresh snow had fallen and there was scarcely a breath of wind. The still air was keen enough with the cold, needing no breeze to sharpen it. Even the brilliant sun, warm where it touched his black clothing and boots, could not soften, much less melt, the powdered snow. He crunched his way at an easy trot to Beverstone, where two drovers told him they'd seen the hunt making south for Tetbury.

Beverstone—indeed the whole, rolling landscape, with its distant prospect of the Midlands plains—was so exactly like the traditional picture of the romantic England, dead and gone, that, when it failed to stir him, Boy could only wonder whether something had gone amiss within. He looked around at the warm and weathered old stone of the houses, with their roofs of thatch and brick-red tile, at the church and the castle ruins, all so perfectly balanced amid the leafless trees, at the remote and secret upland country stretching all around; and he told himself—he had to *tell* himself—that this was the England he had longed for on those long and wearying marches through the lofty Hindu Kush. But the response within him was merely conventional. More than half of him was already homesick for the Northwest Frontier. Where was the thrill of chasing a fox through coppice and dells that you have both known from childhood up, compared with the thrill of hunting tribesmen through mountain passes they know better than their teeth and you knew not at all—where at any moment the roles could be reversed and you would become the hunted! There in the dry, sterile, frozen air of the Cotswolds he began to long for the very smell of India.

The hunt was not hard to follow through the snow; he found them checked at a large wooded covert south of Tetbury.

"Hello, Stevenson. How's India?" It was a voice from the past, but it spoke as casually as if they had parted only last night instead of four years ago.

"Hello, Moncur. I've known it as cold as this. Have you found?"

He and Moncur had been at school and then at Cambridge together. Moncur was now a Grenadier subaltern.

"No scent today. Who are you with these days?"

"No one. Temporarily unattached. Been given a commission to form my own irregulars. Stevenson's Horse."

"Pathans?"

"Mmm. Deuced good horsemen. And soldiers. Goin' to be a high old time."

The laconic phrases and offhand tone masked the sudden sharp wrench he felt merely in talking of it. The rest of his leave, he could see, was going to become a test of his endurance. He was going to have to fight his impatience every hour until he once more boarded the train at Suez and made the last brief overland journey to Indian waters.

"By the way"—Moncur extended his whip vaguely in the direction of another young man—"this is Locke. You don't know it but he's—"

"I know Locke," Boy cut in. "Played in the scrum, one match, when I captained Cambridge against the other place in sixty-two. How d'ye do?"

Locke smiled and bowed.

"Yes, but now he's—" Moncur pressed.

"I know. Captain," Boy said. "Beat Oxford twice last half." He turned to Moncur. "Occasionally, you know, we find old copies of *The Times* washed up on the beach near Bombay."

The three of them laughed; Locke handed round cigars.

"Seen my people?" Boy asked.

"The Master asked them to hold up the far side," Locke said. "I'll ride you round there. We're a bit supernumerary here."

"If I don't see you again today," Moncur said as Boy and Locke walked off, "we'll meet tonight at this ball Steamer's giving."

For a field or two Locke spoke excitedly of the great progress of rugby football at the universities. Almost all the dons were now decent enough to give any undergraduate permission to go to Oxford when the game was away. In Boy's day one Cambridge team had arrived so understrength it actually had a majority of borrowed Oxford men to play it to victory.

Then Locke's conversation began to flag and Boy became aware that something was troubling the fellow. He asked what it was.

At first Locke would not admit he had anything on his mind. But when Boy appeared to accept this assertion and tried to talk of other things, Locke suddenly burst out: "Look, Stevenson. This is none of my business, and you'd have every right to send me off with a flea in my ear, but I'd feel rotten if anything happened to your sister and I'd said nothing."

"Which sister?" Boy asked quickly.

"Lady Winifred. D'you know this—"

Boy smiled. "She's well able to take care of herself, have no fear. I'm sorry—what were you going to ask?"

"D'you know this P. P. Laon fellow she's invited down?"

"The name rings just the faintest bell."

"He came up the year you left. Trinity."

"I didn't know many Trinity men," Boy confessed.

"No loss in this case, believe you me."

They broke off to take a fence; they kept well down from the covert, so as not to interfere with the draw.

"You'd better tell me," Boy said as they began a diagonal climb across some stubble.

"A fellow feels dashed awkward,though," Locke said. "I'm invited to the ball tonight and I'm desperately keen to come, you know. But I hardly can if I've maligned one of your brother's guests—especially to you."

"Don't malign him then," Boy said, dismissing the scruple. "Simply state the facts of the case, without varnish. If the inference is clear to be drawn, I'll draw it. Never fear."

Locke considered this and then laughed. "Jove, Stevenson. I'll wager you make a capital adjutant! Very well, I'll tell you. It was like this. P.P. Laon never had more than a hundred and fifty a year. Two hundred at most. Yet he was in all the high-spending clubs going. Pony and trap . . . faultless dress . . . you know the sort."

"How did he do it?"

"Oh, he never made a secret of it. He made a book—quite openly. But always paid a point under the odds."

Boy was shocked. "But why did anyone bet with him?"

Locke snorted. "You know undergraduates! It doesn't matter to them if they're paid at fives or sixes. The fact was, Laon always paid and was always to be found."

"Which is more than you could say of the average bookmaker."

"Exactly. Worth droppin' a point, d'ye see."

"Well—if he was open about it, that was quite honourable, surely?"

"You listen. He also ran a 'hell' every night. He got Breuvet's to send in a magnificent dinner for eight or ten, and anyone was welcome on the understanding they played 'bank' after."

"Bank?"

"It's more or less *trente-et-quarante*, but he didn't play the *après* rule as at Monte Carlo."

"Don't mean much to me, I'm afraid."

"Well—the way he played it, the odds greatly favoured the bank. And, of course, our friend Laon was always bank."

"Did they play high?"

"I once saw a fellow put a thousand guineas on the turn of a single card!"

Boy whistled.

"Well, one night I asked Laon if I could share the bank, and he agreed. Fifty apiece. But as luck would have it, fortune chose to desert to the players. In less than an hour, the bank was broke. Laon and I then agreed to give the bank a chance and we told the others they could go on punting against an unlimited bank and we'd pay out in IOUs redeemable next day. Well, luck was dead against us and we broke up owing about fourteen hundred—seven hundred apiece. You may imagine how I slept that night! In fact I was still in evening clothes when I went round to Laon's at breakfast. And there he was, bathed, shaved, and cheerful, eating like a king, with the *Pink 'un* propped against the marmalade jar. 'My dear chap,' he said. 'You look awful. Have a brandy and soda. What's the trouble?'

"Well, I told him I hadn't seven hundred in ready—though naturally my guvnor would stump up in the end. But he might have to sell stock and goodness knew how long he'd take. Old Laon smiled and unlocked his dispatch box and took out a bill stamp he just happened to have there. 'How much time d'you want?' he asked. 'Three months? Six?'

"Of course, I was over the moon with delight! He demanded no interest or anything. So I signed the acceptance for seven hundred at three months."

"That was pretty decent of him," Boy said.

"So I thought. Until that afternoon when he had to weigh in with the money. The chaps came round and he said, 'See here, you fellows—we all rather lost our heads last night. You played on to do us a good turn but the luck ran the other way. However, I'm not going to oil out of the debt. I'm not even asking for favours. But fourteen hundred's a lot of scratch—especially since Locke couldn't find his all at once and I've had to take a three-month bill from him. All I have in ready cash is eight hundred. So I thought I'd ask you chaps which you'd prefer—eight hundred now, in full settlement, or a bill for seven hundred at three months' date and another for seven hundred at six months?' "

Locke gave a hollow laugh. "Ask any undergraduate if he'd prefer a hundred now or three hundred in six months! Of course they accepted with delight. 'Devilish straight of you, Laon, old chap,' they said. And I was left as the villain who'd put him in such difficulty. Which was why, he explained to me later, he kept my bill and held my guvnor to the full seven hundred."

"I see," Boy said. Privately he considered that Locke had acted as dishonourably as Laon in betting beyond his capacity; at least Laon had had enough in ready cash to cover his share. The whole tale was one of dishonour masking dishonour. Still, it was good of Locke to put himself in this bad light in order to warn Boy of the danger his sister might run in associating with Laon.

"Those are the facts, Stevenson. Make what you will of 'em. I know they do me little credit but at least I've never gambled again. So some good came out of it. There are your people now. I'll leave you."

"Boy!" Abigail's shriek of delight cut through the crisp, cold air. She left her station and came galloping downhill, taking the hedge in one flying stride.

"Go back," he shouted and spurred toward her. "Mother will be furious," he said as they drew level.

She held out both hands and they gripped each other warmly, if a little awkwardly, over the inevitable gap between two mounted riders. "It's worth it," she said. "How lovely to see you. We'd given you up. Everyone was so disappointed. How long shall you stay? And how is India?"

"And you're letting Steamer down."

She grinned wickedly. "I have already done so," she said. "The appallingly Honourable Mark Caithes was complaining loudly about the social quality of the Hunt these days. And I told him—equally loudly—that it was quite unreasonable to expect *everyone* to be a tailor."

Boy, with theatrical despair, raked the heavens with his eyes; but the jibe was so apt (it was rumoured that Caithes had tried to get his tailor elected to the Hunt in exchange for his wiping out a large debt) that he could not help smiling too.

Satisfied, Abigail turned her horse and trotted with Boy back to her station. "Anyway," she said, "today's a waste of a good hunt. Even if they find, they'll lose the line in half a mile." Suddenly she grew eager again. "I say, Boy, isn't it marvellous! Winnie's brought down ever such a nice person called P. P. Laon and he's going to publish my story."

"How splendid," Boy said. But he was suddenly a great deal more worried than he had been earlier, when he imagined that only Winifred was involved.

They took the jump side by side.

Chapter 10

The ball was a resounding success; even those who came to sneer had to admit it—even as they sneered. The chief architect of this triumph was, in fact, the architect of the building itself. His grand entrance hall at the heart of the house became the ballroom, with the orchestra in the gallery at the end of the wrought-iron bridge. And everything that anyone could want lay only a few paces away. A groaning buffet in the dining room to the southeast; quiet corners and soft chairs in the library and morning room to the south and southwest; space in which to promenade or sit in the drawing rooms and winter garden to the west; a discreet ambulatory for snatched kisses in the armoury (and lots of things to point at and pretend an interest in should others approach); and on the north and east the billiard rooms and the covered entrance court offered a haven to men who had sickened of feminine chatter and who were desperate for a smoke. For those whose thirst outran their capacity there was half an acre of frozen terrace on which to walk it off.

Best of all, there were a dozen places where political and other business could be mooted safely—that is, without imperilling the dancing, feasting, drinking, and other merrymaking. During the course of the evening two new members were recruited to a royal commission of inquiry into docks and waterways, a new justice of the peace was found for the Stroud bench, two candidates were selected for forthcoming bye-elections, a possible new bishop was nominated, and the success of the government's latest Contagious Diseases Bill was as good as ensured.

In most of these affairs John played a prominent part; his presence there was, after all, the sole reason that many of the guests—those with official or parliamentary connections—had agreed to come. In passing, and on his own account, he extended the firm's contract for the new Thames Embankment, agreed to tender for the new Bradford Town Hall, and added his weight to a scheme for financing the nearly completed Suez Canal if the French and Egyptians got into trouble.

John had agreed to the building of Falconwood only with the greatest reluctance; and until tonight he had remained firmly of the opinion that the house was a hostage to Caroline's ambition and Caspar's vanity. Now, after this first public evening, he withdrew all he had thought and said against it. Nora had always maintained that Caspar was the only member of the family who could see the firm as it should be five or even ten years from now. If tonight was anything to go by, she could very well be right.

About three o'clock, when it looked as if the young folk were set to dance until dawn, he sought out Nora to say he was turning in.

"Of course," she agreed. "No one will expect you to stay up. But don't drop off. I'll come up in five minutes—there's something urgent to discuss, something I've heard from Young John."

Whenever he and she went visiting together they were naturally put in one room as man and wife. To avoid embarrassment he usually slept in a portable trestle bed in his dressing room. Nora gave him ten minutes to settle himself and then followed him up.

To her surprise he was still washing. "I'll come back," she said turning to leave.

"Towel!" he spluttered through the soap and water, groping wildly behind him.

She brought him the towel, warm from the fire. Instead of putting it into his groping hand, she draped it over his wet neck and began to rub it dry. Slowly, astonished, he turned to face her, but she covered his face with the towel and went on drying him.

Without warning her heartbeat doubled its rate—which struck her as odd since the rest of her felt quite calm and unemotional. She had no idea why she was drying John in this way, and she rather wished she hadn't started. "There," she said, before she removed her hands.

But he clasped them up and held them fast to the towel that still concealed his face.

"Well?" she asked. For him she did not need to elaborate the question; it meant, *Have you got rid of The Bitch?*

"The Bitch" was Nora's only name for Charity, the ex-fallen, ex-rescued (and now, happily for Nora, ex-young) woman who was John's mistress and the mother of his three bastards. She had been eighteen and very pretty when John had first met her in 1850; she had been even prettier in 1855, when John had set her up in St. John's Wood. But now, at thirty-five, she had grown plump and pasty—and, according to Nora's sources, somewhat inclined to be shrewish.

John clutched the towel from her and began rolling its thinner selvedge into his ears to dry them. If he had heard her, he gave no sign of it.

"Did you talk to Young John?" she asked.

"Yes, we seem to be reconciled again. He's not nearly so priggish now he's learned a bit about the world. He was almost cordial to me."

"Did he talk of Mr. Laon at all?"

"He began to. Yes. But I had to break off to have a word with Bright. What about Laon?"

Nora told him then, everything that Boy had told her (and Boy had kept back nothing but Locke's name). "It's this suggestion to publish Abigail's book that worries me," she concluded. "Winifred's safe, mainly because I control all the school's finances. But Abigail . . ." She sighed.

John, now in his nightshirt, said through the foam of his toothpowder, "The income from one little book! What does it matter? Suppose she lost it all—do her good. Teach her a valuable lesson."

Nora was not convinced. "Let's assume the worst, John," she said. "Assume Laon is an out-and-out scoundrel. And suppose the book sells very well. Suppose the income were over a thousand pounds. It would be a most expensive lesson."

The possibility clearly had not occurred to John. "Is it really so good?" he asked. "Have you read it?"

She shrugged. "I didn't even know it existed. I thought she'd destroyed it—the way she destroys everything. But Winifred is so taken with it—and you know how sparing she usually is of praise, especially for Abigail. And anyone can see how keen Laon is, beneath that mask of indifference. Oh, he has the money itch, all right. So I think we have to assume it could—"

"Damnation!" John burst out. "What is *wrong* with our girls? Are they all determined to shame us! Just when people have grown to accept the fact that the Earl and Countess of Wharfedale's eldest daughter, who could have a million-pound dowry and marry whom she pleased, prefers to run a girls' school, along comes the second daughter, with equal advantages, and now she's going to write for money! And what is Hester doing up in the nursery? Plotting to open a cigar divan in the Strand, I have no doubt."

Nora laughed, relieved that he could joke about it, despite the seriousness of Abigail's proposal to write for money. "At least you're avoiding the heavy hand."

"Oh, I learned *that* lesson. Six years ago."

"Five."

"It seems like sixty. Oh dear, what are we to do?"

"This seems to have turned into a discussion about how to stop Abigail from writing. I wanted to arrange ways of preventing Laon from trepanning her. If that is his intention."

"Or from marrying her."

"Oh, that would be easy. Just let it be known we'd disinherit her. He wouldn't take the risk."

John gargled and spat. "Why not do for her what you do for Winifred?" he asked. "Look after the money side of things?"

"I doubt if she'd let me, John—"

"Let!" he exploded. "Ye gods! Our children now *let* us."

"It's not just *our* children, dear. No one nowadays can tell their daughters who and who not to marry."

"Any more than husbands can tell their wives what—" He bit off the rest of the sentence.

There was a brief silence between them. "No," she said at last.

"I'm surrounded by a conspiracy," he grumbled. "All I get from Winifred is 'Married Women's Property' and repeal of the Contagious Diseases Act. What's gone wrong with women?"

"We're straying again," Nora said. She reached some internal decision, squared her shoulders, and smiled. "Your idea is sound, though. Someone must look after the financial arrangements for her. I wonder if I can persuade Caspar." She laughed. "Yes! He has two dozen good reasons to wish no good to Mr. Laon. Alias Porzelijn."

But the image that kept presenting itself in her mind's eye as she left him and went back to the ball was not of Abigail or Laon or any of them; it was of John's torso, which she had not seen naked for over seven years now. The flesh was a little fallen perhaps, the skin less supple—he was, after all, getting on for sixty—but he still had more muscle than any other man she knew. And not an ounce of flab.

She remembered it. And her body remembered it—that *marvellousness* of him enfolding her. Much later, when the dance was over and the young people had gone back to the hunting field, she lay in her bed, not a dozen yards from him, and, for the first time in years, mourned the loss of him. She grieved that he had wasted himself so long on The Bitch.

Chapter 11

"P. P.?" Winifred said.

"Mmm?" Laon was reading galleys. They were in Winifred's study, waiting for Abigail. Outside two teams of girls were playing lacrosse, the new Canadian game. Watching them, Winifred wondered that anyone could ever have imagined girls to be gentle creatures. Was she being fair, she wondered, encouraging such a competitive spirit? Was it not storing up misery for the girls when they left?

"Yes?" Laon asked.

"Yes what?"

"What d'you mean—'yes what'? You were going to ask me something."

She thought. "Oh yes. Nothing really—I was just about to remark that you are rather young for a publisher."

"Ah!" He gave a knowing grin. "Depends when you start, don't it! At eighteen I was writing reviews for *The Examiner*—*and* got elected to the Savile Club."

"But—I mean—if you quarrelled with your father, how did you get the money?"

He stood up, dropped his proofs, and came to stand beside her at the window. "Marry me," he said, "and I'll tell you the secret."

"Don't be foolish!" she said. But she grinned almost savagely. Her left hand hung against her skirt. He let the back of his hand graze it.

"Stop that," she said, pulling away.

He sighed. "I thought you were about to become serious," he complained. "I thought when a Stevenson gets on to money it has to be serious."

She tossed her head. "How you got your money is a matter of supreme indifference to me."

"Oh. In that case, I'll tell you with pleasure. When I'm in bed at night, you know, I think about you a lot."

She looked at him in owlish surprise.

"And I think to myself: *If I can but keep her indifference alight, I shall surely be counted the happiest of mortals!*"

"You're impossible," she said, delighted at his safe-dangerous foolery.

"I am," he said. "I am the square root of a minus number. The June snowball. The janissary's favourite grandson—"

"I should have known better," she told him. "Go back to your galleys."

He did as she bade; but almost at once he laid down the papers again. "Seriously," he said, "I'll tell you. Nothing to be ashamed of. I ran a book when I was at Cambridge and—"

"Gambling!" Winifred was horrified.

"Wait," he said. "You're going to win, so don't worry. I didn't. Win, I mean. I came down with a paltry few hundred, which, considering the thousands that passed through my fingers, I call as good as losing. So there I was with a first in law and a conviction that gambling was no high road to fortune."

"And a few hundred pounds."

"Yes." He did not welcome the interruption. "While I was waiting to be called to the Bar, I began scribbling for Malthus Roy, the man who then owned three of the magazines I now publish. One day, quite coincidentally, I went into a shop, the toyshop in St. Martin's Lane it was, to buy a clockwork boat for a young nephew of mine, and I was astonished to be charged thirteen and sixpence. When I asked why it was so expensive, the man told me he couldn't get the clockwork under nine shillings. So I bought the boat, but I'm afraid my nephew didn't get it. I took out the clockwork and went to every little workshop in the East End, and even Camden Town. And I couldn't find a single man who'd quote me under eight and sixpence. So I went to Paris. And Lyon. The same story. And Switzerland was hopeless. So I was about to give up. But I thought, 'No, I've put so much into it now, I'll put just a little more.' And—call me Dick Whittington—I found a fellow at last, in a little place outside Milan, where they'd make them for seven shillings. That was two years ago. This year one half of all the clockwork toys sold in England will have motors supplied by me. Same with musical boxes."

Winifred clasped her hands in delight. "How d'you find time?" she asked.

"Oh, I don't have anything to do with the day-to-day running of the business. Malthus Roy does that."

"The . . . ?"

"The same one. It shows how much we all owe to sheer chance. One day Roy said to me, 'D'you know, Laon, I'd rather be buying and selling scrap metal than publishing these wretched rags.' And they were rags, too, in his day. He loathed them. And it showed. Another time he said, 'If I have to read one more account of Lady Whatsit's new furnishings, I shall go out and put every chintz factory in London to the torch!' Oh, he hated it, all right."

"So you simply changed seats? How marvellous!"

Laon chuckled. "Not quite so simply. No. He was losing money heavily. I was making it handsomely. No. I offered him a partnership in a lucrative business in return for the millstones around his neck. And now I've made those profitable, too. This year I do believe we'll really turn the corner."

Winifred saw Abigail's coach turn in the driveway. "I'm so glad for you," she said. "Persistence like yours—and flair—deserve success."

He tapped Abigail's manuscript, still in its folder. "Yet this," he said, "could earn more profit than all my business, and yours, next year. And she was going to throw it away! It hardly seems fair, does it?"

"Here she comes," Winifred said.

*   *   *

Abigail was so nervous she could hardly put one foot surely before the other. The whole day seemed to be ringing and pulsating. Before, when she and Laon and Winnie had talked in general terms about her book, she had been quite calm. But now they were going to look at her actual writing, her very own words. And line by line, paragraph by paragraph, Laon was going to shred them and show her how foolish and—what was his word? She didn't want to remember his word. The memory of how it had sliced through her was enough.

Thank God, Winnie stayed just long enough to see them settled. She wasn't among the most considerate of people, but at least she had tact enough for that.

When they were alone, Laon turned to her. "I heard a good story at the club last night," he said. He seemed in no hurry to start on the manuscript. "About Tennyson. This is going back thirty years. He was dining one night at the Savile with W. H. Brookfield and George Venables, and after the meal he stuck his feet on the table and tilted back his chair like an American. They pleaded with him to sit properly, but 'Why should I?' he said. 'I'm very comfortable.' 'But people will stare.' 'Let 'em!' Tennyson said. But Brookfield had the answer. 'Alfred,' he said. 'People will think you're Longfellow!' And down went the feet!"

Anecdote followed anecdote; Carlyle, Thackeray, Dickens, and his own contemporaries—people like Stevenson and W. E. Henley—he had stories about them all. Small, trivial stories, they were, like the night that Thackeray called unexpectedly to dinner. His host's wife, caught with only a leg of cold mutton in the pantry, sent out for some tarts to enliven the meal. When the tarts were presented and she asked which he preferred, he said unthinkingly, "Thank you. I'll have the *twopenny* one."

Because of their intimate domestic nature, these little anecdotes seemed to invite Abigail into the charmed circle of writers, a circle where such tales must be common currency. She knew, of course, that Laon was doing it deliberately, but that did not make it any the less effective. She had come there like a schoolgirl for a session with her tutor; and within moments he had transformed her into a real writer, while subtly demoting himself to the status of editor, "the clown with the bucket and brush," as he later explained, "doomed to wander the public arena in the wake of the literary elephant."

All his more playful imagery, she found, had this dangerous, earthy tinge, redeemed by his wit or at least by his good humour.

"Now," he said, when he saw that she was properly relaxed, "let us turn to this tale of yours." He opened the box in which the rescued papers had been uncrumpled and pressed flat. "Let us take the opening:

" 'So careless are the folk of The Land of That'll-do you will not even find their country on the map. They do not withhold this information of a purpose (indeed, there are hundreds of seasoned mariners who could take you there in the dark—especially in the dark); they truly intend the world to share the blessed happiness . . .' "

He looked intently at her. "Et—cet—era," he finished.

She cringed inwardly. It did sound frightful.

He glanced farther down the page. "You go on to say that, at map-making time, these folk of The Land of That'll-do always forget to give the mapmakers the necessary details. And that's how you justify your opening sentence. (Incidentally, I think you mean 'carefree' not 'careless' there.) But it's too long-winded, too ponderous, don't you see. Especially for a beginning. I mean, it's a charming *idea*—that there is a mapmaking time, just as there is a haymaking time—but it doesn't sustain an opening."

"It sounds like a bad geography master," Abigail said, "desperately trying to inject some interest into—"

"I'll do the attacking," he told her. "You get out the needle and thread." He turned the page face down to compel her attention. "What does the reader want in an opening?" he asked.

She giggled nervously. "I don't know anything about openings."

"Pardon me, but I think you do. Guess what sort of book this sentence opens: *I have no idea who my parents were; I cannot even name the country of my birth.*"

"An adventure story. Or the tale of a self-made man."

"Not a woman's story?"

"Certainly not. It would be quite unsuitable."

"Indeed? Then what of this, the first line of a short story: *Rosamund had often heard of the phrase 'dance the night away' but the Ball of 1868 was the first at which she both polkaed out the sunset and waltzed in the dawn.*"

Abigail laughed; she loved these games. "Easy! That's for one of your magazines."

"But you told me you know nothing about openings—and I see you know everything. Try this, a harder one. *The long, rainless day was coming to an end, and the sun, now a huge, dull, dusty sphere already nibbled by the skyline, threw before them a pool of shadow in which their fancy (or was it their fatigue?) painted strange and disturbing scenes.*"

Still grinning Abigail gave it some thought. "Gothic," she said. "Decidedly long-haired, artistic, and gothic!"

"And you still maintain you know nothing of openings?" he asked.

"Here's one last one. *So careless are the folk of The Land of That'll-do—*"

He got no further. "All right!" she shouted, her humour gone.

"Good!" He beamed. "It's not the opening to anything, is it?" He turned the manuscript face up again. "Yet it contains the germ of a superb opening. I wonder if you can see it."

She turned her face away.

"Go on!" he encouraged. "Have a good flinch, then read it again."

She read it again.

"What d'you like best—or dislike least?" he asked.

She shrugged. Grudgingly she said, "That bit about getting there especially in the dark."

He rapped the table, delighted. "Exactly! That's your opening, you see: *You cannot reach The Land of That'll-do, unless you go by night.* Now that could not be anything but a children's tale, and already it hints at mystery and excitement. Now let us go on. I'll do a page or two with you and leave you to finish the rest of the chapter on your own during the week. But don't start on chapter two just yet. I want to talk to you about the structure of the book from the second chapter on."

They spent an hour on the first three pages. Abigail, who until then had used commas as mere stage directions, meaning "pause here to draw breath," found it hard going.

He showed her how to make each sentence grow out of its predecessor. "So many of yours are only half-connected," he complained. "I have to read the whole paragraph, trying to hold these half-connected ideas in my mind, and then—somehow—I have to force the connection, once I've grasped the main idea, the main drift of your thoughts. And I mean *drift!* It's such a pity, because the connection is there. The ideas are a delight. The events a joy. But the words! They are like tussocks of grass underfoot. Or squelchy mud."

And he showed her how to make them smooth and firm, how to achieve "the inevitable thread of words." In general he simply rearranged her original, rarely adding to it, but quite often cutting. He was ruthless with her dashes and parentheses and dot-dot-dots wherever they masked a certain breathlessness of thought; out of them he cobbled firm, free-standing sentences.

At first she was excited. It was like watching a good gardener weed a thickly infested shrub border, leaving it neat, showing the form and texture of every plant. But when he had done the best part of a page she read it again and felt a sense of uneasy disappointment. It did *not* flow as he claimed. The shrubs, so to speak, had been pruned too hard and the unity of the border was destroyed.

But then he went back over his work and added half a dozen seemingly empty little words and phrases—"however," "to be sure," "after all," and so on. At one point he tacked a whole new sentence on to the front of a paragraph: "Corney Grain was not the only one to notice that the ship had turned about."

"D'you see how all these little extras help to fill the cracks?" he asked.

And, having just noticed the cracks herself, she had to agree.

He also began a process that was to last through many months of her craft training—the process of rigging literary alarm bells around certain notorious constructions. *Stop* with *-ing* was one. " 'He stopped her coming down the street.' 'He stopped her going to the dance,' " he said. "The first probably means 'stopped her *while* she was coming down the street,' the second probably means 'stopped her *from* going to the dance.' You may say that the context nearly always makes the choice clear. And I say to you that only a bad writer would rely on it. For a good writer the words and the context must point the same way; but if one of them is leaning on the other, they can't, can they!"

Inverted sentences ("Brave would be he who . . .") formed another class of pitfalls.

The position of the word "only" was another.

And there was the illiterate "whom" ("Young Ferdinand, whom they suppose is drowned . . ."). It was a motley collection—inevitably, since it depended on the random illiteracies of her text; but it whetted her appetite for more.

By the time he left she was so fired with the ideals of clear writing and "the inevitable thread of words" that she wanted to go home at once and write the next dozen chapters. Like someone who had just learned to ride a bicycle or swim, she wanted to practise the new skill to the point of exhaustion.

At the doorway, on the threshold of his departure, he turned back to her and, cutting short her delighted thanks, said, "Next time we'd better talk about money."

Chapter 12

They did not, however, talk about money the next time they met, nor the time after that—nor, indeed, for several weeks. Once or twice, as he was leaving, Laon said, "We really must give a thought to the financial side of things." But that was as far as the discussion went. Somehow the editing and rewriting of the story always seemed more important.

They met, as on the first occasion, at The Girls' College, usually in the mornings. Within very few weeks Abigail found that her life was beginning to revolve around "Pepe," as she came to call him. (He, however, refused to call her anything but "Lady Abigail.") She wrote for him alone, or rather for him as arbiter of children's reading. His own private taste in literature, as distinct from what he could approve of as editor and publisher, was far more scholarly. They wasted hours talking of Ben Jonson and Milton and Gibbon; they analyzed Shelley and Wordsworth to dust; they retraced the history of the novel from Defoe and Fielding to their own time and speculated endlessly on the course it might take next.

Yet somehow, despite these distractions, her own story got rewritten and edited and rewritten. And in the process the question of whether or not Laon would agree to publish the finished book (and whether or not Abigail would permit him to publish) was obscurely passed over. Suddenly there was no question at all: The book would be published, and by Laon—his first venture into bound books.

Abigail was careful to keep her growing admiration not only from Laon himself but also from her mother. She knew that if Nora suspected any kind of unsuitable liaison to be developing, the whole thing would be called off. And Abigail now wanted to see herself in print far more ardently than she wanted to go on meeting Pepe.

She did, nonetheless, want to go on meeting him.

But on one occasion—it was one of their rare afternoon appointments—she had to forgo that pleasure. She was driving along Piccadilly as usual, reading her manuscript for the tenth time, and feeling ten times as dissatisfied as she had when she wrote it, when, glancing casually up, she found herself eye to eye with Annie.

There was no mistaking her, despite the gorgeous clothes. An innocent girl might have taken her for a young noblewoman or a leader of fashion out for a stroll; a man of the world would have known, by the slightly too elegant cut of her, that she was an expensive one, not to be approached under twenty guineas; but Abigail knew her at once: Annie, unchanged beneath it all. And Annie recognized her, too; she could see that.

The coach, caught in the traffic, stopped a few yards ahead of Annie. Without thought Abigail opened the door, right in the girl's path. "Do jump in, Annie," she said.

For a fraction of a second she was sure the girl was getting set to refuse.

"We've so much to talk about," she prompted.

Annie, slightly to her own surprise, got up into the coach. For a moment the pair of them sat staring at each other, too shy to speak. Abigail grinned and shrugged her shoulders; Annie tried not to laugh. The coach jolted forward a step or two.

"Let's go out to Richmond and take tea," Abigail suggested.

Annie fished in her bag and pulled out a dark lace cloth, which she draped over her shoulders. "It helps kill them a bit," she said.

Abigail, now laughing, leaned forward and grasped the girl's gloved hands in her own. "Oh, Annie! I can't tell you how glad I am to see you so well."

"You?" Annie asked in surprise. "What's it to you, my lady?"

"Oh, I suffered *agonies* after the Countess dismissed you. I used to go out all over London looking for you. And imagining such terrible things. I've prayed for your—your safety and all that, ever so often. Every night, I should think."

Annie sat back, jutted her jaw, and blew upward over her face, miming the astonishment she felt. "Stupid!" she said.

The affront must have shown in Abigail's face, for Annie corrected herself at once. "No! No, I don't mean stupid. I mean, it was very nice of you. And I'm grateful, I'm sure. What I meant was it was silly to worry. About me. Nice, but silly. I've always been able to look after myself."

Abigail nodded ruefully. That at least was demonstrably true. "So I see," she said. "I must agree you're doing slightly better than you were three or four years ago."

And then, having ordered the coachman to go to Richmond, she told Annie all that had happened to her since. And a lot of family news, too.

There was a little tea room with a glazed balcony overlooking the river, just downstream from the bridge; on this bright, raw March day it was practically deserted. Abigail was still talking as they came in and sat down; any reserve Annie might have felt had long since evaporated. She looked so queenly in her "killed-a-bit" clothes that the serving girl unthinkingly helped her to be seated first. And such was the friendship that had grown between them that Abigail merely laughed—waiting to do so until the girl had gone for the toasted crumpets and strawberry jam.

"Well!" Annie said. "And what have I been doing with myself, eh!"

"You needn't tell me if you'd rather not."

"I'd be more ashamed to confess I'd lived by begging. I've made my own way up. The only way such as I can. Things being as they are."

Abigail wanted to contradict her; she wanted what the girl said to be untrue. But words like "thrift" and "diligence" died unuttered in her throat. For the first time in her life she realized consciously that a secure way of life was not open to everyone. Until now poverty had always been the result of someone's moral failing. Her own mother's childhood poverty, for instance, had been due to her great-great-grandfather's fondness for gambling.

"D'you know how much I've put aside, my lady?" Annie asked.

But Abigail, following up her new insight, was trying to imagine herself in that position—no education, no particular skill, no character. How would she manage? She remembered the time Annie had pointed out the "gay ladies" of Piccadilly to her, saying that they did not even know the men they went off with; and she wondered now, exactly as she had wondered then, how such a thing was possible.

"Best part of two thousand pound!" Annie said. "And I never stinted myself meanwhile, neither. I'm giving it the blow-by next month."

"Giving it up?"

"That I am. Buy me a nice little public, and—"

"But, Annie—you could have given it up a long time ago, surely?"

Annie shook her head with condescending superiority. "Oh no, my lady. Not me. I seen too many gels scrape together just enough to buy a little shop or something and then sweat theirselves to starvelings trying to make a go of it. And then end up back in the way of life. Very few of them ever climbs out twice. They're parson's meat, they are. But not me. Oh, no!"

"What's parson's meat?"

"Food for sermons." Annie laughed. "And they end up getting sermons for food, and all. Out in them refuges and suchlike."

The serving girl brought their tray and they busied themselves pouring the tea and spreading the crumpets. Both took off their gloves.

"But what's it *like,* Annie?" Abigail asked casually, wiping her fingers on her napkin.

Annie licked the butter from her fingers with relish. "Hard work," she said. "Harder than housework. Harder, in some ways, than sewing, or any sweat trade. Yeah," she added, weighing it up. "It can be a sweat trade all its own. March is dead. But April's a riot. Funny, isn't it! Spring and all that. You'd think there's a new army in town in April." She sipped her tea. "I should have got out in February." Then she straightened and her eyes grew bright with a new resolve. "In fact, why not now! Yes, I'll get out now. Meeting you, my lady, was what I needed—the right sort of a shove." She leaned back and her sigh was almost of ecstasy. "Ye-e-s! I've trod the last stone. I've smiled the last smile. That was providence—you coming along." She grinned. "And I almost never got into your carriage, my lady. I almost turned my back on you."

Abigail was startled. "But why?"

Annie shrugged. "Dunno. Afraid, I suppose."

"Of what?"

"Preaching," Annie said reluctantly. Then she chuckled. "Funny—when I go down our street, I'm a queen. I give out money like royalty, too. Penny here, sixpence there. Even shillings and half-crowns. And the little gels come out and stare. And I can see it in their eyes, you know. I know what they're thinking. 'One day I'll be like her. All them fine clothes.' That's me—a queen. And then I see one of your lot, and I see their eyes looking at me, and I feel like a plate of cat's leftovers."

"Not my eyes, Annie dear. I'd never even think that of you."

Annie brightened. "No. Perhaps that's why I come in the end." She looked at Abigail's face, the hesitant smile, the questioning eyes, and something within her divined that she had not answered Abigail's real question. "You mean what's it *really* like?" she asked.

Abigail nodded intently.

Annie screwed up her face. "I got to think back a bit," she said. "I've got my own followers now, regular like. I don't go on parade much, not now. When you saw me in Piccadilly back there, I wasn't parading like. Only shopping. Well—parading on my merry way to the shops you could say." She sighed. "But, thinking back now . . ."

"When you left us, when the Countess turned you off, what did you do?"

"Well, I looked for another place, of course. About ten days I was. Looking. But it was no go, not without a character. So anyway one gel I got to know, she give me an address where she said I could get a good position. Maid-of-all-work, she said. But believe me, by that time I wasn't choosy. I was too hungry. So anyway, it was a poky little place, no more than a floor of furnished rooms, rented by a geezer who called hisself Carey, though I later found out his real name. Of course, the girl what told me was having me on. For a joke, like. The only position there was, as you might say, stretched flat and smiling.

"And even when he opened the door I knew it. Mind you, I'd called four times and no answer, and this was my only hope of a job, so I was near my wit's end, I can tell you. Anyway—I knew it. I could see it in his eyes. He's real old, nearly fifty, and very respectable. He's a railway engineer and very high up. Course, I didn't know all that then. But I knew his game. And—being hungry and all—"

She sought the air around her for fitting explanations. "You know how—did you ever see a cat killing a rabbit?"

"I must have done."

"You know how the rabbit, when it's done screaming but it's still alive—even when it's not bleeding or anything and you'd think it could still make a run for it and maybe escape—but it doesn't. It just kind of sits there, big eyes. Just kind of looking at the cat. And the cat's not excited either. Dead calm. Just looking at the rabbit. The two of them just snug and side by side, looking at each other. And if you was to get their photo like that, not knowing what went before, or what's going to happen, just that moment, you'd think they was real mates."

Abigail nodded, surprised at the sudden beating of her heart. Annie's description was so vivid, and Annie so tense with the relived memory, that Abigail could feel herself almost becoming both animals. She remembered the time when Falconwood was just starting to build, and she had found Steamer and Nick Thornton out on the hillside, and how Nick had looked at her. For one brief moment she had been transfigured by a particular sensation. She had never quite forgotten it, and now Annie's words had brought it back so sharply it might have happened only moments ago. It was the feeling of being those creatures.

"I think," Annie said, "there's a bit of that rabbit in all of us. Women. I think we're made that way. For the sake of the men. God made us for the men, didn't He?" When she saw Abigail's astonished eyes, she added defensively, "You know. Like it says in the Bible, out of one of Adam's ribs and all that. Anyway I can't explain it no other way. I could no more say no to him than that rabbit could run away. All he had to do was he held out his hand and I took it and he led me inside and done it to me.

"Then after, when I was crying, he asked me was it my first time for money. And I said yes and he said that was worth twenty guineas if I'd stay till next day. Twenty guineas! That was more than a year's wages so don't ask why I didn't run away. Even though all I wanted was to go and hide in the dark somewhere."

"But why did he want you to stay?"

Annie snorted a surprised laugh. "Why d'you think?"

"*Again?*"

"Gor-lummy yes. And again. Yeah, that's men for you. But he wasn't bad. He was very nice to me. Not that I fancied him. But there's a long way between fancy and hate. And he was very kind. Learned me a lot. How to go up to a mark—a man. How to flash myself. How to please them. How to avoid the big bay window—you know, the *familiar* way. And how not to get burned." When she saw Abigail's bewilderment she said: "Not to get in for the plate. You know—winning the *heat?* Never mind. He learned me a lot. He was a regular education to me."

She half vanished into her own reverie. "Funny thing is, his wife spends all her time rescuing the likes of me. Got her own refuge and all. I often used to laugh, but he wouldn't never see the funny side to it. Life was all de-dah de-dah de-dah to him. He explained it lots of times but I couldn't never seem to catch on."

Abigail's heart was suddenly trying to force its way up her throat. She knew who this "Carey" man was! There couldn't be two senior railway engineers around the age of fifty with wives who devoted themselves to the rescue of fallen women. It could only be her "Uncle" Walter—Walter Thornton, Nick's father, and one of their oldest family friends.

"What sort of things did he say?" she asked, hoping her agitation did not show. She could not believe that dear, mild, *respectable* Uncle Walter could do and be all the things Annie had said. Yet Annie could have no possible motive for lying. She could not even suspect that her "Mr. Carey" was known to Abigail.

Annie shrugged.

"Was he a *respectable* man? I'd love to hear how a respectable man might justify such things."

"I only go with respectable men. I got twenty-two regulars, and all above three thousand a year. I got a bishop. A man who was cabinet minister. An equerry. Four lords, five honourables, two baronets. A tea importer. A shipowner. Three barristers—"

Abigail cut short the laconic recital with a laugh. "Very well, Annie, I believe you."

"And clergy."

"But I'd love to hear the justification."

Annie made the necessary effort—and let Abigail see clearly what an effort it was. "Well, he went on about health a lot. And some kind of energy. I don't know—settoral energy, he said."

"Would that be sexual energy?" Abigail asked after looking carefully around.

"Maybe. I don't listen to dirty talk from men. Just let them rattle on and smile every now and then. But, of course, I did listen to him, what with it all being so new to me. And he said God had made all the extra women so that men with lots of that what-you-said energy could, like, use it up. But without defiling the pure ones." She laughed. "He's a funny one. He's nicer to think of than be with. Here! He writes it all down, you know, everything that happens with him and the women he has. Soon as he's dressed—dip, dip in the inkwell and he's away. 'What did you think when we did so-and-so?' he asks. And 'How did you like it when such and such?' I try not to laugh, and of course I don't tell him I was thinking about the public house I'm going to buy one day, and what sort of colour I'm going to paint the walls." She giggled like a naughty girl.

"Isn't it fun then, Annie?"

"It is for them. Times you'd think they was breaking down the pearly gates."

"But only for them? Not for us?"

Annie tilted her head reluctantly. "I agreed with the Countess," she said. "I done wrong to tell you. It's not—you shouldn't—you needn't know. While there's gels like us, men'll leave you be. And it's best that way."

"You said it was the best fun ever."

"Did I? I've said a lot of things. Well, I've just had four years of the best fun ever, and here I am, this very day, saying goodbye to it all. And what is it? It's the happiest day of my life. So—there's your answer. Now!"

"So!" Abigail challenged. "You agree with—" She gulped. She had almost said "Uncle Walter"! "With this Mr. Carew—"

"Carey."

"Mr. Carey. You get the surfeit of their energy so that we may be spared any of it? What a mess we all seem to have made of things. If it really is such fun, you'd think we could arrange it all better."

"Oh yes? Better for who? How would gels like us make our living? I'd like to know."

"We'd have to arrange that better, too."

"Who's all this 'we' then?"

Abigail smiled ruefully. "I don't know, Annie, I'm talking nonsense. I'm talking about things I know nothing of. Anyway, I'm glad you're happy."

"Oh, I wasn't miserable *before*, my lady—"

"Don't call me that. You don't work for us now. It's absurd. Call me Abbie."

"Lummie! I couldn't do that!"

"Please. Annie and Abbie. It's better, isn't it?"

"Lummie!"

"Anyway, you were saying—you weren't miserable *before*."

"No. Not always. Not often even. But I mean, when a man's grateful and says you made him very happy, even if you felt nothing at the time, you can still feel good when he says that. And a lot of times, too, I've had men go upstairs with me and kick off their boots and just lie there on the bed and talk. Talk for two hours—don't do nothing, though I'm right by them. Only talk. And then pay me just the same. And say I made them happy."

"It must be a gift you have, Annie."

"Oh, I don't mean dirty talk. But just gassing on about ordinary things. Anything. You know—family . . . business . . . buying houses . . . rows with their wives. Sometimes I reckon we're the only people they *can* talk to. Really talk, you know."

Abigail did know. It was how she and Pepe were. He was the only person she could really talk to, as Annie meant it. They could pass hours just talking in exactly that way. But she felt the quick stab of jealousy, for their talking was always in carefully guarded situations; the thought of lying on a bed beside Pepe with their shoes kicked off, talking of all the things that interested and engaged them, was such a picture of bliss that she envied Annie the so-casual achievement of it and, she was certain, the equally casual waste of it.

In the carriage, on their way home, Annie said: "I've not yet told you the best of it. Can you keep a secret?"

Abigail laughed. "I didn't keep your last one very well, did I! And I didn't even know I was giving it away."

"I'm to be wed," Annie said. She spoke rapidly, thrusting the words out as if they were a challenge; then she bit her lips into her mouth and stared at Abigail with bated breath.

"Annie! How marvellous! Who is he?"

"A follower." The glint in her eye was truculent now. She watched Abigail trying not to ask the obvious, hurtful question, then she answered it unspoken: "You'd be surprised at the number of gels who get out through marrying their own reg'lars. I know I'd like a pound for every proposal I've said no to. I'd be rich and all."

Abigail shook her head, as much as to say that the ways of people were beyond her understanding. "Tell me about him," she said.

"Well . . ." Annie settled herself with relish. "He's a gentleman. Oldale's his name, Roger Oldale. Just turned forty. Not much of an income, but this pub will take care of that. And he's ever so nice and jolly. Fond of a good laugh and I like a good laugh myself."

"And what does he do?"

"What *doesn't* he do! He's dug for gold in Bolivia, that's where he got his money. He was a surgeon in one of their armies."

"Qualified, you mean?"

"No—of course not. What else? Oh, yes—he was a photographer down in Brighton. He was town agent to Lord Lucas. And—I don't know—lots of other things. Just now he's a gentleman of leisure. Well—almost. I mean, just to have something to do he canvasses advertising for the *Graphic*. But he doesn't . . . need to . . ." Her recitation petered out. "He doesn't sound very good, does he?" she added. "But if you knew him, you'd see."

"I'm sure I would, Annie. Though I must admit your description isn't—"

Annie cut in with a defiant laugh. "Funny, when you was talking about your Mr. Laon, I was thinking just the same. 'You'd better watch out for that one, gel,' I said to myself. I suppose we're all afraid of unknown men, I suppose that's something that's in us. But it's different when we know them."

"And when you say he's a 'follower,' d'you mean—still?"

Annie looked out of the window. "I told him no. I told him we ought to stop. The minute it was on like, between him and me. But it only made him—" She shrugged. Then she chuckled. "He still *pays* me and all for it. We both have a good laugh but he won't stop." Briefly she looked at Abigail. "You be glad you'll only have one man to please. The *different* ways they can take their pleasure! You be glad."

"Do you love him, Annie?"

"I need him. I can't run a public house without a man."

"But—*love?*"

Annie's gaze had returned to the outside; this time she did not turn back as she spoke. "I dunno, Abbie," she said flatly. "I don't seem fit to love nobody very much no more."

Chapter 13

Pepe was angry the next time they met; she could see it even before she spoke. And when she did speak, she unthinkingly told him the truth: She had met a former servant who had been dismissed and—out of sheer charity—had spent some time with the girl. (Well . . . it was close enough to *pass* as truth.)

Even as she spoke she realized what a thin—not to say outright insulting—excuse it was. Yet, curiously enough, Pepe not only accepted it as natural, he even became quite jovial about it. This struck her as such an odd response (it was almost as if Pepe said "Oh—*that* girl!") that she began to wonder if he and Winifred had ever discussed the affair of Annie. If so, what gloss had Winnie put upon it? The implications of such a conversation were rich. She decided to press a little.

"Yes. Poor Annie," she said. "I don't know what Literature would have made of her, but Life has made rather a mess."

It would be wrong to say that Laon grew excited. Indeed, only someone who knew him as well as Abigail would have noticed any change; but a definite undercurrent of interest was there . . . a tension that she could not help feeling.

"Poor soul," he said, straightening all the papers and fiddling with his pencils.

"Yet I *do* know what Literature would have made of her. Nothing! It would have passed over Annie in discreet silence."

"You mean—" He could not continue.

"I mean she is, or until that day was, *une fille de joie*. Though I doubt she would concur in the description."

Pepe was trembling. It was the first time Abigail had seen a specifically sexual emotion at work in a man. (She still could not think of snatched kisses behind potted palms between dances as having any such connotation.) She found it just a little frightening—but, like a safely caged beast, a little exhilarating, too. If the mere mention of what Annie had been could produce this degree of disturbance in someone usually so possessed of himself as Pepe, then what a very powerful emotion it must be. And, in that case, why did she feel none of it?

He cleared his throat. "I trust that—ah—as soon as you—er—discovered—um—you broke off all connection with—er—"

"Why do you 'trust' any such thing, Pepe?"

"Because, Lady Abigail, I mean, because . . ."

"If I told you I had met a *slothful* girl, instead, would you equally 'trust' I snubbed her on the spot? Or a gluttonous one? Or one puffed up with pride? Or one who told lies? Indeed, I could name you a dozen girls in each category; but I'm sure you would not tremble at the mention of it as you tremble to hear of poor Annie's trade."

He looked at her speechless. His eyes begged for strength. "It is not a fit topic of conversation." His laughter was an apology for having to state something so obvious.

"Why?" she asked. "I spent two hours talking about it with Annie. It seemed to me a most fitting and serious topic of conversation. It *is* a problem, you know."

"You—?" His face was a mask of suffering. "Oh, no!"

It was as if she had confessed to cutting off all her hair or mutilating herself.

"What's it to you, Pepe? You don't—as Annie would say— 'fancy' me, do you?"

Of course, she had no idea of the emotions she was playing with. She had intended this rhetorical question to be the ridiculous exaggeration that would close the conversation and bring them back to their proper business, just as when she had once said to him, about her story, "Let's sell it to everyone in the world and make a million pounds and buy the Isle of Wight from the Queen and live happily ever after!" She expected him to give that familiar, tolerant laugh of his and say "Dear scatterwits!" or something of that kind.

But he did no such thing. He stared like a man frozen, a man transfixed, a man mocked.

At once the truth hit her, with a visceral might: he did fancy her. He loved her! A frantic terror took root and grew as swift as thought. She was close to destroying something in him. The mockery in her taunt would, if allowed to fester, soon cauterize that feeling and leave him, in some way, a lesser man.

Instantly she stood up and went round the table to him. "Get up," she commanded.

Still shocked, he obeyed her.

"Kiss me," she begged, lifting her face.

For a moment it seemed he had not heard. Then . . . oh then! The wonder that flooded his face! The glory that filled his eyes!

Tenderly he took her head between his hands, as if it and the moment were too fragile for any sort of grip, however light. Slowly he lowered his lips to hers. Until then it was like any one of a hundred kisses she had stolen: experimental . . . a toe-in-the-water affair. But the moment their lips met, a new and unexpected drowsiness invaded her. She could not breathe. Her stomach seemed to be falling. Something was burrowing and squirming at the pit of her lungs. It was the sweetest, most poignant sensation she had ever felt. It was—marvellous—stupendous. It must endure forever.

She put her arms around him and hugged as if she would squeeze their two bodies into one. He struggled and broke free—no more than an inch.

"Such strength!" he said.

She hugged herself back into his embrace. Next time they broke he took her face once more in his large, gentle hands and gazed deep into her eyes, filling his own with wonder.

"Oh, Abbie," he whispered. It was a new form of music. "Abbie, Abbie. Oh, my dear!"

"What is this?" she asked. His gaze was a physical pressure on her skin, weighting her eyelids, making her tingle.

"I never dreamed it," he told her. "I never dared to dream it. Or is that all it is? A dream."

The softness of his sentiment disappointed her. She wanted . . . she did not know. Something different. "I wonder," she said, and stood on his foot.

"Ouch!"

"No dream," she told him. "So what are you going to do about it now?"

Laughing, he took her in his arms again and hugged her. "Oh, Abbie! You are the most startling, wonderful—*stunning* girl. I have no right to do this. It is madness."

"You don't really think that," she said. "You're only saying it because you think it's what I expect you to say. You should know me better."

"It's not you, love. It's your people. The Earl and Countess will never agree to anything between us."

She broke from him, took his hand, and began to walk him around the room, round and round the table. "The Earl and Countess," she told him, "are those two people who wanted Boy to take his share of the business. Boy, however, wanted nothing so much as the Army. And where is Boy now? The Earl and Countess wanted Steamer to join the colours. But Steamer never desired anything but the industrial side of our firm. And where is Steamer now? The Earl and Countess wanted Winnie to marry a frightful, frightful man called Blenkinsop. A real *pederast*, Steamer called him. But Winnie always wanted to manage her own school. And where is Winnie now? I hope, by the way, you noticed the nice rhetorical balance of that paragraph."

Winnie, at the door, cleared her throat. "A pity," she said, "that they won't forbid you to do this book. Their permission is almost an omen of failure."

Abigail turned to him in delight. "You hear, Pepe? Success is guaranteed!"

Chapter 14

"What do you and Papa want for me, Mama?" Abigail asked one evening. She had chosen a moment after one of Nora's musical soirées, when her mother would be more than a little tired, in case it came to a fight.

"Only to be happy, dear."

"Only?"

"Well—first and foremost."

"Isn't happiness a bit of a mare's nest?"

Nora sighed. "It's not as easy as most people imagine."

"I mean, looking for happiness is like taking a bucket and going out in search of *heat*. Instead of looking for kindling, or coal."

Nora smiled. "What book is that out of?"

"No book!" Abigail said indignantly. "I didn't even think it out before I said it."

Nora dipped her head in apology. "Undo my necklace, there's a poppet."

"Can I comb out your hair?"

"If you'll be gentle."

Abigail was delighted; she'd always felt very close to her mother when she was allowed to comb out her hair.

Nora watched the girl's studious concentration. "You're getting quite a wise head on those shoulders, aren't you? I'm sure I'd never have thought so clearly about happiness at your age."

Abigail pulled a face. "You'd probably experienced a lot more of it though."

"Oh, don't say *that!*"

"But isn't it true? At eighteen you had next to nothing, when you met Papa. At twenty-one you were well on your way to fortune. And you did it all yourselves."

Nora, unwilling to speak, merely nodded. She tried to think about those times as little as possible nowadays—those days when she and John had stood and lived and fought the world side by side. They had been marvellous. She would never know their like again. And now? Now she had more money than even she knew what to do with. She had all the formidable power of one of London's leading hostesses. Houses and villas all over Europe. And so much influence in so many directions its exercise sometimes frightened her. Yet she could not think of it as anything but mere compensation—compensation for all that vanished glory. How could she tell Abigail that?

"I met Annie the other day," Abigail said.

"Annie who?"

"Annie Barnard, who used to work for us."

"Oh, *that* Annie."

"She went on the streets, you know."

Nora was silent a while, watching the careful nonchalance in her daughter's face. "You are growing up."

"I wonder what I'd have done in her situation."

"You wouldn't have done *that.*"

"You're very sure, Mama. I wish I could share your certainty. I imagine myself sewing shirts for pennies a day—barely enough to buy the candles to see by. And I imagine some kindly gentleman holding out twenty guineas. . . . How can I judge Annie?"

"Twenty guineas!" Nora sneered. "You didn't believe that, did you!"

"Guess who gave it to her!" Abigail, who had always had a facility as a mimic, dropped into Annie's argot: "He was a railway engineer, ever so high up. About fifty. Ever so old. And after he done it to me and I was crying, he asked if it was my first and I said yes and he said then it's worth twenty guineas and he made me stay all night. Learned me a lot, too, he did and all. About men and that. And all the tricks. And the funny thing is—'Ere! 'Ere's a funny thing. His wife spends her life rescuing the likes of us. Got her own refuge and all. Only he never could see the funny side of it!"

Nora's face blanched, but not for the reason Abigail believed. Like Abigail, she recognized Walter Thornton at once. But what Abigail could not possibly know was that all those years ago when she "was eighteen and had next to nothing," she had met up with Walter Thornton, then a young railway engineer, and had exchanged her only commodity for a golden sovereign. It was Walter who had told her she might get a shakedown among the navvies on his railway, and that was how she had met John and helped him win his first railway contract—and all that followed.

And now here was Abigail thinking that, through Annie, she was making one of the discoveries of the century! Even suppose she wanted to enlighten the girl (which she emphatically did not), where could she possibly begin such a tale?

"I'm sure there are dozens of senior railway engineers with wives like that," she said calmly.

"Mama!"

"Dozens," Nora insisted.

Abigail smiled and resumed her trade of coiffeuse.

"You imitate her very well. What else did she tell you?"

"Oh, she's saved up two thousand pounds and is going to buy a gin palace down east. And she's going to get married—to one of her regulars." She watched her mother for a reaction. "Don't you condemn her then?"

Condemn her? Nora thought. In *this* world? "I suppose there are degrees of—er—turpitude."

"Don't say 'turpitude,' Mama. It's what Anglicans say when they're afraid of being taken for Methodists. There's nothing wrong with good, plain 'wickedness.' As a word, I mean."

"D'you wish me to write it out a hundred times?" Nora asked.

Abigail laughed and hugged her. "Sorry."

"As I was saying, there are degrees. Annie appears to have kept her wits and her money. And she is now going into a relatively respectable trade—by comparison. Anyway, it is not for us to condemn the person. Only the sin."

"Yet if Annie had been one of those courtesans, *une grande horizontale*, we would not even condemn the sin. She would be feted and welcomed everywhere. At Ascot and the opera, gentlemen would vie to do her little services. How money sanctifies!"

"Let us be thankful for that, dear. If we had not made so much money, I'm afraid very few people would consider us even respectable."

"Good," Abigail said.

Nora caught the tone. *That's round one!* it meant. She wondered what tortuous plan the girl was following. "How's Mr. Laon?" she asked, not consciously making the connection until she saw Abigail's face in the looking glass; then she was sure there *was* a connection between the girl's devious leading of their conversation and Laon.

"Very—ah—helpful," she answered, too casually. "The book will be finished before the end of April."

"I'm glad." Nora took the brush from Abigail and trapped her hand. "Sit down, dear," she said. "I know this is like commanding you to go and marry the man by special licence, but I wouldn't form anything other than a professional attachment to your Mr. Laon."

Abigail breathed deeply to contain her anger. "May a woman of twenty-one ask why?" she said at length.

"We've heard some disturbing things about his time at Cambridge."

"He ran a book, you mean?"

"Not just that," Nora said and told her what Boy had heard at Christmas.

"But we do that in business every day, surely. If we undertake to build a bridge for such and such a sum and then the price of bricks or the wage for bricklayers falls, I'm certain we don't go to the proprietor and say, 'We can now build your bridge even cheaper—here's a few thousand pounds back.' "

Nora laughed at the notion. "Business is different, dear."

"But Pepe ran a *book*. That's business."

"All right, dear—but it's very borderliney, isn't it? Just don't become involved with him in any— What has he said about publishing? Has he offered you a contract?"

Abigail grinned. "The last time I asked, he told me of a theatrical friend of his who was forced into signing a contract with a young girl dancer. The girl's mother had drawn it up—pages and pages. Among other things it stipulated that she should not be required to dance in any group larger than three. To keep her out of the *corps de ballet*, you see. Of course, the first thing they did was to put her in the *corps*. But never dancing with more than two others. And the girl's mother could do nothing, because the fact that there were *other* groups of three on the stage at the same time had no bearing on her contract."

"And that's Mr. Laon's last word on contracts, is it?"

"For the moment. Anyway, I trust him. I think one should trust people."

"It's a very good way to get hurt."

"So is horse riding. That's what makes it fun, surely?"

Chapter 15

"But you can't possibly publish it under your own name!" Laon laughed. And his laughter, even more than his words, told Abigail how preposterous he thought it was.

"Why not? Anyway, it's a fine time—to wait until the book is at the printer's and then tell me."

"It just never occurred to me that you would dream of using your own name. No! It must have a man's name."

"But why?"

"Because everyone knows that women writers are a dissatisfied and resentful bunch of creatures. Happy women, women whose lives are rounded and complete, do not need to buttonhole the world: all they want is the calm, daily tide of household duties and pleasures. It will do you no good, you see."

"What rubbish! You might as well say that any man not actually engaged in charging down the enemy, sabre clamped between his teeth, is equally 'dissatisfied and resentful'!"

Laon smiled tolerantly. "Quite possibly true," he conceded. "But it has no bearing on what all the world knows about women as writers. Whether they hide it like Jane Austen or parade it like Mrs. Gaskell, they are as sour as sucked lemons. I won't let you expose yourself to the charge. No—come now, let us think of a suitable name."

"George Stevenson!"

"Oh, do be serious, darling."

"I am serious, Pepe. Good heavens, it's only a children's story. If a female may not write such a book, then what *may* she do?"

"You see, that's where we differ. You believe it's 'only a children's story.' But I believe it could attract a much wider readership. It has intellect and wit. Incidentally, that's another reason to publish under a male name. Women writers are notoriously lacking in both qualities. With a woman's name on it, the book will never acquire that wider host of readers. Anyway, what does 'Abigail Stevenson' sound like? A scullery maid!"

Pepe was on his home ground, of course, in his own editorial office, or he never would behave so officiously. Abigail paced up and down in front of the two tall windows, hating him with an intensity that was possible only between those who are deeply in love. More than all, she hated the truths that gleamed behind his arrogance. Most women *were* happy not to write. Whatever Jane Austen and the Brontë sisters were famous for, it was certainly not their wit and intellect. And if her book did, indeed, have qualities likely to attract a serious adult reader, "Abigail Stevenson" was not the author to recommend it. "Scullery maid" was close to the mark.

But she was not about to yield easily. "How long could we keep it secret?" she asked scornfully. "Dickens saw that 'George Eliot' was a woman before he was ten pages into *Adam Bede*. In less than a year everyone knew."

Pepe was smiling. "Naturally the secret will out. But it won't matter by then. The book will have made its mark. Why do you not trust me, sweet? I trust you as a writer. Why don't you trust me as a publisher— even if you can't see the argument yourself?"

At that he convinced her. She could feel her mind yielding to his persuasion. And though she might yet muster an argument or two, she would not be able to make them sound convincing. With a speed that would have done credit to her mother in her most nimble-witted days, she sought crumbs of comfort and advantage.

"I agree on one condition," she said, with every show of reluctance. "That I write a regular article for one of your papers under my own name."

Again that tolerant, tolerant smile. "Don't you think you could do a great deal better," he asked, "than *my* humble papers? Why aim so low?"

"Better?"

"What would you say to reviewing for *The Examiner*? Or a column on the galleries for *The Spectator*? Or stories for *The Cornhill* or *Blackwood's*? I think you should try your hand at some journalism now—but not at this parochial women's level." Thus he dismissed his own stable.

Her first instinct was to laugh at the grand folly of his suggestions— the very idea of it, that she should write for such august journals! But then something she had not expected to find within herself grew angry at that nascent laughter. Indeed, why should she not write for them *all!* It was that necessary touch of blind arrogance which is to a writer as a shell is to a turtle—a shield against the desiccating heat (in her case, the withering heat of endless self-criticism) and against the claws of enemies. Yes, why should she not write for them all!

Because she was still angry with him for being so sure of himself she did not reward him with ecstatic cries of *darling!* and *genius!* "Yes—why not?" was all she said.

Until a few moments earlier an invisible mental barrier had stood between her awareness of herself as a writer and the columns of journals like those Pepe had named. In fact, it had hardly struck her that those columns were written by flesh-and-blood people in lodgings, in taverns, in offices, in comfortable libraries and studies—by people as inwardly uncertain and as conscious of their own fallibility as she was of hers. The barrier had suddenly dissolved and she found herself standing on the far side of the line it had once taken.

"Yes," he echoed. "Why not indeed? You'll never know what you're made of until you try."

He tapped his desk impatiently. She could see he was working around to dismissing her. "If you were mainly interested in money, we would go about things in a slightly different way. But you're not, are you?"

"No," she said grandly. "Of course not."

"So there's an end to it."

Now that the clash between them was over she could permit herself once again to see him as the man she loved. And she loved him to the edge of distraction. The air around him was electric with her love.

"Kiss me and I'll go," she said.

He looked guiltily at the door and then at the windows. He laughed nervously. "I feel so inhibited here," he explained.

"Overwatched by the shades of all your dear lady contributors?"

He snorted a single laugh. "Something of that sort."

"And am I not strong enough to banish them?"

Of course, he could not let his gallantry fail that test. As his lips closed on hers she felt once again the overwhelming obsession for him that her body seemed to have developed quite independently of her wishes or even of her will. In those moments, he became the infinite. He filled the universe for her.

And her effect on him was the same. She could tell it by the way he fought all those emotions when they were writer-and-editor together—for she fought them in precisely that way, too.

When she left him that morning, the memory of him travelled in the carriage with her. No, she thought, not the memory—more than the memory—the *fact* of him travelled with her, all around her, like an envelope of some especial warmth. She wondered if anyone else had ever felt like this, and knew that, of course, they had—and yet she was amazed that the whole world did not ring with the sheer glory of it.

With amused self-contempt she remembered her erstwhile dread of being possessed by a man, *invaded* by a man. She tried to remember the shiver of revulsion she had felt at the mere thought of such an approach, but now the man who drew near in her imagination was Pepe, and the shiver he induced was certainly not born of revulsion.

The delicious, dangerous thought of him followed her up the Strand and across Trafalgar Square. Sir Edwin Landseer's new lions at the foot of Nelson's Column almost convinced her of their dignified ferocity, but at the last minute their subfusc, pussylike quality burst through the sculptor's intentions and ruined their pretence. They would never roar; if some Merlin touched them with his wand, they would mew sheepishly and slink away in shame.

She determined then, for no greater reason than that Landseer's name was in her mind, to go to the Royal Academy exhibition. Landseer had recently refused election to the presidency of that august body. It was too late for her to write any criticism of it, of course, the season was nearly done; but she could at least practise. One advantage of being over twenty-one, and (almost) a professional writer, was that she had, willy-nilly, acquired a lot more freedom of movement than could possibly have been granted to a younger girl.

It so happened that a few days earlier she had gone to the new National Portrait Gallery exhibition in South Kensington, where portraits from 1688 to 1800 had just been added to the display. So, as she walked around the Royal Academy, amid acres of pompous, bombastic, tired canvas, lacking both soul and wit, she still had the clearest memory of Kneller and Hogarth, Reynolds and Gainsborough. She had once heard an eminent R.A. tell her mother that Hogarth had no sense of beauty—that Hogarth couldn't paint.

And there in South Kensington had been Hogarth's "Miss Rich," a simple, blue-eyed angel in a mobcap, as alive and fresh as she had been a hundred years ago. And there, too, were the Reynoldses—"Lady Lincoln" with her harp; "Jessamy Bride," adored for her own loveliness and endeared to generations of readers by Goldsmith; "Lady Powis" in her blue beaver and white-sprigged mantua, walking her parkland; "Countess Spencer" with her straw hat and bridal muslin—and others. In six canvases Sir Joshua told more of humanity than any six hundred of the Academy's jejune array. In *one* canvas—"Lord Mendip"—Gainsborough did the same. Even Kneller, whose gritty, big-boned Dutchmen had seemed crude in such company, even Kneller outshone this tired Royal Academy show as the sun to a candle.

She left the Academy three-fourths unvisited, having seen it all before at the start of the season and feeling that today's quarter-reminder evoked the memory of the rest sufficiently for her to want to escape it entirely. A depressing weight settled on her spirit.

It demanded to be written about; but what could she say? What value was there in the opinion of a girl just out of school, and with no more critical qualification than her own profound conviction that the show was bad, bad, bad to its very heart?

She could not even think of an opening sentence. Nevertheless, she did as Pepe always advised—she put a blank piece of paper on the desk before her and took up her pen. And, for once, the miracle happened immediately. As she moved the pen to dip it in the inkwell, she had no notion of what she was to spill forth upon the page. As she dipped the pen, she remembered that the Academy dinner was about to be held, this week or next. As she put the pen to the paper, she wrote: "My Lord, your Excellencies, etc. . . . Gentlemen! . . ."

And what followed was the purported speech of the president, Sir Francis Grant, replied to by Lord Derby for the government, and by the Chancellor of the Exchequer speaking on behalf of Money. It was cruel; it was accurate; it was devastating; and it was very funny. The academicians' pursuit of money and social rank at the expense of artistic values was flayed mercilessly—seemingly out of the sublimely (if unconsciously) revealing utterances of their own president. The government's philistinism shone through every line of Lord Derby's reply, which was mostly taken up with a petulant attack on the few Noble Lords who had artistic taste—they would keep delaying the government in its attempts to put up new buildings like the National Gallery and the Law Courts or to beautify existing buildings with coloured brick, patent glass frescoes, and the like. The Chancellor confined himself to congratulating the Academy on keeping its finances so utterly secret that no one could even guess what they did with the ten thousand pounds they received from visitors to their exhibitions each year. Certainly the paltry three hundred lavished on the dinner came nowhere near it—nor the five hundred or so they spent on the Academy Schools. Perhaps, he concluded, he and they might enter a partnership; all his life he had sought someone clever enough to conceal the government's management of money from the Audit Office and the House of Commons.

When she read it over—and had finished hugging herself in

delight—she began to wonder where all the jibes and thrusts had come from. A few she recognized—comments made by people at her mother's salon; others she had no doubt read and forgotten; but most had sprung new-minted from her own mind. Indeed, not even from her mind but almost from the tip of her pen; she had been as astonished to see them take form on the page as any onlooker would have been.

She knew she could never sign this with her own name. Too many of her mother's friends were—if only by implication—skinned in it. She signed the pseudonym *l'Abbé*—"the Abbot"—at the foot of the page and blew the ink dry.

Then she took it back to Pepe, finding him just on the point of leaving for dinner at Stone's. "Come and eat," he suggested, thrusting her manuscript in his pocket.

"Women aren't allowed there, surely?"

"Then we'll go to the Café de l'Europe. No! I know. That place in Russell Street, the Albion. They have private rooms there."

Private rooms! She had heard the words whispered and giggled at in ballrooms.

When he saw her hesitation, he said, "Oh, it's quite respectable at the Albion. That's one thing we could learn from the French. I mean, where in this city can a man take his wife and daughters to dine? There's only Simpson's, the London Taverns, and the Albion. If you want mutton, we'll go to Simpson's, otherwise I'd recommend the Albion."

Instead of getting back into her carriage she grasped him by the arm and pushed him along Drury Court toward Drury Lane. "Oh, come on," she said. "I don't care if we eat dry bread and water. I want you to read my piece and tell me where you're going to sell it."

She let Dilks, the coachman, see the Albion and then told him to return in two hours. They were shown into a magnificent room where a dozen might dine and not feel cramped. They had two waiters apiece.

"This had better be a good article," he joked, "or I shall be well and truly out of pocket."

They ordered turtle soup, cod à la crème au gratin, and roast snipe, with poached eggs and spinach to finish. It was a four-and-sixpenny dinner even without the wine.

"Is it a very good piece?" Laon asked, looking at the list of wines.

"The best," she promised.

"Then," he told the waiter, "we, too, shall have the best: Tokay d'Alsace and a Château Curé Bon la Madeleine."

"Are you going to *read* it?" she asked before he had even finished the order.

"I suppose I might." He looked around the room. "Nothing better to do." With great ceremony he took out her manuscript, laid it flat, ironed it several times with his hands, and then, when he could find no more cause for delay, began to read.

He did not laugh once. His fingers gripped the paper ever tighter. His nostrils dilated, his eyes hardly blinked, but not a smile stirred his lips, not a chuckle escaped him. Abigail, watching him, was close to screaming with frustration before he had finished.

He tapped the paper two or three times, folded it, and then raised his eyes to meet hers. "Stunning," he said.

"D'you like it?"

More to himself than to her he added, "I wonder what Swift's first piece was like?" He stood abruptly; if there had been soup on the table he would have spilled it. "I want a second opinion. Shan't be long." And the door closed behind him before she was halfway through asking him where he was going.

A waiter came with their soup; she told him to take it back until Pepe returned. She waited ten minutes, committing the wallpaper pattern and the decoration of the cornice to memory; then she sent for her soup and the Tokay, consuming them alone. The suspense made her ravenous; she almost sent for his soup, too.

She was into the second glass of Tokay when he returned, bursting with delight. "I sold it!" he said incredulously. "Just like that! I sold it!"

"To whom?"

He settled himself and smiled at her. When he spoke again he was a great deal calmer. "Ah—that shows you're not yet a fully fledged writer. A true professional's first question would be 'how much?' "

"Who *to?*" she said insistently.

His soup came. He maddened her further by eating like a Frenchman—in reverent silence, as if the soup came straight from the kitchens in paradise.

She took a loose spoon and held it threateningly over his plate. "If you don't tell me, at once," she said, "I'm going to let this fall."

Grinning, he pushed the spoon away and prepared to tell her. "You don't deserve it," he warned. "Things like this aren't supposed to happen."

"Things like *what?* I shall scream in a minute."

"Winifred talked of omens. Good and bad. Well, here's an omen that couldn't be better."

She changed her mood abruptly then, sipping her Tokay and looking at him coolly. "The grape, I would say, was plucked an hour too early in the day." She sipped again. "Perhaps half an hour."

He told her then: "I suddenly remembered that some of the fellows from *Punch* dine here. Francis Garfield's up there." He pointed to the floor above. "At this minute your manuscript is about twenty feet over our heads. Next week it will be in every drawing room in England. Men in all the London clubs will be puzzling themselves into *rigor* over who this remarkable satirist who signs himself *l'Abbé* can possibly be!"

She said it then: "How much?"

"He offered fourteen."

Her jaw dropped. Her heart skipped a beat.

"I told him it wasn't intended for *Punch* and I was on my way to *Once a Week* with it. Immediately he said twenty! So I didn't try to nudge our luck any further."

"Twenty pounds!" Abigail shrieked.

"Guineas!" he roared back. "Waiter! A magnum of the Bollinger '62!"

He was not serious again until the cod had been dispatched. "Why didn't you tell me about it when we met this morning?" he asked.

"I hadn't done it then." And she told him how the piece had been written.

He accepted the account because, as he said, the thing read as if it happened in just that way. "Can you do more? D'you want to?" he asked.

"What other exhibition is there? The British Artists?"

"No, no. Not just art. Any journalism. *L'Abbé* could be a general sort of wasp."

She grew thoughtful. "We've forgotten my parents," she said.

"That's for you to consider, certainly."

"Pepe, why did you quarrel with your father?"

For an irresolute moment he stared a little to one side of her. Then he said, "At the risk of sounding repetitive, for I believe I've recently used the words in another connection, it's not a fit topic for conversation."

"Is it something he did? Or something you did?"

"It's something he—does. Have some more Tokay."

"In the best society one never says 'more' like that. Even if it's the person's fiftieth glass, you offer it as if it were their first."

He laughed. "You can always do an etiquette column in one of my lot. Once you have sorted out your pronouns."

She smiled and then let a silence grow, for she wanted him to understand that her next question was serious. "Do you like your magazines, Pepe? You're sometimes very disparaging about them."

He, too, became serious. "I—if I had to sell up, they would be the very last things I'd let go. I couldn't say this to another man. He'd be bound to take it the wrong way." He laughed, more in embarrassment than in humour. "I don't know that I could say it to a woman, either—to anyone but you, my darling. I feel that part of me *is* a woman."

He lifted the bottle and peered at the gaslight through it. "Talk on!" he said to the wine. She realized then that he had laid this confession before her exactly as she had laid her article before him: full of trepidation—a potential sacrifice to laughter.

"Why?" she asked, wanting to frame a more specific question but lacking all the words for it.

Committed, he plunged on, as he emptied the bottle into their glasses. "Ask me what I really want in life and it isn't riches or influence. All I want is to know what it's like to be a woman. You think differently. You feel differently. You do not approach anything as we do. We are certainly not mere mirror images of one another—that is, you do not respond to us as we do to you, not even by opposites. Nor do you respond to yourselves as we respond among each other. I don't mean that the differences are great. In fact, they are minute when you think of all that we have in common. But their very minuteness . . . I mean, you'd think something so small would easily get bruised or rubbed away. But they *don't!* They persist, these differences. I'm sure they'd resist every conscious effort to efface them. And that stubborn, ironclad persistence is what makes them so eternally fascinating to me."

In the silence his embarrassment returned. He looked at his thumbnail and found nothing. "If I said that to a man, he'd think I meant it as a highfalutin' way of excusing something unworthy. And I'm sure most women would believe I was out on an obscure 'fishing expedition.' But you understand, don't you, Abbie?"

Smiling, she took his hand between hers and nodded. Even the strongest words would have been less reassuring.

"It is an impossible ambition. I realize that. But if I can know one woman as intimately and as *entirely* as I think I know myself. So that when I touch her here"—he stroked her gloved forearm—"I almost feel it here." He touched his own forearm, and laughed. "Does that sound ridiculous?"

The laughter was a welcome relief. "It depends, my darling," she said, "on which woman you are talking about."

He became serious again; but it was a different seriousness, not tense with confession, but beautiful. "You know it is you," he said. "We are bound at the wheel of each other now. We could not imagine, we could not even contemplate, a life without the other. Lord knows what sort of life we may have together; I know it won't all be 'a bank where the wild thyme grows.' But a life apart is unthinkable."

Chapter 16

Next morning at breakfast there was a large package directed to her in Pepe's handwriting. It contained the previous week's issue of *Punch*, folded open at a certain page, and the cryptic note: *Care to bite the hand that feeds you? P. P.*

The piece he referred to was not one of *Punch*'s sprightliest—a tired page that might have condensed to a wry paragraph, mocking Mr. Bright's proposal to enfranchise female property owners. Mr. Punch could not decide whether to laugh or be angry, so he sputtered between the two; his main argument was that the female mind was incapable of grasping, propounding, or following a logical train of thought and would therefore make a mockery of elections and Parliament.

Abigail, who suspected that no mind, of either sex, was capable of logic when deep interests were threatened, thought *Punch* would be easy game. And so it was—too easy. The Abbot's technique was to show folly and stupidity caught *in flagrante delicto*. Royal Academicians had been mocked out of the mouth of their own president—so let it be with parliamentarians (for it was they, not Mr. Punch, who would deny Bright's motion). The parliamentary reports in *Hansard* would supply all her texts.

It was a mere hour's work—and most of that spent in simple copy-ing—to cull half a dozen prime samples of inane masculine logic from those distinguished columns. Mr. Punch's argument, suitably condensed to that one wry paragraph—and looking so much the better for it that even the editor himself could hardly complain—made her opening; and the simple assertion that "there must be at least ten million female minds in this country incapable of grasping, let alone following, the logic that shone forth from every parliamentary word" made a nice rounding-off conclusion.

And yet . . . and yet it lacked the sparkle of the Abbot's earlier piece on the Academy. She read it again but could not see precisely where "he" might add that sparkle. He had a good opening—that is, he took the argument he was going to attack and summarized it better than its original advocate could have done. His examples were amusing—doubly so when wrenched from their context. And his conclusion was both logical and pithy. But the whole thing remained ordinary. Indeed, if the tide of public and journalistic opinion had not been toward the other camp, you could have read such a piece in a dozen journals over a dozen signatures.

Laon's opinion of it was even lower than hers. "It's a mere answering of like with like," he said. "Everyone knows that women are inane, empty-headed creatures given over entirely to petty frivolities. If we are going to make any dent in that knowledge, we shall have to do ten times better than this."

He dropped her manuscript back on his desk. Then he saw her crestfallen face and sought to comfort her. "It's merely *good*," he said with a smile. "You're never going to be merely good. You're going to be the brightest star in the firmament."

And though she smiled back, his words descended on her like a great, gray weight. He was not joking, for all his jocularity. He meant it. And she knew that whatever talent she might possess, whatever occasional flashes of achievement it might serve up, she had not the sustaining genius to fulfil his prediction or to answer his hopes.

"The good thing about this," he said, picking up her piece again, "is that it shows you can turn out an ordinary, acceptable piece of journalism any day of the week. I'll sell this for you, if you want. Not for twenty guineas, mind; more like three or four—if that. But I'd prefer you to take it away and try to come back with something more worthy of the Abbot's signature. But the choice is yours."

The choice is yours! she thought, not once but many times over the days that followed—days in which she wrestled with the impossible task of matching the Abbot's first fine, careless (or did she mean carefree?) rapture. With a little more maturity and experience she would have seen at once what was lacking: she was no barrister, ready to argue for or against, up or down, black or white, at the drop of a guinea or ten; the fact was she didn't care a straw whether Mr. Bright got his motion or not. That was Winnie's sort of obsession, not hers. She felt no identity with Womankind, and so could recognize no common cause with such a large and vague abstraction. She was too busy writing *her* book, loving *her* Pepe, discovering *her* world and selfhood, to engage her energies in anything so diffuse. "Enfranchisement of Propertied Women"? It sounded like a private joke among political philosophers.

So, she began to ask herself, what *did* she care about; beyond, that is, her own immediate concerns? The only thing that absolutely sprang to mind was painting. She had always cared about painting. From her earliest girlhood she had never been able to go into a gallery or look at others' collections without forming the strongest opinions as to the merits and failings of the works on show.

Yes, but did she care about the wider aspects of the thing? she went on to ask. It was all very well to respond to this or to that particular painting, but what about Art? What was it *for?* And was the present generation serving that purpose well or ill?

Even as the questions formed—and long before any answers occurred to her—she felt stiffened by a certain rapt concentration. Later she was to recognize this tension as the final stage of verbal pregnancy, the moment when ideas within her came to term. On this afternoon, though, sheer instinct guided her to take up her pen, brush aside her earlier drafts, and begin writing at the dictation of an inner voice that thought only a fraction of a second ahead of the moving hand.

"In our common vision of the future," she wrote, "do we foresee a time peopled exclusively by a mildly philosophical middle class, drifting through Arcadia in aniline-dyed druid costumes? I fear we do. And for that appalling vision we have no one to blame but the Pre-Raphaelites, unless it be ourselves."

She read back through the opening and changed *middle class* into the more exotic *bourgeoisie*, a word just coming into vogue. Then she went on to develop a scathing attack on all schools of modern art, and most especially the Pre-Raphaelites, for their backward-looking vision of beauty. It was something, she felt, that could proudly bear the signature *l'Abbé*.

"But it's all about art again," Laon objected when he had read no more than the first paragraph. Yet he read on. And she could tell by his rapt, unsmiling face and his fierce grip upon the paper that she had written another "stunner."

"Superb," he said when he had finished.

"You don't think—" she said hesitantly. "I mean, the trouble is, it doesn't suggest any alternative."

"But that's what's so good. You understand without being told that the whole point of this kind of writing is simply to attack . . . destroy . . . tear down . . . ridicule . . . lampoon . . . flay. Look at the letters of

Junius—the grandest and most biting political attacks in the English language. Yet you'd scour them in vain for any alternative political philosophy. No, Abbie. You must ever dip your pen in acid. The Abbot must never elect himself pope!"

He glanced back through her piece, this time allowing himself to chuckle. "Yes, I'll try *Blackwood's*, or *The Saturday Review*. All the same, Abbie, I wish the Abbot could interest himself in something other than art. I can see him bestriding a much wider stage."

*   *   *

Next day her first article, the satire on the Academy dinner, appeared in *Punch*—a rare, signed piece in a journal most of whose pieces were anonymous. That night all the talk at her mother's salon, among the artists anyway, was of this stinging attack on artistic orthodoxy. Speculation as to the Abbot's identity ran wild.

The consensus seemed to favour Rossetti, who, as chance would have it, put in one of his infrequent appearances that night. He denied it, naturally, but Abigail could see he was pleased to be thought a candidate. Later in the evening she engaged him in conversation, which was not difficult since she had the long neck and disdainfully curved lips he adored. She soon managed to steer their talk around to "the Pre-Raphaelite vision."

And he (as she knew he would) was provoked into asking her just what she imagined that vision to be.

Whereupon she, as if she were plucking the words out of the air, said, "It is of a world peopled entirely by a mildly philosophical bourgeoisie drifting through Arcadia in aniline-dyed druid costumes. Surely daunting enough!"

Rossetti roared with laughter, but behind his merriment she could see his eyes at work in revaluation of her. She did not mind. The secret of the Abbot's identity was certain to come out sooner or later; when it did, Rossetti would remember this evening and would resent it if she had given him no clue.

"Oh, Lady Abigail," he said. "For you to be so beautiful is unfair enough on the rest of us poor mortals. But to be so witty as well!"

Nora, overhearing the remark, took it for a rebuke and later added one of her own. The secret of running a successful salon, she said, was never to compete with, much less to outshine, its members.

Abigail found herself resenting this advice. With each new achievement, and especially with the success of the *Punch* piece, she felt herself to be less and less an auxiliary hostess to her mother and more and more a salon member in her own right.

Chapter 17

The publication of *The Land of That'll-do* put all problems of journalism to one side, if only temporarily. Abigail had chosen the pseudonym "Abe Stevenson," arguing that when the facts inevitably came out, the name would be deemed less a violation than an accommodation of the truth. From the first week of June, and all summer long, Abe Stevenson was rarely out of the public print, as the dailies, the weeklies, fortnightlies, monthlies, and, finally, the quarterlies had their successive says.

Acclaim was not quite universal; but even those who disliked the book damned it in terms that made it sound interesting. Dickens, writing in *Household Words* (Dickens, who had seen the woman in "George Eliot" within the first ten pages of *Adam Bede*), pooh-poohed the notion that "Abe Stevenson" too was a woman. The tale was too witty and intellectually inventive for that, he said. Nevertheless he found it too dry for children, too coy for grownups.

T.W. Sturgess in *The Week* called it a tale without a single redeeming feature—and spent two pages on the demonstration, as if even he were uncertain of his own conclusion. An anonymous lady in *Hearth & Home* (Abigail was sure it was a lady—and one who, moreover, had divined "Abe's" real gender) found it nauseating and amoral.

But these and a few others were solitary voices against a general roar of approval. *The Times,* with unconscious irony, began: "*M. l'Abbé* may rail against the present state of artistic orthodoxy in England, but even that stern Cato will surely approve the heterodox spirit that now pervades our literature." *The Examiner* was the first to suggest that "Abe Stevenson" was a woman—"one of the new breed now knocking at the doors of the university examination halls—not your simpering, vaporous misses so beloved of the three-decker novelists." *The Spectator* classed it along with Aesop and some of the *Arabian Nights*—a tale ostensibly for children, yet one to divert and delight their parents, too.

This flood of enthusiastic reviews confirmed Nora's worst fears. She had read the proofs of the story with very mixed feelings. Her pride as a mother had been stirred at the inventive brilliance her daughter showed. For long chapters she could forget that these were the words of that frightened, ecstatic, emotional girl she had nursed through so many of the crises of growing up; the writing was so assured, so mature. Yet she could not bring herself to believe that Abigail, the person as opposed to the writer, had also made that transition. She feared all the harm the successful writer might do to the immature woman.

She watched her with Laon, who was now a fairly regular visitor to Hamilton Place, both to the salons and *en famille*. She saw the two of them together, Abigail so plainly and hopelessly in love with him, and a terrible foreboding would seize her. Few parents are given tangible signs of their children's coming independence; Nora saw it in every line of *The Land of That'll-do*—and what is independence, she thought, but the chance to ruin your own life?

She managed to convey her alarm to John, who, though usually far more sanguine than she, soon came to share her fears. Both of them, influenced by Boy's story about Laon at Cambridge, were convinced that any kind of liaison with the man (even the now-inevitable commercial relationship) would be for the worst.

"You must just forbid her to see him," John said. "Except in your presence."

Nora did not really need to answer that. "If we wanted children who'd respond to that sort of treatment," she said, "we ought to have started when they were three or less. I should have met them once a day, you once a week. We should never have let them share our table, or our conversation. We all know one another too well."

He seemed to be only half listening. "We can't have an open battle with Abigail," he said. "We've already lost any battle of that sort. We lost it the moment Young John joined the colours, the moment I agreed to get Caspar back from America, the moment I gave in to Winifred over her school."

"You don't listen. I told you the battle was lost long before all that."

"Can we buy Laon off?" he asked. "You must know him quite well by now."

She sighed out her bafflement. "I've thought of it, of course. But he's not an easy man to assess. If we're wrong about him, and we try to buy him off, it would be disastrous for us."

"We could always say we were testing him."

"Yes. We could always *say* it."

"Well, dammit, Nora—what is the answer?"

Despite the fact that she shared his anxiety, she could not help smiling.

"I see no cause for amusement," he told her.

"I was thinking of the time you abducted Winifred and—"

"A father cannot abduct his own daughter."

"—and put her in that prison—"

John made an exasperated grunt.

"—and I tried to get her out. And I found a mother had no rights. No rights at all. No power."

"Do we have to drag up all this ancient—"

"Well, I hope it is ancient, John. I bring it up now merely to remind you of the futility of force. Even with Winifred, where you had legal right and actual power—I mean, you could have made her penniless—even there it failed. But Abigail is both legally of age and, thanks to this book of hers, independent."

John nodded, accepting the logic of her argument. "It's even worse," he said glumly. "If we play a heavy hand, we'll only drive her straight to him. We must, at all costs, prevent them from marrying."

"All costs, John?"

"I would say so."

"For instance, you'd prefer her to become his mistress rather than his wife?"

He looked at her. His jaw fell slack. "My God!" he said at last. "It must certainly not come to *that*."

"Quite," Nora said. "So you see how clever we shall have to be, John."

*   *   *

The trouble was that Nora no longer felt competent to read Abigail as a person. For example, she was sure her daughter would make a great drama out of reading her reviews—either taking them hysterically to heart or disdainfully refusing to read them at all (and then devouring them secretly in her room). In fact, Abigail read them with an olympian detachment, as if "Abe Stevenson" were no more than a distant relative. Of course, Nora was not then aware that Abigail was also the Abbot and so was able to divide her interest between the personal and the professional.

Only when Winifred came sweeping down from Highgate with armfuls of papers could they provoke in Abigail any of the excitement the rest of the family felt at her success—even Nora, despite her long-sighted reservations. Laon came too, and any paper or journal that Winifred missed he had. Only then did Abigail realize how rarely she saw Winnie and Pepe together these days; she wondered if it was an accident, or if Winnie had taken to avoiding Pepe whenever she, Abigail, was around.

They took turns to read the reviews aloud, laughing scornfully at any adverse comment—as if amazed that any intelligent person could so parade his ignorance or want of taste in public—reading twice or three times all the bits that made Abigail's ears burn red.

John, who now and then dropped in for tea even when Nora was not At Home, happened to be there that afternoon: he contributed the best news of all.

"I thought you'd like to know," he said, "that your book was mentioned in the House this afternoon. Lord Culffe asked Lord Derby if he was conscious of being the prime minister of the United Kingdom because up until now he had behaved more like prime minister of The Land of That'll-do!"

"But that's marvellous!" Laon said. "That's worth a hundred good reviews. When your book passes into everyone's consciousness—even those who have never read it—when every idler is automatically called 'Lackadoo,' when every venial mayor is nicknamed 'Corney Grain,' when exasperated parents shout the taunt of 'Grace Grasshope' after every flighty young miss . . ."

Abigail's eyes gleamed. "Oh, Pepe! To give new words to the language! D'you think that's possible?"

"It's already happening," Laon said, extending his hand in John's direction.

"How are the sales, Mr. Laon?" Nora asked.

Like a man with secrets to give away, Laon put his hand to an inside pocket, withdrew an envelope, and passed it, without a word, to Abigail. She opened it at once.

"A thousand guineas!" she said, holding up the cheque. She passed it to her mother, as if it would not become genuine until Nora decreed it so.

Nora scanned it with thin-lipped, almost disappointed approval and passed it on to John.

"Lady Abigail sold me the rights," Laon explained, "for a hundred pounds. This"—he pointed at the cheque, which John was then handing back to Nora—"makes the distribution of profits more equitable."

Nora delayed the cheque a moment on its journey back to Abigail. "You mean," she asked, "you have no legal obligation to pay this?"

"I have a moral obligation," he said.

He smiled then. Abigail thought his smile so devastating it must surely vanquish her horribly suspicious mother. "I know, Countess," he said, "how much you disapprove of the lack of formal contract between Lady Abigail and me, but I truly believe that contracts force people to cheat each other—or, at least, to think of cheating each other."

"Contracts are also for people who die, or become insane, or go bankrupt, or suffer any one of a thousand shocks and reverses," Nora said.

"Oh, if I die, I have already returned her the rights in my will. If I am adjudged insane or bankrupt, there is a power of attorney ready signed in her favour." He paused and then added, "I am no longer an improvident fool, Countess!" He grinned hugely to show that his words could not possibly be intended as a rebuke of her mean-spirited fears.

And Nora, for her part, swallowed her chagrin and smiled back, knowing that he had rebuked her and that the rebuke had gone home. Her only justifiable answer—that contracts were also for people who fell out of love—could not be made, not merely because the very idea of love between Laon and Abigail had yet to come out in public but also because any mention of the subject would give him a chance he was much too clever to overlook.

His eyes were so full of challenge she was sure he read those thoughts. For a moment they sat thus, smiling at each other between the rounds of an undeclared battle; and for that moment she found herself taking quite a liking to him—indeed, almost trusting him.

But it was only for that moment.

*   *   *

Abigail saw Pepe to the door. "Let's celebrate this," she said.

He looked surprised, not certain of her meaning.

"Tonight," she said. "Let's go out to dinner. Let me take you out to dinner."

"Certainly not. Anyway, your mother won't permit it again. Not that she exactly permitted it last—"

"What d'you mean *again?* What are you talking about?"

"She made it quite clear to me—her disapproval of our dinner at the Albion. And she's right. It was thoughtless. Reckless. Just because *we* know it was innocent, we are the worst judges of the case."

"Oh, I can hear her voice there, all right." Abigail's expression hardened. "Just you be waiting for me. I shall call at seven and we'll go to—No! That'll be a surprise."

He grew worried. "Don't fall out with your mother over me, darling. Please."

She looked hastily around and pecked him a quick kiss, for reassurance. "Don't give yourself airs," she said. "If I fall out with her, it'll be over *me*. Not you."

He left, not the least reassured.

Abigail waited until her mother was alone and then said, "I shall be out to dinner tonight, by the way."

"Oh? Whose invitation?"

"My own. I am taking Pepe out to celebrate our first thou."

Nora fell into the trap; she could not resist making the trivial financial point before the far more important social one: "*Your* first thousand, you mean! You may be sure Mr. Laon has made a great deal more than that."

An idea surfaced briefly in Abigail's mind, something to suggest to Pepe. It vanished, less than half glimpsed, as her mother made the point she ought to have made at the very first: "It's out of the question, anyway. One rash act, like your dinner at the Albion, may be overlooked in time. But two? Never! You must put it out of your mind."

Nora, annoyed at having to make this point belatedly, and therefore more vehemently than was wise in any dealing with Abigail, prepared for a scorching row. Nevertheless she was determined to remain immovable on this prohibition.

Abigail stood up and began to pace the room, calmly, sedately, like a monk at contemplation. She spoke quietly, at times barely audibly, as if thinking aloud and only slightly aware of her mother's presence: "Everything I have done until now has been—experimental. I mean part of me has stood aside and watched me."

"Abigail!" Nora laughed. "Anything less probable is hard to imagine. You? You who throw yourself into everything with such fury? Experimental?"

Abigail treated the objection as if a voice within herself had made it. She replied not to Nora but to the windows, the clock, the air about her. "Until recently I would have agreed," she said. "But now I have done something that does not feel experimental. Oh, I wish there were a better word; 'experimental' is so cold. You know when you try on different bonnets? That 'I wonder' feeling you have when you first put them on? That's what I mean by experimental. And you know how there are some bonnets that as soon as you put them on you *know*. That's the right one. You don't pause to ask. You just know. Well, that's the sort of certainty I'm—"

"You mean your writing, darling? But you've been doing that for years."

"Not that writing. Not the book. That's not what I'm talking about." And she went on to tell her mother about the Abbot and some other pieces she had written—pieces that were in what Pepe had called the "merely good" class, like her piece on the Enfranchisement of Propertied Women.

She went to her room and brought them all down for Nora to read. And Nora, glad that what had looked set for a fierce argument had instead taken this mild and serious turn, read them with a doubled pleasure. "They are good," she said. "More than good."

"Thank you," Abigail said. "But in a way that is irrelevant to what I'm saying. The difference between literature and journalism is very simple. If a book is good, no one can *really* say why. They can only make guesses at the reason. That's what criticism is—an interesting guess at why a book is good or bad. The *real* reason is the book itself, of course. But if a piece of journalism is good, anyone can say why: It's good because an editor paid money for it and printed it."

Nora smiled at this cynicism. "If you said that at a dinner table, I wouldn't let it pass," she warned. "However, for argument's sake, I will. You were saying that the excellence or otherwise of these pieces is irrelevant. Now why?"

"Because of that feeling I'm talking about. When I wrote these, nothing in me was saying 'I wonder.' It was not experimental. In a way it's absurd, isn't it? Here I am with—what? Four or five pieces to my credit. It's *nothing!* Yet I'm asserting—I'm saying I'm absolutely convinced that's what I'm going to do in life."

"How can you say that?" Nora, suddenly seeing where this oh-so-calm and reasonable conversation was going, felt a twinge of alarm.

"Yes!" Abigail laughed, even calmer, even more reasonable. "How can I? Yet it is so. I once told Winnie that we are born knowing all the important things we need to know—whether or not we like strawberries, or *really* believe in God, and so on. The learning we acquire, *her* sort of learning, is trivial by comparison. When I said it, I was just saying something clever-sounding to prevent a real discussion—or so I thought. Now, since making this discovery about myself, I think it was more profound than I knew. And when I told you I was never going to marry—" She looked intently at Nora. "*Did* I ever tell you that, by the way?"

Nora laughed, beseeching the heavens with her eyes.

"When I told you that, I said it in a sort of panic, not knowing what to put in place of marriage. But it was that same kind of knowledge. The kind we are born with. The kind that never makes us say 'I wonder' about whether or not it's true."

"It's wrong to be so certain about *that*," Nora said. She herself felt a sort of panic—about this conversation. Abigail furious, Abigail hysterical, Abigail in the miseries of remorse—these she could cope with. But Abigail sitting like a god in judgement on herself . . .

"Why is it wrong?" Abigail asked, still without a hint of provocation in her voice. "What is so special, so marvellous, about marriage?"

Nora, stung and drawing breath to reply, saw the calmness vanish from her daughter's face. At once she understood that the girl had asked the question in a general sense, wanting Nora to interpret Society's edict. But as soon as the question was out she had realized that, for her mother, it had a much keener edge. Seeing the girl's discomfiture as her chance to penetrate that godlike calm, Nora (who had been going to point out that marriage was as old as mankind, and develop the argument from there) said instead, "I would not undo *my* marriage, for all the sorry thing it has become. If I could go back and undo it, I would not." Her voice faltered. She had started this line of argument coldly enough; but now its sentiment overcame her. The room swam with her tears. She lowered her head. "I would bind it a million times more firmly."

Abigail ran to where Nora was sitting, fell to her knees, and threw her arms about her mother, hugging her tight. "Oh, Mama! I didn't mean . . ." She, too, broke down and wept.

Nora, tearful but triumphant, stroked her daughter's head and neck. "I know, popsie. I know you didn't. But if I can say that about my marriage—which has been no marriage these ten years and more—if I can say that, how can you, who have experienced none of it, talk of these things with such certainty?"

A new sort of calm stole over Abigail—the calm of self-disgust. This emotional outburst had happened so quickly it had caught her unawares. But her mother's words changed nothing. She lay there, gathering her thoughts, letting Nora think she was soothing her, until she was self-collected enough to stand again and say, "But it changes nothing, Mama. The 'experience' you talk of is yours, not mine. Just as your mother's experience was not yours. You did what you knew you had to do. And I'm sure no one could have talked you out of it, could they?"

Nora, who sensed her own failure not in Abigail's words but in the return of that immovable calm, said, "Things were so different. I had nothing. I was as far outside Society as it is possible to be. It mattered to no one what I did. But you are in Society. You have—"

"I shall live outside Society," Abigail said.

Nora ignored her interruption. "You have a father prominent in the country's affairs; a mother whose position in London is no less prominent." All softness had now deserted her. "You have brothers and sisters who, not being blessed with your outstanding talent for dashing down amusing pieces on this and that in return for the odd handful of guineas—"

"Mama!"

"—will have to make their way within the bounds allowed by Society."

"I will make my own way. I will earn my own place. Painters and writers are all acceptable now, as if I need tell *you!*"

Nora, realizing that cold opposition would get her nowhere, smiled and held out a hand for Abigail to take. When the girl was seated—warily—beside her, she said, "Not for a woman, dear. That path just isn't open to a woman. Men, yes. But a woman's only way into Society, in her own right, is by marriage."

"Her *own* right! You call that her own right?"

"Don't pick me up on words, dear. I mean a woman can make her own way only *after* she has secured a firm base in marriage."

To Nora this fact was so obvious it seemed to her like the clinching argument. She was astonished then to see Abigail smile—an I-thought-as-much sort of smile.

"You are saying that Society has nothing to offer me but marriage?"

"Not at all. It has everything to offer."

"But only after I am married."

"Well, that is self-evident. Society exists to regulate marriage and the family. How can it possibly offer rewards to a young girl who shuns both?"

Again that smile. "Perhaps," Abigail said, and there was in her voice an edge of wonder that such a thing was possible, "perhaps Winnie and I are actually fighting the selfsame battle!"

Nora hesitated. Years ago John had been furious with her for neglecting all her social duties, for inviting painters and writers and such people to her dinner table; he had virtually commanded her to drop them and to enter Society properly and on Society's own terms (which then excluded almost all painters, writers, university people—everyone she found interesting). Instead she had carried the battle into Society's camp and, through her salon and her dinner parties, had made *her* friends acceptable from Windsor to Westminster. A few of the Old Aristocracy, rotting somewhere out in the shires, might turn up their noses still; but they were no longer a force that counted for much. And Nora had done far more than one mortal's share to bring about this change.

And now, with Winifred and Abigail, each in her own different way, threatening to teach Society another new trick, how could she, of all people, object?

Abigail saw the hesitation. "You could do so much to help us," she said. "If you wanted."

Nora slumped where she sat. Her chin fell to her chest. For a moment Abigail thought she was crying again. "Oh darling!" she called and put an arm around her. But Nora was not crying; no emotion of any kind showed.

"Don't you want to?" Abigail asked with all the relentlessness of her convinced and self-absorbed youth.

"Want!" Nora said flatly. Then she turned her gaze on Abigail. "I'll tell you what I want! I want your father back." She spoke in that same level tone. "I am almost ready to accept anything. Even . . ." She could not say it.

"Even the fact that he—"

"We both know what I mean," Nora interrupted firmly, even icily. She never wanted to hear the name of Charity nor the word "mistress" from anyone's lips. "But that is not the only price. It would be out of the question for me to engage in yet another battle with Society."

"Even if you were sure of winning? And you would win, you know."

"Especially then. Your father began his . . . I mean, the breach came into our marriage the very week—I think it was the very week—he as good as ordered me to take up my social duties and I told him it would be on my terms or not at all."

"And you were right."

Nora's stare was full of pity. "I sometimes think that's the worst thing any human may be: *right*."

Abigail, thinking the statement absurdly dramatic, began to laugh, a cajoling laugh to pry her mother out of this unaccustomed, dour humour.

But Nora added: "It's what the Crucifixion was about, after all. Being intolerably right. Right beyond the endurance of other mortals. Don't imagine you and I cannot have our own share of it. Little crucifixions are possible in every life."

Abigail, now that her mother was out of emotional danger, became calm again. "If they were not, darling," she said gently, "d'you think it would be worth living?"

Nora, hearing this easy courage from her daughter, was suddenly cut off from all certainty. She no longer knew which of them was right—she, with a weight of experience she could not even begin to impart; or Abigail, brave as a blind girl on a cliff top.

"What is it you are thinking of doing?" she asked.

Abigail came suddenly to life again; all that unwonted calm was gone. Her eyes gleamed; her voice shook with excitement. And Nora understood that whatever she had said, whatever invincible arguments she had mustered, it would have been as if she had said nothing. Abigail was set on her own destruction—or at least, she thought (snatching what comfort she could), on the destruction of all that the first twenty-one years of her life had made her.

"I am going to become the writer whose pieces no one can afford to miss—whom no editor can afford to reject, if he cares at all about the number of copies he sells."

"All by yourself?"

"No. Pepe will help. He'll be vital to me."

"You'll marry him?"

"I told you: No."

"But you do love him."

Abigail paused to stop herself gushing into confession. "Winnie loved Nick Thornton once. I think she loved Pepe, too, a bit, before she introduced us. She wouldn't marry either of them. Or anyone else. What do you say to her?"

"But Winifred is not you, popsie. She has not your temperament, nor your gift for self-destruction. Well . . ." She sighed and turned to the practicalities of her own surrender. "There's the house in Halkin Street. I suppose you'd better have that."

Abigail laughed. "Halkin Street? What are you talking about?"

"We acquired it in a forced sale last year. I've had it redecorated and I was just about to put it back on the market. Quite a nice, modest little place. Six bedrooms and a mews. You could manage it all with just a dozen servants."

Abigail was already laughing. "Mama! Haven't you understood *any*thing? I aim to live by my pen! Not by your dole! 'Just a dozen servants'! I shall take rooms *en pension* where I shall live with just one maid. And I shall write."

"But you are *Lady* Abigail Stevenson! How can you even think of . . ."

"It's only a courtesy title, Mama. I'm really a commoner."

"Legally, yes. But you'd still be seated above the wife of the eldest son of a marquis."

Abigail's hand flew to her mouth. "Good heavens! I never thought of that. What can I *do?*"

For a moment Nora was deceived. Then she put the echo of her words against this monstrous change that Abigail was proposing in her life—and, of course, she was unable to stem the laughter that seized them both.

"But what can *I* do?" Nora asked as they drew breath and wiped the tears from their eyes. "I must do something to help you. I gave Winifred the money to found her school, as soon as I was sure it was what she really wanted."

"It doesn't have to be anything to do with money," Abigail said. "All I want from you is never to say 'I told you so,' never to deny to anyone that I am your daughter, and never to close your doors against me."

Nora, looking at her daughter's bright eyes and eager smile, and knowing what innocence and vulnerability—what capacity for pain—were there, smiled back when she could so easily have wept.

"Of course I won't," she said. "As if you even needed to ask!"

Chapter 18

Annie's pub, The Old Fountain, where Abigail had decided to take Pepe for dinner, was in Little Jewry, less than a quarter of a mile due north of the Tower of London. The Tower, the Royal Mint, and Trinity House—all within a stone's throw—had prevented the utter decay of the area; yet an equal distance away to the north and east were slums as wretched and as deep in depravity as any in London.

But it was a good place for a pub, as a delighted Annie explained when she had overcome her surprise enough to show Abbie and Laon around. There was a spit-and-sawdust public bar for the poor Scots and Irish from their teeming rookeries off Aldgate and Whitechapel. There was a superior public bar for the brassfounders and artisans of The Minories and the area around the Royal Mint. There was a saloon bar for the City clerks—and here Annie took them to the window and pointed at the overhead railway lines into Fenchurch Street station, terminus of the London & Blackwall Railway.

"They pour in and out here," she said, "from Stepney, Poplar,

Limehouse, Bow. I remember the Countess' once saying a man could make a fortune just buying land near railway stations. And it's true here. I thought of that when I bought this place. Put a pub near a railway station—you can't lose."

"But wasn't the pub here already, Annie?" Abigail asked.

"Pub!" Annie said pityingly. "I wouldn't have kept coals in it!" She looked about her with satisfaction. "No, dear. I made this place. I put in all this cut glass, all them lights. What's a City clerk want after a day in them dingy offices? What's a stevedore want? Or a ragpicker? What's a blancher want, or a press cutter, coming out The Mint? I'll tell you—they all wants a palace, like this."

With its opulent mahogany and walnut and its scintillating cut glass, it was a palace, too; a place where poverty could be deceived awhile, if not forgotten.

"And for the gentry . . ." Annie led them to the other half of her empire.

Until then they had imagined that the gin palace—the part Annie had just shown them—which sprawled along half of Little Jewry, was all of The Old Fountain. But the part to which she now led them was, if anything, larger still. It fronted discreetly (so discreetly, indeed, that their coachman had driven straight past it) onto the main thoroughfare, named Crutched Friars after a religious house that had once stood there. Its name was painted high on the wall—and in a side street, at that.

This was the "gentry's" pub—private bars, a lounge bar, newspaper rooms, a chophouse, and supper rooms—for City gentlemen.

Like all the best English pubs, The Old Fountain was, indeed, a faithful microcosm of its district.

But the tour was not complete until she had shown them the cellars—an immense warren of tunnels and chambers full of tuns and firkins, hogsheads and kieves.

"Used to brew their own once," Annie said. "But I doubt we'll go back to them days. 'Ere!" She led them to a corner below the coalholes that opened into the pavements of Crutched Friars. "What about that, then?"

A mouldering heap of stone projected into the cellar.

"Bit of the old Roman Wall of London, that is," she said with pride.

Annie may have made the pub, as she claimed; but, Abigail thought, the pub had certainly made Annie. It was an empire, and she its queen.

"What did it cost, Annie?" Abigail asked as they returned upstairs.

Annie laughed. "A lot of silver." She laughed again, even louder, and pointed into her wet, open mouth. "And a silver tongue."

"And where is Mr. Oldale?"

Her laugh was now continuous. "Sleepin' it off, the old devil!"

"Sleeping what off?"

"Only got hitched two days back, didn't we? He's not sober yet! No, but he'll wake up. Then he'll pull his weight." She held open the door of her most sumptuous private supper room. "Or I'll know the reason!"

They had a small argument over whose treat this was, Abigail's or Annie's, which both won; that is, Abigail said, "I'll never be able to come here again or bring friends here if I fear you're going to be so foolishly generous," and Annie said, "If you let me treat you this first time, I give my word it'll be the last. Go on—I'm giving out free dinners to likely regulars all week!"

They had potted meat, jugged hare, oysters, and galantine of mutton, washed down with a warm, summery ale.

"A good City meal," Laon told Annie. "Good English food. Not the frenchified muck they serve up west." He could not have pleased her more.

"I like him," she said to Abigail as she took her up to the privy in her own apartments. "He's not at all like what you made out."

Abigail laughed. "I don't suppose Mr. Oldale fits your description either."

"No! He's worse!"

When their laughter died Annie said, " 'Ere. You want to be—you know—left alone with your Mr. Laon? Know my meaning?"

Abigail's heart dropped a beat and then raced to catch up. She had not even considered it; but as soon as the words struck her she knew that she did, indeed, want to be "left alone" with Pepe.

"I don't know," she said.

On their way back downstairs Annie opened a bureau drawer and took out a long, limp silken envelope, something like a miniature balloon. "Don't let him do anything unless he's got this on," she said, giving it to Abigail.

"On what?" Abigail asked.

Then understanding dawned and she blushed, thrusting it back into Annie's hands. "Oh, I couldn't!"

Annie looked at it and then at Abigail, seeing the impossibility of it. She stood her ground, unwilling to let Abbie return to Laon before some arrangement was made. "There's things you can wear," she said, "but only after, you know. Only after a time or two. He's got to use this. First time anyway."

"But Annie, it would look so calculating."

Annie nodded. "Well, don't let him—you know. Fingers is all right. But don't let him—"

Abigail rescued her. "Don't let him put Nebuchadnezzar out to graze—or work the hairy oracle!"

"Ye-e-ah!" Annie's face split in a widening smile as the dimmest of dim memories grew brighter. "Blimey! That's an age ago and all, what, 'my lady'!"

"A lifetime it seems." Abigail was suddenly at her ease. Those ridiculous resurrected phrases had worked some soothing magic and she was no longer afraid of going back to meet Pepe, no matter what happened. She was ready for him; yet she did not think about *him*—what he would do, how he would treat her. All she could think of was, *Will I be any good at it? Will he like me or will I disappoint him?* She remembered Annie's image of the cat and the rabbit.

"Remember, love," Annie said. "If it goes wrong, if you take on more than what you bargained for, if you know my meaning, come straight to old Annie. It's not the end of the world." Then she whispered her final words, for they were now back outside the supper-room door. "I'll see you're not disturbed—until you call."

Pepe was sprawled across the divan, staring at a recharged tankard of ale. A fresh tankard awaited her on the dresser but she left it there, preferring to drink from the same one as Pepe.

"So where d'you go now?" he asked.

Over dinner she had told him of her decision to leave home.

"I'll stay at home until I find a suitable place."

"If you had enough friends like Annie, you could move around for months and never come to rest!"

"Why not forever?" she asked, sipping his ale.

He looked at her, suddenly more alert. "What a marvellous little article that would make!" he said. "How to cadge a living off your friends!"

Abigail saw it at once—and saw better. "Let's pretend there was once this woman—one of those dull, solemn, well-meaning creatures who writes for your rags—and she wrote a book called—er—'How I Managed My Household on £200 a Year.' What name shall we give her?"

"Mrs. Warren? Does that sound solemn enough?"

"Yes! Well, I'll pretend to be Mrs. Warren's flighty young daughter.

And I'll write a piece saying how *I* get by on two hundred. An income of two hundred and an expenditure equivalent to eight hundred—all done by staying at friends' houses."

"You'd have to be married—I mean, you'd have to write as Mrs. Warren's married daughter. It wouldn't be funny to hear a single girl boasting of doing that."

Abigail thought about it and realized he was right; then she laughed. He asked why.

"It's almost exactly the point my mother was making earlier—from a different angle."

"Marry me, Abbie."

He slipped the words in as casually as if he were asking whether she wanted more ale; but he watched her with unblinking eyes and bated breath.

She kissed him, long and gently, their lips barely brushing. "I love you, Pepe," she said as they separated. "I will never love any other man so much as this."

But despite these words she managed to convey that she would not marry him. She saw his disappointment.

"Listen," she said, taking the tankard from him and putting it under the divan. "What would marriage be for us? A house to maintain. Servants to pay, to organize, to watch over for their honesty, to guard from each other's spites and jealousies. It will mean children—strangers to come between us, to claim you from me, me from you. I will not be chained at the mill of childbearing till I am dry and you are grown fat. Is that so very wrong?"

"There need be no children," he said.

She looked at him, fearful of his meaning.

"There are ways," he said. He pulled her head to him, brushed the hair from her temple, and kissed the delicate, blue-veined skin there. "This fine, beautiful head," he murmured, "of this fine, beautiful girl—so quick of wit, so graceful, so intelligent, so gifted, so astonishing, so original, so—so absolutely *stunning*. And so wrong!"

For a long time then he kept his lips pressed to her head.

"Pepe?"

He heard her gentle voice coming up from below. "Mmmm?"

"If there were no children, there needn't be any marriage. Nor any house. We could just be together whenever we wanted."

He shook his head from side to side, still brushing his lips on her temples.

She chuckled and pulled away to look him in the eye. "I hope all our arguments are so gentle."

"I am not arguing," he told her.

"No!" Her vehemence was pretended but he could see the grain of genuine annoyance at its heart. "You just sit there knowing you're right and I am wrong. Why do I *feel* wrong?" She turned her anger on herself. "I know I'm right."

Now, laughing at her own confusion, she threw her arms about him and pressed kiss after kiss all over his face. "Oh, Pepe," she whispered. "Let's just see, eh? Let's just see."

His hands caressed her shoulders. She shivered. He undid the lace between her neck and the top of her bodice, which was by no means low cut. His hands, still barely touching her, gently stroked the skin the lace had partly covered. She shivered and gave a little moan of pleasure.

She longed for his hands to stray below the top hem of her bodice; but they did not. She marvelled at his self-control. She marvelled, too, that she, feeling as she did, yet made no move to show him he could go further; but she did not see that as having anything to do with self-control. It was simply the rabbit again.

At length he said, "We really ought to go."

And twenty minutes later they did manage at last to tear themselves apart and leave—thanking Annie profusely for everything. Abigail contrived to gesture a "no" at Annie's questioning eyes; and Annie understood that Nebuchadnezzar had not grazed.

"Pepe," she said when they were almost home, "d'you keep accounts and all that sort of thing to do with my book?"

"Of course!" He laughed.

"Would you let my mother see them?"

He stopped laughing. "Why?"

"Oh," she said lightly, "it was just a thought that occurred to me when I was talking with her earlier. I can't think why now."

"Did she suggest it?"

"Heavens no! No, it just—struck me. I've forgotten why. Still, it would do no harm. You, I mean. It would do you no harm with her."

"She shall see them tomorrow," he promised.

When they drew up at Hamilton Place, she said, "Annie says we can go back as often as we like. We'd never be disturbed there."

"Good." He was shivering as he kissed her. "Tomorrow then?"

"Friday," she said, it being three days away.

"Bring your two-hundred-a-year piece. Mrs. Warren's married daughter."

Later, when she was in bed, she relived the evening with him, caressing her own shoulders as he had caressed them; then she let her hands slip to where his had failed to reach. It was a pleasure, but only for as long as she could forget the hands were really hers. Breasts were for keeping her own hands warm between on winter nights.

As she fell asleep she wondered why—when every minute away from him was a sweet torment—why she had put him off until Friday night? Was it because she wanted him never to take her for granted? Because she wanted everything about their love to be a surprise?

She did not think so. The decision seemed to have come from much deeper levels within herself than that.

Chapter 19

Laon brought his books around the very next day. Nora had not looked at them above a minute before she smelled a rat.

People who worked for her asked her how she did it. Once, for a wager, John had got a City accountant to doctor a set of books—for an imaginary company, of course—in which the embezzlement was as perfectly buried as human ingenuity could manage. It had taken Nora the best part of a day but she had found it. "How did you do it?" the accountant asked, echoing a hundred others.

The only way Nora had ever been able to explain it was by a parallel. "Imagine a chess game," she would say, "between two first-rate players. Suppose you stop it halfway and then move a piece—a pawn, say—just one square. A trivial little move that most ordinary players wouldn't even notice. But ask another master of the game to look at the board and he'd sniff something wrong at once. He'd tell you that there was no possible play between first-rate players that would result in such a board. He might even put the pawn back where it belonged and say, 'Now if that pawn were *there* . . . !' Well, that's how I am with account books that have been tampered with. I smell it at once, however long it takes me to run it down."

Laon knew none of this when he presented his books to Nora. And she did not want him to know until she had all his accounts there; these were only his publishing records.

"You are your own printer, too, are you not, Mr. Laon?" she asked.

"It's a separate company, Countess."

"Nevertheless you own both?"

He agreed he did.

"Then—though this is plainly a farce, for these accounts look immaculate to me—I think for completeness' sake, and to satisfy the dear girl, I had better see the printing accounts, too."

His face fell—confirmation enough of his guilt. And he redoubled her certainty of fraud when he took back his publishing accounts. Obviously that was to enable him to doctor the printer's accounts so that both told the same lie. With a hunter's relish she waited for him to return the following day. At last she would have solid evidence against Laon to lay before Abigail.

He was most ill at ease when he came back with the books next day; had someone breathed her reputation to him?

"Lady Wharfedale," he said with a strong tremor in his voice, "I obviously cannot bind you to such a promise in advance. But when you have satisfied yourself as to these accounts, I am going to ask you to promise never to reveal to Lady Abigail what you have seen—nor anything you think you may have discovered."

I'll bet you are! Nora thought.

Five minutes later she was ready to confess that these were the most bewildering accounts she had seen for years. They were doctored; there was no doubt of that. But she could see no way in which Laon had benefited from the doctoring.

"You seem to have made no profit at all as a publisher," she said.

"Yes," he said in a voice eager to persuade. "Here, see!"

"But no," she said. "That actually belongs here." And she turned to the ledgers of the printing company. "And see—it is exactly wiped out by these three entries. *Exactly.* Now, how can that be? In truth, you have made no profit at all—either as publisher or as printer. These books smell worse than all Billingsgate Fish Mart. Yet they reveal you not as a swindler but as a fool."

"Damn!" he burst out. Then he turned red and apologized. But when he saw she was not really shocked, he said it again. "Damn! She might have told me how good you are at it!"

"But . . ." Nora laughed, still completely baffled. "The only person who has made any money out of it at all is . . ." Her voice trailed off as enlightenment reached her at last. "Abigail!" She waved her hands over the books. "You've given it *all* to her." She was shocked.

Miserably he nodded.

"But why? To entice her away from us?"

Now it was Laon who was stung to shock. "Of course not! I simply did not wish to make a profit from her. I took care to make no loss—as you have discovered—but I have also made no profit."

"Because you love her?"

He looked angrily at her. "Did you need to say that? And now I must ask you to make that promise, please?"

"But why?"

"Because I do not wish her to know. It would cheapen the whole thing."

"If it came from you, yes. But not from me, surely?"

"Please, Lady Wharfedale, I do not want her to know. It is best if she believes we have normal business relations as far as her writing goes. It is important for her to believe that. Just as it is important for me to know I have not profited by her. This"—he pointed at the book—"reconciles those demands."

Nora smiled. "Does it! I could show you a dozen ways of doing it less clumsily. But I apologize to you, Mr. Laon. You are obviously a man of fine feelings."

Laon also smiled. "What did you really expect? That I was making money out of her?"

Nora shrugged.

"Really!" he said. "Making money is no problem. At least, I have never found it so."

"Come, Mr. Laon! You sound more eligible by the minute."

He barely noticed her compliment. "But Abigail!" he said, more to himself than to her. "She is unique. There has never been, and never will be again, such a girl as her."

And Nora, who had feared for Abigail's vulnerability and Abigail's capacity for pain, now saw that the boot was on the other foot.

"Poor boy," she said. It was almost a whisper.

"She will not marry me."

"She is still young. Here." Nora touched her own heart.

He looked at her with his dark, piercing eyes. "Help me," he begged.

And Nora, to her own utter astonishment, heard herself saying, "Of course I will."

Later she wondered what on earth could have induced her to such agreement. Of course she would not honour it; but now, more than ever, she worried for Abigail in her dealings with this man.

Chapter 20

"You'll never guess what," Laon said that Friday evening. "Rossetti thinks *I* am the Abbot!"

Abigail joined his laughter until she realized it was not entirely at Rossetti's expense, nor at the exquisiteness of their secret; it was at his own cleverness—that he was the sort of person who could be mistaken for the Abbot even by someone as perceptive as Rossetti. It seemed to her then that she was the victim of a trick, that something precious had been filched from her. But it was only a passing feeling, and Laon was so charming and attentive she soon forgot.

"How's Mr. Oldale?" she asked Annie, who came to supervise the clearing of the banquet.

Annie pulled a sour face. "I've seen ostriches fly better," she said. But then she laughed, so Abigail understood it was nothing serious, especially as Annie left them alone with a solemn wink.

They were in each other's arms at once, almost bruising their lips with the passion of their kisses. Again she revelled at the sweetly aching emptiness he made at the very centre of her, felt her breathing turn to disorder.

In the midst of this abandon he said, "Tell me what it's like."

"What!"

"Oh, please, Abbie darling! I have never known a girl like you. No one has ever had this effect on me. I want to share it. I want to know it all. Please?" His dark eyes, so full of pain and hope, held her pinned to his will. "Help me!"

For this dinner she had not put on her evening gown with its fashionable low-cut bodice and yoke of lace (and its myriad hooks and buttons). Instead she wore a much simpler, flowing gown of her own devising. Its inspiration was Pre-Raphaelite—very much the "aniline-dyed druid costume" the Abbot had mocked. At a distance, and in silhouette, she might have been taken for a Quaker girl in an older sister's dress; but no Quaker girl ever wore such lustrous silks, so richly amber in colour.

She reached a hand inside, where she hoped his hand might have strayed, and delicately eased out a button she hoped his fingers might have discovered.

"What are you doing?" he asked.

"Telling you."

"Not that way."

"It is the only way I can."

"Telling me what? Say it!"

"That I love you. That love sanctifies us. That I feel no shame. That I am yours in every way and always. That we might do anything—things that in words might seem shameful—and we would make them . . . glory."

She had meant to say "holy" and could not understand why she had blurted out "glory," with all its overtones of battle and victory.

Gently he pulled her hand from the folds of her gown; gently he took her back in his arms; gently he murmured into her ear, making her thrill again at the vibrant nearness of him, "I'm sorry, darling. It's just—I want to know you better than I know myself, better than anyone ever knew any other being. You are the warmest, loveliest, most breathtaking, most captivating, sweetest, brightest, most astonishing girl who ever lived. You are magical. The whole world is different just because you are in it. Wherever you go, the stones and trees beside your path—the very air you walk through—are all transformed, because they have shared a little in the rarity of you."

His hands invaded the folds of her sleeves and, finding no resistance, were soon caressing her shoulders and shoulder blades and, through her chemise, her spine.

"That's what it's like to be me," he said. "Heaven and hell. And the hell of it is *not* knowing you—not *being* you. What is it like to *be* you?"

The room dissolved in a shimmering; her voice became a quicksand for her own self-possession. "I don't know," she stammered. "You help me—to find out."

She threw herself back on the divan and, with clumsy urgency, began to undo the inner buttons between her neck and waist, until his grip stayed her. He lay mostly on the divan, only slightly upon her, and gently parted the long, open folds of her bodice, kissing the line of her jaw, her cheekbones, her ears, running his lips down her long, slender neck.

His fingertips, and sometimes his fingernails, strayed where her body lay peeled—over her shoulders, her arms, her ribs, down her breastbone, to the taut skin of her stomach—everywhere but her breasts. She shivered until the divan itself turned to jelly; her heartbeat was a thunderous ripple, in her scalp, in her toes. A strange, glowing fluid seemed to irrigate her, a solvent of all her senses. It reached into everything, every part, uniting in a way she had never before experienced—a mysterious sweetness that felt like strength yet left her overcome with drowsiness.

"Please!" she begged, not knowing what she begged. "Oh, please!"

"Yes!" he promised, not knowing what he promised.

His fingers stole to the edge of her breast. She drew a deep breath; her lost voice meandered in and out of her breathing.

His hand covered her breast. At once that inward glow turned to incandescence. A distant cry, her own, echoed through the sudden infinity she had become. Delight so great it was also a terror seized her, again and again—then there was a quick and overwhelming fear of death.

She knew—beyond certainty she knew—that she was close to death. Her skin burned in uneven flushes. Her heart would not beat; it squirmed in its weakness. She pulled his hand off her and crept at once into his embrace, straining herself to him, wanting to die in his arms.

Now his hands comforted her, dowsing the fires that had turned to terror, gently easing apart that awe-full unity, restoring all the separate parts of her body to her own possession.

"There," he said, kissing her salt-soaked cheeks.

Feeling hot she drew away from him and blew down her front to cool herself. Where her skin had burned there were lingering patches of discolour. "Something is wrong with me," she said.

"Mmmm?"

She repeated herself in more matter-of-fact tones.

"I'll poison any doctor who confirms it," he said. His voice was lethargic, all his movements leaden; he was only half awake.

"Seriously," she said. "I just had a seizure of some kind. Epilepsy. Or a heart attack."

He laughed, a comatose attempt at a hearty laugh, and hugged her to him. "Oh, Abbie, Abbie! I love you."

"What?" She did not like to be unwittingly funny.

"Don't you understand?"

"No."

"You saw the Great God Pan," he said. "And so," he added, pointing at a damp mark on his pantaloons, "did I."

When Abigail went to Annie's boudoir to tidy herself, she tried to explain what had happened—and found herself hesitating and stammering as if she had to say it in a language she had only half mastered. She—the writer whose sales were rivalling those of Dickens, the journalist no editor had yet refused to print—could not begin to describe what had just happened to her.

"Blimey!" Annie said. "And all he did was touch you? There?"

"Yes."

"You must love him, gel. That's all about it."

"Is it? Why?"

"Didn't you like it?"

"I don't know. It gave me such a fright."

"First time? Never happened before?"

"Never. What was it, Annie?"

"Next time you'll be expecting it. Then you'll see."

Abigail stared, trusting Annie's words more than she understood them.

"It's what it's all about, gel," Annie said.

*   *   *

August passed into September and the days were noticeably drawing in. Now and then a damp, salty mist would drift in off the Thames and make the year seem even later than it was.

They dined at Annie's as often as they could, sometimes four nights a week. For both it was a time of marvel; they knew where it was leading; Abigail did not fear it; Laon was not consumed with impatience. Day by day each unravelled more of the mystery of the other's body. She learned the things that gave him ecstasy and discovered where her own thrills were released. In Annie's phrase she "saw the elephant"—saw it, felt it grow, held its gristle, squeezed its sinew, contained its throb, and looked in wonder at the starchy residue on her fingers.

She realized this was the stuff with the power to quicken her. She had no idea how; but that only made it more magic and potent She feared it. But the fear was not of mere social death; it was of something deeper and far, far more ancient.

And Pepe feared her, too. She could sense that. He approached her body with a sort of awe that was only part in worship; the other part was dread. She would catch him staring into her eyes as a man might stare at a bomb whose appointed hour for explosion has come and gone. Then *he* was the rabbit; though she did not feel one whit more like the cat.

With time these taut moments began to slacken. The fear, the novelty, the awkwardness all diminished. The magic remained. Though their love was, as yet, unconsummated, and therefore ought to have been tense with anticipation, she found she could relax—even bask—in his sexuality, without fear, without anxiety, and with a longing untinged by desperation.

"When?" she asked once, in that rich language that had grown between them, threadbare only in its words.

"When we need to," he said. "Soon."

But as "soon" drew near, his proposals of marriage became more insistent—as if he were hoping to make the one act conditional upon the other. He did not press, nor did he grow angry; but his quiet resignation, his sadness, which he took no pains to hide, cut her to the quick. She grieved for him that he could not see her fear of marriage and domesticity as anything but juvenile.

Fortunately it did not affect her work, nor his impartiality as her editor and agent. And as September came on, pushing back the enervating heat of August, she fell into a spate of work that extended her in every direction, from the aloof wit of the Abbot to earnest and sincere trifles on cookery (helped by Anton, her mother's chef) for Laon's own magazines. She came to love the wearing of all these different hats and being all these different people—insatiable people, each of whom wanted to write her (or "his") piece and damn the others. She averaged around seven thousand words a day, which excused the fact that she was still living at home, still merely talking of moving to a place of her own.

One day, after delivering a shoal of articles and a couple of short stories to Laon, she was sauntering up the Strand, wondering what to write next, when the delicious thought stole upon her that she would write nothing at all. A crisp, early autumn sun was filling the city with silver; the overnight rain had settled the street dust. It was a perfect day in which to loaf; a day to be young in. She would buy the first book that seized her fancy, take it home, sit out on one of the balconies in the sun with the glorious throb of the city at her feet, and read it from cover to cover. The ambition was easy to achieve, for that part of the Strand was full of secondhand bookshops (not all of them quite as proper as their outside stalls would lead the casual passerby to imagine).

Some angel must have guided her steps, she afterwards felt. For the book that took her fancy (more for its rich binding than its title) was a facsimile edition of one of William Blake's prophetic poems, *Visions of the Daughters of Albion*. Idly she opened it and read:

The golden nymph replied: "Pluck thou my flower. Oothoon the mild,
Another flower shall spring, because the soul of sweet delight
Can never pass away." . . .

And she almost ceased to breathe.

Then Oothoon plucked the flower, saying: "I pluck thee from thy bed,
Sweet flower, and put thee here to glow between my breasts;
And thus I turn my face to where my whole soul seeks."

Her hair stood on end. Blake, who had lived in Fountains Court, not two hundred yards from where she now stood, knew! He was telling her all those things she felt and yet could not articulate.

The man did not want to sell the book to her—seemed annoyed that it had been on the stall where she had found it. But Abigail insisted. And when Abigail insisted on anything, few men could deny it her for long. She hurried home. By teatime she knew the *Visions of the Daughters of Albion* by heart. It was the textbook for her life: "All that lives is holy."

That evening the mists off the Thames were thick and the fires that people kindled only served to make them thicker. Abigail and Laon had a fire set in their supper room at Annie's. With the fever of Blake's *Visions* still on her, Abigail ate lightly and the meal was soon over. Soon, too, they were lying naked, side by side in near contact, touching only with their fingertips and lips.

He was aware of this new excitement in her and she could see his eyes posing a question his tongue could not quite frame. She wished she could babble the whole poem to him in one great superword, so that he could see it the way you see a painting; she wanted him to share it, but instantly, not dragged out in time—time during which their lust would clamour, throats would dry, scalps itch, noses need blowing, fires tending, and a thousand other mundane irritations intervene.

He drew breath to speak, to stumble at that still-forming question. She leaped upon him, on all fours, straddling him, hanging over him. She spoke barely above a whisper, kissing him lightly at every pause, until he could relax no deeper.

"Thy joys are tears, thy labour vain, to form men to thine image.
How can one joy absorb another? Are not different joys
Holy, eternal, infinite; and each joy is a love?"

"What's this?" he asked, smiling up at her in wonderment. He began to caress her spine and hips, gently, with raking fingernails.

At bay to her own desire she said urgently, "Listen. It's for us. It's about us:

"With what sense does the parson claim the labour of the farmer?

"Forget about parsons and farmers—it's *us*," she insisted.

"What are his nets and gins and traps, and how does he surround him
With cold floods of abstraction, and with forests of solitude,
To build him castles and high spires, where kings and priests
*   may dwell,*
Till she who burns with youth, and knows no fixed lot is bound
In spells of law to one she loaths? And must she drag the chain
Of life in weary lust? Must chilling, murderous thoughts obscure
The clear heaven of her eternal spring; to bear the wintry rage
Of a harsh terror driven to madness, bound to hold a rod . . ."

"Oh darling!" he said. "It is wrong, wrong, wrong!"
"Listen!"

But he would not listen, not to *her*, only to the words, turning them into "cold floods of abstraction." His merciless fingers gave her longings no rest.

"Please, Pepe," she said, hearing the bewilderment of her straying voice. "It's all the things I don't want to happen to us.

"To turn the wheel of false desire; and longings that make her womb
To the abhorred birth of cherubs in the human form
That live a pestilence and die a meteor, and are no more . . ."

"I don't want to . . . I want . . ." she faltered.

"I want," he whispered. "I want, I want, I want."

He slipped beneath her to kiss her hanging breasts and suckle her. His hands moved to her thighs, up and up.

"Pepe," she murmured. He had not heard. He listened and understood but he had not *heard*.

Yet that was in the *Visions* too!

. . . Take thy bliss, O man!
And sweet shall be thy taste, and sweet thy infant joys renew!
. . . The moment of desire! The moment of desire! The virgin
That pines for man shall awaken her womb to enormous joys . . .

The words had heaped her day. The longing for him was now insupportable. She moved down upon him. He pulled her home, to the hilt of him.

Time ceased. In that infinity of pleasure all thought came to its stop. They surrendered every faculty but sensation.

He toppled her, smothered her. She became their bed, the room, the house, the whole Earth; it was at once the strangest and most natural thing to lack fingers . . . toes . . . all extremities, all defined boundaries—to vanish and yet to become everything.

At last she returned to herself, spiralling down the memory of one long voiceless moan that still lingered on the air of the room. Every muscle in her body collapsed. The movement made her aware that Pepe was no longer in her. His dead body breathed into her ear. Her hands found him, found the napkin between them, felt its dampness.

She remembered language but not the need to use it. Not yet. The firelight was warm and golden on their bodies. The clock began to tick again. When Pepe stirred to ease his weight on her, a sudden stab of longing for him came, fierce as ever—*don't go!* A little memorandum from her flesh—to remind her of its sovereignty "in lovely copulation."

I cry, Love! Love! Love! happy, happy love! free as the mountain wind!

She whispered the words to him.

"It's no true recipe for life though, is it?" he said, not stirring. His breath made a furnace in her hair and on her neck.

"I want it to be. It feels so *right*. I know it goes in the face of everything."

"Especially of logic."

"Yes. Especially that. To want such utter freedom. Free! Love! The two most beautiful words. To want that freedom and yet to want to share every moment and morsel of it with you! To be in thrall to you, and yet to call that slavery the most perfect of all freedoms!"

He raised himself on one elbow and pulled off the damp napkin, revealing himself shrivelled and boneless. "I could have stayed inside," he said, "and ended all these fancies."

She wanted to weep. He had gathered nothing! All her ideas and feelings, as clear and sharp to her as a thousand suns . . . he stared straight through them as if they were not there.

"Never think *that!*" she said fiercely. "I would even bear your child unmarried. A hundred children."

He slumped, shut his eyes, and lay beside her a long minute.

Later, when she dressed and went up as usual to Annie's boudoir, she found a stranger, a nervous middle-aged woman, there. "I'm Annie's auntie, dear," she said, offering no name.

At first Abigail thought her nervousness was a form of embarrassment at what she knew must have been going on with Pepe in the locked supper room. But when she asked the "auntie" where Annie was, and saw the shifty look in the older woman's eye, she knew it had something to do with that.

"She's out on an errand of mercy, love," the aunt said. "Be away all week, she will."

Abigail was still overwhelmed by Pepe's inability to comprehend; she had no time to bother much at Annie's absence.

Chapter 21

One day that autumn—it was the week before Abigail finally left home—Wilkie Collins called on Nora. He was an even less frequent visitor than Rossetti, and Nora soon discovered he had come to see not her but "the remarkable young author of that remarkably witty book *The Land of That'll-do*." The secret was breaking; the ripples spreading.

From the writer of *The Moonstone*, an even greater recent success than Abigail's book, this was praise indeed. When Nora rang for a footman to fetch Abigail, Collins expressed a hope to see her at her desk, saying one could learn more about a writer from that than from a dozen drawing-room conversations.

Nora knew how terrified Abigail would have been of this encounter less than a year earlier, so it was with some misgiving that she agreed to take Collins up to the room which Abigail had made her study. But when she saw how easily the girl coped, greeting Collins almost as an equal (which he did not, Nora noticed, entirely welcome), she understood just how much her daughter had matured these last months.

They found her correcting the galleys of a short story Laon had "syndicated" for her. The term was new to Collins, and Abigail had to explain it for him. "This same story appears in five or six different country newspapers, you see," she said.

"And you get five or six times as much money for it?"

"Naturally." Abigail laughed.

"Your Mr. Laon sounds a very clever man."

"Oh, it's not his own idea," she said. "They do it a lot in America. He heard about it from a friend of Walter Besant's, a Mr. Watt, who got it from someone called Tillotson."

Collins held out his hand for the proof. "May I?"

He read the story with deep attention and declared it very good. But the ending he said, could be greatly improved—not by changing it, but merely by telescoping two or three incidents. "Don't you see how much stronger that would make it?" he asked.

She agreed.

"D'you mind if I alter it?"

She said she would feel honoured.

He whipped out a pencil and soon not just her ending but the whole galley was a mass of excisions, links, and transpositions. Nora watched aghast, until her eyes met Abigail's and Abigail winked.

"There!" Collins had finished. As he looked at the ruin of the galley and remembered where he was and why he had come, his face fell. "I am most awfully—" he began.

But Abigail took the galley from him and put it straight into an envelope already addressed to the *Bristol Times & Mirror*, the journal for which the piece was destined. She rang for a servant to take it directly to the post office at St. Martin's. "It will arrive tomorrow," she said. "How delighted they will be."

Collins forgot then whatever slight affront he had felt and began discussing writers and publishers and the book trade without reserve or condescension. After a while Nora quietly withdrew, but Collins did not notice her absence for a full half hour. When he did, he was shocked.

"Good heavens!" he said, looking around him as if the floor had collapsed and he was left isolated on a single, infirm pinnacle. "This is most—most—er—irregular. I—"

Abigail cut him short, not concealing her impatience at his social scruple. "You have not talked of yourself, Mr. Collins," she said. "What is your next book to be?"

Politeness (reinforced, to be sure, by natural inclination) forced him to answer, and in doing so he forgot the cause of his embarrassment and talked on for another half hour.

"That was so nice of you, popsie," Nora said after Collins had left.

"What was?"

"Not to protest when he began scribbling all over your story—and to send it off at once, so that he could be sure you wouldn't just throw that proof away and use another. I don't know any other writer who'd allow such a thing."

"But he was right!"

"Even less of a reason, to most people."

"You're talking about men authors. Maybe they're different. I must write at once to Bristol, though, and tell that editor what happened."

But that letter did not go until the following day.

*   *   *

Two days later Pepe was waiting for her at Annie's with an amused grin.

"Read and learn," he said. And he passed over a couple of letters from the editor of the *Bristol Times & Mirror*. The first said he had already had a sample of Mr. Abe Stevenson's impertinence and had been in two minds about taking this new story; now his doubts were confirmed. If Mr. Stevenson thought his compositors had nothing better to do than decipher Chinese hieroglyphs . . . , etc. The second begged Mr. Laon to ignore his first letter and to convey his warmest feelings to Lady Abigail. ("How the ripples do spread," she chuckled.) He had no idea she was acquainted with Mr. Collins. . . . Could she perhaps beg some trifle from him for the *BT&M* . . . She might feel every assurance that past misunderstandings were past and would never recur.

She laughed and they sat down to their meal.

"BT&M!" She snorted. "I'd like to kick him on his B,T,M! I should have thought of it when I wrote that first time."

"Yes," he said. "I don't understand that. What was it? I didn't know there'd been a fracas between you."

"Oh, it was over that first story you syndicated, 'The Weaker Sex.' Remember he changed the ending?"

"Yes. But I said to let it pass."

"Well, I tried to but I couldn't. All I did was write and ask him why he'd done it. I mean I really wanted to know. And he had the effrontery to write back and say he'd assumed there was a page of manuscript missing. The story had no proper end, so he wrote it himself."

"Was that all?"

She took a morsel of food to avoid answering; she held out her empty wineglass to distract him.

"Was it?" he repeated as he filled the glass.

"No. I wrote again," she said.

He drummed the table with his fingertips, looking at her wearily.

"I told him," she said defiantly, "that the village editor has no more right to adulterate literature than the village grocer has to put chalk in the flour."

"Oh my God!" Laon sank his head in his hands.

"And I added that I knew the practice was rife in the second trade but had not until now been aware of its spread to the first."

Laon silently shook his head. At last he raised his eyes to hers and held her in a long survey while he gathered words.

"You got away with it," he said. "But the lesson is nonetheless plain. Your book, your *one* book, may have sold as well as *The Moonstone*—it may even have outsold it—but that does not even begin to turn you into the sort of literary figure Wilkie Collins now is. This"—he held up the second letter—"fawning and grovelling is entirely due to the magic of his name. Not yours. It will be a long time yet before you can give yourself literary airs. Until then, darling Abbie, never never forget that you are writing for a market. For a *dozen* markets. Always remember that each piece has a market."

"Market!" she said, feeling too diminished to attack his main argument. "What is a market!"

"A market . . ." he began and then paused to think. A slow smile transformed his face. "A market is a strange mixing—a chimera composed of ninety-nine percent pure editor and a trifling one percent adulteration known in the trade as 'The Reader.' Yet 'The Reader' gives his name to the entire beast!"

His witticism amused him. She, too, laughed, though more in relief that he had not grown angry with her. He would have had every right to be angry.

"Forget it at your peril," he said, closing the subject.

Before she left that night she went as usual up to Annie's boudoir. The nameless auntie was still there.

"Annie's away a long time," Abigail said. It had been nearly four weeks.

"Oh, no, dear, she's back," the woman answered. "She came back while you and your gentleman was—er—eatin'."

Abigail was delighted. "Oh, but tell her I'm here, do! I'm longing to see her again."

"Well—I don't know. I'm not sure."

"Not sure of what?"

"She may not want to see you."

For a moment Abigail did not know what to say. "Why ever not?" she asked at length.

The woman shrugged, plainly embarrassed, and, going to the door, said, "Well, I'll tell her then."

Annie's appearance appalled Abigail. She looked *old*. And beaten. Though she smiled bravely there was an air of defeat about her that not all the would-be girlish squeaks and hugs could mask.

"What is it, Annie?" she asked.

"I'll soon be right as a rainbow," Annie said. She laughed. "And twice as crooked, you're supposed to say."

"Right from what? What's been happening to you?"

"I don't want to talk about it, love. Me sister, the one in Wales, did I ever tell you? No? Well, her little one took ill. That's where I went. He died. Oh, it was chronic. But don't talk about it. Tell us about you."

She looked around as if she had forgotten something, saw the decanter of port on a small credenza, and almost ran to pour herself a glass. Abigail realized she was already a little tipsy—"obfuscated," as Annie called it.

She sipped the port and pulled a face. "Decoction of brewer's apron," she said. "Well, gel. Have you made the addition?"

Abigail heard "edition," and did not understand.

"Have you lost your stakes?" Annie laughed. Her tone grew a little wild. "Has he been all there but most of him? Swopped a bit of hard for a bit of soft, did you? Take the starch out of him?"

"Oh, Annie, don't! It isn't like that."

"Like what?"

"It's not a battle. Nor a game."

"Try it with the chill off!"

"What's the matter, Annie dear?"

Annie made obvious efforts to rally herself. "Sorry, love. Tired, that's all. Just tired. All be different in the morning." She grinned—genuinely—and seemed to relax. "Seriously," she said. "Did he?"

Abigail smiled. "*We* did. We *do*."

Annie clapped hands and laughed. "Straight? What d'you think of it, then? D'you take to it?"

Abigail could only grin back at her; she could not follow Annie's animalistic line. The thing itself was too sacred; it would have been a betrayal.

"Bet you do!" Annie challenged. Then she grew serious again. " 'Ere! He wouldn't break your leg, would he?"

Abigail shook her head, but Annie took it as a sign of incomprehension. "Leave you with a lapful? In the familiar way?"

She shook her head more forcefully. "He has—those things. Like you showed me."

Annie was only half reassured. "They're better than nothing. But what you want is one of those things we can wear. What they call a Dutch cap. It's a new idea but they say it's the best. Shall I get you one?"

Abigail had no notion what Annie was talking about; the only images in her mind were all from Rembrandt and Van Dyck—girls in starched white bonnets.

"What are they like? What do they do?"

Annie explained and showed one of her own. "It's me Sunday one," she said with a wink.

Abigail thought it would be a good idea.

"Well," Annie said as she downed her third port, "got to give *my* old man his supper I suppose."

Just before she went Abigail asked why it was called a Dutch cap.

"Well, it *is* a cap, isn't it?" Annie said.

"Yes, but why *Dutch*?"

"Don't you get it?" Annie said in surprise. "*Low countries!*"

Abigail still did not comprehend, though she knew some kind of double meaning was involved. Later she wondered at Annie's utter inability to talk about men, women, and copulation without elaborate, joking circumlocutions and double meanings. She and Pepe could talk about it, straight and unabashed, but that was a private language. The only person she knew who could manage it in public was William Blake, in some of his poems; and the only place you could get those poems was in the dirty bookshops.

Dirty bookshops!

Someone, she thought, *has got the marching orders wrong!*

Chapter 22

Abigail took a large set of chambers in an old house near the river end of Buckingham Street, just south of the Strand near Charing Cross. The new embankment was nearing completion, much of it built by the Stevenson family business. Often when looking out of her windows she would see her father or Steamer on one of their regular visits to check on the progress of the works; sometimes she would run out and join them and be taken on a tour of the new sewers and underground railway and all the other marvels. Usually there was another man with them, Joseph Bazalgette. Her father introduced him as "the gentleman who made it possible for you to live in Buckingham Street without choking on the stench of the river."

Bazalgette was, in fact, the architect of London's modern sewerage system, not yet complete, and the chief begetter of all the new Thames embankments.

"D'you know when the guvnor and he first met?" Caspar asked her once, when the two older men were out of earshot. "It shows the value of old friendships."

"Does it?"

"Those two first met the year before you were born, Abbie. The guvnor got up at half past four one morning, especially to meet that man—and found him with his surveyor's tools at the bottom of a twenty-foot trench in Fleet Street."

"Hurt?"

"No! Working, silly. No one had ever heard of Bazalgette then, but they talked for an hour, enthusiast to enthusiast. And that's why we've got so large a slice of this!" He looked around the workings with crisp satisfaction. "I mean, they trust each other."

Abigail, watching her father and Bazalgette, envied so long a friendship. Of all the people she met now (apart, of course, from Pepe), whom would she still know and work with twenty-five years hence?

Steamer, unconsciously echoing her thoughts, said, "So, Abbie dear, the moral is plain—when you go to meet your grand publishers and all those great editors, be sweetest of all to the office boys!"

*   *   *

Her family took far more kindly to her unconventional choice of life than she had dared to hope—perhaps because she was so careful to keep all possible taint of scandal from her. Naturally she and Pepe still dined together and made love several times a week, at Annie's pub; but they always arrived and left separately, even by different streets. And Annie had the builders in to stop one of the passages short and so allow a private access between her own apartments and the supper room. Abigail never entered that room until the food was in and the servants gone. For the rest, the men who came to call on her invariably found her chaperoned by

Mary, the young daughter of the married couple who looked after her, Mr. and Mrs. Stone.

Society, as she had hoped, took an ambivalent stance, neither accepting nor condemning—that is, for every one who condemned, there were two who would defend her. And since blame shouts the louder, that proportion appeared as perfect balance. True, her style of dress was unconventional, but it was plain and modest, and she carried it with assurance; and when the occasion demanded, she would don all the crinolines and petticoats and ribbons and lay bare as much of her shoulders and chest as anyone (or any other woman) could desire. And those women who might otherwise have condemned her the loudest were quite pleased to see how dowdy she looked; and to call her "dowdy" to one another was almost to admit her into their warmest friendship.

But women do not look at each other with men's eyes. Their "dowdy" indicates no more than a departure from fashion's latest dictates, even though that departure may be next year's high-water mark of chic. No man who looked at Abigail found her "dowdy."

And thus she earned the gratitude of both sexes insofar as it was due—or important.

Her own explanation for this remarkable acquiescence was, naturally, her talent. She had more than fulfilled that early and outrageous self-prediction: "I am going to become the writer whose pieces no one can afford to miss—whom no editor can afford to reject." She still wrote under a variety of pseudonyms. The Abbot, now a regular columnist in *Once a Week*, still flayed the pretensions of the art world. Her unsigned but unmistakable satires appeared almost as regularly in *Punch*. Short stories by Abe Stevenson were in everything from *Blackwood's* to *The Pall Mall Magazine*. She wrote as a glutton eats, by compulsion; she turned down nothing. She was "Mrs. Madge Challis," adviser on etiquette and domestic matters to *My Lady*. She was "A Chef to the Aristocracy" in *The Drawing Room*. She wrote sly, risqué pieces for *The Girl of the Period* as "Drucilla Getz."

All these names and activities were more or less widely known in London Society. And when it was clear that hers was no mere skyrocket of a career, that she was in earnest, that she could write with style and wit and always find at least one of those phrases that make people say, "Why didn't I think of that!" it was also obvious that she simply could not be ignored. Besides, her book had become a modern classic, selling steadily and capturing the imagination of all who read it.

Laon's explanation was different. "You have your mother to thank," he said. "You know this extraordinary swath you have cut through the social forest this past year or so?"

"One cuts a swath through a cornfield. Through a forest one cuts a trail."

"You leave my lines to me, miss." He called her "miss" quite often these days. "Did you notice all those blazes healing on the trees as you passed? They were cut by your mother."

Abigail sniffed. "I really must get around to reading her books sometime."

"The single most remarkable thing about your mother is—do you know?"

"Ten million pounds."

"That's unworthy, darling. The truly remarkable thing about her is that she has no enemies—or none who amount to anything. Don't you think that's extraordinary? There she is, with a Yorkshire accent she doesn't disguise, and as a girl she worked in a cotton mill and lived in a hovel, none of which she tries to hide; and now here she is a countess and the benevolent dictatrix of an important section of metropolitan Society—and the only words you'll hear to her discredit are those stupid little sneers *all* women make about one another, even about their closest friends."

"I don't."

He looked at her as if the point had never occurred to him. "No," he agreed at length. "That's true."

"Nor does my mother."

"Perhaps that's the secret, then."

"Collapse of stout theory!"

He shrugged and smiled, but the gesture conveyed that he knew better—that she was too obtuse to recognize the truth. From anyone else it would have infuriated her, but she would take it from Pepe because it was probably true. He had always had that air of being one secret ahead of her.

She sought a gesture of appeasement. "The truth is in between," she said. "What Society worships is *success*. In any form. My mother's —mine—*any* success. Why, if a man were to—" she sought for some activity that would violate Society's supposed values to the ultimate limit. "If a man were to sell little girls into vice, so long as he made a fortune at it, you'd find some section of Society willing to . . ."

She faltered. Pepe was staring at her, aghast.

"You—*Judas!*" he cried.

And then she remembered: Percy Laon . . . Porzelijn . . . the man who had sold Mary Coen—and countless other girls—into French brothels.

"What?" She tried to brazen it out, but the memory had shown in her face and he was not deceived.

"Don't make it worse," he said.

For what seemed an eternity they stared at each other. A million things clamoured to be said; she was so crammed with things to say that her tongue could not pry loose one of them.

"Oh—Pepe—!" she stammered.

His bloodless lips parted. Out of the black of his mouth she heard a voice that was barely his say, "I will write to you when I am myself." He went to the door. "But there can never be anything more between us."

With an anguished cry she ran to him. She reached the door just as it slammed behind him. She would have followed him into the street but the terrible finality of his last words stayed her: She was afraid to hear them repeated. Instead, she rushed to her bedroom, pulled the clothes over her head, and howled herself dry and voiceless. Twice, unknown to her, Mary Stone came and stood at the foot of the bed, only to tiptoe away again.

The third time Mary had a letter, brought by messenger; it seemed important enough to justify disturbing her mistress.

Abigail saw at once that the envelope was addressed in Laon's hand. "Put it on the table, Mary," she croaked. She did not want to open it, for the same reason she had not followed him into the street.

"Please, my lady, my mother says are you in to dinner?"

"I am in but I shall not dine," she said tonelessly.

*   *   *

The letter was still unopened when she went to bed. Its pale outlines challenged her from the dark corner where it now lay. Again and again she had picked it up, turned it over, stared at it, and put it down once more.

"But I love him so!" she told the emptiness, as if to prove that none of this could be happening.

The emptiness was appalling. How, she wondered, could one person support such loss? Why did the grief not kill her? What a monstrous prison her body had become—a prison where time and memory lay shackled together, each pinning fast the other, fouling their sweetness.

But what sweetness! Pepe's dark eyes . . . Pepe begging her to marry him . . . Oh, the folly! The folly of those proud refusals! "Yes, I will, I will!" she called at the dark.

"I love him so," she whispered, drowning the ghostly room in hot salt.

In the small hours she arose and dressed. Two lines of pain ran from her neck up the inside of her skull; her bruised eyes saw dual images of everything; her nose could smell nothing but the brine that had swilled it raw. The movement of each racked muscle was a miracle, but no mercy.

From room to room she wandered unconsoled. Mary, hearing her movement, rose and came as far as the door.

"Go back to bed, Mary." She had to force the words through thickets of phlegm.

Mary did not go back to bed. Five minutes later she came from the kitchen with a candlelit tray on which stood a glass of hot milk and a buttered wafer.

Abigail wanted neither; but her dry throat and cavernous stomach won. She sipped—and was amazed at the relish of it. She ate—and never had such simple food tasted so good.

"What prisoners we are," she said glumly. "What power our bodies hold over us!"

Mary nodded.

The milk tasted odd.

"There's a drop o' comfort in that, m'm," Mary said.

How like Annie she talked—the same chirpy cockney. All confidence. *No one puts it over me,* it proclaimed. *I seen it all. Twice!*

She would go and see Annie tomorrow. No—she looked at the clock—*today*.

"Were you ever in love, Mary?" she asked.

Mary grinned. "I am, m'm. I was going to ask as if I might be allowed a follower. He's a p'liceman but he's ever so respectable."

In the face of such enthusiasm Abigail could not avoid a smile, a brief, wan, sad little stretching of her lips, but a smile no less. It felt like a split in her face after so long an absence. She wanted to say, *You see what has happened to me—and you still want to risk it?* But that part of her mind which silently spoke her words in advance of any possible utterance heard the melodrama and silenced her.

"My lady?" the girl pressed.

"I shall have to talk to your mother. For myself I have no objection. You must ask him to call on me."

Only the knowledge of her mistress' grief kept the girl from dancing.

When Abigail was alone again she went—or, rather, her body went, by long habit—to her desk. She took a spill and lighted the gas; the dancing fishtail of flame was absurdly jolly. The whole world seemed bent on mocking her grief.

The first papers beneath her hand were some pages of a short story Pepe had returned with his comments. "Can't you get it into your head . . ." one of them began.

The tears sprang unbidden to her eyes. She could hear his voice, feel his presence, in those words. "Oh, I love him. I love him!" she said.

But she had to clench her eyelids now to force the tears to roll upon her cheeks; the luxurious floods of yesterday were gone. A drab sadness claimed her. She sat and read.

"Can't you get it into your head that casual accidents—*truly* casual accidents—are not permitted in literature? There must be purpose in everything. The reader is not looking for more cloth off the same loom that weaves his or her own seemingly unpatterned experience. He wants *you* to show him it need not be patternless. He wants to watch you play at God—and make a mess of it, like everyone else; but at least he wants you to *try*. So go on—*play* at God! Enjoy it, too! Your writ is brief enough."

In some obscure way—and not just because she heard his voice in every word—this one-paragraph essay brought immense comfort to her. She took up her pen and began to revise the story to accord with his suggestions. And in that way she kept him comfortingly near her until dawn.

Mary was by now quite accustomed to sweeping and dusting the room around her mistress, for Abigail was often at her desk an hour or more before the girl arose at six. Today, when the girl had finished, Abigail sent her round to Pepe's office with the revised manuscript; as an afterthought she put in his letter, still unopened. Whatever he had said in it, in haste, in hurt, he would know she could not hold it against him. It was a kind of apology. Well . . . *almost*.

She even managed a light breakfast.

Midmorning brought another letter from him. It had a different envelope and was promisingly fat; eagerly she opened it—and gave a cry.

Out fell his letter of yesterday, still in its original envelope. And there was another piece of paper, a note: "I am glad you at least are calm enough to work. For myself the desolation is terrible, to know that all this time I have adored someone quite different from the person you have turned out to be. Please read my first letter. I did not write it in haste. It contains a number of practical suggestions for our future—or, I mean, our futures—

which you must consider and answer. For the meantime I must—and will—continue to act as your agent. To act otherwise would do us both quite needless harm. And you can hardly deal directly as a male author could."

She was too numb to weep. She stood at the window and watched the squalls of rain sweep across the wintry face of the river; she felt like a machine whose sole purpose was to stand and watch the world yet comprehend it not at all. Everything was pointless. The stirring of the branches in the wind, the flotsam bobbing along the rain-filled gutters and falling into the drains, the soot stirring in random eddies where the window ledge was still dry—all these were at one with the dull heartbeat within her, all meaningless.

She stood thus for an eternity, until Caspar's voice pierced her silence. "I say, Abbie, what's up?"

She turned and looked at him, standing at the door. "Up?"

"I've been watching you." He came to the window and put an arm about her. "With the survey telescope. You didn't move or—"

She leaned into his embrace and tears she did not know were left inside her fell like rain. "Oh, Steamer—Steamer, I'm so miserable—I just wish I could die. If he's going to leave me, I will die. I know I will."

Caspar held her, saying nothing, just hugging all the comfort he could into her.

Eventually she was calm again, but still he held her. He spoke over her shoulder. "You're talking about Laon, of course."

She nodded; after-tears hiccups shook her.

"What has he done?"

"It's what I've done. I said something—he thought—I didn't mean—but he—"

His hug stifled her. "Calm!" he said. "Be calm. Tell me just a bit at a time. What exactly did you say?"

His stillness and good sense reached into her. She nodded and made the effort. "We were talking about success. About how Society worships it and will forgive anything if it makes money. And I said—you know how one exaggerates for effect?"

She felt him nod; his jaw grazed her hair. "What I said was—" She choked.

"Go on," he urged gently.

"I said a man could spend his life selling little girls into vice . . . of course it was ridiculous, but you know how one sometimes . . . ."

"Go on," Caspar repeated, but this time his voice was laden with foreboding.

"I said if such a man made enough money, Society would applaud."

"You said that to Laon?"

"Yes, but I'd *forgotten* about his father. I swear it! I haven't thought about Porzelijn for years. I didn't *mean* that. God! Of *all* the hyperboles I might have chosen, why did I choose *that!*"

"Indeed, Abbie. Why did you? He will never believe it to be accidental."

"Oh, Steamer!" She broke down again.

He let grief work its way and then nudged her gently toward the sofa. "Let's talk," he said.

When they were seated he continued. He spoke gravely, not as if he were out to comfort her. Indeed, he seemed to speak more to himself. "You remember how Mr. Ignaz Porzelijn first—what shall I call it?—impinged on our lives?"

She nodded. "Mary Coen."

"I was in love with Mary Coen. For six months after she vanished I went through the sort of hell you must be going through now. I know it feels unique, but it isn't. Everyone you meet has gone through it."

"But that—" she began in her disappointment.

"I know," he cut across. "But that makes no difference. I know. I wasn't going to try and pretend otherwise. It makes no difference. I wasn't even going to say that I got over it in the end. But I *did* get over it. I stopped crying myself to sleep every single blessed night. I stopped whispering her name to make my guts turn over. I stopped hoping to see her round every corner." He gave a contemptuous laugh. "I used to ride round Yorkshire—Yorkshire!—knowing she was vanished off the face of the earth, and I'd look for her behind every bush and down every lane! Yet I got over it. Oh, I was quite myself again when Nick told me he'd seen her in Paris. And what did I do? I nearly broke my ankle jumping off the ship. Oh, I'd got over her! I didn't rest until I'd reached Paris and tracked her down. But I'd got over her!"

His full meaning dawned upon her. "Oh, Steamer! You . . . still?"

He nodded, not taking his eyes off her. "*And* Laney, that girl in New York. Don't imagine you'll ever get over it. You just get used to *not* getting over it—until one day you'll suddenly realize it's been years since you even thought about it. But even then don't deceive yourself. It's a sleeping volcano, that's all. If Laney was to come walking down the street one day next week—or Mary Coen—I don't know if—"

She touched his mouth with the tips of her fingers. "Please!"

"Oh, you haven't heard the best of it," he said. "I think I know why this is. That's what I really meant to tell you. It's the only comfort I can honestly give."

"What is it?"

He looked at her, summoning resolution. "You're a big girl now, Abbie. So I suppose I may tell you. I loved both those girls. Not with the pure love of a medieval knight, you understand—but with a *real* love. I craved them."

"I know," she said. "I know what you mean."

But he seemed not to hear. He was now embarked not on a story but on a compulsion to tell a story. "The way Society goes on you'd think men and women need only five seconds to beget the next generation, like flies. I mean, that's the longest time we allow the two sexes together unchaperoned. Well, Mary Coen and I passed two nights in bed together and nothing happened. I mean *everything* happened, but not that one particular—you know what I mean."

She nodded. Her silence made him look at her. "Shocked?"

She smiled and shook her head.

"What I'm saying is that because I was denied—or denied myself—that ultimate joy with them both, I never ceased to long for them." He squeezed his torso at the ribs. "This—*thing*—is such a tyrant to us. To men, anyway."

"And to women."

"I doubt the tyranny is so immediate. But no matter. Even if it is, that's just what I'm saying. The fact that you and Laon are not married is bound to intensify . . ." Her smile made him falter.

"Dear Steamer!" she said. "Now *you* think your experience is so unique!"

He sprang to his feet, aghast. He moved away from her as if she had admitted having cholera. "No!"

"Oh?" She was stung to the edge of anger. "It is all fine and beautiful for you—but not for your sister!"

"That is different." Spit flew from his lips. "Of course it is different."

"I'll tell you *how* different, brother dear. Pepe and I went not two nights but two months of nights before we felt ourselves ready for that joy you speak of—"

"Stop! I want to hear no more!"

But her anger was up now. She stood and seized him by the shoulders to shake him. "This tone of high disgust has the reek of hypocrisy," she said. "I warn you, Caspar, my experience is every bit as beautiful and holy to me as yours obviously was to you. If you behave as if it were something foul and disgusting, you and I will part company. Now!"

"But Abbie . . ." He was in anguish.

"Choose!"

Defeated, he sat again on the sofa. She sat beside him and took his hand. "Very well," he said. "Not disgusting. But"—he looked at her searchingly—"*dangerous!*"

"We are careful. People who know us well, even intimately, have not the slightest suspicion of what we are doing. If they did—"

He cut in: "But someone must see him come here."

"Here! He hardly ever comes here."

"Where then?"

"Neither you nor anyone else will ever know."

It was a foolish thing to say and she regretted it at once; Steamer loved nothing so much as a challenge. Still there would be time enough to worry about that.

Then she realized what that last thought of hers implied: hope! The bleak conviction that all was finished had lifted from her. Somehow Steamer had brought her comfort after all.

*   *   *

She slept for sixteen hours and awoke ravenous enough to do justice to a four-course breakfast. During the night an unexpected transformation had worked in her. It showed itself first when she thought by habit, *I must call on Pepe*—and then felt a twinge of doubt.

She still wanted to talk to him . . . explain . . . see him . . . touch him. None of that had diminished in any way. But alongside it had grown a conviction that if she went to him she would lose something. What it was she could not say, any more than she could say in plain words why she was still so full of terrors at the thought of marriage. But the loss would be permanent. It had something to do with the marvellous symmetry of their love, hers for him, his for her. If she went to him now, it would introduce a permanent inequality between them; the symmetry would be destroyed. "Symmetry" was another aspect of her freedom.

Beneath this reasoning, barely perceived by her, was something of that same inexplicable impulse which, at the beginning of their affair, had made her postpone for three days an assignation with Pepe that she longed for. But that was beyond her fathoming.

She rose from her breakfast and went to the window, intending no

more than to see what sort of a day it was, and found that she was searching the street for the sight of Pepe! It was the same all day, just as Caspar
had described it. She followed the usual round—visiting the galleries, calling on friends—and everywhere her body prepared her for an encounter
with him. It was not quite so absurd as it had been with Caspar and Mary
Coen. Laon's public path did occasionally cross hers, after all. But she
knew that if she were in Paris—or Peking—she would be looking for him
in that same way.

Chapter 23

A week later she still had not seen Pepe; neither had she opened his first
letter. Each day she said, *Today I will go and see him*. And each day that
reluctance to be the first to act held her back. She longed for him, wept for
him, sighed for the loss of him; yet long habit would not let her believe
that it was final. They would be together again, soon; but the move that
would reunite them would be his.

Each day, too, she resolved to go and visit Annie, who had been away
on one of her periodic visits to Wales, where her sister always seemed to
be in one kind of trouble or another. Abigail was not even sure Annie was
back, but she ought to go and see. After a week she realized that the same
reluctance to meet Pepe was keeping her from visiting Annie. Of course,
that was absurd. The last place in London where she'd be likely to run into
Pepe was at Annie's.

It was Sunday. She went to early evensong at St. Paul's and then took
a cab to Crutched Friars. Sunday was a quiet evening at The Old Fountain;
they'd have lots of time for a chat. She knocked at the private door. The
maid, recognizing her, took her up.

"They're having such a jolly party, m'm," she said. "The missus and
all. It's just like when we first come here."

And it was a splendid party, too. A real East End booze up, with
oysters and whelks and jellied eels, with porter and milk stout and rum,
and with dancing and comic turns and songs. The only people Abigail
knew were Annie and her husband and a couple of the waiters. But that
evening everyone was her friend. She never quite fathomed what exactly
they were celebrating—a win on the horses, Annie's return, or a general
deliverance from some unspecified but awful fate; but that they *were*

celebrating was never in doubt. Annie made an immense fuss over Abigail and set her in a place of honour at her left.

"Fetch a plate o' whelks!" she called. "And champagne." She leaned conspiratorially toward Abigail. "You think you know about fun up them palaces up west. Well now, just see how *we* can cheat the worms! And don't mind me, gel. If you see a bit of prairie—go!"

Her laugh filled the room and became the signal for their interrupted fun to start again.

"So anyway," said a foxy little man with a red moustache who had been speaking when Abigail came in, "he's stuck for lodgings so he knocks on this door and this landlady comes out. 'Yes?' she says. And he says, 'I'm stopping here.' And she says, 'Well stop there then!' And she shuts the door in his face so he knocks again and she says, 'Yes?' 'You're cracked,' he says. 'I know,' she says, 'but you'd never notice.' "

Everyone howled with laughter. The foxy man grinned wickedly around. "That's what I like about you," he said. "You're *quick!* So he says, 'No don't mess around now. Can't you see me all right for tonight?' So she looks up and down the street. 'Just yourself, is it?' she asks. 'Only I don't want no children.' 'Now then,' he says, 'I'm a married man myself.' So she takes him in and in the parlour he meets this pal. 'Hello, me old china,' he says. 'How's the missus?' 'I don't know,' he says, 'I left her home in bed, smoking.' "

The man suddenly looked at Abigail. "Jerusalem," he said. "There's a lady present. I can't finish this one."

By now the tears were streaming down every face. "Don't take it amiss, love," Annie gasped to Abigail. "He always says that about someone. There's no proper end to that one."

"You mean you've heard this before?"

"Scores of times."

The monologue went on, a formless, quickfire tale full of lodgers, black eyes, infidelities, illegitimate children, risqué puns, contrived misunderstandings, and catch phrases, until people were calling "Stop!" and "More!" in the same breath.

At last he did stop, though (on the line "You marry whichever one you fancy, son. *He's* not your father, anyway!"), and gave people a chance to wipe their eyes and rub their aching sides.

"Still," Annie cried breathlessly, "like the gel said—the more you cry the less there is to piss! I hope that's not still your first glass of champagne, love?"

Abigail downed it guiltily and held out the glass for a refill.

Spontaneously, from a corner of the room, an angelic young girl in white stood and sang "Home Sweet Home" in a pure, flutelike voice. At once the mood changed. The raucous crowd, which only moments earlier had bayed the roof with laughter, sat still and leaned their heads to one side and sighed and looked far away.

"She's beautiful!" Abigail whispered.

Annie merely nodded. But when the song was over she added that the girl had been "on the turf since the age of ten, though you'd scarce credit it."

Indeed, Abigail did not credit it—until the girl, with that same winsome innocence, sang "Whoops—I lost it!" and looked around with mock surprise at every salacious laugh.

Then there was dancing. Then a fat woman stood and recited "Living, alias Starving," followed by an awkward, rubbery sort of man who declaimed a parody of Hamlet: "To woo, or not to woo?"

The high spot of the evening came when the guvnor himself, Mr. Oldale, sang "Up in a Balloon" and "Slap Bang Here We Are Again." He had a fine boozy baritone that "needed only ale to oil its squeaks," as Annie said. But he could put over a drinking song with great verve, which brought everyone to a rousing cheer at the end. With elaborate courtesy he dedicated the cheers to Annie, kissing her hand as Queen of Revels.

"Oh, he'll feed the dumb glutton tonight all right," Annie told Abigail with a wink.

Later Annie said, "What you going to do, gel?"

"Do?"

"Yeah. Sing? Recite? Do a patter? What?"

"Oh, Annie! I couldn't!"

"Course you can! Everyone does."

"But I—"

"They'll think you're giving yourself airs, if you don't."

"I had no idea."

"Don't you sing nothing?"

"I know 'The Last Rose of Summer.'"

"Luverly!" She clapped her hands for silence and Abigail, to her horror, heard the announcement: "And now, straight from her success at the Olympic Theatre in the Strand, The Old Fountain proudly brings you Bessie Power to sing 'The Last Rose of Summer.'"

At the time, Abigail could have killed her; but later she realized it was a kindness Annie had done. For by the time that first awful sinking of the stomach hit her she was already well launched into the song, and the moment for nerves had passed. What nervousness there was merely gave her voice a not unpleasing vibrato.

Of course no one was deceived. By the third line everyone knew she was an ordinary domestic performer like themselves; but then Annie's elaborate introduction worked in her favour—everyone *wanted* her to live up to it.

By the middle of the second verse she actually found herself enjoying it. Until now she had sung only on private, family occasions; to see perhaps a hundred eyes, all fixed on her, was oddly exciting—frightening, but exciting. They fed something back to her, something that her song imparted to them. They were moved to sadness at the thought of the rose "left blooming all alone"; and the repetition in "withered . . . faded . . . plucked . . . gone" struck a deeply nostalgic and tender response among people whose lives never strayed far from the margins of death and loss.

She caught the mood from them. Its ineffable sadness almost felled her in the last verse.

> *So soon may I follow, when friendships decay,*
> *And from love's shining circle, the gems drop away.*

Her voice broke at

> *When true hearts lie wither'd, and loved ones are flown . . .*

She could see many in her audience beginning to weep and, curiously enough, that helped to rally her. It was as if, by imparting her own sorrow, she had lost it. What she had caught from them she now gave back. She felt a strange mixture of love and contempt for them—love for those who shared her sense of loss, contempt that they could do so only through this doggerel song (and contempt for herself, too, that *she* could be moved by it as deeply as they).

So she roused herself easily for that final line:

> *Oh, who would inhabit this bleak world alone?*

A long gasp of ecstatic sentiment erupted into the greatest applause of the evening; even as their tears still ran, they shouted and stamped and whistled. "Encore! Encore!"

But Annie plucked at her sleeve. "Don't trump your own ace, gel," she advised. She, too, had been reduced to tears.

Some time later, Annie's husband was overcome by drink and the heat. Annie had him carried up to the private apartments; Abigail followed.

Annie stood over his bloated figure, loosening his cravat. It seemed an affectionate gesture until she said, "Who needs them, anyway!"

There was a challenge in her eye as she looked up at Abigail. "And what's come over you, gel?" she asked.

"What d'you mean?"

"Why'd you come here alone? Where's your Mr. Laon? And the way you sung? Think it don't show, love?"

Abigail, already light-headed with the champagne, suddenly found herself wanting to share it all with Annie. Annie would understand. Annie knew everything about love; she would know what to do.

"Oh, Annie," she began. "He—I—he thinks—" The tears brimmed again.

"Stow that!" Annie said harshly. "There's not one of them is worth it. Not one that ever lived." She looked at the sleeping Mr. Oldale. "Not Jesus Christ hisself."

Abigail saw then that Annie knew nothing—nothing but her own bitterness and disappointments. Her impulse to tears was choked in a new pity. "Oh, Annie!"

Annie turned on her angrily, "Oh Annie, oh Annie!" she sneered. "You don't know *nothing*, gel. That bastard there is killing me. And you want to cry to me about love? If your Laon said ta-ta, you don't know when you're well off. Love? It's a gallows tree for us."

Abigail hardly knew what to say. "Why d'you let him drink so much?" she asked. She suddenly felt like a visitor from the Poor Law guardians.

"I hope he may die of it," Annie said calmly. She even smiled. "If I knew a way to get a bottle of brandy down him now, so help me I'd do it. I'd kill him with no more feeling than I'd pull the head off a flea."

Her composure was dreadful. If she had screamed the words, Abigail could have discounted them. But Annie was as cool as a teacher of anatomy standing over a cadaver. Abigail saw that whatever comfort she herself might need, it was as a dimple compared with Annie's well of grief.

But how could she comfort her?

Annie spoke again, still in that same flat voice: "I'd have more luck saving Margate beach from the sea!"

How could she tell her that life need not be as hers had become?

"Men!" Annie said.

And she spoke with such utter contempt that Abigail knew there was no way to tell her. Annie needed to believe in her own cosmic scorn—to know it was justly universal. Perhaps she could be made to see that, if it was true at all, it was true only of the men she had known and chosen. But what would be the use of that? It would only bring the blame too close to home. She would just pass from one kind of despair to another—from despair against men to despair at herself. It was a terrible thing to realize that here was another woman, a fellow human being, whom she loved as a sister, who was beyond any possible comfort. The desolation of it appalled her.

But Annie was suddenly bright and cheerful. "Come on, Abbie love!" she said. "Or we'll have the brewers complaining!"

An hour later Abigail and "Auntie"—the only two who were even halfway sober by then—were putting a drunken Annie to bed beside her comatose husband. Her brow was still furrowed; not even oblivion, it seemed, could bring her peace.

"Poor mite," the older woman said. "It's all the ease she has now."

Chapter 24

All next day Abigail thought far more of Annie's wretchedness than her own. By evening she was drawn irresistibly back to the pub in Crutched Friars, where she had learned so much of joy while Annie had tasted so much bitterness. It did not deter her to know that Annie was beyond comfort; she wanted to try to help, or at least just to be with her.

Annie was in a dangerously joyful mood, brightly sharp.

"How's Mr. Oldale?" Abigail asked.

Annie cackled: "Sobered up, sat up, drank up, pissed up, threw up— and I wish he'd bleeding well give up!"

It was a piece of comic patter that belonged to yesterday's party— intrusive in real life.

"You said some terrible things last night, Annie."

"You think they was wrong? You think your Mr. Laon's so maaarvellous! *Lay-on*—that's the name for him all right!"

"What d'you mean?"

"I hope you may never find out, love. Better live sweet, innocent, and foolish than be like me."

Abigail sighed. If she left, she knew she would only be doubly miserable; but to stay seemed worse than futile.

She sat down to a meal, though, and gradually realized that her presence was, in a curious way, a comfort to Annie. Time and again Annie laughed or sneered at Abigail's supposed innocence, hinting at secret knowledge—*superior* knowledge—until Abigail saw that Annie needed to score over her in this way, as a salve to her bruises. Then she did not mind so much.

But when Annie saw she did not mind, her crowing grew even more bitter. Once, after Abigail had turned aside one of Annie's jibes, Annie said, "Words! That's all you think it is, gel, don't you! I bet you couldn't walk in there and talk so calm and lovey-dovey." She nodded at the private door to the supper room.

Abigail hesitated, not wanting to give Annie best, yet not certain she could face down such a challenge.

"Yeah! I thought as much," Annie said.

At that moment the private door opened. The angelic-looking young girl who had sung "Home Sweet Home" last night stood angrily at the threshold, dressed only in a shift. "A right hanging Dick you lumped me with!" she shouted at Annie.

But Abigail, after that brief instant of recognition did not look at the girl again; for there beyond her, naked in the firelight, stood Pepe.

Annie laughed, an eldritch cackle of triumph that filled Abigail with a cold rage. She marched upon the room. The girl stood her ground but Abigail, fed on meat since birth, flung her aside like a straw doll. She slammed the door behind her and locked it.

"Me cloves!" the girl shrieked.

At first Abigail intended to ignore the shrieks and hammerings but the smell of the girl's clothes was overpowering, rank flesh and perfume. She gathered the whole bundle and unlocked the door just long enough to hurl them out.

"See!" Annie mocked from beyond the closed door. "Now who's right, gel?"

All this time, from the moment he had first recognized her, Laon sat with his head in his hands.

"How *could* you!" Abigail shouted at him.

"That's the whole point, isn't it?" he said, still not looking at her. "I couldn't."

"What d'you mean?"

"What d'you think all *that* is about?" He nodded at the door and stared her in the eye at last.

He looked ghastly . . . thin, haggard, ten years older. She wanted to stay angry, to punish him for all the suffering he had caused her; but pity won. Pity and love—a sudden brimming incandescence of love. She was about to run to him, the cry of his name was in her throat, when he slumped upon the divan and said: "I cannot endure it any longer. You are everything to me—my life, my whole existence. I don't care what sort of person you are. I don't care how much contempt you feel for me. I don't care if you mock me all your life, I can never leave you again. Did you ever hear anything so abject! Was there ever anyone more spineless! But it is your doing! Look at me—it's your handiwork."

His self-pity left her no room to speak. How could she say all that she yearned to say—that she had been miserable, too; that she would do any-thing, *anything*, rather than lose him again, even marry him—how could she slip all that past the seamless armour of his self-pity!

She sat beside him and pushed him down, supine. She lay beside him and kissed him, whispering his name. Their tears mingled, though neither was crying—or, at least, they were not sobbing.

She kissed his body and saw his excitement swell in the firelight, saw it grow firm and hard. It kicked in her hand when she toyed with it. Greatly daring, she kissed it and then, filled with a sudden terror—like an invisible suffocation—she threw herself upon him and kissed his cheeks and lips and throat and ears with a hurtful passion.

He had half her buttons undone before she realized it; she sat up and tore the clothes off her. Then their bodies were at a riot with each other. There was no finesse, no gentleness now. She gripped him like a succubus; he hammered at her like a demon.

"No!" she shouted, though if he had stopped she would have killed him.

She wanted to kill him. She bit his shoulder. She sank her nails into his ribs.

He gave a cry. He grabbed her hands and pinned them above her head. She was racked beneath him; for a moment of frenzy their eyes locked—and each was appalled at the pools of hate in the other's.

She heard the familiar cry of his ecstasy, felt the pulse of it. And then there was a new sensation—the hot stabbing of his ejaculation. Then she was rent apart and scattered to the universe.

Usually he stopped at that point, but tonight he went on and on, whimpering all the while as if it were an exquisite pain. And she went on, too, rising again and again for that magical moment when all the sweetness and tenderness in the world seemed to melt and flow into her.

"No more!" she begged when the glory grew unbearable and verged on torment.

They lay gasping and panting until both fell into a brief, shallow slumber. She was the first to awaken.

"I couldn't have lived another day without you, Pepe," she said.

He came awake like a cat: instantly. "Who told you?" he asked.

"Told me what?"

"About—my father."

How calm they were, suddenly. Where had all that passion fled?

"But I've always known."

He snorted with impatience and at once grew dejected again. "You've no need to lie," he said. "I've told you—I am yours on any terms. You can say anything. Even the truth."

"But it is the truth. We had a servant girl once who was abducted and sold into a house in France. And the man involved was called Ignaz Porzelijn. Well, it's hardly what you'd call a *common* name!"

His jaw fell. "So you *all* know!"

"No!" She lied. "Only Mama. She doesn't even know *I* know. I mean, I read it all in her diaries."

"When? Recently?"

"No. Years and years ago."

His eyes were full of wonder. "So you've always known!"

"Yes—long before we met. So long I'd forgotten all about it when I . . ."

"And it made no difference?"

She took his hand. "Oh, Pepe! Is *that* what you were afraid of?"

He crept into the shade of her. "Abbie, Abbie! I've done you such a wrong. And you are so noble. Will you ever forgive me?"

Mention of forgiveness must have stirred his most recent memory, for he sat up and looked at her earnestly. "Let me explain to you. About—" He nodded at the door.

"There's no need."

"But there is. Don't you see? I think we should tell each other everything from now on. There should only be honesty between us. If I'd told you about my father and my feelings of shame, I wouldn't have been such a fool this last week—God, is it only a week?"

She lay back and pulled him on to her. "Don't stop touching me," she said.

"I bought a copy of Blake's prophetic poems," he said. "And I found it hard to read. I've found it hard to do anything since— Anyway, I thought if I came here and read it, I'd be able to understand better. And to understand you better. Or try to."

"And did you? Do you?" She was deeply moved.

"I had no chance. As soon as I'd finished the meal, Annie came in with that girl—d'you know, that's her young sister!"

"Annie seems to have a million sisters," Abigail said bitterly. She could see it all now.

"She said I looked as if I needed a bit of consoling. And she left me alone with—whatever her name is."

"But I've been with Annie for the past hour, so . . . " She didn't want to say the obvious.

"We talked," Laon said. "Mostly about her. D'you know she must have been with over a thousand men, and she's not yet twenty. And she's never known the slightest—not even the most passing pleasure in it. What a terrible thing. She hates men. And after talking with her, I almost feel the same."

"But—Pepe! You *were* naked. And with her."

She wished he had not begun this "explanation"; it diminished her and left him dishonoured. So he and that girl had "talked" for an hour, had they—"mostly about her"! She could just hear it: "Tell me what it's like to be you"! and his dark, begging eyes launching the words. Did they rise to his throat automatically at the sight of female flesh? And did he imagine that this explanation would satisfy her—even in the most narrow, logical sense?

He nodded. "That's in a way what I mean. All the beastliness in sex was put there by men. Oh, Abbie—I missed you!"

"I missed you, too, darling. Only God knows how much. But it would never even have *occurred* to me to find solace with any other man. Even men I feel quite attracted to. And what was that girl to you? You don't even know her name. And she reeked."

"I know. I know!" Pepe said. "But you don't know. You have no idea what it's like to be a man. I'll bet you don't think about you and me—in between—"

"I think about you all the time."

"Yes, but not about *us*. Not actually together, here, naked, in each other's arms. Me *in* you. I'll bet you never actually picture that and get excited about it."

"Of course I don't."

"You see! Now if I made such an answer, with a hundred men to witness, then a hundred men would know instantly that I was lying."

"You mean—you—?"

"I mean all men. *All* men. I think about you and me, like that, a dozen times a day. More!"

"But why? Where's the point in it?"

"The answer's in our stars, not in ourselves. I mean we're all born that way. Take the cow to the bull. If the cow's ready, the bull is. But not the other way round. It's the same with all animals. The male must be ready—always."

Despite his penitent tone there was smugness in the way he aligned the whole of nature on his side and consigned all blame to the world of beasts. She stood and began to dress.

"It seems," she said, "that there was hardly any point in our struggling to the top of the evolutionary tree!"

It was an easy rebuke to allow, for it touched him not at all. "Why d'you think Annie hates you so?" he asked.

Abigail smiled. "You don't understand women at all. She did it because she loves me."

She did not want to add that Annie had done it out of hate of *him*—for bringing her, Abigail, so much happiness.

She would be very kind to Annie, who had worries enough and more without adding to them the remorse of her own treachery.

"Funny kind of love."

Yes, she thought, looking down at him. *Funny—and deep. You wouldn't understand it.* She barely understood it herself, not in so many words. There was a sense in which love between men and women was shallow; they might *feel* it deeply but that did not make it deep. And when they hurt each other, it filled in part of their love, making it shallower yet. The language was different. This thing Pepe had done—he might very well see it as a cry of anguish, a way of saying to her, *See how miserable I am!* But how could she think of it like that? It was not something she herself could do without revulsion, not even in imagination; therefore it conveyed nothing to her—except that same revulsion. And when he said, "I am like that—all men are like that," it shut off part of him, and part of all men, from her forever.

Annie had hurt her, too; but the language of the action was one she recognized. Through it she saw a little more deeply into Annie's confused and lonely bitterness. Annie's cruelty made the love between them more profound; Laon's cruelty made part of him a third person to her. What was the difference? The only difference was the flesh. The love between Annie and her was entirely human and purely of their spirit; but her love and Laon's? He had been right to invoke the animals.

She had the first intimations of carnal love not as an enrichment but as a means of battle.

When she was dressed, she looked down at his exhausted, still-naked body. Something was missing, she felt. It was a moment before she could place it, but when she did, her heart dropped a beat. "Pepe!" she cried. "You weren't wearing anything!"

But his jaw did not drop. He did not sit up in alarm. Instead a slow smile spread over his face.

"Well," she said. "Two rousing cheers for honesty!"

*   *   *

Annie showed her how to use the douche. "The bastards!" she kept saying. "But we'll cheat them yet, you'll see."

"Take a glass or three of gin each night, now," was her parting advice. "And a bath as hot as you can stand it. When's the cardinal due?"

She had to explain that.

"Oh," Abigail said. "This week, I think."

"Might be lucky then." Annie was full of confidence.

On the threshold Abigail turned and said, "It's what you told me all those years ago. You remember? 'Then they've got you where they want you,' you said."

"And wasn't I right? Wasn't I just. Still—you've got the idea, gel. Don't never marry him. Take your fun, like what they do. Keep yourself free, like what they do."

On his appointed day, the "cardinal" came, which was no extraordinary relief after Annie's supreme confidence. But Abigail could not get out of her mind what Laon had tried to do. He had used his body, his seed, as a weapon to trap her. It was like . . . She tried to think what it was like. But it was like nothing that had ever happened to her. Her mind went back again to the time Annie had first told her The Secret and she had tried to imagine what it would be like to let a man into her. That shrinking-into-herself feeling—it was something like that. A recoil from him.

Then one day, walking through the Bond Street Arcade, she saw a shopkeeper sticking pins through dead butterflies and impaling them on silk panels. He seemed to be smiling as he worked; in fact, it was only his concentration, but the smile was Pepe's smile. At last she had an image to contain her raw feeling—something she could point to and say, *"That* is what it was like!"

Chapter 25

To the world she was a confirmed and contented spinster, a wise virgin, a regrettable, slightly-to-be-pitied, but in no way reprehensible thing to be. She was still far too nubile to be allowed an independent social status; she could not, for instance, entertain anyone in Society—or anyone anxious to get in. And that was irksome, since most writers and painters were in one of those two categories. They could meet at others' entertainments, and she could accept their hospitality, but she could never return it as her own hostess.

Laon frequently stressed these disadvantages to her until she stopped him by threatening to marry the first derelict whom a doctor could guarantee to be on his deathbed—for, as a widow, she would enjoy all the independence and advantages of a married woman.

"But never mind," she said. "In ten years or so I could put about a not-too-ridiculous claim to be forty, and the conventions will quietly relax their grip."

Laon could see this as nothing but cruelty. "You will not release me," he said. "Indeed, you cannot. I am bound to you by ties that neither you nor I nor any earthly power can undo. You say you love me, but you will let nothing come of it. Only miseries."

"So it is misery, meeting me here?"

"No, it is misery *not* meeting you here. Every moment we are apart is misery."

"But Pepe, we see far more of each other than most husbands and wives. We enjoy far more of each other—at work and in love. Why must you want what you can never have?"

For all the determination of her words, there were many times when his misery touched her so deeply that she was on the point of yielding to him. Then Annie's vehemence came to stay her resolution and reprieve her from that sacrifice.

But Annie was often away these days, visiting her sister. And The Old Fountain was showing signs of neglect. Oldale was worse than useless.

When he was not dead drunk he was entertaining his betting companions in the private rooms, kicking up a shindy, driving away custom, and eating into the pub's dwindling profits. Annie was often in tears at him—not soft, feminine tears but tears of bitter hatred. "If there was a legal day for murders, gel," she would say, "how many men would be left, I wonder!"

Abigail could understand Annie's desire to be away from the place as long and as often as possible, but it was no real answer, for it could lead only to bankruptcy. Even now, she noticed, all the fine ornaments and nice furniture Annie had started out with were gone from the private apartments, to be replaced by plain deal of the cheapest make.

"When your home goes, everything goes," Annie said.

And so her absences grew longer and more frequent.

During one of them, when Abigail was almost desperate for the spinster courage Annie was so good at furnishing, she got help from a quite unexpected—indeed, almost unremembered—quarter. Late one night, Mary brought her a letter that had just been pushed through the door. It read:

Dear Lady Abigail,

I presume upon an acquaintance that, even at its warmest, was too slender for the weight I yet hope it may bear. In truth, I know no one else to whom I may turn, and if you cannot help me, then I shall know I am truly friendless and must bear my situation alone. I mean, you are my last hope. It is years since I first conceived the idea of enlisting your aid; I do so now only in an extremity.

I know you must receive many begging letters, so let me at once say I need no money. It is probably the only form of assistance I do not need. All I ask is a little counsel, and from one whose words to me (almost ten years ago now!) and whose public writings since have proved her to be among the most sagacious and understanding of people.

You may remember you cautioned me against a hasty marriage? It was a warning I was too impetuous to heed. I married directly from your sister's schoolroom. What indignities, what monstrous miseries, I have since endured, I cannot set upon paper. Now I can endure no more, but I know so little of the world that I am utterly at a loss how to proceed next.

I have followed your astonishing career from the moment the true identity of your various *noms de plume* became common knowledge. Even when my miseries first began, which was the first night of my marriage, it was to you that I was impelled to turn. But you seemed to move farther and farther from my small ambit until you were impossibly beyond my reach. Now, only my desperation furnishes me with sufficient boldness to attempt the bridging of that impossible gulf you must see between us.

I shall, if I may, call upon you tomorrow morning at eleven o'clock. If I find you "not at home," please take this as my heartfelt gratitude for having read thus far. Be assured I shall not (for all my despair) do anything rash, nothing you might fear to reproach yourself with should you find it impossible to receive me. I shall return to my ordinary life and endure it as best I may, thinking none the less warmly of you.

I sign myself as you may remember me and as I wish, ten thousand times a day, I still were,

Celia Addison.

She looked awful. She was dressed well enough, even richly, but she was as drawn as a waif. Abigail divined that, since delivering that letter last night, she had been wandering the streets.

She had seen Celia Addison coming up from the direction of the Embankment and had herself gone to the door to greet her. Celia, expecting the maidservant, was thrown into confusion.

"I cannot furnish you with a card, nor give you my married name," she said. "In view of what I must tell you, it would be treachery to my husband."

This breaking of convention seemed so great a worry to her that it drove out all other fears.

"I will call you Celia, and you shall call me Abbie—as of old. Why should the passage of mere years change all that," Abigail said.

The woman was not as relieved as she might have been; Abigail guessed that she had wanted the distraction of the social solecism to draw attention from whatever she was now going to have to confess. Certainly once they were seated she was in no hurry to begin. She prattled a lot—about the weather, about the most recent of Abigail's articles, about the charm of Abigail's apartments, about how well she was looking. . . . All the time she smiled, nervous smiles that flashed and faded like sparks and did not distract Abigail one moment from the gray lines of her face, her bloodless cheeks, her hollow eyes—eyes that had long ago shed every tear they possessed. Never would Abigail have recognized her as the plump, rosy, frivolous Celia Addison of the Highgate Girls' College.

"You must be famished," she said, stemming the flow of inanities. "You look as if you had no breakfast."

Celia began to protest but Abigail took command, making her go into the bedroom and have a good wash and tidy-up. She sent Mary in to help her and meanwhile ordered a hearty breakfast from Mrs. Stone. It was a somewhat restored Celia who sat with her an hour later, with no further excuse for prevarication.

It was then that a thought struck Celia—apparently for the first time. "Dear me," she said. "You are so prominent a person, Abbie . . . you write so . . . wisely, that I had quite overlooked the fact that you are not married!"

You did no such thing! Abigail thought, seeing for the first time a hint of ruthlessness beneath that browbeaten exterior. "Well, I don't intend to get married," she said. "Not even for you, my dear."

Celia laughed but was quickly serious again. "Oh, I would not wish it on my deepest-dyed enemy."

Still she volunteered no information. Abigail waited.

"Even to ask you to listen is to pollute your thoughts," Celia spoke half to herself.

"I doubt it," Abigail said.

Celia looked at her wide-eyed.

"Let me remind you that I write regularly for at least four ladies' magazines. I frequently have to deal with letters from distraught readers who—believe me—are far from reticent in what they commit to writing. I doubt if you can tell me anything more 'polluting,' as you call it, than I see a dozen times a week."

The remark stung Celia—the idea that she could rank somewhere lower than first in a league of that sort. "More polluting than *this?*" she asked, pulling a sheet of paper from her bag and thrusting it into Abigail's hand.

At once she regretted the impulse and half drew it away; but Abigail clenched it tightly and read, with a bewilderment that turned to horror:

Frolic of August 16th 1874

The title was written and underlined in three differently coloured inks. The text ran:

She will come to my bedroom at ten of the evening, bathed, perfumed, and dressed as in the Frolic of December 14th 1867. She will stand before me and I will walk around her and touch her where I will. She will permit me to lift her robes and see her Jewel. [That word, too, was in coloured inks.] I will stand above her and peer down on her Beauteous Orbs. [Again in three colours.] She will kneel before me and with loving caresses divest me of my Inexpressibles. She will stand and lift her robe that I may kiss her Twin Pillars.

On and on it went—a whole page of coy, multicoloured directions for lechery.

"Your husband's handwriting?" Abigail asked.

Celia, relieved that Abigail was not shocked beyond speech, nodded.

"And you found this by accident, I suppose?"

Celia looked away. "No. He sent it to me."

"*Sent* it!"

"I mean, they are there beside my plate every Sunday at breakfast. And every Wednesday. He puts them there."

"They?" The sofa and the chair seemed to have become insubstantial.

"That's only the first page. They run to four or five pages usually."

"Your—let me hear now—your husband writes—*things* like this and leaves them for you to read, twice a week?"

"Yes, he—"

"Does it occur to you that this other woman may not exist? This is surely some mental aberration. He writes these pages to consume his sick fantasy—but that is all."

Celia began to laugh—a wild laugh that soon turned hysterical. Abigail let the storm pass. When Celia was able to speak again she said, "The other woman is *me!* These are not letters, Abbie. They are instructions. I must learn them by rote, though they are all mere minute variations in the same most loathsome, disgusting ritual. I must learn them and . . ." She lowered her eyes. "And perform them."

Abigail could not move. The implications of this terrible confession pinned her mind to a repetition of those dreadful last words—"and perform them."

Perform them!

"Why?" she asked.

"I don't know. I think he's mad. He's driving me mad."

"I mean, why do you consent to do it?"

Celia looked at her pityingly.

"Have you told anyone else?" Abigail asked.

"I told my parents. In the beginning. I ran away, you see. I ran back home. But it wasn't like this then. He didn't write it all down like this."

"But?"

"He just told me what to do. Or pushed me into different—poses. Like clay or something. On our wedding night I had to sit on a sort of throne and he undressed me and"—she swallowed—"and hung jewels and flowers on me. I was petrified. He looked—he was—he looked so *odd*."

"Did you know what to expect at all?"

Celia shrugged. "My mother told me to drink plenty of champagne and not to be surprised at anything Henry did." Her hand flew to her mouth. "There! I meant never to tell you his name!"

"Oh, Celia—after all this you can still be loyal to him?"

"He is my husband."

"He is your torturer."

"He has never hurt me."

"He has degraded you. Anyway, what did your parents say when you told them these disgusting things?"

Celia closed her eyes, unwilling to relive the memory. "I wanted so much to go back home. I wanted everything to be as it was before."

"But what did they say?"

"They said I couldn't come back. They said I belonged to him. Of course, they were unhappy—my mother was miserable—but they said he had the right to do whatever he was doing. And I must endure it."

"And for ten years you . . . Was there no one else you could confide in?"

Celia shrugged at the impossibility of it. "I hinted I was unhappy to the vicar. I think he suspected that Henry was not as—as *nice* as he seems. He lent me books on fortitude and resignation. He reminded me I married for better *or* for worse—that was my vow. He is a marvellous man. A great comforter to me."

"What of your children? Do you have any children?"

"How could God bless so wicked a union!"

"Is that why you are now desperate enough to—well, to write to me as you did? You feel the wickedness?"

Her heavy eyelids fell as she nodded; to open her eyes again seemed a labour in itself. "Also, it gets worse. Last time it began at ten and finished at four next morning. I cannot go without sleep as he can. I am worn to a frazzle by it."

"So I can see." Abigail thought it odd that in all this recitation, which must have cost her every bit of courage she had, Celia had not once seemed close to tears—not even when she had laughed so hysterically.

"For better or for worse does not mean for impossible. If God is asking the impossible of me—I have tried it for long enough, and I can try no more."

A silence fell between them.

"Does it not sometimes make you cry, Celia dear?" Abigail ventured.

"I used to cry, but he liked that."

The silence returned. In a while Abigail spoke again: "What do you want to do? If I may help, in any way, even with money—despite what you said—you have only to ask. Whatever is in my power I will do."

Celia drew a deep breath and smiled so radiantly that Abigail suddenly understood that she had been waiting to hear this offer; without it she would have asked nothing. "I want to leave Henry. I want to live alone. I don't know how a woman of my education may earn a living." She laughed. "Lady Winifred was so right! And we used to think her so—" She shook her head. "I don't even know if the law will permit it. Can he force me to return to him? I thought you would know all these things."

"I know where I can find out. And as for you—you look as if you could sleep forty-eight hours straight through."

"Oh, I could!" Celia said rhetorically.

"Then do so. There is my bed. I shall go and see some friends. And in two days I shall return with all you need to know."

*   *   *

"Pepe? Do you know the laws on divorce and separation and that sort of thing?" she asked that evening.

He grinned knowingly. She asked why.

"A man in Smithfield market recently showed me how they get a wily heifer into a pen when all normal persuasion fails."

"How?" Abigail smiled, half guessing.

"Open the gate at the far side. Show the apparent exit. They always fall for it. So of course I know the divorce law—backwards to Jericho. And of course I'll tell you. I'm delighted you ask."

She laughed and gave him a kiss for persistence.

"Why *do* you ask?" he said.

"It might make an article."

"It's been done. Mary Morris did it. It's in this week's *Companion*."

"So you really do know the law."

"It so happens I do. Marriages can be dissolved on grounds of—"

"Yes, yes. I know all the old reasons. But the new ones. The offences."

"The Act of 'fifty-seven?"

She nodded.

"The husband can divorce the wife for adultery. Just that alone. But the wife has to prove adultery plus one other offence. I mean one of a number of offences. If he's cruel, for instance—beats her, starves her, slanders her—that sort of thing."

"Degrades her?"

"In public?"

"Or in private."

"What d'you mean by degradation, then?" he asked.

"Makes her wear indecent clothing and pose indecently for him."

Laon looked dubious. "Devilish tricky to prove. You wouldn't get the courts interfering there . . . unless . . ." He looked shifty.

Thinking she was on to something, she pressed him: "Unless what?"

He squared himself and looked at her coolly. "What's a pederast, Abbie?" he asked.

She frowned. "It's what Steamer once called a schoolfellow of his. It's not very nice."

"Indeed not! Is that all you know? I've been meaning to ask you for years and thought the chance would never arise."

"What is it then?"

"It's a man who takes no pleasure—*there*." He touched her. "But *there*, instead."

She cringed in disgust. "But what did Steamer mean?"

"You think, Abbie. Boys' school. Strong passions. No women. You think!"

She hid her face.

He smiled indulgently. "So be careful how and when you use that word next time, my darling."

She hugged him, still not wanting to show him her face.

"Adultery plus that would be grounds for divorce. Also incestuous adultery—even with the wife's brother's daughter. But not with his own first cousin. Aren't we marvellous! When we are at our most logical, then we are at our least reasonable."

His bitterness startled her, so that she could face him. In response to the question in her eyes he said, "I think this is a monstrous law, Abbie. And if you want to strike at it—as only you could do—I will print it wherever it will be most effectual."

"Why, Pepe—" she began.

"Look what the law of marriage has done to your friend Annie. Oldale can booze and gamble this pub—*her* pub—into bankruptcy. Because the law says it's his. He could spend all her money on a mistress and she can do nothing to prevent it. If she tried to, he could go to law and force her to yield." He looked at her solemnly and said, "And now tell me—who else are we talking about?"

"Who else?" She gulped.

"Your curiosity has none of the signs of disinterest. You are asking these questions on someone's behalf. If we are to help her, I must know what's what."

So she told Pepe—told him what she had only just promised Celia never to reveal to anyone. Before she finished the tale, his head had sunk into his hands. He was a long time silent; she even wondered if he was crying.

"There is no escape," he said at last.

"For her?"

"For all of us." He looked up. She wanted to hug him, he seemed so forlorn. "When I found out how my father made his money—the money that had paid for my education, fed me, bought all my comforts—when I found out that, I didn't know where to go for the shame."

"Did you have an argument with him?"

"Argument? I didn't—I couldn't even *look* at him, nor bear the sound nor smell of him. I remembered all the comforts and advantages I'd had, and I thought of the cost in lives made foul, in violated bodies—bodies of little girls of twelve. Or even less! I was in a fever for weeks. I almost died of my own disgust." For a long moment he could only breathe, as if breathing needed all his concentration. "And then I came to realize that my father was not alone to blame. He was not the *cause*. There was no cause. No single cause. There were thousands—hundreds of thousands of causes: *men*. This terrifying, implacable urge that possesses all of us, to get over a woman. All of us—you see? *I* was guilty, too, in thought if not in deed. Oh, Abbie—what would I have become if I had not met you?"

"Why?" She laughed in surprise.

"You remember how long it took us to—copulate." He snorted. "Even that word, which is usually spoken in sniggers, or with a sort of forensic challenge, even that word—you have taught me to find the love and beauty inside it."

"You were saying—how long it took . . ."

"Yes. That was not coyness."

"Hardly! I always thought you were being considerate of me."

"I needed time to—to discover the love and beauty in it. Not just in the word but in the act. It was I who needed time, not you. If you had not taught me that . . ." He shrugged at the inexpressible vastness of the alternative.

"What? You have to tell me now! You can't just leave—"

"I hated all men. I loathed us for what we are and how we degrade women. I wanted to become a woman." He laughed. "Why else did I take over those women's magazines? And when I first met you, I wanted us to enjoy the most wonderful, pure, platonic love that ever was. We were to be the arrow's tip of a new revolution in human love! And we almost succeeded. But then you met Annie and told me about her. And *bang!* I exploded inside. You were as near to being raped then as you ever were in your life. And that was the craving and the violence in me, which I fought and fought—until you taught me how to yield to it, how to make it gentle and lovely. If I hadn't met you, I would have gone on hating my masculinity, craving everything feminine." He laughed. "I'd have become a sort of male lesbian."

She had to ask him to explain. Celia's revelations—and Pepe's—blunted the distaste she would otherwise have felt.

"Perhaps," he said reluctantly, "perhaps I already am. Perhaps that's why I accept what few other men would accept from you—your refusal to marry me. And then I hear this dreadful ordeal of your friend Celia's and I feel you are right. Oh God, Abbie—has anyone ever known what to do with it? Will any society ever get it right?"

"What?"

"What to do with sex."

"We have, I think. I mean you and me."

"We are not Society. Nor could all Society do as we do. This beautiful *shape* of flesh I have here, and this beautiful space you have here, which accepts it with such ineffable sweetness—they are tied by an unbreakable thread, which we cannot ignore, to remote questions like who gets this bit of land or that boxful of gold when flesh and space are gone to earth and dust again."

"It's so vast," Abigail said, wondering at the scope of his vision. "How will anyone ever get *all* of it right at the same time! And meanwhile there is poor Celia."

Chapter 26

It was Pepe who pointed the way out of Celia's difficulties. If she set up alone, even if she could find work, her husband could sue for restitution of his rights over every penny she earned and every stick she possessed. And any man who employed her could risk an action for criminal conversion of her affections brought by her husband.

"He would never dare," Abigail said. "Look at all the things she could tell the court about him!"

"A woman has no right to be heard in a crim-con action. Only the husband and the man he accuses. It's between them."

"But that's monstrous! Two men could act in collusion to damn a woman forever—and she'd have no right even to be heard?"

"That's the law. Such injustice must have happened often. But what I'm suggesting for Celia is that *you* should give her employment."

"Good heavens!"

"Don't you see the advantages? With a married lady as your companion, you could be your own hostess. I know that tongues have more or less ceased to wag about you, but it would ensure that they'd never grow loose again. And look at the thousand ways she could be useful, even if she has only half a head on her shoulders—the errands she could run that you now cannot entrust to Mary; the tedious letters she could answer; the tiresome people she could see on your behalf; copying; looking things up. And when you visit Paris or Rome—the arrangements she could make in advance and also supervise during your travels. How *have* you managed without her!"

Within very few months Abigail was asking the same question. Celia was like a spring unstoppered. With the burden of her husband's attentions removed, she grew jolly, rosy, and plump again; she recovered well enough for Abigail to be quite angry with her at times, for she could be both forgetful and extravagant. Mostly though, Abigail was delighted she had followed Pepe's suggestion; despite these occasional lapses, Celia was an invaluable secretary and a boon of a companion.

Henry Crabb, her husband, made several attempts to enforce her return. He tried personal entreaty. He tried suing for restitution but dropped the case before the first hearing. He even waylaid them in the street, but Celia, newly assured of her legal status, would not so much as glance at him. Abigail thought he looked so pitiable and abject that she asked him to call on them the following day.

Of course, that was just bait. She sent Celia out on an errand well before Crabb was due; she thought if she could see him alone, she might get him to understand that there could never be any question of Celia's return. But he found it impossible to accept.

"She's my wife!" he kept saying in a bewildered tone. "She cannot run away. It's against a woman's nature. It's against the duties she was brought up to respect." And he turned to Abigail as to another person of sense. "Can't *you* make her understand that, my lady?"

She realized then, as no amount of letter writing or arm's-length dealing could have done, how possessed he was, and how that possession unhinged him.

"Tell her I adore her still," he said just before he left. "Tell her that everything I did was done in adoration of her." He broke down then. "Where in all the world am I to find a woman to worship as she let me worship her? I never harmed her. I never defiled her. I never burdened her—"

He was still listing his own virtues as she led him to the door.

They never heard of or from him again while he lived; but the memory of that sad encounter pursued Abigail for years. She was never able to think of the things Celia had endured and rouse herself to quite the same pitch of anger as before; the pitiable figure of Henry Crabb would not sustain it. At times Celia was now so cheerful that Abigail almost thought her heartless.

*   *   *

Abigail had a rough-and-ready rule that her writing should support her. Thus, when the successful "Abe Stevenson" and all her other personae lived at the same address in Buckingham Street, they could pool their income and live in fair style. But when the Abbot or one of her even less-well-paid aliases went to Paris (or Rome, or Vienna, or Berlin) to report on the latest exhibitions and the work in the studios, she insisted they do so without subsidy from the others—who, figuratively at least, remained in London and fed their editors from a literary larder built up over the previous months; so the Abbot could spend three weeks in Rome while Drucilla Getz sent her regular copy to *The Girl of the Period*—and so on with all the others, too.

Celia at first did not like the arrangement. When Abigail had said "Rome!" Celia had had visions of wafting into the Hotel Bristol—or the Grand or the Inghilterra—on bouquets of flowers, trailing a comet's tail of page boys and luggage. There would be rich food in dazzling restaurants . . . nights at the opera . . . days amid romantic ruins . . . sumptuous beds . . . and an attentive servant for every little want.

"There is a very pleasant little pension in the Via Campania," Abigail said. "Run by an admirable woman, Signora Facetti. I have stayed there before. It is clean and comfortable, less than a kilometre from the station and a hundred miles from the Forum and the Colosseum and all the other flypapers, and there are some pleasant and cheap cafés not too far away."

But after a few days in Rome, Celia saw how right Abigail had been.

"High living consumes so much time," Abigail said. Living modestly as they did, they could visit the studios and exhibitions in the mornings, when those places were mercifully empty of all the tiresome people (who were at that hour still caught up in the toils of "high living"), stroll about the city and go into the first trattoria that took their fancy, eat a light luncheon, and return to the pension.

And there, while sensible Romans slept through their siesta and high-living tourists sweltered in the flypapers, Abigail could sit in the cool shade of the balcony, look out over the Borghese Gardens, and write the copy that would be paying for it all. She did not tell Celia, but it pleased her to think that this part of the city was the site of the fabulous Gardens of Sallust—"an immoral man but a most artistic writer."

Then, when real Rome awakened for the evening, out they went, bathed and refreshed, to enjoy the sights of the modern city for an hour or two before taking up the serious business of the day: dinner. If Abigail had written something especially good—something that would be sure to earn a good fee—she would claim an instant reward and take Celia, and any artist or writer they met or whose lodging they passed, to the Falcone, there to feast on Maccheroni alla Napolitana, Cinghale all'Agra Dolce, and the sweet, delicate wines of Orvieto. The Falcone was a shabby, sombre crypt, so old that the Caesars had been its patrons, and the waiters could even point out a grease mark left on the wall by the head of Augustus—just as the waiters in The Cheshire Cheese point to that mark of Dr. Johnson's.

After the meal, whether it was eaten at the Falcone or some cleaner, humbler place, they invariably went to a café. Usually it was the Nazionale Aragno in the Corso—the biggest and most sumptuous of all the cafés in Rome. There, amongst an infinity of mirrors, gilding, and blue plush, while the waiters pirouetted around them with their little nickel trays held high above their heads, they could sit and drink coffee and toy with the pastries and marzipan, and talk, or read a two-day-old copy of *The Times* or a ten-day-old *Daily News*.

If they had found no companion before, they needed one for the Nazionale, which would not admit unaccompanied women (there being quite enough of *them* in the streets outside). All Abigail's friends in Rome were writers or artists—mostly painters; and even the writers were agreed that painting was the doyen of the arts (though whether or not she agreed that Rome was its capital depended on whether she was in Rome or Paris). Often they would talk until one or two in the morning, debating hotly whether the artist's purpose was to convey his own excitement at the appearance of things, or whether things themselves, and the light and colour that revealed them, were the true heroes of the pictures.

Italian was at that time more of a literary than a living language—even Cavour, for example, when he was prime minister, had spoken in French to King Victor Emmanuel. Celia, who had learned literary Italian at school, very soon adapted it to the Roman dialect. Abigail, whose French was near perfect and was almost universally understood in her sort of circle, had less incentive to improve her Italian. It was her greatest regret each time they left Rome; if she could stay just a few months longer, she felt, she would soon be as fluent in it as she was in French. But, as things were, each time she returned to Italy she seemed merely to recover the linguistic ground she had lost since the previous time.

But each such visit had to end. Four weeks would exhaust the journalistic possibilities of a Roman season; Paris could be covered in three. And then all those other literary selves she had left in London would clamour for rescue from their depleted larders, and she and Celia had to return. The sugar on the pill of this disappointment—for Abigail—was the knowledge that her Pepe would be waiting for her with three or four weeks of longings to squander.

Celia's companionship was the final crowning of a life that had grown steadily more pleasant with the passing of the years. She could now entertain on her own account. A little circle of friends, mostly fellow journalists, would drop in on a couple of evenings each week—Mondays, when the week's issue was nail-bitingly uncertain (but the coup of the century still possible), and Fridays, when the edition had gone to bed as exciting and run-of-the-mill as ever. She could give dinner parties to some of the grander people who attended her mother's salons. She became one of the arbiters of London's taste. People sought her opinions on plays and books, they asked her to judge this or that picture they were thinking of buying; to an extent she was even lionized.

It could have gone on for the rest of her life; but one day she awoke with feelings of nausea—and she realized that the cardinal was long over-due.

Chapter 27

She was thirty-two years old and she was pregnant. She had made her own life, had built it around a rare talent, had become a person well above the common run, had skirted convention and been allowed to get away with it, had *settled*. And now a tenacious little bud of life—a natural tumour—had fastened itself like a tick into the wall of her womb and, in four or five months' time, would swell visibly enough to wipe out everything.

How had it happened! Had they not taken every care? What terrible will could circumvent two stout blockades of rubber and a toxic bath of quinine jelly, and then turn into this mindless, microscopic vandal of her life? She raged that there was no way of communicating with it, for she longed to shout within herself and let it know it was doing itself no good by fattening there; it would destroy both of them. In despair she reverted to an Abigail she thought she had abandoned several milestones back in her life: she fled to Caspar.

But Caspar was not at Falconwood—was not expected for two days. So for two days she practised the new art that was to sustain her through the next nine months and more: the art of laughing when her heart would burst, of eating while her gorge rose, of conversing lightly when her thoughts were congealed, of smiling when she lived within an ace of a scream.

Caroline, who sought her opinion on paintings, colours, furnishings, flower beds, was deceived. Her nieces and nephews, whom she hurrahed on their ponies and pushed on their swings, were deceived. But Caspar, when he came, was not, though he laughed and joked as expertly as she.

As soon as they were alone—it was a hot Saturday in July, and they took a walk in a new plantation of balsam poplars—he asked what was wrong.

"I'm ruined," she said.

"Money?" He was jovial.

"No. Really ruined."

He fell silent. "The Old Fountain!" he said bitterly at last.

She remembered how she had stressed to him the care she and Pepe took over their meetings. He would have taken that as a challenge; she did not want to know how he had found out. Anyway, what did it matter now?

"Won't Laon marry you? I assume—" he began. "Well, of course."

"Yes, of course it is his. And he doesn't know yet."

"You think he would refuse?"

"I don't want to be married."

"That's a bit academic now, isn't it? I presume, then, that he would marry you."

"It would send him over the moon with happiness."

"But you don't love him? Not that that is of much—"

"He is food, he is wine, he is everything to me. Except my own life. And I still want my own life."

Caspar walked on, a long way, before he spoke again: "Abbie, you know you would never be turned away from here. You could go on the streets—commit murder—and you would always find a refuge here. But you would join *us*. I could not join you. I could not go against Society. To be specific, you would have to retire to your room whenever others called or visited; no one could meet you and we could not risk asking anyone to do so. Yet this would be a *friendly* house, Abbie dear. Think what the world would be like! Think how absolutely unfriended you would be. You and this new life you hold—what a life for both of you!"

"So," she said, as forlorn as she had ever felt. "It's public ruin or private ruin."

"Is he really such a bad chap as all that?"

"Not him! *Me!* I shall change— Oh, it's no use. You'll never understand. No man will ever understand. Annie understands me."

"And a fine friend she proved to be!"

Abigail, hating the frailty that pressed her to it, burst into tears—not because Caspar's condemnation of Annie was true but because, of all he had said, it was the only lie.

*   *   *

Celia, when Abigail confessed it all to her, agreed at once with Caspar. Since leaving Henry Crabb she had seen enough of the world to know what an oddity that man had been; she had no fear her advice might deliver Abigail into a similar fate. Her good-humoured calm did much to restore Abigail.

"You're a brick, Celia," she said. "Not to judge me."

"Judge you? *I!* Judge *you!* Abbie dear, even in the schoolroom I'd not have judged you. I've lived a thousand years since then."

Abigail smiled. "No. You aren't that sort of person. That's your fate. If you were, you'd not have stood two weeks of your marriage. It's what makes you such a lovely and loving friend."

And so she decided to marry Pepe by special licence before a registrar, as soon as it could legally be done. She went to tell Annie the news— Annie, who, from the little she had seen of her lately, could do with some cheering up herself.

*   *   *

The Old Fountain was closed—that is to say, its doors were wide open but no customer was inside and there was neither barman nor maid nor waiter on the premises. The doors were open to let the broker's men in and out—in empty-handed and out with what furniture and knickknacks remained.

"Where's Mrs. Oldale?" she asked one of the men.

"Gawn scarlet," he said, not stopping.

"What d'you mean?"

"Vamoosed," said another. "Scarpered, as the gypsies say."

"To Wales?"

The men laughed. "West of here, anyway," one said, and with such heavy humour that Abigail understood at once that he meant she was on the streets up west.

"And Mr. Oldale?"

"Drinking the last keg." The man nodded toward the gin-palace end of the establishment.

"No he ain't," his partner said. "He's kipping if off upstairs."

"And no one else is here?"

"Shouldn't be."

"How much is wanted?" she asked.

"Albert!" one of the men called.

A fat bowler-hatted man with drooping moustaches and an air of self-importance waddled slowly from the direction of the kitchens, licking his fingers and belching. He coloured when he saw Abigail. "Not so much of that," he said to the man who had shouted. "Mr. Williams to you."

"Lady wants to know the distraint."

"Lady who, may I ask?" He looked at her truculently.

"The Lady Abigail Stevenson." She gave him her card.

His manner changed at once. "Begging pardon, your ladyship—er—the distraint?" He consulted a notebook. "One hundred and fourteen pounds eleven shillings and fourpence three-farthings."

"Owed to?"

"Er—sundry creditors. Most of it to Whitbread's."

"Put everything back," she said. "I will bring you the money directly."

"I have a bill of exchange prepared, my lady. Payable at sight. If you will put your name to it, I'm sure that will satisfy me."

She signed and endorsed it with her banker's name. Within twenty minutes everything (and it was little enough) was returned. She gave them two bottles of rum out of the newly restored stock. They left delighted.

"I'll leave the key with your ladyship," Mr. Williams said.

When they were gone she went around the place, locking every door and barring every window. Then, taking a bottle of brandy from the bar and a funnel from the kitchen, she went upstairs in search of Mr. Oldale.

Wales!

Now it was clear where all those trips had been. Annie had ten thousand such sisters in *that* Wales. And that was what had kept this pub stumbling along all these years, had given Oldale his betting money and booze: Annie, driving herself back, time and again, to the trade she loathed.

Her easiest way to the apartment led through the private supper room that had been "hers" and Laon's for over ten years now. Emptied, it was no longer anybody's—a room on the market. She tried to imagine it, telling herself, "There we sat . . . there we lay together . . . there I conceived. . . ." It was meaningless in the context of this day.

She walked through to Annie's boudoir, empty save for a single deal bed and a cracked ewer and jug. On the bed, in a pool of puke, lay the purulent, blue-veined wreck of the man Annie had chosen among hundreds because, like herself, he was "fond of a good laugh." Why had she really married him? Was her own self-opinion so low that *this* was all she could find to match it? Decent men must have proposed to her, too. Had she been afraid of their decency? Had she feared it might illuminate all that she found unworthy within herself?

What was wrong with Annie and with Celia, the two women she knew and loved the best? What was it in Celia that had allowed her to endure so many years of Henry Crabb's vileness so meekly? And what in Annie had sent her back to a vileness ten times as bad, not once but repeatedly, for the sake of this rubbish now dying on the bed and for the tawdry splendours of this place? Was there something in all women—or something lacking—that made them endure and submit? Did they cast themselves as victims and then go out and seek a man as instrument?

And what of herself and Pepe . . . ?

Before she could pursue that thought, the remains of Roger Oldale stirred. Without further ado—and certainly without pity—she took up the funnel and the brandy bottle, bit through the wax of the seal, pulled out the stopper—*like*, she thought, *pulling the head off a flea*. It was a kindness, to him and to Annie. She never considered it to be anything else.

Twenty minutes later she was on her way west.

*   *   *

By eight that evening she returned, alone and exhausted, to Buckingham Street, not to rest but to snatch a meal and refill her purse with half-sovereigns. She had bribed her way into more alleys and courtyards, bars and night houses, than she had ever dreamed existed—and all within ten paces of streets she had known and traversed all her life.

She had been mistaken as competition and reviled. She had been mistaken as competition and proposed to; one man, panting at her angry heels, had gone as high as forty guineas. But when she still refused, he had shouted after her, "What are you, anyway—old spinster carrion?"

By nine o'clock, changed and half-refreshed, she went out again, determined not to rest until Annie was rescued. Celia had begged to go with her but Abigail was adamant. No one would see Annie in that trade and condition who might afterwards see her in quite another.

It was near midnight before she finally tracked Annie down. A "kaffir," or whore's bully, who had taken half a sovereign off her earlier in the evening, came running up behind her. "Still got the glims out fer Annie B?" he asked.

She said she was still looking. She had established earlier that Annie went by her maiden name, Barnard, in these parts.

"There's a little casa round in Panton Street, Haymarket end. Looks like a drinking gaff but really it's a body ken." She was not sure whether he said "body" or "bawdy." He winked. "Your noffgur's in there, dying of barrel fever with a party of bulkers. Don't ask me why."

"Is it certain this time?" she asked.

"Didn't I just cut from her?" he answered.

She offered him more money but he pushed her hand down with a grin. "No, lady, you paid already."

A strange flirtation with honour, she thought as she made for Panton Street, by a man who certainly would not scruple to rob her.

She was well down the Haymarket, almost at Panton Street, when she was brought to a dead halt by a man who came tripping out of a night house with a laughing young girl on his arm. Abigail knew him at once; it was her Uncle Walter—Walter Thornton, Nick's father. She had known him all her life, for he and his wife Arabella were old family friends; in fact, Uncle Walter had been the company engineer on her father's first railway contract.

Walter recognized her in the same instant. Give him his due, he had enough presence of mind for twenty. He smiled broadly, even graciously—certainly without a trace of embarrassment. "Why, Lady Abigail! Is anything amiss? May I help in any way?"

Even as he spoke these few terse words he managed subtly to change the nature of his grip upon the girl's arm. When she first spotted him he had been a cavalier carrying off a wench, but now he was something more like a parish beadle with a petty wrongdoer. It was skilfully managed. The girl played along, too.

"I'm looking for a former servant of ours, Uncle Walter. You wouldn't remember her, I'm sure, but her name is Annie Barnard. I'm told she's round in Panton Street."

The irony of it! she thought, hoping the thought didn't show. This was the man who had been Annie's first customer. In a sense he was her seducer.

Walter was looking back up the Haymarket, over Abigail's shoulder, as if he expected to see something there; his disappointment at apparently not seeing it was keen. "Did you not pass Aunt Arabella?" he asked.

"Not knowingly—obviously," Abigail said, wondering that he took her for such a fool. His immediate assumption that his nimble wits and cool head would easily deceive her was intensely annoying. Her own set of friends was not smart or racy, but it was sophisticated—well beyond this sort of schoolboyish bluff. The fact that Uncle Walter was twice her age only made his childish arrogance the worse.

"She must have the carriage up there in Jermyn Street," he said, half to her, half to the girl. Then he turned wholly to the girl. "Look, my dear. Walk up to the corner of Jermyn Street and if you see a growler there, perhaps with other unfortunate women in it, go up to it and make yourself known to my good wife. Otherwise wait for me there. Be assured I shall not desert you." The girl moved off in obedience. "Nor will the good Lord," he shouted after her. "God is close to you tonight!" He contrived to face Abigail back toward Panton Street before she could see how the girl might respond to this afterthought.

"I will not allow your Aunt Arabella into places like that," he said, nodding at the house he and the girl had just left. "Nor, by the same token, can I permit you. I shall find this servant for you, if she is to be found at all. What was her name? Amy?"

"Annie. Annie Barnard." Abigail described her and translated what she thought the kaffir had told her.

Annoyed, she had no choice but to play Uncle Walter's game; to do otherwise would be to give the lie to him openly. Perhaps he even knew that—knew she was not deceived and did not care. Now *there* was real cause for anger; it revealed a view of womankind she had almost forgotten. Her success, the esteem she had earned, the equality with which she competed for, and won, space for her writing (which was *herself*)—these had isolated her from her sisterhood and the way men patronized them.

She looked at Walter, at his arrogant, twinkling eyes, as avuncular as his courtesy title, and felt a sudden welling up of hatred that surprised her. She would feel insulted enough if he imagined his charade deceived her; but if he knew it did not, and himself did not care so long as convention forced her to play his game, that was far worse. Beyond her surprise she was self-aware enough to know that at any earlier point in her life, at least part of her would be amused at catching out Walter in this way and at watching his calm (even if perfunctory) saving of the situation.

What had changed her? Annie. And the things that had happened to Annie. The chances Annie had never known—to find what love truly is, to own a little dignity, to possess her own person—and all because arrogant, twinkling-eyed men like this "uncle" walked abroad with Annie's food in their bellies, Annie's cloth on their backs, and Annie's cash jingling in their pockets, for so it now appeared to her.

"We'll soon see if there's honour among thieves, me dear," Walter said as he walked in through the open doorway of the house the kaffir had described. Ironically enough, this was the night house where she had made her first inquiry of the evening. Walter paused just over the threshold and surveyed the interior; a change in his expression showed that Annie, or someone of her description, was, indeed, inside.

Abigail could bear the game no longer. She strode in past Walter and turned toward where he had been looking. It was Annie right enough.

If she had earned anything this evening, a good part of it must already have vanished down her throat. She sat at a coverless table, the centre of a rank of five girls, all drinking but none so drunk as Annie. She stood out in more flattering ways, too. Even drunk she was handsome—dark-eyed, angular, sleek-skinned. The years and troubles had not marked that skin; the four other girls were puffy-fleshed, fuddled, and blowsy. "Blowsa-bellas," Annie had once called such girls; and so they were.

"Annie, dear. The pub is yours again," she told her.

It took Annie a moment to recognize the source and then the bringer of this news.

"It's yours," Abigail said again. "The pub is yours."

"Welcome to Wales!" Annie said, half falling over the table as she tried to gesture around the room.

"Mr. Oldale will never trouble you again."

She did not take it in. All the self-disgust Abigail guessed was there suddenly came welling up. "Piss off!" she shouted.

"You ungrateful wretch!" Walter said. "Come home now, as your mistress commands." He turned to Abigail. "This is exactly the sort of thing I forbid Aunt Arabella to expose . . . ." His voice tailed off as he caught Abigail's eye.

"You don't even recognize her, do you, Uncle Walter?" Abigail said, taking no care now to hide her contempt.

"Recognize . . . ?" He looked back at Annie in bewilderment. "Ah! Lady Winifred's maid—of course. Yes, of course. Dear, dear!"

Clearly he did not know her from Eve. To be rid of him Abigail pretended to share his triumph of memory. "What facility you have, Uncle Walter! But I think it best for you to go now. I know this girl very well and I'm sure I shall cope. Besides, Aunt Arabella might begin to wonder what you're at!"

The eagerness that showed in his face was at the thought of escaping this place and her company, and returning to the Haymarket to resume the more wonted role of cavalier with the laughing wench. Abigail's disgust did not survive his departure by a second; he was too slight an entity to bear what properly belonged to that vast segment of man-kind—or *man*-kind—who nightly and daily made the whole mess possible.

She turned back to Annie, who was staring at her with a swaying, angry absorption.

"Come home with me, Annie dear. I'll look after you."

"Fuck off! Just—fuck off!" Annie burst into tears and fell over the table, sending glasses sprawling.

A bully came over; until now he had been lurking in the dark to one side of the bar. "Enough of that," he said to Abigail. His accent was Welsh.

"I came to tell her her husband is dead."

The man looked at Annie, still sobbing heavily. "You told her," he said.

"I want to take her back home."

The man jabbed a finger in Annie's back, making her wince. Her sobbing stopped. "You wanna go home?" he asked.

She shook her head with such weary slowness it was more final than her obscenities or any word she might have spoken.

"So." The man turned back to Abigail. "You may flit off."

I tried, Abigail thought as she went outside. At the door she heard Annie scream. She turned back, but Annie was fighting with one of the blowsabellas and the Welshman was once more weaving his way toward that table.

A moment later Annie was pitched out into the street, still cursing the other girl, the Welshman—the world. Almost at once she was picked up by two policemen, who started frogmarching her up to the wagon at the top of the Haymarket.

Abigail stepped in their path and handed them her card. "This girl is one of my servants," she said severely. "Bring her home in half an hour and I have two guineas for the police widows' fund."

She turned and called up her cab to take her home.

*　　　*　　　*

Annie slept a full eighteen hours—in Abigail's bed since there was none other for her. Abigail, who slept but fitfully beside her, heard her toss and turn and call out strange half-words all night.

The following morning Abigail went back to The Old Fountain, this time with Celia, where she "discovered" the dead Roger Oldale and called in the police. Her story (especially when later confirmed by half a dozen broker's men), the evidence of their eyes, and their own common knowledge of the man himself satisfied them he had died—as indeed he had—of drink.

She had arranged to travel abroad, she said; would it be possible for her and Mrs. Crabb to swear a deposition giving formal evidence of finding the body to satisfy the coroner? The inspector was most sympathetic; their affidavits were sworn well before lunchtime.

*   *   *

She and Annie lay awake long that night, talking in the dark, tracing
the silver and black of the window mullions where they splayed their
shadows over the ceiling. Annie spoke of the whole mess of her rotten
marriage; her hatred of Roger had inflamed into a hatred of all men—all
the men in history, it seemed. There wasn't a good one among them.

"Yet you were going back into that trade, Annie. You were going
back to please them."

"Please them!" She snorted. "I want to get poxed. You think I'd
normally go in a fleapit like that? I want to *burn*. I want to go out among
them like a fireship!"

"Oh, Annie—don't do that, *please*."

"I don't see no other way out."

"Come and stay here. Stay with me."

Annie sat up. Her eyes gleamed with light borrowed from the street.
"Straight?" she asked with hushed breath. "Oh, I'd do anything for you,
Abbie. I'll cook and skivvy and slave for you. I idolize you, honest. You
know that."

The fury of this devotion took Abigail aback. In a flash she saw how
impossible a situation it would be. Annie was too mercurial. She'd be
"devoted" now; in two days she'd be hurling pots downstairs.

She laughed. "What are we talking about, Annie! He's gone. You
don't have to come here. The pub is yours. I'll lend you the money to get
you going again."

But Annie shook her head, sighed, and lay down again, accepting that
Abigail had offered only a temporary refuge. "No more pubs for me,
love," she said. "I'll sell it. That's what I'll do. Open a little haberdasher's
down Pimlico. Victoria way. Do me a treat. Nice quiet little
business—don't need no bleedin' man. I'll just sit there and grow old
respectably." She giggled at the idea that such a thing really was possible
for her.

"You and Mr. Laon will have to find new quarters," she said.

Abigail told her then. "I tried all the things you suggested last time,
but they didn't work," she finished.

"No, this one's got your name," Annie said. "Listen, I know a lady as
keeps down the census—by Aldgate pump. I've heard gels talk about
her."

"I couldn't do that, Annie. It's myself I hate, not—it."

"So you'll marry him, and that's all about it!"

"I suppose so. As you said"—she imitated Annie—" 'I don't see no other way out.' "

Annie kissed her warmly and settled herself to sleep. "We'll see about that," she said. "Time for a little think."

Abigail lay back contentedly. Annie would think of something; it might be mad, it might be impossible—it probably would be—but it would be all Annie.

I am lucky, she thought. Celia was a dear, good friend; and Annie was . . . a sister? No—even more than a sister. A strange twin self. They could share joy and suffering without a word passing between them.

She awoke drowsily in the small hours. The first light of dawn filled the streets, lending a pink flush to the window glass and filling the room with a sense of peace. By some telepathy Annie awakened, too. She snuggled against Abigail and put an arm over her neck. Abigail kissed her forehead lightly.

"I thought it all out, gel," Annie said. "You don't need to marry him. You can go away and have your baby and come back and carry on just like before. You can even keep the baby by you. And all without one whiff or sniff of a scandal. There, now!"

Abigail smiled at the ceiling. She ran her fingers lightly through Annie's hair. "Dear Annie!" she said.

"You think I'm dreaming?" Annie shivered and trapped Abigail's fingers at the nape of her neck.

"Sorry," Abigail said.

"No, don't stop. It's nice. I'm not used to it, that's all—not for a century."

"Tell me how I can live this miracle."

"Let *me* have the baby for you."

"Oh, willingly!"

"No, straight. Here's how. D'you know a safe house in France or somewhere? Italy?"

"And if I do?"

"Here's me—friend of yours. Widow in black—thick veil and all. Carrying. Tragic case. Needs to get away. Here's you—how long since you writ that book, *Land of Whos's 'name?*"

"A lifetime!"

"There you are then. For years you wanted to write another, didn't you? Go around telling people that. Dying to write another. Remind them how you've been saying it for years."

"But I haven't."

"That won't stop them remembering it." Annie assumed a lah-di-dah accent. "D'you kneow, I rahthah think I'll take may deah friend Mrs. Eoldale to Frahnce this heah wintah. She can do her kitten and I can wrate may book."

The idea, and Annie's mockery of Abigail, were both so farfetched that the two women fell into helpless giggles.

"Annie!" Abigail said, wiping her eyes.

"It would work," Annie said, growing serious again. "You could lace in so nothing'd show for six or seven months. I've known gels on the turf lace in till the foal's dropped. And meanwhile I'm wearing black with a little bustle basket around the front." She giggled again. "And the little basket's getting bigger every week, isn't he!"

Abigail sighed and shook her head.

"Tell me one way it wouldn't work. In the last two months you're desperate to finish your book. Night and day you're at it—anyone can see the light in your study. Don't want no visitors thanks. I'll lay any odds you're not the first writer what ever done that."

Abigail felt a certain tension grow within her; she was actually considering this preposterous idea! Something within her desperately wanted it to happen—just as Annie painted it. *For heaven's sake!* a wiser self sneered. But her mind's eye did not relinquish its hold on that little foreign villa—somewhere—with its high wall, its groves of sheltering myrtle and cypresses, and the sad, stately figure of the English widow with her belly out. And her good friend, the dedicated writer-recluse, the celebrated Lady Abigail, desperately trying to finish the masterpiece that still lurked within her. And, of course, Lady A's companion, the demure, jolly—and jolly respectable—Mrs. Crabb.

Mrs. Oldale . . . Lady Abigail Stevenson . . . Mrs. Crabb . . . by thunder, it could work! The very madness of the idea almost guaranteed it. The real temptation, Abigail realized suddenly, was the idea of writing another book. How had Annie thought of that? She herself had hardly realized, until now, when the possibility was handed to her, how much she wanted to write another book. She was tired of journalism; she might even be getting stale.

And what a book it would be! No children's fable now. She would write of a real modern woman and a real modern man. She would write of love—real love. Not the absurd histrionics of Heathcliff and Catherine, nor the sugar-water innocence of David Copperfield and child-bride Dora, nor that all-suffering, all-forgiving, ever-constant Agnes. But a real woman—one who would make even the "shocking" Madame Bovary seem tame.

"And if I was always around," Annie said, "what's more natural than that she'll be around, too?"

"She?"

"The baby, of course."

"Suppose it's a he?"

Annie hugged her. "You won't have no man-child, gel. Got too much sense, you have." And she gave Abigail an embarrassingly passionate kiss on the cheek.

"You're a baby yourself," Abigail said.

*   *   *

Celia, to Abigail's surprise, thought the idea little short of genius; perhaps ten years of enormity had accustomed her to take any idea in her stride. But Abigail put her finger on its moral weakness: "It isn't very fair to Pepe," she said.

"Fair!" Annie snorted. "Was it fair when he shot you in the giblets that time? He done it deliberate and all."

"It was a long while ago, Annie. *This* was not his intention."

"When were you born, gel? They're all the same—sweet as figs, but they'll put the white swelling on you, easy as laughing. You don't owe him."

"I do, love. I've just realized what I owe him. I owe him the chance to find a life without me. Since I cannot give him his child, that will have to do."

And that was how she put it to Laon. "All this time I've been saying I was so afraid of being a wife . . . the woman who's always there . . . your own tame Agnes whom you never need to woo or win . . . your bond-woman. Yet that is what I have made you, my darling. How many times have you yourself said it: that I cannot release you. You are my bondman. So I will take a year off to write this book. Poor Annie is with child and quite alone, so she will accompany me—and Celia, of course. And you will have a year to—" She almost broke down. "Oh, Pepe. I'm going to be so miserable."

"Then don't go. For heaven's sake, it's not as if—"

"I do have to. I must. I'm so unfair to you—holding on to you and yet swearing I'll never marry."

"Let me be the judge of that."

"I am, darling. That's what this time is for."

"And if, at the end of it, I am still of the same mind?"

"I may change."

His eyes filled with hope until she added, "I may change in ways you don't welcome, too."

*   *   *

Celia saw another flaw that had escaped both Abigail and Annie. When Abigail said she knew just the place—the Villa Mancini on Lake Como—Celia said, "Suppose you were not circumstanced as you are—is that where you would choose to go?" And Abigail had to admit that it was not.

"What would you do then?"

Abigail considered. Her mother had many years ago bought a lot of land and foreshore at a place in Normandy called Deauville, opposite the fashionable resort of Trouville; there were hopes of making an equally fashionable resort out of Deauville. Those hopes were still only half-realized, but the scheme had already borne certain fruits, among them a number of fine villas, any one of which Abigail would have begged if her sole purpose had been to write a book.

Annie looked at Celia with a new admiration. "We'd best keep you by us," she said, "in case we turn to crime. You'd flannel a good line on any turnover."

Celia blushed at this barely comprehensible praise, though she did not like Annie's use of "we." As far as she was concerned, she and Abigail were taking Annie along.

Nora was all in favour of her daughter's scheme. She was glad Abigail had never married Laon—and almost glad she had never married at all. She saw this year-long break as the beginning of the end for Laon's chances.

"From September you may have your pick of the villas," she said. "But in fact the best is vacant now. Countess d'Aligny was to have had it, but her husband is ill, poor lady. She would be glad, I'm sure, to have the rent returned."

"Which one is it?"

Nora had sketches of all the villas. "This," she said. "The Villa Corot—after the painter, you know. He stayed there a few years ago and we renamed it in his honour. There is a little studio in the garden."

It was charming—romantic, even anarchic, but in a very controlled French way. "Perfect," Abigail said.

"And you can go over and see Tante Rodie every day if you wish."

Ah! She had forgotten Tante Rodie—Madame Rodet—her mother's great friend. The year she had spent in France perfecting her French had been passed in the Rodets' Paris house at Saint Cloud; she had forgotten La Gracieuse, their home at Trouville.

"I had thought of that, of course." Abigail smiled. "But Tante Rodie's nearness may turn out to be the disadvantage. I hope she would understand."

"What?"

"I *must* write this book. If I find Deauville too distracting, or if I can't settle, or the weather's bad, I'll have to move on. I thought the Villa Mancini near Como—you remember? The Rodets took it that summer I stayed with them."

And so she laid the grounds for a move that would be inevitable, never mind the weather or the distractions of Deauville or how well or ill she settled; there could be no question of being within a hundred miles of Tante Rodie from the moment the swelling became visible.

In case she harboured any illusions about what she was relinquishing by this mad notion of hers (Pepe's words), Laon arranged a testimonial farewell dinner at the Albion. Editors and writers returned from grouse moors in Scotland and from moorings in the Solent to be there; many a Grand Old Writer on his retirement would not have been so honoured.

G. V. Simms, in a witty but pointed speech, made it clear that the book she was going to produce had better be a masterpiece, or she would have deceived her admirers twice over. Jimmy Whistler brought the roof down with his selection of readings from the Abbot's columns, artlessly choosing only those passages that referred to him and innocently ascribing their reference to some unknown painter whom he longed to meet—they might have sued Ruskin together and doubled their damages! At the end, with that extraordinary ability of his to ring a sudden change, he paid her a most moving personal tribute as a lady above reproach in all things.

Another painter, Bob Stevenson, who was later to be immortalized by his more famous cousin Robert Louis as "Springheel Jack," then presumed to welcome her to France, on no greater pretext than that he was working over there at the moment and their names were the same. R. L. Stevenson called Springheel Jack a "loud, copious, intolerant talker." Bob's speech that night was certainly very strange. Abigail had only the vaguest knowledge of him. Their ways had never crossed. She had never written about his work. Yet he spoke as if he owed his very life to her or, rather, he hinted as much in one breath and withdrew it in the next. It was a topsy-turvy speech, full of paradoxes and extravagance, yet all spoken with the most solemn earnestness.

Afterwards, in conversation with her, he apologized and said he had stood up merely to fish a coin from a very deep pocket but then, finding himself on his feet, had been carried away by the occasion. It transpired that he was then painting at Barbizon, near Fontainebleau, and was a close friend of another painter, a Frenchman also painting there, who knew her well and also knew of her forthcoming visit to Deauville: César Rodet. Perhaps they might call on her some day this autumn?

César Rodet! He had been a remote, godlike figure, a taciturn giant of twenty-five years, when she, a babe of sixteen, had stayed with the Rodets. He had flitted in and out of the house twice in that year. She thought he had been a doctor, not a painter. She could hardly remember him now.

"You will like him," Bob Stevenson said. "He never utters a word. The very best kind of conversationalist, *I* always find. We look forward to seeing you in France."

Laon could hardly bear to say goodbye. "It will be a wasted year," he said in an angry sort of grief. "A needless hole in our lives. You could stay away for twenty years and yet find me as much your captive as I am at this minute. Your tragedy is you still think life is long. You have not yet grown up."

PART TWO

The Aventine Hill, 1879

Chapter 28

They settled at the Villa Corot in Deauville during the fashionable middle two weeks of August. Abigail was seen everywhere: at the Casino, in the party of M. Rodet; at a concert, squired by an officer on leave from Boy's regiment; and at a ball, where her companion was none other than Bob Stevenson. Her constant chaperone was the jolly Mrs. Crabb.

At quieter hours, in the morning, the two ladies could be seen assisting a third, a tall woman in widow's weeds who, to judge by Lady Abigail's solicitude, was in an interesting condition.

In September, when fashionable London had returned to fashionable London, taking with it the firmest memory of these images, life at the Villa Corot settled to a more natural routine. Its centre was Abigail. Her baby and her book were all that mattered. Annie and Celia vied with each other to ensure the safe gestation of both—to such an extent that Abigail had at last to intervene with a list of the services she required, and to say which of them was to furnish each. Then, with autumn fast drawing on, something like peace settled in among them.

It was a kind of peace Abigail had forgotten, a peace almost from her childhood. Each dawn, as she woke up, her mind automatically reached for the matter she would cover in today's articles—the galleries she would visit, the periodicals she would scan, the people she would see—and she found . . . *nothing!*

At first it was unnerving, like an unnatural silence. Then, imperceptibly, the silence became natural. For the last ten years she had been pursued by a noise—the noise of success, the noise of her London: "What happened? . . . What's next? . . . Did you hear? . . . Did she really? . . . I don't *believe* it! . . . What do *you* think?" Journalism had consumed her, at five—six—seven thousand words a day. She fed it words; it gobbled words and said "Good!" and to say *good* was to say *More! More words!*

And now the endless chain was broken; the treadmill was silent. And the silence itself had become natural. Would she be forgotten as easily? Was the silence of the Abbot and Madge Challis and Drucilla Getz equally natural in London now? She found she did not mind.

Partly, to be sure, that was the baby inside her. She could not feel it yet—not as a lump, though there was the occasional squirm, a vertigo of the midriff. But the knowledge that it was there was strangely comforting. She had heard of girls who had endured the most terrible privations, girls for whom the final refuge of the workhouse was a heaven, and all for the sake of that little life within them. She understood them now.

These were new thoughts, though—too new to have wrought so profound a change within her. That change led her back to an inner simplicity she had forgotten. It was not a thought, nor even a feeling, but something much more raw: it was a sensation. Complex but immediate. It hit at her from the morning air and the autumnal light so that she reeled under the shock of it and had to probe and reason her way back into herself.

It *was* the morning air. It *was* the autumnal light. As simple as that! How long since she had smelled such fragrance? How long since she had seen the unmarked world, the stones, the cracks in the pavements, the sea pinks, the distant white horses, with such clarity? How long since her mind had been so empty of worldly trivia? Empty enough to be filled—more than filled: possessed—by such simplicities?

If she had said, or even thought, *I am going to France to rediscover myself and my directions,* she would have cringed at the solemn portentousness of such a wish. Yet, wish or no, it was happening to her just the same.

She had thought herself happy in London, and so she was. But the happiness had been stretched—a serial. She was glad to be living. Here she was something far better: she was glad to be alive. It meant being young again. It meant the joy of aimless strolling, the warmth of woollen stockings, the taste of hazelnuts, the crispness of white linen. It meant the gladness of a life that could be consumed in such ordinary things.

*   *   *

Within ten weeks her new novel was finished, save for the last chapter. But she knew exactly how that would go; she left it unwritten because she feared the emptiness that would follow—for it would be three or four months yet before she could send it to Laon.

When she had outlined the book to herself, the night Annie had first broached this mad idea, the theme had depressed her. Such a story, such a love as she had envisaged, could not end happily—not in this century; the time was too far out of joint. How could you bring Blake's vision of love to an age whose preparation for it was "Drink plenty of champagne and show no surprise!" And it was Blake's vision of love on which she built her tale,

as she had tried to build her life. To make that clear, she called the book
Into a Narrow Circle and prefaced it with the quotation:

> *And they inclosed my infinite brain into a narrow circle,*
> *And sunk my heart into the abyss, a red round globe hot burning,*
> *Till from all life I was obliterated and erased.*

But though her lovers, William and Catherine, ended tragically, theirs
was a tale of terrible joy; even their death, in the final, yet-to-be-written
chapter, would be a hymn to the holiness of love. For herself the story was
a hymn to Pepe and all she had learned with him; while she wrote it she
could not miss him, for his presence was as strong in the room as the
ticking of her clock.

None of these elements—not the peace of the Villa Corot, not the joy
of their little sorority, not her passion for Blake, not her loving memories
of Pepe—accounted for the speed with which she wrote. For that she had
no one to thank but César Rodet, Bob Stevenson's painter friend. To call
him "taciturn" was the understatement of the century. On his first three
visits he spoke not a word, neither *bonjour* nor *adieu*. He merely watched
them with his dark nervous eyes.

Tante Rodie, his mother, who called at least twice a week, waved her
hands in eloquent despair. "That one!" she said. "Is he even French?
How can we know?"

Then one day César came visiting alone. He did not knock at the door;
in fact, he climbed through the hedge at the bottom of the garden.
Abigail, who had taken to doing a little sketching out in the studio each
afternoon—just as a break from the tyranny of writing—watched him
walk boldly up the lawn. Boldly? No. In anyone else his unconcern would
have been bold; in him it was simply—unconcern. Nothing he ever did
was ambiguous. Incomprehensible, perhaps, but not ambiguous.

He caught sight of her and turned at once toward her—no embarrassment, not even the slightest hesitation. He did not say hello, but he smiled
dazzlingly. How could she dislike him! He looked at her drawing and
pointed at a shape; a puzzled frown knit his brow.

"It's that house," she said nervously. "See?" She spoke in French out
of courtesy.

He nodded dubiously and pointed at another shape. "It's that tree, the
cypress," she said. "I moved it nearer to help the composition."

He pointed at other features—each quite obviously whatever it was
supposed to be: a building, a bush, a cloud. And, feeling increasingly
foolish, she identified each in words.

He grunted, smiled at her (was it with a hint of pity?), and sitting down beside her, pulled out his own sketchbook and began to draw. He sat at an angle that just prevented her from seeing his work without craning over rudely—though why should she feel that to be rude, she wondered, after *his* little performance?

In only a few minutes he stood again, tore off his sketch, and handed it to her. "Here is how you draw," he said, also in French. "But already my drawing is superior to yours." And away he went, back through the hedge.

His voice was so beautifully bass, like a flowing liquid, black as his beard, that she did not at first grasp the meaning. And the drawing did not immediately help. It consisted of the capital letters HOUSE, TREE, and CLOUD, each distorted into the shape of a house, a tree, and a cloud. When a person can draw, he or she can draw anything—a matchstick man, a little sketch map of how to reach the nearest post office—it doesn't matter what; the talent for drawing will show. Abigail could see César's talent in every line of his little joke. When he said "my drawing is superior to yours," it was not vanity but simple truth.

But was it a joke? she wondered. Something in his manner had made it seem more important than that. Was he also making a serious point? If so, then he was telling her—no, showing her—that she was not drawing things but concepts. That had been the idea behind his point-and-frown charade. She was not drawing the shape of the house, the shape of the tree— No! Even that was too verbal.

Forget the words! Forget "house." Forget "tree." Forget "cloud." Just look!

Over there is a—a mass, and there another mass, and there another mass. In each there are parts— No! Parts need names. Forget parts.

In each there are—there are *surfaces!* Surfaces that come toward you . . . twist . . . go away . . . face upward . . . overhang . . . fold in on themselves . . . flicker . . . scintillate.

Was that what César was saying? Look at a landscape and forget the name, the function, the history, the associations of every element in it. Look only for masses, surfaces, movements, directions.

With a feeling of excitement, as if the discovery were uniquely hers, she began a fresh drawing. Ten minutes later she had achieved a shattering insight—shattering because it was so obvious she ought to have seen it thirty years ago.

Next day he came again, just as before, through the hedge. As he drew near she said, "The shapes between things are just as important as the things themselves!"

He laughed! He danced on the frosty lawn. He ran to her and kissed her. It was not a sexual kiss. She felt that if she had been a male student of his (and without doubt she was now a student of his), he would have done the same.

His face fell a little when he looked at her drawing, but then he gave a Gallic shrug that said, "It will get better from now," and sat down to draw beside her, a proper drawing this time.

After five minutes she asked, "Where's Bob?"

He did not seem to hear. It was half an hour before he spoke, by which time her fingers and toes had frozen to numbness. "England," he said.

She looked at his drawing and felt a sort of despair. It was the scene before them—its essence, its spirit. Her own drawing was full of local colour, texture, imposingly deployed clouds, and "artistic" vignetting—shading off—at the edges. His was a modest display of everything she had missed. A passing tourist might have admired hers far more, but she was not deceived.

"Why draw?" he asked. His deep voice was so warm.

"For amusement . . . relaxation . . ."

He shook his head. "There is only one purpose: painting. You draw to be able to paint. Drawing for drawing's sake?" He pulled a face and pointed at her sketch. "Full of tricks and self-congratulation."

These encounters came at an important moment for Abigail— just as she was about to embark on the first full draft of *Into a Narrow Circle*. She saw at once how relevant were these new insights from César Rodet. His drawing might look as if it were tied to a particular scene—this unique arrangement of houses, trees, clouds, and so on; but his genius was to extract from that arrangement something that was true about *all* masses and shapes and surfaces, regardless of the names that might be pinned on them. So he could do a drawing that was accurate to the last leaf without limiting it to a time and a place. It remained universal.

That universal feeling, of being accurate about a time and place without being tied to it, was exactly what she wanted in her book. And how to achieve it? That also came out of César's drawing lesson: *the shapes between*. In a flash of insight she saw at once what was so wrong about Dickens—and what had made Pepe once say that she was "every bit as bad." Dickens' writing was "every bit as bad" as her drawing: full of rich local colour, full of texture, imposingly deployed elements, and artistic vignetting. Just the thing for the passing tourist. But the shapes between? Mere accidents, all of them.

She knew then what to avoid in her writing. She did not yet know how to find those shapes between—the elements that related Catherine and William to each other and then to the world—but that was now her goal: to find them. It pleased her especially to realize that she had achieved this insight all by herself; every other discovery of hers had actually been placed in her path by Pepe, who had always been "one secret ahead" of her. Then with a slight wrench of sadness she realized that Pepe would probably never have planted this discovery. Even if she explained it to him, he probably wouldn't see it—"Shapes *between* people? In a *story?* What airy rubbish is this?" She had passed beyond him, and not in some trivial area of her life but in the most important one of all.

Because she knew, from the very first line, what she was after, the story grew with remarkable fluency. She had a mental sieve that allowed or blocked each possible development as it occurred to her. She never floundered, never wavered. Best of all, she did not miss Pepe's guiding hand, the constant nudge of his editorial goad. At last she stood alone.

César came almost every day; he was living at his parents' home in Trouville now. When the weather was mild, he, Celia, and Abigail went out sketching along the seafront. When it was not, they sat and drew from one of the windows. Celia did watercolours—light, fresh, charming little landscapes and seascapes. César praised them, rather extravagantly, Abigail thought at times. They weren't *that* good, surely? And Celia wasn't really doing what an artist ought to be doing—what César himself did, and what she, Abigail, attempted. Celia wasn't out to discover anything. For her, each blank sheet of watercolour paper was another chance to display a skill that was learned and completed years ago; if she continued until she was ninety, her paintings would look just as they did today. Abigail thought it very unfair of César to praise Celia so much and yet be so hard on her own much more honest work.

Once, when Celia was not with them, she told him so.

"But she's not an artist," César said. "What she does—it's nothing to you and me. You want Molière to write fashion reports? That's all Celia can be—a fashion reporter. An illustrator. But she's a very good one. So I tell her." After a long silence, twenty minutes during which they sketched, he added, "Besides, she can make a living perhaps. It can be useful."

There were, she realized, depths to this man.

*   *   *

Annie did not like César; she pointedly left any room as soon as he entered. More tiresomely, she grew very jealous of the time Abigail spent with him, though it was only an hour or two a day.

Around this time Annie began to suffer night terrors—on account, she said, of never having slept alone. The only cure was for her to sleep with Abigail. At first, Abigail, who had never regularly shared a bed with anyone, not even as a child, resented it; but Annie was such a compulsive and colourful talker, had experienced so much that Abigail would never (she hoped) experience, and was so richly revealing of herself that Abigail soon looked forward to the nightly flow of Annie's chatter.

But she also realized that the words she had once jokingly spoken, "You're a baby yourself," were close to the truth. When Annie went over to London to attend the sale of her pub, and actually received quite a bit more than she had originally sunk into it, she came back to France and handed the whole lot over to Abigail. "You keep it, gel," she said. "It's all for you. Just give us a bit at a time." Of course, Abigail transferred it all to an English bank in Annie's name.

Annie loved to cuddle up to Abigail, to put her ears to the barely perceptible mound of Abigail's stomach and swear she could hear "the little gel's heart a-beating." And she could not sleep until Abigail had stroked her hair and neck. She talked endlessly of her childhood; it seemed to amaze her, no less than it amazed Abigail, that despite all the outward trappings of misery they had been so happy. The days when her father got steady work and was able to take the rest of them out of the workhouse and orphanage—Annie could make that joy ring out all over again.

Annie talked a lot about their future, too: how happy the three of them were and always would be, how they'd find a little place somewhere and settle down and "never need no bleedin' men except for chopping logs and fetching coals." The one thing she never talked about was men—the hundreds she must have known in her years on the streets. She behaved as if she had wiped them out of her life. But Abigail wondered if that was really so.

She put a lot of Annie into Catherine, the heroine of *Into a Narrow Circle*—not, of course, her misanthropy, but her honesty, her sensuousness, her glad acceptance of each day, her childlike but fierce loyalty to those she loved. In the same way William, the hero, owed a lot to César. He had the same apparent simplicity, the same animallike directness in satisfying his few basic wants, the same lack of guile, the same dedication to himself, the same generosity. It was a pity Annie and César did not get on; they were very alike once you penetrated their obvious differences.

Chapter 29

By the end of November they decided it would be wise soon to transfer their household to the Villa Mancini. Soon not all the lacing in nor all the loose-flowing "druid costumes" would be able to disguise Abigail's condition. Annie was delighted, of course, for it meant leaving "that blackbeard beggar" behind.

Abigail tried to break it to César gently, but he merely smiled. "I'll come, too," he said.

She laughed. "That's out of the question."

"It will be better."

"No doubt! Better for whom?"

"Better for me. The light is better in north Italy. Also the mountains and the lake."

"There won't be room for you."

"I know the Villa Mancini. There's a tower. No one else could live in it in the winter, but I will."

"I'm sorry, César," she finally had to insist, not without a feeling of panic, "but no!"

"It'll be better to have a man when the baby comes."

"But you know very well that Mrs. Oldale doesn't like you."

"I mean your baby."

She sat down abruptly. The assurance in his smile ruled out any bluff on her part. She felt dead; it had all been wasted. "How long have you known?" she asked.

"Long enough."

"Does your mother—have you told anyone?"

"Of course not!"

"You still can't come with us, César. It's out of the question."

But he came with them all the same.

Of course they did not own the train; they could not push him back onto the platform. His ticket was as valid as theirs. They could not refuse his help with their luggage nor the coffee he procured en route when no one else could find so much as a glass of water. Abigail was furious but she could see that Celia was secretly delighted. More surprisingly, Annie, who was outwardly even angrier than Abigail, was obviously excited at this development—she protested far too much.

*   *   *

The Villa Mancini was a large, dignified house in the Borgo Vico. It stood facing south, on the shore of Lake Como at its southwestern end, opposite the town of Como itself, which was fifteen minutes away on foot. It had a high-walled garden stretching down to the lake edge, broken only by a small wicket gate that allowed access over a pebble shore to the water. Because of this wall the lake was visible only from the upper floor of the villa and from the tower. In December the level was usually low, but with the spring thaw up in the Alps, the waters rose over the pebbles and nudged into the garden itself. On the northern side of the house was a formal garden and courtyard, also enclosed behind a high wall. Only when the heavy iron gates were opened could the house be seen, and then only from the road.

Abigail had forgotten the tower until César mentioned it, but it was the ideal place for him. He could stay there out of the way, making what mess he wanted, and, yes, it would be useful to have a man about the house. As soon as she herself was settled, she went up to see that all was as suitable as she had remembered it. He was unpacking and arranging his paints and other materials.

"It's good," he said.

"Why did you really come here?" she asked.

"I love women," he said. "Especially Celia, Annie, and Abigail."

"I'm still very angry at you," she warned.

"It'll pass." He grinned again. "Life is too short."

She stumped back down the stairs. Her complaints against him were so bitter that even Annie was moved to say, "Come on, love. He ain't doing that much harm."

Between then and Christmas, Abigail stayed in her room, finishing *Into a Narrow Circle*. The final chapter seemed to take as long to write as had the rest of the book. It concerned the events that led up to the death of Catherine and William, and she fought against this inevitable climax every word of the way. For hours she stared at the blank garden wall, trying to conjure up the shape of the Alps and the face of the ice-floed lake, and plotting ways to save the two lovers; when that became impossible, she would pretend she was a painter, gathering information for a picture—anything rather than complete each sentence. But at last they were both dead, and the respectable world had tut-tutted and clucked them into the grave, and there was nothing left for her to do but to put the manuscript away until she could safely send it to Pepe.

Had César developed some strange telepathy with her—was that how he had divined her pregnancy? The very day after she finished the book he stood below her window and blew a kiss at her.

She had a suite of rooms at the eastern end of the house, on the ground floor; a French window gave out onto a balcony and then down five stone steps to the garden. She pulled on a stout woollen cloak, for despite the crisp sunshine the day was cold, and went out to join him. His smile was so warm, she could not prevent herself from smiling back.

He took her arm and, saying nothing, led her with a measured tread around the lawn. Now she was glad he had come; in a strange way, she was even glad he knew about the baby, too. He pointed to a network of shadows on the ground, where the sun shone through the branches of a Judas tree. "Blunt lace," he said.

She laughed, it was so strange and yet so apt an image. It was all he said in the entire twenty minutes of their stroll, until she was on the point of going back indoors. "All will be well with you," he said.

She was more than glad he had come, and did not need to tell him so in words.

*   *   *

As near as they could reckon, the baby was due toward the end of February. Annie still slept with Abigail, not only because she needed to and because Abigail wanted her there, but also because it was now becoming expedient. The villa was tended by an old housewife and her somewhat simple daughter, who was also pregnant, though not so far advanced as Abigail. The daughter's husband did a few hours of unspecified work in Como each day and spent the rest of his time pottering about or asleep.

From the moment they moved in, Abigail naturally had become "Mrs. Oldale" (mourning and all), Annie was "Mrs. Crabb," and Celia was "Lady A." And it was "Lady A" who dealt exclusively with the servants; they understood that neither of the other two ladies had any knowledge of Italian. If they also chose to infer that "Mrs. Oldale" was French, because she spoke so much French to the monsieur in the tower (and perhaps he was her cousin?), no one bothered to disabuse them.

It was pretty watertight. No one would ever inquire, of course, but if they did—if any ultrasuspicious people came poking around—they would soon be forced to conclude that the old woman and her simpleton daughter were good for nothing in the way of information. Anyone who could imagine that cockney Annie Oldale was French . . . !

It did not occur to any of the three women to ask what would come of the deception if Abigail died in childbirth.

*   *   *

The pains began one wet afternoon in the middle of January. Abigail, who had seen no doctor (who might have detected that she was a month out in her reckoning), had no idea what to expect. Neither Annie nor Celia had borne children, so they had no firsthand knowledge either. But Annie had seen a number of births in her childhood and teens and it was on her "authority" that the others hoped to rely.

Each pain was searing; it seemed to rip a path inside her, from her knees to the pit of her neck. She wondered at her survival when each had passed and she lay bathed in cold sweat.

Celia went at once and told the housewife to send for the doctor. Moments after she had returned to Abigail, then in the throes of another pang, the old woman herself came bustling into the room and elbowed them all aside.

"I told you to get the doctor," Celia said.

"It is done. And what have we here?" She looked at Abigail and shook her head. "Get some hot water," she told Annie. Celia had to translate. "You," she told Celia, "build up that fire. Get the Frenchman to help until my son-in-law returns." Celia ran to obey. Somehow the old woman radiated a competence they dared not question.

"And now, signora," Abigail heard through the receding mists of pain, "I know you don't understand me, but if I know that doctor, we'll probably have to get this baby into the world all by ourselves. And it's twenty years since I was last a midwife." Her smile conveyed none of the sense of her words.

She threw off the sheets and began to push her strong fingers into the mound of Abigail's stomach. She did not like whatever it was she felt.

When Celia returned, Abigail, keeping up the pretence, asked her to find out what the old woman had said. "I said the doctor would be here soon and she was not to worry as I am the midwife in these parts." Her fingers went on exploring the lump of the baby. "It is presented the wrong way," she said. "Tell the signora I must try to turn it. She may drink some wine if she wishes—or something stronger if you have it." Abigail waited for the translation before she refused.

If the earlier pains had been bad, the pain that now racked her, when the woman made the first attempt to turn the baby, was beyond endurance. A fierce claw seemed to seize her guts and tear and crush them. For a moment she passed out; when consciousness returned she heard her own voice, far off, whimpering.

"But the baby must be turned," the woman was saying.

They covered her hastily while César came in with fresh logs and built up the fire. He stared indecisively at Abigail until the glares of the women sent him out.

An hour—and three more futile attempts—later, Abigail was held in constant pain; and the birth itself had not even started. The pangs were mere crests of torment in a sea of suffering; she had not known there was so much pain in all the world.

The son-in-law returned and said the doctor was on his way; twenty minutes later the doctor still had not come. The woman made one more attempt to turn the baby. Abigail's screams filled the house Until that moment she had prayed to live, if only from moment to moment; now she prayed for death to intervene and separate her from this agony.

There was a commotion outside: someone was striding toward the bedroom door. The doctor! But it was César. Yet he was carrying a doctor's bag.

"What game is this?" Celia asked sharply.

He threw off his jacket and pushed the women aside.

" 'Ere!" Annie cried.

He paid no attention but, taking an auscultation tube from his bag, placed it on Abigail's chest, above her heart. At the same time he felt her pulse. His businesslike attitude brooked no further questions. He put the tube to her abdomen. He nodded. "It lives," he said.

He felt it as the old woman had done. He looked at her and nodded grimly. She nodded back.

"It should have been turned weeks ago," he said, almost as if he blamed himself.

He sorted through his bag and pulled out a bottle of ether and a frame. He hesitated before standing the frame over Abigail's face. "But we have no choice," he said.

When the frame was above her face he let several drops of ether spill upon it. Abigail's eyes were closed. From time to time he raised an eyelid and peered into her flickering eye. Once he felt her pulse again.

At last he was satisfied. Her face was relaxed. "Watch her face," he told Annie in English. "Tell me if she frowns or if her mouth moves. Also watch her breathing." He gave her a small mirror.

"Now," he said and took a knife from his bag. "Bring a lamp right here."

"No!" Annie called when she saw the knife.

"If you have a voice," he said, "pray."

Before he made his incision he told Celia to get the largest embroidery needle she could find; then he set her to work threading it with as many silk threads as she could poke through its eye, each about two yards long and doubled. He poured a bottle of phenol into a bowl and told her to soak the needle and thread in it when she was done.

He swilled his own hands and scalpel in the phenol and, for good measure, he held the scalpel over the lamp. As he carried it to her he made the sign of the cross with it. The old woman crossed herself, too. His glistening fingers walked and probed over Abigail's abdomen. They stopped, pushed, splayed, and waited. He glanced at her. At Annie.

Annie nodded. Still breathing.

"Look away," he said.

None did. He heard their gasps as he cut through the skin.

Twenty minutes later he was tying the last silken knot and their gasps were of relief. He alone knew how premature they were.

The baby, a struggling, uncoordinated, eight-pound boy, would certainly live, barring accident. But Abigail . . . ? He did not put her chances high; he should have operated hours earlier.

Chapter 30

For nine weeks she hovered at the frontier of death. Sometimes she would recover consciousness, recognize one or other of them, smile, half say something, and then fall back into a shallow doze. At other times she would beat her head against the pillow repeatedly, and with as much vigour as it would take to ride a horse.

"That's a good sign, surely?" they would say to César.

He would only shrug, not wanting to admit how long it was since he last practised medicine. But during those weeks he could not have done more to make up for lost time. Not once did he go out to paint or sketch. He was never farther from her than his brief walks to the gate by the foreshore took him. For the rest of the time he was either at her side or asleep on a truckle bed behind a screen in the corner of her room. Annie and Celia, who shared the bed next door, took turns to mind the baby or to sit by her.

Their anxiety was compounded by the deception they had practised, and were almost daily making worse in their correspondence with Pepe and with Abigail's family. Time and again, especially when her life seemed at last to ebb, they were on the point of sending telegrams summoning Lord and Lady Wharfedale at once, only for Abigail to rally and so give them hope they would not have to betray her. Celia answered the letters from England, saying that Lady Abigail was immersed in her novel as she had never before been immersed in any other undertaking and begged their indulgence a few days longer.

But a few days cannot be tricked out into nine weeks; and before six of those weeks were up, Caspar was ringing at the main gate and asking for Lady Abigail. He was more than a little surprised to be presented to Celia, but she, having dreaded such an encounter for weeks, was prepared.

"Steamer darling!" she cried. "Thank God you're here. Do come in." And she shut the door quickly behind him.

He did not even stay overnight. A week later he was back, this time with John and Nora. Primed by him, they greeted Celia as their daughter before the door closed on them. By good fortune Abigail was on one of her crests of apparent recovery. She was conscious and in no pain. She had even taken nourishment. She was weak, of course, and a little bewildered. She did not ask for the baby; indeed, she appeared to have forgotten it. But no one could doubt her delight at seeing her parents again.

"Both!" she said. And she sighed such contentment it would have seemed all her life's ambition to see them so.

Soon, however, she was unconscious and rambling again, and they understood how precarious was her hold on life.

César told them the circumstances of her delivery. For John it was the recapitulation of a nightmare. Over thirty-three years ago, when Abigail herself was born, Nora had undergone just such an ordeal; for weeks she too had lingered at the point of death. He remembered it as a fact. Now, looking down at the pallid, wasted figure of his daughter, he remembered it as an experience as well.

Over the days that followed, more memories of that time returned. He had been up at Stevenstown, near Stockton, when news of Nora's near-death came through. Hudson—poor old George Hudson—had laid on a special train to take him down to her, near Hertford. He remembered how he had sought some magic to keep her alive until he arrived, how he had conjured up her image, there in the rattling dark of the railway carriage, and had reached out and grasped her and shouted his love to her above the roar and clank of the speeding train. He had imagined himself to be some night eagle soaring over Maran Hill, where Nora lay; and in that way he pinned her soul to the house and drove off the angel of death.

Remembering that, and looking now at Nora, he longed to take her in his arms again, as he had not done for twenty years or more; he wanted to tell her of that same love, which once had dimmed but now burned bright as ever. But the imminent possibility of Abigail's death somehow stayed him, as if he feared it would be an intrusion into Nora's quite separate anxiety.

When the atmosphere in that sickroom became too claustrophobic to bear, they took to going on long walks around the lakeshore. Sometimes Caspar would come with them; more often he would stay and talk with César. For all their differences in temperament, he and César got on like twins.

Nora knew exactly what was happening to John—knew from the way his conversation kept going back over the circumstances of Abigail's own birth and his relief at her, Nora's, eventual recovery. But she felt unable to help him turn these memories into a springboard for the plunge back into her life, despite her almost desperate longing for him. Once before, the best part of twenty years ago, he had broken down and begged her to let him back and she had agreed, rapturously thinking he intended to give up his mistress, Charity, and their children; but he had been labouring under the opposite delusion—that she would agree to share him with Charity. This time (if there was to be a this time) she would say nothing until he spoke.

Not until the eighth week of Abigail's illness, when César dared to hold out some crumbs of hope, did John begin to make even the first overtures. "I'm near seventy," he said, apropos nothing. And then, as if to belie the words, he hurled a pebble far out into the lake.

Nora watched the ripples spread. "Eay, what's this then?" she asked in broad Yorkshire. "Second childhood?"

He looked at her askance. "What do'st mean?" he answered. He had not spoken to her in their native dialect for years. It held a special richness, not to be squandered on trivial moments.

"When thou were forty," she said, "it were all 'hush of life' with thee. I never thought thou'd make it to sixty."

He hurled another stone, and another. The ripples became enmeshed. "Eay, Nora," he said. "We've seen some times, thee and me."

She said nothing and shortly afterward they returned to the villa. But from that moment on, she knew it was a matter of time only. Somehow this idle little exchange had contrived an obscure breach in the wall that divided them. Inexorably the rest of its fabric would now fall.

Next day it was raining too hard for a walk. They paced up and down the verandah upstairs, listening to the drumming of the raindrops on the tiles and the gurgling of the waste where it gathered. Nora stopped at one point where the gutter had a pinhole leak. In the black of its belly she watched the points of light swell to ripeness and fall . . . fall . . . fall. She caught one in her hand and tried the softness of its water on her cheek.

"You did me a great wrong," John said suddenly.

"Aye," she agreed.

The silence swelled like the ripening drops of rain.

"I regretted it," she said, "the minute it happened. But I don't regret the fruit of it. Sefton will be a credit to you."

Sefton, her youngest son, had been fathered by a rising young painter with whom Nora had had a passing affair when she had first discovered John's infidelity. Nora had made sure John knew he was not the father. That painter was now a senior R.A., and Sefton was off to Cambridge this autumn. So long ago!

"It was a great wrong," John repeated.

"Put a measure on the provocation."

He placed his hand over hers. She pulled away, longing for him to follow—fight her—force her to yield. "I will yield," she wanted to shout.

But he had lost too much of his assurance with her to know what she might be thinking; he could judge her only by her outward behaviour.

"You were off to India for six months," she said, deliberately keeping the heat from her voice. "You came home to me for one night—and slept like a eunuch. Because where had you been?"

"Provocation!" he said, in a tone that implied he knew a thing or two about provocation. Then, hearing her draw breath, he headed her off. "What is Abigail to do now? What are we going to do about this baby?"

Nora gave a grim chuckle. "You think we can have any say? You've known Abigail all these years and you still think that?"

"Maybe Annie knows what's on her mind, since the boy's going to be legally hers. I blame Annie for a lot of this."

"So did I, at first. But now I think that would be unfair."

He leaned over the edge of the verandah and called softly: "Mrs. Crabb, are you down there?"

Annie's head poked out of a window, squinting up against the rain. "My lord?"

"At your leisure, if you might spare us a moment."

Annie nodded and withdrew.

"Abigail was twenty-two or three when this—liaison—began," Nora said. "She would not have stopped just for lack of suitable premises."

"Suitable! An East End pub!"

"Caspar told me he had to compare two separate reports by two different inquiry agents before he could work it out. How much more discreet do you—"

"If Annie hadn't provided the means—"

"Abigail would still have—you don't know her. Either that or you've forgotten the strength of the passions we're talking about."

Their eyes dwelled in each other's. "D'you think I could ever forget that?" he asked.

Annie opened the door of one of the rooms that led onto the verandah. Nora turned toward the lake and cursed softly. John at last dared to give her arm a squeeze, but there was time for no more than that.

"My lord?" Annie stood at the door.

"We were wondering, Mrs. Crabb, what arrangements have been made for the little boy?"

"Or," Nora added, "even talked about."

Annie spoke so low that no eavesdropper, not even one with perfect English, could have overheard. "I'm staying by Abbie. The little boy'll be mine—in law, I mean. But he'll have two mothers—three, I daresay, if Celia stops." She gave a little laugh. "Three women, ruined by men, bringing up a man! I don't think God has much time for women, somehow. Either that or He's fond of a good laugh!"

"At least," Nora said, "the boy will grow up knowing what not to do. Shall you all come back to London?"

"Abbie talked of staying awhile in Rome, my lady. So it's parley-voo Italiano for me, though I doubt I ever will."

Nora laughed, despite herself.

"We'd like to settle something on you and the baby," John began.

Annie drew breath through flaring nostrils. "I got two thousand five hundred of me own," she said, tossing her hair. "And what's mine is Abbie's and what's hers is mine."

"Well," Nora cut in quickly, seeing that they had no hope of a swift and rational settlement, "don't say no. Don't say yes. Think about it. Think of all the accidents and reverses in fortune that can happen in life, how the best of friends can fall out, how money can be lost. And think, too, how nice it would be to know of some small and steady income that would be safe and unfailing."

"You're a pioneer in new country," John told her with a smile. "Pitch your tent near the spring."

It was exactly the right image to reach into Annie; it carried no censure and made her seem the brave one. She smiled back and said she was sorry if she'd started a bit of a slang and she'd think about it.

Nora had forgotten how good John was at managing people.

"If you do want to make Abbie happy—" Annie began. But then she thought better of it and shook her head.

"What, Annie?" Nora asked.

"No, my lady, it's not my place. I was forgetting myself." She left but had not reached the inner door before she turned and came back to them. "I'll say this," she added. "And it's not impertinence but love for her as makes me, so you'll please to take it as it's meant. We've had many and many a jaw, Abbie and me, and at such times as no secrets is kept back. And if she's told me once, she's told me a dozen times as how she hopes to be spared until—well, until things is right at home. There—now I said it." She looked at both to be sure that they took her meaning, and then she was gone.

John turned from Nora to face the lake. She saw how white his knuckles were from their fierce grip upon the iron balustrade. Suddenly she could wait no more for him to take the initiative. She was in hell until he did. "Well, John," she said, "and shall you now forsake your canvas bed?"

Still he did not turn. When he spoke, his voice was strangely altered by the power of his emotion. "I'd easier climb yon mountains than say what must be said."

"What? Just say it."

He slumped. "Eay, Nora! She's fifty years old!"

"And I'm near sixty."

He snorted. "You're twenty compared with her."

Silence returned.

"Is that all you've got to say?" she asked.

"But what good am I? I blighted your life and I ruined hers. How can I ever make that up to either of you?"

"Well, not by prolonging the offence, that's certain."

He turned to her then, clumsily, and took her in his arms—though he leaned so heavily he would have fallen if she had not been there. His kiss, which she had not felt for so long, was exactly as her body remembered it. The Bitch had taught him no new tricks, then.

She felt twenty again, as he had joked. She craved him with all the intensity she had so long fought to suppress. Now unbound, it consumed her, became the be-all of her. Nothing else mattered. There was nothing else to matter.

"Come on," she said, pulling him toward their bedroom.

For a moment he resisted. "But I'm near seventy," he said. "And you're—"

"I'm twenty. You may be what you please but if I'm to bear the weight of you, I'll choose the manner of it."

They were older, of course; their skin was less supple, their muscles slower, they were more careful of their joints—but these were trifling changes. From the moment he pulled the bedclothes back over them and straddled her, seeking the old positions, she knew how much they still belonged to each other. And the knowledge made her as good as twenty—and him as good as thirty-two.

An hour later he cleared his throat and said, "We must get up."

"Just once more," she wheedled.

Twenty minutes later she asked, "Where did all that 'hush of life' go then?"

"I must have left it in St. John's Wood. There's been an epidemic of it there!" After a silence he went on. "We must talk about— arrangements and things."

"What did you mean, John, saying 'she's fifty' like that?"

"Like what?"

"The way you said it. You know the way you said it."

"I meant where's the harm in it now?"

Nora laughed. "Well, now you know!"

"Eay, Nora! We've not done this for—she and I—for . . . I don't know. It can't be as long as ten years, but it feels like it."

"Listen, John." She was serious now. "If you live to be a hundred, I shall be eighty-nine. And if on your hundredth birthday I hear you so much as passed the time of day with her, I'll blind you with these fingernails."

"But the lads are all grown up and gone," John said. "She's alone."

"What fifty-year-old mistress isn't! All right, John. I'll accept that your continued interest is kindness of heart, not lust—"

"It never was lust."

"Oh? What was it then brought you and her to bed?"

"Nay, love—no recriminations. It doesn't matter now. It doesn't matter if it was lust or—or a common fear of spiders. You were in the middle of accepting the fact that I have a kind heart."

"Aye. So I'll say this—because I'll match kindness with kindness. You may see her to settle what affairs you have to settle, and you may then see her but once more: when you give her away on her wedding day."

"Wedding?" He was astonished.

"If we can't find her a nice settled widower who'd rather have the company of a wife than a housekeeper, the world has changed too much. Especially a wife with a pension." She chuckled. "A small pension, of course. You'd not want to attract gold seekers."

"Well . . ." he said uncertainly, but could find no obvious flaw.

She grinned and kissed him. "Of course you never thought of it," she teased. "You're the dog with three beef shinbones and but two jaws!"

She tried to excite him again.

"Eay, no, Nora love. It hurts, it truly does."

"Goo-o-d!" she whispered.

Chapter 31

In the ninth week of her illness Abigail rallied. "Did the baby live?" she asked.

Annie brought him to her. "Oh, it's Pepe's face," she said as she took him. "What's he called?"

Annie looked at her in surprise. "You never said no name."

"And you waited for me? How old is he?"

"Nine weeks."

"I must have been very ill."

"Ill enough to bring Mr. Caspar and the Earl and Countess—surely you remember when they came two weeks back?"

She thought hard. "I seem to. My brain is like—blunt lace. That's a quotation from something." She looked back at the baby. "I don't feel anything about this one. I suppose that's a wicked thing to say. Someone's looking after him well."

"There's a wet nurse comes from Como every day. He sleeps all night now, thank God."

"Oh, Annie, I'm so sorry." Tears surprised her. "So much trouble for everyone. And all for such passing pleasure, too. Why can't we do without it!"

"Speak for yourself!"

The baby began to cry as well. Instinctively she gave it back to Annie. "Call him William. He'll grow up a good and kind lover of women, into an age that understands us better."

"César wants to circumcise him. I think so, too." Annie calmed him again by lifting his petticoat and blowing rasps on his tummy. "It's cleaner," she went on, "when it grows into a big belly-ruffian. Ooh, look at him! Ooh, he's full of sauce! Yes he is! Yes he is! Little William. Shall we cut his little willie? William's little willie? Cut it with César's knife? Only don't let Annie do it! No—Annie'd only cut the bleeding thing right off!"

"César? Oh, yes—César."

" 'Ere—did you know he was a doctor?"

"Yes, I always thought that. Then I thought I must have remembered wrongly. You mean to say he . . ." She looked at William.

"Yeah. He saved your life, gel. If all the men in the world was like him, I could just about stomach them. He's never been farther from you than that gate where he is now."

"You'll find someone yet, Annie. They're not all rotten."

Annie leaned over the bed and kissed her on the forehead. "I don't need to, me old love," she said. "I don't even need to look." She stood and took the baby away. Then she threw open the window and called César, who was talking to Caspar.

They both turned and hurried toward the house. John and Nora, who also heard the joy in Annie's call, came from the drawing room next door. They walked and stood arm in arm.

Abigail saw the difference in them at once. "It's over!" she cried.

"It's over," Nora said. "You don't remember what we were like together, this impossible man and me. But you'll see now!"

"Because of me?"

"It wouldn't have happened without you," John said.

"Steamer!" she called as he came panting in at the French window. "It's over! The Great Schism is over!"

Caspar joined her laughter, overjoyed that she could laugh. "I know! They've even redrawn their wills. We don't exist now— they've left it all to each other. For eternity."

"You'll show some respect, young Caspar," John warned with mock severity. "The days are gone when you could go to your mother for an ally against me, or to me against her."

"Curses!" Caspar said, twirling imaginary moustachios.

"César." Abigail held out her hands, which he took and squeezed. Silent as ever, he stared into her eyes. She pulled him onto the bed. "How can I thank you?" she asked quietly. "I never can, of course. I owe you my life."

He shook his head, not in mock modesty but sincerely. "Thank those who gave you the strong body you have. And the will to fight away death."

He took her pulse, looked at her tongue, made her squeeze his wrists with both hands, peered at the whites of her eyes, and said, "I'll go painting tomorrow. The light is better every day."

*　　*　　*

She walked a few steps that day; quite a lot more the next. The following day she sat up for several hours by the fire, taking it in turns to read with Celia. Only then did César follow his promise and go out painting.

He brought it to her that evening like a hunter with a trophy. It was of the villa—but more than that, it was everything she had felt about the villa. He felt it, too.

"You don't start, as I was taught," she said, "with all the dark parts, painted thinly, and then work up to the highlights using more and more linseed oil?"

He laughed. "When you write, d'you put in all the nouns first and then go back and add the verbs? What's wrong with shadows that I should drown them in turpentine? Shadows are rich, too."

Then he brought her a portrait he had done of her to stop himself going mad of anxiety at her bedside. At once she saw how ill she had been.

"I did it," he said, "because it was all I thought was left of you. But now, when spring comes and you can run again, I'll do better."

"Why me?" She laughed.

"You are Hélène Fourment, you are Mademoiselle Murphy, you are Saskia, you are la Donna Isabel. You are one of those rare women of each age who demands the revelation of painting."

For César it was the equivalent of a four-hour speech; she hoped it was not also a declaration of love.

*　　*　　*

The following day was warm; spring was a week premature. She went for a walk in the garden and then sat under a moth-eaten parasol to read and doze. No one could doubt that all she needed for a complete return to health was time.

"Will you come back to us now?" Nora asked her. "Or at least back to London? If so, we'll wait here. If not, we'll leave soon and expect to see you in the summer."

Caspar said he had to leave tomorrow anyway.

"I think the least question-raising course is the best. We'll all go to Rome, and become ourselves again, thank God! Then I'll send my novel to Pepe and see." she said. Then, thinking it a little unfeeling after all they'd endured, she added, "I'd love to come home, but we must be wise."

"Yes," John said. "Now and in the future."

"Dear me," Abigail said. "I must be getting well if you can warn me of that."

When she went to bed that night, she asked for Annie to come and sleep beside her.

"Old Celia's glad, I'll bet," Annie said as she slipped between the sheets. "She reckons I prattle far too much."

"So you do. And is she no talker?"

"She said enough! 'Ere, she needn't bother with no divorce. She can get an annulment any day."

"Are you serious? How? What has she told you?"

"She don't know it. I never said it to her. But old Crabb, he never touched her."

"Oh, pardon me, Annie, but I saw—"

"He never touched her! She's a virgin still. Look, don't try and tell *me!*"

"Are you sure?"

"Sure as I am of the Henry Crabbs of this world. Cover you with beads. Slobber all over you. But can't raise so much as a smile!"

"But all that ritual—what was it for?"

"Search me! What's any of them *for?* Except theirselves!"

" 'The best fun we ever have.' "

Annie laughed. "Did I say that? Well, you can tell it to Cheeks the Marine—it's like the fisherman's lucky creek. No one knows where it is!"

"Except the fishwife."

"Yeah? Well, tell me *her* name! I know it's not Annie. And it's not Celia. And I don't think it's Abigail, neither."

"Well—I'm too tired to think of all that now."

This time it was Annie who cradled Abigail's head in her arms and stroked her hair and forehead, and kissed her to sleep.

It was marvellous being with Annie again.

Chapter 32

On their third day in Rome, César found the ideal place for them—an atelier on the (modern) top floor of the ancient Teatro di Marcello. It stood between the old Vecchio Ghetto and the Capitoline Hill, just outside the original city wall.

"Romans and Jews—it's The Old Fountain again!" Annie said.

The Teatro had been started by Julius Caesar and completed by Augustus Octavius, who named it after his late nephew, Marcellus; at its opening twenty-five thousand civilized spectators watched the slaughter of six hundred "savage beasts" so called. In the Middle Ages it had served as a castle for a succession of powerful families, during which time it had lost its top layer and its bottom layer had been half buried in rubble. In 1712 it passed into the hands of the Orsini family, who built the Palazzo Orsini on the rubble inside the semicircle of the theatre. They still owned the whole area when César and the three women moved in.

The rest of the Teatro was a ruin. The massive walls still stood but their decorations, which had at one time been the finest Doric and Ionic in Rome, had crumbled beyond recognition. Six of the half-buried ground-floor arches had been cleared and let off as workshops; and where the now-missing top floor had been, there stood what amounted to a semicircular terrace of modern houses, built at various times between the seventeenth century and the present, in all shapes and sizes.

In one of the narrowest of these, facing north and looking directly at the church of Sant'Agnolo Pescivendolo, César had discovered the perfect studio in a former sailmaker's loft. Four other rooms, two on the same floor, two below, went with the loft. They thought the place was cheap because of the permanent smell of fish, for the fishmongers' Oratory, attached to the church, was also used as a fish mart; when the catch was big, the market—in best medieval tradition—spilled over into the church as well. It was not until winter that they discovered the real reason for the cheapness of their atelier.

They stood, that bright spring afternoon, at the large windows of César's studio, looking down at the church and the pathetic remains of the once splendid Portico d'Ottavia.

"The Temples of Juno and Jupiter once stood there," César told them. "And the church is on the site of the temple of Mercury. What vanity! And here, too, is where every victorious Roman general started his triumphal ascent to the Capitol. And what is it now? A fish market and a ghetto! That's the way to treat history, if you want to rejuvenate yourself: start again; become the Eternal City!"

After that he spoke only monosyllables for four days; but the women hardly noticed. They were too busy arranging for the atelier to be cleaned, furnished, and stocked—or, rather, Celia was too busy doing that, for Annie spent half the time with her baby (and none of them now thought of William as anything but hers), and Abigail, still convalescent, had to give her novel a final revision before sending it off to Pepe.

When it was sent, Abigail tried to sketch but could settle to nothing. She thought of visiting a few galleries and doing a piece for one of the London papers on spec; but her spirit recoiled so violently from the notion that she began to wonder if she'd ever be a journalist again. So she and Celia—and Annie, whenever she could persuade César to mind William— took to strolling aimlessly about the streets, visiting whatever palaces and ruins and catacombs they chanced upon. She could do nothing serious until Pepe answered.

"César is right about rejuvenation and this city," Celia said. "It has learned the secret—neither dwell on nor forget your own past. But use it. I think it's marvellous the way they just build on top of the old Teatro. And the way the Jews and poor people built their houses all leaning against and wedged between the pillars of the Portico d'Ottavia. And then plastered them over and recarved them. The Forum and all the old imperial ruins are dead. But our part of Rome is alive."

"And how will you apply this secret?" Abigail asked.

Celia laughed, a little embarrassed at her own effusiveness. "I don't know. Does it matter? I just feel it's possible. And more possible here than anywhere."

"I hope Annie can feel that, too." Annie was at home that day.

"I feel so sorry for her," Celia said. "What a terrible life!"

"Well, you saw the man," Abigail reminded her, "even though he was dead."

"I didn't mean that. I meant on the streets—'on the turf' as she calls it."

"Did she tell you about that?"

"Oh, my dear, she talked about nothing else. Why?"

"Strange. She never talks to me about it at all."

"She can make me hate the very idea of a man." Celia laughed. "Mind you, after Henry that is no great achievement. But then I think of Pepe, and your brother, what little I know of him, and César, and I wonder—are they *two* people, each of them? And can a pure woman bring out the best in them, just as an impure woman can bring out the worst? In other words, was I to blame for the way Henry behaved?"

Abigail began to tremble, her mind was so packed with things to say. Again she yearned to find that *superword* which would cram the whole vision of Blake—or, now, the whole of *Into a Narrow Circle*—inside Celia's mind at one swoop. Why could Celia not even glimpse what was so self-evident?

"You think I was?" Celia interpreted her silence.

"No, no, no!" She answered so vehemently that tourists all around turned amused or outraged faces toward them. They were walking on the bank of the Tiber, just below the Palatine Hill. Abigail changed direction abruptly to cross the square called Bocca della Verità; there were fewer people there, and most of them were clustered either around the fountain or at the "mask of truth" that gives the square its name.

"It's the division into two people that's wrong. Don't you see? They do it to us. Then we accept it. And then we force it on them." She looked at Celia's uncomprehending face and raged at the ineptitude of her words. "Look." She tried again. "We are worshipped—idolized—adored by men. Yes? They raise us far above them in purity, sweetness, and virtues like that. You agree so far?"

Celia's smile was half a sneer. "It's what they *say*. It's what Henry was always saying. But—"

"Forget Henry. I mean he was very—" And then Abigail paused. "No," she said in a different tone. "Don't forget him. He's a caricature of what I'm talking about. I'm not talking about the actual truth, but about the conventional, accepted belief in Society about us. About women. We are vestal virgins, spotless, above reproach, etcetera, etcetera. And we connive at that. We—"

"But isn't it true?" Celia asked, a little shocked at what Abigail seemed to be hinting.

"No, Celia. It isn't. But let me develop this my way. We connive at the division. Why not! It's very flattering. What a wonderful, noble thing it is to be a woman, we are led to think. Until we discover the cost."

"*You* discovered the cost."

"We all did, Celia. That's the point. You, Annie, and me, in our different ways. The cost is to vacate half of our true natures. We inhabit, as it were, the north of ourselves—tend it, embellish it, beautify it. Our cool northern self. But the hot south? Here you are in Rome, in the spring, does it not call to you?"

Celia blushed and gulped, looking around for distractions.

"If you don't feel it," Abigail said, "I'm wasting words. If nobody does, then I've wasted a whole bookful of words."

"*Into a Narrow Circle?*"

"Yes."

"The whole book is about—*that?* What you call 'north' and 'south'?"

Abigail was silent for a while. "Let me tell you what it's about. It's about the fact that 'north' and 'south'—or 'pure' and 'impure'—are mere ideas. There is only *one* country. We are one. There is only one woman inside each of our skins. In their heart of hearts men know that. They say we are Purity, they beg us to elevate them, and yet look how they flock to the night houses and to all the girls like Annie—or like Annie was—all the thousands of them!"

"Oh, they are the hypocrites all right!"

"No, Celia. That is not true. That's Annie talking, but she is deluded. It's not hypocrisy. In a way it's honesty. The hypocrisy is ours for letting them divide us as they do."

At this Celia began to grow heated. "I don't know how you can say that, Abbie. If the truth about baby William ever got out—or even if it were known that you and Pepe passed one night together—you'd be shunned by Society forever. You know it! Men would cease to recognize you. Yet those very same men feel quite free to make the same slip with girls like Annie, any night of the week. Or they go home to degrade their legal wives as Henry degraded me. How can you say there is no hypocrisy!"

"I know, Celia. Seeing what happened to you and Annie made me very bitter against men for a time. If I hadn't had my love for Pepe—well, never mind. I only know that Annie's sort of bitterness and misanthropy is no answer. It won't serve. We have to sweep all our notions away and begin again. We have to make men understand that we are not vestals or—or Annies. They must understand that those two are not incompatible."

Celia laughed with a nervousness that bordered on hysteria. "But they *are!* By definition they are."

"Then we have the definitions wrong. Oh, Celia, my dearest wish for you is that you will meet a man you can love, a good man, a man who understands himself as Pepe does—who knows he is capable of adoration and lust not at different times but at the *same* time. That's the important thing, Celia—the same time. It is a big, big emotion and it stretches all the way from adoration to lust. Love, real love, is both at the same time." She paused for breath as if they had been running, though they were, in fact, walking so slowly that they had not even circled the piazza once as yet.

In Celia's eyes she thought she glimpsed the first sign of hesitation. Something inside was nudging Celia's thoughts toward this impossible notion.

"It is part of life," Abigail said. "Henry made it foul for you. But for your own sake you must rise above that view. You must think of him as a caricature. He is what happens when 'adoration' is carried to a preposterous length. Annie is what happens when 'lust' is carried to the other extreme. We must all draw back from those extremes. We must find the middle ground. Where 'all that lives is holy.' "

"The middle ground, it seems, is where babies happen!"

Abigail stopped and turned to her. Smiling radiantly she grasped both of Celia's gloved hands in her own. "Yes, Celia darling. It is. And in the world I want to see, that would be no sentence of social death. It would be a joy. I would not be giving my baby away. I would not have had to flee from Pepe."

"But then—you want an end of marriage itself!"

Abigail let go and walked on. "I certainly want an end to the sort of marriage that can serve up Roger Oldales and Henry Crabbs—and bind decent, good women to them for life. If you call it life. Look!" She turned toward the church. "The mask of truth. I'll show you."

In the portico of the church, Santa Maria in Cosmedin, was a large human mask carved in marble. At some time its mouth had probably formed a decorative opening to a small Roman sewer, but after it was rescued and set up at the church the legend had grown that this was the mask of the Great God Pan.

"Lovers come here and put their arms in his mouth," Abigail said. "Then they declare their love. Anyone who lies—the god bites off his hand. Or," she said as she thrust her own arm in, "her hand. Now listen."

To the blank eyes of Pan she said, " 'All that lives is holy. Life delights in life.' "

For a moment the flesh of her arm tingled; she had managed to half-convince herself of the legend. Celia saw the change in her face and went wide-eyed. Smiling, Abigail withdrew her arm and tested its integrity. Celia, relieved, took her other arm and together they began to stroll back toward the Tiber.

"Now you may start believing me," Abigail said.

Neither spoke until they reached the river, when Abigail said, "I wonder if Annie will be able to settle in Rome? She'll obviously never learn more than a few words of Italian. It won't be much fun for her if I decide to settle a while."

"Annie will stay where you stay."

"D'you think so?"

"I know so. Poor Annie!"

Abigail laughed. "Dear me, Celia—is it so bad a fate?"

"No!" Celia squeezed her arm. "I was thinking how she hates men so much and yet how she loves William. She absolutely adores him. And she's so angry with herself for feeling like that."

"I think Annie's changing underneath and doesn't know it. Not one of us has commented on how odd it is that the four of us are still together—that the three of us women have moved into César's atelier as if anything else would have been—I mean, as if it hadn't even occurred to us not to move in. I thought Annie at least would cry havoc."

Celia walked beside her in silence.

"Don't you think?" Abigail prompted.

"You did not live through what *we* lived through at the Villa Mancini," Celia answered.

Chapter 33

Pepe was in Rome within the month. Abigail came back one afternoon to find a pageboy from his hotel standing before the Teatro with a note for her: "Found the theatre all right but the labyrinth on the top floor defeated me. Perhaps it would be best for you to come here! Hotel Minerva."

She was disappointed. She wanted to ask the pageboy, "But didn't he say anything about my book?"

He could at least have written something. One word would have sufficed: *Marvellous!*

She told Annie where she was going—just over half a kilometre away—and set off to meet Pepe.

He was sitting in the hotel lounge, which was, in midafternoon, almost empty—but not empty enough to permit them more than a chaste embrace. He sent for some tea.

"You are thin," he said. "Are you not eating?"

"It was hard to eat when all I wanted was to hear from my editor."

He smiled and raised his eyebrows—an ambiguous gesture. Then he laughed: "All?"

"I also longed for my lover. Oh, Pepe—let's go back to my room now!"

He tapped his briefcase. "Don't you want to talk about this?" His smile was warmly mocking.

"No," she said. "I'm afraid suddenly." She looked around uncomfortably. "Why did you choose to stay at the Minerva? Only priests stay here."

"I didn't know that when I booked. But now I think it'll suit me very well. Priests don't run up and down corridors. They don't sing grand opera or stay up late. And say what you like—they're enthusiasts for comfort and good food." He looked steadily at her for a moment. "No, but you're right to be afraid. You know, of course, that it's out of the question to publish this book?"

For a second she lost the thread and could only stare at him.

"Oh, dear," he said. "I had hoped you weren't serious."

"What d'you mean 'not serious'! Have you read it?"

"I mean I hoped it was like a long—extended private letter to me. I was touched and deeply moved by it. But I hoped you realized it could never be published."

"But it must be published. People must see—"

"People must?" he interrupted. "What's all this? People must? Are you turning into one of these polemical novelists?"

"Damn your labels. I am what you made me. What's in that story is everything I've learned through— Pepe! You're not serious, are you? You will publish it?"

Obviously hating himself, he shook his head. "I'd be sent to prison. And you'd be reviled, high and low. They'd pick up horse dung in the streets and pelt you as you passed. That's no exaggeration, either."

"Have you not enough courage to face that?"

"Easily said. Just look at the trouble Zola is having with his new book, *Nana*. And he's got the Socialists behind him. Have you read it?"

She shook her head.

"Well, it's modesty itself compared to some of your scenes."

"But they're true. They're honest."

He frowned. His patience was getting short. "Oh, come now, Abbie. What has happened to your instinct—that marvellous journalist's instinct—for what the public will accept? Of course your William and Catherine are true—and honest, and real, and moving. But you cannot bludgeon people with truth and honesty! You must surprise them—ambush them—then let them escape back into their own comfortable ways—then ambush them again . . . and so on. Until, imperceptibly, they find they've arrived at quite a different destination from the one they set out for. Good heavens! You used to know that so well I never had to tell it you."

She wanted to weep. He was right, of course. She had not lost the instinct, only the will to apply it. She was weary of the tricks, weary of journalism. How could anyone who saw, as clearly as she could see, that the whole of Society was *wrong* and would have to stand all its ideas on their heads—how could she feed that massive insight to them in little ambushes? Suppose that all those cool-headed, sensible people you get in every society, the Pepes of this world, had told Jesus to give out the Sermon on the Mount at the rate of one sentence a century! He'd be at it still.

She looked across at Pepe and the gulf between them might as well have been infinite. "Come back to my room now," she begged.

He clenched his fists, as if to prevent his hands from agreeing. "We must settle this first. Tell me at least that you see my point of view, even if you—"

"This longing for you will burst me."

"Oh, Abbie—have pity!"

She stood and walked out, past the waiter who was bringing in their tea. Pepe sprang after her but did not catch up until she was out in the square. "What's happened to you?" he asked breathlessly. "D'you think if I'd found your rooms and we'd gone to bed at once—you think I'd have said anything different?"

"You're like a fly that's found a wound," she told him. "Talk of something else. Look, there's the Gésu church. Talk about that."

He stared in bewilderment, at the church, at her. But she was already walking on. "I'll talk about it then," she said. And without looking at it she began to point out how the facade, which was at first sight stolid and imposing, was a hotchpotch of uncomfortable detail and restless elements. "They lost all their confidence while designing that church," she said.

"It's a moment when history turned over. Reason, proportion, harmony, humanism—all the triumphs that had secured the Renaissance—were beginning to fail them. The old, dark forces were creeping back. In a church for the Jesuits, naturally! Look at that facade and you can *hear* Savonarola thundering. Oh, Pepe!"

She drew him into a deep doorway, barred with iron. "Kiss me! Kiss me, my darling! Stop me talking like this. It isn't me."

After the longest kiss they had ever enjoyed, he broke and murmured, "It was you. You used to write like that."

Arm in arm and silently then they drifted back to the Teatro. In a half-dream she led him to their atelier. He admired César's painting; César nodded at him and carried on at his easel. He admired little William and told Annie that things had turned out well. Annie linked arms with Abigail and said, "Don't I know it!"

Then Abigail held out her hands to Pepe and led him to the door to her room. Glancing back she saw Annie staring at them in bewilderment, not to say horror. When she opened the door, Annie shook her head violently but Abigail misinterpreted the gesture until it was too late.

She slipped out of her clothes and stood, a silvered silhouette, facing him. He ran to her. She began to undress him but he stopped her with a kiss. He kissed her neck. Her shoulders. His lips and breath ran down to her breasts, shattering her self-possession. She clutched his head to her. Down he went, grazing the skin of her stomach with his lips.

He stopped.

The scar!

How could she have forgotten the scar!

He stood and began to turn her into the light.

"No!" She crumpled and sat on the bed.

Winded, he sat beside her, all excitement drained. "So that was it," he said tonelessly. "My God!"

She could tell him nothing.

"Of all the humiliations you heaped on me, I never dreamed—"

Her cry was almost a scream. "No, Pepe—not humiliations!"

"What a simpleton I am. What a fool you must think me."

"Oh, Pepe, why? Why? It isn't like that. I did it for love of you. To keep—"

He laughed, though the tears ran down his cheeks. "Love? What love is it that gives away its fruit—its *jewel*—and to a whore like that!"

He stood up and strode from the room, too swiftly for her to stop him.

She called his name but, being naked, could not follow. Enraged at herself she fell upon the bed and howled into the pillow.

A door slammed. Then Annie was at her side, soothing her, urging her between the sheets, stroking her hair, saying nothing.

An hour later she stirred. She thought of rising but there was nothing to rise for. Nothing! She tried to contemplate the infinity of that nothing.

"My life is finished, Annie," she said.

"Yeah. I know."

"Truly. I've often wondered why I didn't feel more at giving William to you. More sense of loss. I thought it was because I was ill so long and he'd grown to be yours meanwhile. But that wasn't really it. I know what it was."

"Mmm?"

"I had another baby. My book. I was so sure Pepe would publish it."

"And he won't?"

"No. Nor anyone else. It tells the truth about love and he says—"

"Better burn it," Annie said. " 'Cos you don't know love from a horse's hoof."

When this produced no response she added, "Stop in bed now, I should. I'll bring your supper when the waiter comes."

They usually ate out but sometimes they had the nearest trattoria send their dinner up in a pail.

"I shan't want to eat."

"We'll see."

Annie was right. By half past nine, when the dinner came, Abigail was ravenous. It was saltimbocca alla Romana; she could have eaten it twice over. She and Annie finished a whole bottle of Chianti with it. Annie took away the debris and came back with William, fast asleep.

"He's taken to that goat's milk a treat," she said. "So there's a weight off our minds. That and his circumcision. Perhaps we'll get some peace now." She bent and kissed him. "Sleep, you little rascal," she murmured. "Hear me? Ooh, don't they smell good when they're all washed and clean! I reckon angels smell like that."

She heaved off her clothes and sniffed at her own armpits. "I'll do." She laughed. "Gawd, I reckon I wash meself four times a day here." She put on her nightdress and slipped in beside Abigail.

"Well, gel," she said cheerfully as she snuffed the candle, "what's it like out there at the end of the world?"

Abigail almost hurled herself upon Annie. "Oh, Annie—thank God you're here! Without you I'd be lost."

Annie held her in her strong arms. "I'll always be here, love," she said. "I'm not a man. I'll always be by you."

She soothed away her tears and caressed her to sleep. Abigail was actually dropping off when she was brought back to full consciousness by an entirely new sensation. Annie was kissing her on the lips! And Annie's hand, which had been soothing her hair and shoulders—like the soothing hand of a mother—now fell to her breast and began to caress her with the soft urgency of a lover.

She lay petrified with the shock. And the shock was not just at what Annie was doing but at her own response to it. Something in her—all those parts that had so recently yearned for Pepe and had been thwarted—now began responding to Annie's . . . to Annie's what? What was Annie doing?

"Annie," she whispered. "No!"

Annie was trembling. "I love you," she whispered back. "Oh, Abbie, I thought I'd never be able to tell you. Never show it."

"I love you too, Annie," Abigail said. "But not like that." She slipped her hand between Annie's and her breast but did not turn her lips away. The gesture stilled whatever it was that had begun to respond as a lover.

"Don't draw back now, gel. You come so close to it." She kissed her again and again.

Abigail neither withdrew nor responded. "I haven't, Annie. Honestly. Please be like you were before. I can't give you . . . whatever it is you want."

And what *did* Annie want? How could they *do* anything?

Annie began to cry. Abigail wanted to comfort her but now was shy of it.

"That night you come and got me—" Annie sobbed. "That night down the Haymarket—life began again for me. I was as low then as what you was this evening. You give meaning to my life, Abbie. You're all I ever want."

"What? What do you want?"

"To be with you."

"But you can be—you know that. Always."

"I mean—completely. Live together. Sleep together. Love each other."

"But *how?* I'm sorry—I don't mean to sound shrill."

"I don't know! I've never loved another woman before. But I love you. You're the only one I ever loved—man or woman. And if you could love me, we'd find ways."

Abigail was silent. She wanted to say that it was unnatural but could not hear, in her mind's ear, a kindly intonation for the word.

"I s'pose I disgust you."

"No, Annie—of course you don't."

"I do."

Abigail sat up abruptly and pushed Annie onto her back. At first Annie resisted and struggled to get up, but then Abigail kissed her, full on the mouth, as if she were Pepe and Annie her. Annie yielded with a sigh.

"I can do that, Annie," she said, suddenly quite calm. "I can even do this." And she kissed her again and slipped her tongue into Annie's mouth. "Or this." She began to caress Annie's breasts, still unsexing herself with the half-belief that she was a man.

Annie moaned in pleasure.

"I could probably—as you say—'find ways.' I know where my own pleasure arises. Yours is probably the same." She snaked her hands down over Annie's body. "There? And there?"

Annie gasped and drew up her legs, spreading them wide.

"The point is," Abigail said, withdrawing herself a few inches and taking Annie's hand, "I would feel nothing—certainly not that sort of passion."

"Oh, Abbie," she whimpered. "Why can't you?"

"Why can't you feel it for a man? Could you even do this with Celia? You don't want me to pretend it for you, do you?"

"Yes! Only try and you'll see."

"But Annie, you of all people can't want me to pretend it. You know what that sort of fraud is. And you know what opinion the pretender soon forms for the one who accepts it as the real thing."

"I don't."

"You do."

"I don't. I only know I love you. I love you so much, I'd take anything."

"I love you too, Annie. But only as a sister. More than a sister—a twin. In almost everything I'm closer to you than to Pepe—but not in that one thing. I could share everything with you, be closer to you than I could with any man, but not in that one thing. If I could live with you twenty-three hours a day, and Pepe one, that would be heaven. I'm much happier with you than I am with Pepe, much more at ease, but I need that one thing from him. And only from him."

She was lying, of course. The truth was far more complex—beyond the simplicities of "happier" and "more at ease." But Annie did not need the truth from her, any more—she realized—than she needed it from Pepe.

*　　*　　*

Next morning when she awoke, Annie had gone. So had her clothes. But William was there. Abigail rose and dressed and heated up his goat's milk. She had to wake him to feed him. He was growing almost as taciturn as César.

She tried to feel some kinship with him, but he had become Annie's, in fact as in law. He was so registered at the embassy and on her passport.

Annie came back shortly before ten; she avoided Abigail's eyes.

"I'm going, love," she said. "Back to England. Back to the Smoke."

"No, Annie!"

"I'll never settle here. And you won't go back there."

"But—"

"I just seen Mr. Laon. He's off on the night train and he agreed to squire me—and William. He sired the little bleeder, now he can squire him."

"Annie? Please stay."

Annie showed her rail ticket. "I pinched the money off of you," she said.

"This is because of—last night!"

" 'Course it is."

"But don't pay heed to that, Annie. I was cruel. I didn't know what I was saying. It was losing Pepe made me like that. Don't leave me!"

"I must, love. Cruel or not, you was right. Don't make it hard now, eh?"

"I'll do anything, Annie. Anything you want, only don't leave me alone!"

Annie smiled. "I don't think you'll be alone too long, gel."

"I'll pretend so well you'll never know."

"Oh dear!" Annie's lips began to tremble.

Abigail seized her arms. "Come on. Come back to bed now. I'll show you!"

With a superhuman effort Annie wrenched her arms free and drew a deep breath, both to steady herself and to bellow "Celia!" at the top of her voice. Celia came running from the studio, watercolour brush between her fingers. "Give us a hand, there's a love," Annie said. "I'm going back to England today."

She even managed a laugh.

Chapter 34

"What will you do?" César asked. "Will you write another novel?"

She shook her head. For days she had not left the atelier. She had drifted from room to room, staring out of the windows, following cracks in the plaster, wanting not to be alive. She had found a shawl left by Annie and had almost worn it out passing it through her fingers, raising it to her face to sniff the last trace of her.

She missed Annie far more than she missed Pepe. He had half gone from her life a year ago. She still loved him, but the companionship, the kinship of obsessions, had gone. *Now*, she thought, in vindication of her life, *suppose we had been yoked in marriage!*

Annie was the real loss. She thought of her all the time. Wherever she turned, a part of her prepared to welcome Annie. Her dark eyes and angular features were everywhere. She remembered her voice, her tread on the floor, the rustle of her clothes, her laugh, her angry, tender love for little William. At night she would wake and reach for Annie's body before memory returned. She remembered Annie's lips on hers and Annie's hand on her breast. Had she been wrong and Annie right? If she had yielded, would she have *seen?* Had her love for Pepe been a mere apprenticeship for the love she might have found with her?

At first, in the depth of her double loss, she believed that to be so. But as time staunched the immediate flow of her grief, she came to doubt it. Some part of her wanted it to be true; but the rest of her was too honest, and too self-aware, to connive at the wish.

By the time César judged it right to ask her what she would do, to face her again toward the future, she knew that if ever she loved again, it would be with a man; yet because of what Annie had offered—and she so nearly accepted—she would understand that love far more deeply than before.

"If not a novel, then what?" César persisted.

She smiled then. "I might even paint."

He nodded judiciously. "It could be good." His rich, dark voice was comforting.

But even as the thought occurred to her, she shied away from it. *Oh, dear,* she wondered. *Am I going to look for comforting things to lean on all my life?*

So when he stood up suddenly and said, "Let's go out to the Cavour. Music and sparkle and officers in uniform! My eyes are starved of spectacle!" she was just in the mood to accept with something like the beginnings of enthusiasm. With gratitude, anyway.

When the spirit took him like that, he was marvellous company. He danced with both Abigail and Celia equally, paid them lavish but equal compliments, made sure they both became equally tipsy, and gave them equal support all the way home. It was the first night in many that Abigail had not cried herself to sleep.

In the small hours, sometime between three and four, she came wide awake with the conviction that she was being a fool. She had lost Pepe. She had lost Annie. She had lost her baby. And she had lost her book. The four most valued things in her life. But how was it going to help for her to hide herself away in Rome? What would a new career as a painter—a very minor painter, she felt sure—achieve? How, when the grief had passed, as all griefs pass, would she come to view herself for her wet acceptance of all these losses?

True enough, there was little she could do about the loss of Annie; if she had any ally there, it was time, and time alone. There was nothing (short of resigning the world and all the acquaintance and connections that sustained her in it) to be done about little William, beyond what she had already done. But Pepe? Was she going to accept that loss as absolute? And his refusal to publish—had that become her own refusal, too? Was she not still a *Stevenson?*

What would her parents do in the face of such reverses? Or Steamer—Boy—Winnie—any of them? Shrug it off and settle for a new life at something they knew was second rate? Very likely!

She rose and began to pack. She and Celia were a week behind Pepe and Annie in their return to London. César smiled when he saw the boxes they left in Rome, "to be sent on when we have found a place."

"I'll still be here when you come back," he said. "And your rooms will be ready for you."

From the wistful way Celia hung around until the last moment, and the way her eyes drank greedily at each last sight of Rome, Abigail could see how miserable she was at leaving; but naturally it was impossible for her to remain alone with César, quite apart from the obligations her gratitude owed to Abigail.

*　　　*　　　*

They put up at a small hotel in Holborn, conveniently close to the publishers with whom she hoped to deal. But she was tactician enough to know that no reputable house would take the book without the strongest assurance of her mother's support. Even then, to judge from Pepe's response, they might still balk at the idea; but without the Countess' support the book had no chance at all. Abigail decided on a flanking move, via Winifred and Steamer; if her mother was in two minds, she'd be bound to consult one, if not both, of them.

At least she started with one great potential objection removed: her parents were reconciled, so her mother could not play *that* card a second time. First, however, there was the manuscript to be recovered from Pepe.

For a writer she showed a remarkable distrust of letters; but she remembered how she had ignored that letter from Pepe during their previous separation, and she could not believe he would behave differently if she wrote to him now. Instead she walked in upon him in his office.

He was looking through some proof prints with one of the engravers. The man stared at her in surprise; Pepe's stare was something more fierce. He nodded at the engraver, who left without a word.

"I came for the manuscript," she said.

He opened a drawer, took out a packet, and handed it to her. "Or shall I have it sent?" he asked.

She let it lie on the desk between them. "I suppose you haven't reconsidered—and won't?" she asked.

He made an exasperated face.

"Then it simply means you don't understand it," she said. "It's not just a tale—an idle invention to divert fat ladies between one chocolate and the next. It's a truth. It demands to be told. If you understood it, you'd see that. If you understood it, you'd be moving heaven and hell to see it published."

He savoured these words as if they were a professional offering, not personally touching him. "I see," he said. "To understand all is to forgive all, eh?"

"If you're quoting Madame de Staël, her actual words were, 'The more we know, the better we forgive; whoe'er feels deeply, feels for all who live.' Hah—it might almost be Blake himself!"

"And I suppose I know nothing and feel nothing! I tell you, I feel about as betrayed as it is possible to feel."

"And you won't even let me—"

"Lady Abigail," he began. Then, hearing how petulant the snub made him seem, he softened it: "Abbie—Abbie! You gave away my son. I didn't mean you to have a child. I didn't—" He sought a violent word. "—*inject* the baby there, use myself as a weapon to subdue you. But the child formed itself nonetheless. We made it. Together. It was ours. But you alone concealed it. You alone disowned it. You alone gave it away for a common, ignorant whore to raise. If 'all that lives is holy,' what name can you give such blasphemy? And what can you expect between us now, except—at the very best—a sort of baffled aversion? One day, if my prayers are answered, I'll stop hating you. But that day is not this day."

He spoke mournfully, without passion. And mournfully, and without passion, she nodded, picked up her manuscript, and left without a backward glance. Then and later she wondered that his rejection, so absolute, did not reduce her to tears. Or was her spirit now so low that even tears would have been an elevation? Perhaps his very absoluteness was a kind of cautery, sealing the wound beneath an instantaneous scar.

*　　　*　　　*

She left *Into a Narrow Circle* with Winifred, expecting to be invited back to Highgate a week or two later. But the following day Winifred called at the hotel, with the manuscript in a sealed envelope inside her bag. She gave a laugh that was almost apologetic. "I thought I'd better get it off the premises as fast as possible!"

Abigail's heart fell. "As bad as that?" she asked.

Winifred did not at once answer. Abigail saw that her sister was trembling. She sent for some tea to be brought up; at all costs Winnie must be put at her ease.

"What d'you think of *Jane Eyre?*" Winifred asked the moment she was seated. It was a prepared gambit, an academic's nonquestion with, no doubt, a dozen prepared nonquestions to follow, depending on her initial reply. She saw the point at once, of course. Jane Eyre, when faced with the prospect of becoming the mistress (and what is more, in the circumstances, the almost blameless mistress) of the man she so passionately loved—the man she had only hours earlier been on the point of marrying—Jane Eyre nonetheless chose to run away to friendless poverty and starvation because that was the only virtuous course open to her. But Catherine of *Into a Narrow Circle* did not for a moment hesitate to make the very opposite choice when faced with an almost identical decision. Even at the time of writing it, the contrast had struck Abigail.

"Charlotte Brontë was trapped in a house of sermons. She wasn't free to write as she pleased."

Winifred let this shallowness answer itself. She merely smiled and shook her head, a relaxation that delighted Abigail.

"*Jane Eyre* the book or Jane Eyre the woman?" Abigail then asked. "Either."

"The book is a marvellous piece of storytelling, of course. But it's flawed by the choice that Jane makes—to run away from love. In order to settle matters and bring the lovers together again, Miss Brontë then has to arrange a startling sequence of coincidences—of a kind that our own Great Author so consistently fails to arrange in real life by way of reward to those who, like Jane, set cold righteousness above all else."

The reply astounded Winifred. "You mean you've stopped believing in God?"

"Of course not, Winnie. Of course I still believe in God—but not as a good way out of a literary error. The happiness Jane is given at the end is a cheat. All the time we see that someone has been standing outside her story; and at the end that someone says to Jane, 'You were a good girl not to take the cake when it lay open and inviting on the table, so now I'm going to give it you.' I'm not interested in writing books which cheat like that. The happiness my Catherine wins, even in facing her own death, is some-thing she's earned; it grows out of everything she's done—and you can't say she had an easy time of it. No primrose path for her! I don't cheat."

At least Winifred was no longer trembling. But Abigail could see that, of all possible answers to that opening question, she had not expected this. At once, in a clap of insight, she understood why it had been wrong to involve Winnie in this whole business. *Jane Eyre* was a red herring. Jane was no counterpart to Catherine. The true counterpart was Winifred herself.

Winifred's refusal to marry had little to do with her often stated reasons. She did not fear a husband's ownership of her school; she feared the passion of love itself—the husband's ownership of her. In a curious way, though they had travelled such utterly different routes, she and her sister were now but a hairsbreadth apart. Yet, as Abigail discovered, it is quite possible to be so close and yet to face in opposite directions.

"Then I'm sorry to have to say this, Abbie dear"—Winifred steeled herself to continue—"but I wish you had 'cheated,' as you call it. I think *Into a Narrow Circle* is a pernicious book. Precisely because it is so moving and tender and—yes, if you force me to it—so true."

"You . . ." Abigail laughed in bewilderment. "I'm speechless."

Winifred tapped the manuscript. "A pity. This conversation comes a year too late."

Abigail froze. Did Winifred know? She *couldn't*—only those at the Villa Mancini knew. Then Winifred touched the manuscript, and Abigail understood that she had meant the book, not the baby.

Abigail challenged her: "How can truth be pernicious?"

". . . asked the serpent! Truth, you say? You mean merely that life is as you describe it? Love is as you describe it? That sort of truth? The accidental truth of a photographic snapshot! Surely literature—*all* art—must aspire to a higher truth than that? As *Jane Eyre* does. Charlotte Brontë directs us toward a higher moral choice and away from sensuality. You not only do the opposite, you also try to claim some sort of moral justification for it. Fortunately no one will ever publish the book. I strongly advise you never to show it to anyone else, not even to Pepe. And for yourself—well, I believe you have some thinking to do."

Her understanding of Winnie, and of all the deep reasons for this inability to face the honesty of Catherine's choice, prevented Abigail from feeling utterly downcast at this rejection. She even managed a smile. "Come," she said, "if we are to set each other tasks, then I have one for you."

"Oh?" Winifred, who had feared a blistering row—tantrums—tears— was delighted that Abigail should take her harshness so bravely.

"Yes. Right at the end of *Jane Eyre*, where Jane takes in the tray and candles to poor blind Mr. Rochester, what does she call him?"

"I don't remember!" Winifred laughed.

"Guess! 'My love'? . . . 'my angel'? . . . 'darling'? . . . 'precious'? After all, they had sworn undying devotion. They had stood side by side before the altar. And they are clearly going to marry, now that Rochester is free at last. So what does she call him? She calls him 'my dear master.' *Master!*"

"Well?" Winifred shrugged, not seeing a point. "It's not surprising."

"Of course it's not. Not when you consider what sort of woman Jane was—a woman who lived in perpetual submission to one authority after another. *Your* problem, Winnie, is that you want to educate your girls into freedom from precisely that sort of submission. You want them to have Catherine's intellect, Catherine's insight, Catherine's independence of spirit. Yet, at the heel of the hunt, you want them to make Jane's moral choices. I believe those are two metals you'll never alloy."

Winifred pretended to accept this dilemma as her "task." But Abigail could see that her sister's monumental self-assurance—the crust of a dozen years' headmistressing—was not even dented. Perhaps, in the end, that was the only quality essential to a headmistress: a self-assurance no one and nothing could dent.

They talked then of family matters and Abigail's recent illness, and then it was time for Winifred to go back and conduct evening prayers.

Abigail had learned from her sister that Caspar was at the firm's London offices all this week. Five minutes later, a messenger was carrying Abigail's manuscript to him, with an accompanying letter to say that she and Celia would be at Falconwood on Saturday unless she meanwhile heard that the visit would not be convenient.

*   *   *

Falconwood was maturing well. Wistaria and Russian vine were thickening on the walls; the copper spire had collected its verdant patina; the vast tree plantations no longer looked like scars over the hilltops but were resplendent in their new spring mantles of green. The lakes, grassed to their edges and girt about with walks and rides, might have been there since the last glacial retreat. Peacocks strutted beneath the cedars; roe deer cropped nonchalantly at the lawns. The fountains played for two hours each afternoon. The gravelled court was raked into patterns of oriental complexity after every passing carriage. Eighty indoor servants, twenty-four gardeners, four dozen gamekeepers and estate workers, twenty stable hands and coachmen, a bailiff, two managers, a chaplain, a tutor, a governess, and a chef all went unobtrusively about their business of tending Caspar, Caroline, their five children, and their guests.

Caspar was not in a literary mood that weekend. He had newly installed an electrical generator, driven by the steam engine that also powered the hydraulic lift, and he had brought down an electrical platewarmer as the first demonstration of the new magic. This had made it necessary to raise some floorboards in the servery and butler's pantry to get at the copper bars he had buried there more than twelve years earlier.

The trouble was that neither he nor the engineer had remembered to bring down cable to join the platewarmer to these copper conductors.

"We'll use garden wire," Caspar said.

When it was brought the engineer looked dubious. "Iron," he said, shaking his head. "And very thin. It'll get hotter than the wire in the platewarmer."

Caspar overruled his objections. Everyone was summoned to watch the new marvel perform. A chain of servants carried the message "Now!" to the engine house. The engineer slipped the belt that drove the generator.

After a long, tedious wait, there could be no doubt that the miracle of electricity was making the plate somewhat hotter than any hand might bear. For several minutes Caspar basked in the triumph.

Then his youngest daughter, Charlotte, perhaps because she was only three, and thus was nearer the ground than the others, pointed at the floor beneath the plate. "Pity!" she giggled in delight. "Pity! Pity!"

And though she meant *pretty* she was actually nearer the mark with the word she uttered; for the wire beneath the plate was glowing and the floor beginning to smoulder. Caspar tried to operate the switch but the heat had fused it. The engineer began the long run back to the engine house. Dismayed, the rest of them watched the flames begin to kindle among the joists.

"Here, this won't do," Caspar said and, standing, he gave a heavy kick to the platewarmer. The white-hot wires drew out to thin threads and sputtered into an incandescent divorce, showering sparks.

Imperturbable Lucas, the butler, passed Caspar a soda syphon. Caspar played its jet at the burning joists and cooling sherds of iron until everything was black and sodden.

"Pity! Pity!" Charlotte giggled.

The galvanometer needle fell back to zero; the engineer had succeeded in throwing the drive belt. Everyone breathed again and looked at Caspar to see how he would take this failure. He surveyed the charred and still-steaming floor and the welded, shattered scraps of wire. "Pioneers," he said, "must expect the occasional setback."

"No!" Linny shouted. It was a long dining hall and her voice carried back to them as she strode away, the full length of it. "I shall never complain of gas again. We may even go back to oil lamps. But electricity? Never! Never while I live here!"

Caspar was then, after lunch, rather glad to escape into the higher realms of literature.

"Linny will come round to it," he said confidently as they descended past the fountain and went down into the park. "We've heard that Armstrong is determined to light Cragside with incandescent electrical lamps next year. And we're equally determined to beat him to it."

For a while she talked about his new paintings. He had bought quite a lot since she had left for France the previous summer: a Poussin, a Tintoretto, two Gainsboroughs, three Rubenses, a Rembrandt, a Titian, and he had on approval a Stubbs and a Watteau. Over the previous decade she had helped form his taste; in this recent spate of purchases he was casting himself as ex-pupil, sealing his independence.

"Still," he said when enough compliments had flown, "you came here to talk about your art, not mine." He looked briefly at her. "Plain talking, eh, Abbie?"

"By all means," she said; but her heart sank.

"Well, it's not what you'd call a funny book, is it?"

"*Funny!*"

"Yes. Funny. Life's full of comedy. Even the sort of intimacies you talk about—they've got their funny moments, too. But not your book. There's not a single laugh in it. Not one you intend, anyway."

She caught the qualification at once. "What does that mean?"

"Well—your utter solemnity is very funny at times, though I'm sure you don't mean it to be. Frankly, Abbie"—he grinned his kindly intentions at her—"your Catherine and William, between them, are a bit of a hardwood bench."

"Oh!" She had been prepared for every criticism but that. "You mean," she said, brightening, "if I popped in the odd rib-tickler, the book would be—"

He was already shaking his head. "I merely thought, why loose off the big gun when the peashooter will do as well!"

"What's the big gun?"

"Their view of love—presumably your view, too?"

She nodded.

"Suitable only for untenanted tropic islands. You could do that, you know. Shipwreck your Catherine and William on some island. Then you'd get away with it all. It'd still be a shocker, of course; but you'd just about get away with it. Or set it in some mythological Arcadia—perhaps even in a future Utopia."

"Oh, but that would be cheating, Steamer."

"Really? You mean the love you're writing about is not a universal love but just a very local one, found only in England in the 1870s? Pity, as young Charlotte says."

Abigail laughed. "Oh! You are . . . insidious."

"I mean it. A lot of us could get to be quite fond of your William and Catherine—just as long as neither of them tries to move in next door. Or next year."

"But why? If it's true, then—"

"Of course it's true! Who's denying its truth?"

"Well then!"

"Well what? We don't want all truths to get around, do we? It's true that it's very easy for a titled person to get a forgery entered on a passport at a foreign legation, eh?" He looked knowingly at her. "But we don't want that truth to circulate too widely, do we? And it's true that women can take as intense a pleasure as men can in—hmm—copulation, as dear Kate and Bill insist on calling it with that implacable solemnity of theirs. Or yours. But we don't want that truth getting about too widely, do we?"

"Don't we?"

"Of course we don't," he said. "Not among our unmarried women-folk anyway." She drew breath to object but he went on. "Because—and I'd hardly have thought *you* needed the reminder—married or not, young women can have babies. And babies have nasty habits. They make messes. They mess up the whole business of inheritance and property. So a few years of ignorance and lost opportunities on the part of young females seems to me a small price to pay for social stability."

"If it *were* the only price," she said.

"What's that mean?"

She told him then of the night she went searching for Annie and found Uncle Walter. "Until then, Steamer, I thought the few girls one saw in Piccadilly and the main thoroughfares were all that the Social Evil amounted to. I had no idea of those teeming courts and back alleys. I thought there were perhaps a mere hundred girls in London. There must be tens of thousands."

"There are a lot, I know."

"And I thought they were sustained by a few thousand men of low class or of depraved natures. But how can that be? Are there hundreds of thousands of men of that kind? Of course not. It's all kept going by normal, apparently decent family men like Uncle Walter. And by all those earnest, hard-working bachelors who have to marry late. There's another price—a price in family life based on deceit and hypocrisy. And what of the price Annie has paid? Her ability to love blighted by disgust. The same thing must have happened to others, to most of them perhaps. I don't think it's so small a price, Steamer."

He shrugged. "What's the alternative? D'you want men of our class to find their outlet with *women* of our class!"

"Yes! With love as the basis, not cash. As between William and Catherine."

"And tiny feet?"

"Well, there are various Malthusian devices—"

"Which you and Pepe had never *heard* about, I'm sure!"

"They can be perfected."

"They had *better* be, if you're anything of a prophet."

She could not brush Caspar's objections aside easily. Winifred's she could explain away in terms of Winifred's life and circumstances; but Caspar obviously spoke for people in general—and for their most tolerant wing, at that. Years of journalism, that is, of daily exposure to judgement, had taught her to accept such outright rejection or, at least, to make a convincing show of it. She knew how to smile with interest, and how to raise her eyebrows with a gesture that said: *Oh, really? Do tell me exactly how bad it is—I long to know!*

It had not happened often. In a decade of sustained work she had had no more than two dozen pieces rejected outright, mostly short stories. And she could remember every one. She could almost quote them word for word, though others that had gone through with a smile and a nod had vanished from her memory like the ephemera they were. Sometimes she would come across articles that bore one of her pen names and wonder, *Did I write that?* But rejected pieces lived on within her like unhealed cysts beneath the skin.

Worst of all was a rejection by a friend, for it could be ascribed to nothing but honest opinion, even to a care for her own best interests. (Indeed, she had noticed, editors always universalized their own objections: "Any reader with good instincts will scorn this creaking manipulation of the plot," they would scribble down the margin. Or, "Your reader, I fear, will already have skipped to the end of this paragraph—if not of this *chapter!*") At such times she met, or renewed acquaintance with, the demiurge that did her real writing for her. That implacable creature was no rational, urbane, polished young woman such as Abigail took pride in being. She-it would consider Pepe (and most rejections had naturally come from him, as first in the line of fire) with a smouldering hatred, seeing only a perverse, insensitive fool who stood between her distillation of wisdom—wit—pathos—and its proper achievement on the printed page. If she felt sorrow, it was for all those thousands of millions of readers, from now until the end of time, who were to be denied their share because of this doltish, illiterate, barbarian *editor!*

For hours after she and Caspar had parted company that afternoon—with all outward show of affection and, on her part, of gratitude—she strolled through the park, scheming every possible means of putting *Into a Narrow Circle* before that vast and grateful army of readers whose property it rightly was. She could print a few hundred copies herself and employ out-of-work but respectable people to leave them in railway trains about to depart, squeeze them into library shelves, pop them through reviewers' letterboxes until a groundswell of clamour and curiosity forced Pepe into doing a proper edition. Or she could do as Caspar suggested—recast the tale as an allegory, set in the twentieth century (*Into a Future Circle*—what an intriguing title! Who could fail to want to read it!), and then, when it was accepted in its theatrical clothing and had passed into that special oblivion reserved for last month's *causes célèbres*, she would hurl the real book in the public's face to let them see just what it was they had accepted. *Into a Narrow Circle?* Yes, the change would carry a double irony.

She began to grow quite excited by the idea. If she had picked any other phrase but "hurl . . . in the public's face," she might have been so fired with enthusiasm that she would have tried it. But that phrase had been Ruskin's when he had accused Jimmy Whistler of "hurling a pot of paint in the public's face." Jimmy had sued him for libel and won; but a British jury had awarded him no more than a farthing's damages. She remembered it not only because she had covered the trial but also because Jimmy had made a joke about it at her farewell dinner. So, in her mind, futility clung to the very phrase, "hurl . . . in the public's face." Before the trial Jimmy had been so sure, so convinced of the rightness of his cause—as convinced as she now was of hers. That memory alone was enough to tip the balance of her judgement back from hot to cold, until at last she saw, with bleak resignation, how impossible it was for her book to be published. For the first time in her life she hated her own country and its people. A land of philistine jurors.

That evening she told Celia, "There seems no point in showing my parents this book. I think I'll just lock it away."

"Just like that."

"No, Celia!" She was sharp. "Not 'just like that.' But let's pretend, eh?"

"Sorry."

"You look it."

Celia was hurt. "Oh? Should I be sorry? What've I done?"

Abigail, forced to concede her own unreasonableness, smiled. "Of course you shouldn't. I just wish I lived in any other country or any other time."

Celia smiled too. "Ancient Rome?" she asked.

"They probably knew it all."

"Knew what?"

"What I try to say in my book."

Celia grasped Abigail's arm, suddenly alive. "Abbie! Let's go back to Rome! Just for the summer, you know. Just painting and reading and—and not deciding anything!"

"We'll see," Abigail said. Something in her leaped up with joy at the suggestion.

Just after she turned out the gas, Celia said, "D'you think I might read this book, Abbie?"

She read it on the train back to London. She almost finished it on the train to Digswell. And she read the last few pages in the coach to Maran Hill, one of the Stevensons' country homes, where the Earl and Countess were passing a few weeks by way of a midseason break.

"Well?" Abigail asked as she finished. They were driving along the foot of the Maran valley, one of the loveliest in all Hertfordshire.

"It's an idyllic tale," Celia said. "But lord, what a fool I am!"

"Why?" Abigail laughed.

"I'm ashamed to tell you."

"Tell what?"

"I had no idea—why men and women—you know. Of course it's obvious. Yet I'd never seen it. I never understood."

"But—Henry?"

Celia shook her head. Then she laughed bitterly. "To think I was afraid to tell you about him! And all the while I was the ignorant one. Is it really like—as you say? Such an exquisite joy?"

"But what did Annie tell you? In Rome you told me she talked of nothing else."

Celia hid her face and chuckled. "I thought they did to her what Henry did to me. Just decorated her and—and drooled."

An intense green light reflected off the water meadows beside the river; it filled the cab with an unearthly radiance.

"Damn Henry!" Celia said, looking up again.

"Never mind, Celia. You're young yet. You'll still have your day."

Perhaps, she thought, I should lend this book to all England— one reader at a time! Only the rational parts of her would ever learn to accept the impossibility of seeing it published.

It was marvellous to see her parents together again, especially as they were so obviously relishing a second honeymoon still. Over dinner they relived for Abigail's and Celia's benefit the triumph of their first railway contract—Summit Tunnel on the Manchester & Leeds, over forty years ago. John had been no more than a navvy ganger when the tunnel started. Then the contractor had gone bankrupt and Walter Thornton, the company's engineer, had taken a big risk to his own reputation and had proposed John as the man to finish the job. The same day Nora, tramping from Manchester to Leeds, had come into John's life with nothing but a faded blue dress, a gold sovereign, and a phenomenal gift for figures.

Together they had slaved through the night working out all the costings "every way from Jericho." When John went before the Manchester & Leeds board the following day he dazzled them with Nora's sums; without her, he swore, he'd never have been trusted with so great an enterprise—the world's then-longest tunnel. He'd come straight back to the Summit workings and asked Nora to marry him.

Nora was so carried away at the retelling of this tale that she ran upstairs to get the very blue dress she had been wearing—as if the story would not become real until everyone had seen it and felt it.

"I've not washed it nor anything," she said. "I left it as it was, to look at in case we ever got too proud."

"What's this?" Abigail asked. "Blood? It looks like blood."

Nora smiled and nodded. "Next day, while John was in Manchester, I went to help break up a rabbit warren. Conies, we called them. Breaking warrens and squandering conies was a great country sport in those days."

"You were always a huntress, weren't you!" Abigail said. "I'd never realized it went back that far."

"And further!" Nora answered. "I got two dozen conies that day. That's rabbit blood on that dress."

"I can't imagine you like that," Abigail told her. "I can only ever imagine you in places like this."

Nora grinned at John. "He can," she said. "He proposed to me in that lane, dead rabbits and all. And me barefoot, in that dress." She put her hand in his. "He said—you'll excuse the Yorkshire, but it means nothing in any other tongue—he said, 'I hope I may always remember thee like this, Nora, my . . . most precious.' " Her eyes began to swim. " 'Dusty. Loppered with blood. Bare of feet.' " Her voice broke. She could not continue.

John supplied the rest, speaking only just above a whisper; his lips scarcely moved. He took both her hands between his. " 'There's grand changes agate, they'll sweep up thee and me and carry us I know not where. But I hope thou might never lose this . . . sunshine in thy spirit.' " He did not turn from her. "And she never did," he added.

"And never will!" Abigail ran between them and put an arm around each. "Oh, I'm so *glad* about you two. We all are."

"Amen," Nora said.

Later, when they were preparing for bed, Celia said, "What is it about some people—they can make life so much more real than it usually is? They carry an extra sort of electricity around with them."

"My parents, you mean? Yes, they have—"

"But you too, Abbie dear. You also have it. There's always more life when you come into a room, and it departs with you. You don't have to say anything, or do anything. It's just something that's . . . you!'"

At that moment Nora came in. "I suppose I may read this book that's doing the rounds of the family?" she asked. "So as not to feel entirely superannuated."

"I shan't publish it," Abigail warned. "Winnie and Steamer have persuaded me." She handed the by-now-tattered envelope to her mother.

"From all I hear," Nora said, "that'll simply quadruple my pleasure."

She finished the book shortly after lunch the following day. Abigail had watched her from safe hides, through cracks in doorways, peeping in mirrors. But Nora's face had given nothing away. Now, as her mother crossed the ballroom, she was afraid to turn and look at her face. She stood in the large bow window, peering out through the lavender-tinted glass at the lawns and a small fountain down near the ha-ha.

Nora put her arms around her from behind and, kissing her on the ear, gave a gentle hug. "I want your father to read it," she said.

Abigail was too delighted—and astounded—to know how to respond.

"There's so much in it," Nora went on, "that we both know and have rediscovered, but we'd never have the wit to say."

Abigail began to laugh. "I thought Winnie and Steamer would be for it and you'd be dead set against it. Have I changed so much? Or is it you? Or did I never really know you?"

"Who knows that side of anyone? I didn't know it of you. I didn't know you saw it all so deeply." She sighed. "Oh Abigail, what shall you do? You're no lass for these times. You'd want eyes as narrow as one pair of cufflinks to be sure of happiness. Chain and all. Aye! What shall you do?"

"I'm finished with Pepe," she said. And she wept, quite spontaneously. All the tension of these last weeks suddenly brought her down. A child again, she turned into Nora's arms and cried for the sheer comfort to be found there.

"You never could do the easy thing," Nora said, clutching her hard. "Not from birth. The first thing you ever drew—you remember that? A flower pot? The first thing that wasn't just scribble?"

Abigail, her sobbing only part stilled, shook her head.

"In this very house it was. Above this very room. If you covered one sheet of paper, you covered twenty before it satisfied you. There never was such a child for going on and on, through anger and tears, on and on, till you got it right. I wonder if any of us ever changes. You said last night I was always a huntress. My earliest memory of a great excitement is going ratting with a stray terrier. And if I live to be a hundred, I'm like to die in the hunting field."

Abigail's weeping had subsided. A void was replacing the sorrow. "Let's go along the linden walk," she suggested. And when Nora turned back toward the hall, she said, "No. No hats. No gloves. And damn who meets us! If that old blue dress were down here still, I'd say put that on and kick off your shoes as well."

The ha-ha was less than a hundred yards long, little more than the width of the lower lawn, which it made seem continuous with the deer-cropped parkland beyond. At each end, behind a concealing shrubbery, its ditch rose to a wrought-iron fence, with a wicket gate to give access to the south park. From the western gate stretched an avenue of ancient limes that had probably been planted in Elizabethan days. This was the linden walk Abigail had suggested.

"I still can't publish it," she said when they had gained the avenue.

"No question of that."

Abigail laughed, with hardly a trace of bitterness. "Somehow the disappointment of it is outweighed by your approval. That means more to me."

"Then you may be thankful your next crust of bread didn't depend on publication!"

Abigail stooped to pick a buttercup, trembling in the breeze. "D'you still like butter?" She held it below her mother's chin. "Yes, you do. So do I." But she did not test herself. "I used to have a sort of rule that I'd try to live by my earnings and leave my income untouched. But I never applied it absolutely rigorously. Perhaps I should do that. Is there a way of locking up my income against any weakening in my resolve?"

Nora snorted. "You'd be as ridiculous as a steam engine with sails! I was making the opposite point. Because you have an income, because you don't depend on your earnings, you can be that much more honest in life. If it's true, for example, that my approval means more to you than publication, you can accept that fact and say so. You must also accept what you are—a rich woman."

"But how?"

"That's what I asked. What shall you do now?"

Abigail sighed.

"Still," Nora went on quickly, "no need to make up your mind all in a hurry. Time's on your side. Celia told me at breakfast that you're thinking of going back to Rome and spending the summer painting. I think that would be excellent. You need a long break from everything. And painting was always a kind of second love, wasn't it?"

"Love!" Abigail laughed. "That's what I need a long break from! A long, long break. I think if I met someone I liked, or even someone with nothing I *dis*liked, I'd marry him. Liking's easy. Love is so hard."

"What about César Rodet?" Nora ventured.

"Heavens, no!" She laughed. "There's only one love in that man's life—painting. Oh, no—the man I liked would have to *adore* me, absolutely and to distraction."

They both laughed at her egotism.

"It is possible, though," Nora said, "inside marriage. Love."

"So I see," Abigail answered, throwing away the buttercup and linking arms with her mother. They reached the end of the walk, where the long avenue of limes marched down the ridge to mingle with a deep belt of fox covert. For a moment they stood, looking out over the sunlit valley beyond. Then they turned and made for home. "Even so," Abigail continued, "you had your 'long, long break,' too."

"Aye," Nora said.

"If you *are* a huntress," Abigail pressed, "why did you tolerate it so long? Why didn't you go and rout out— Can we say her name now?"

"Charity. I don't know. Well—I do. But—"

"You don't have to say," Abigail cut in. "It's none of my business really."

"But I will tell you," Nora said. "There's no other living soul I'd tell—for fear of not being understood." She gathered her thoughts. "Also, you'll maybe see why I'm not so lacking in understanding of you." She began to walk in a different manner, swaying awkwardly, as if to transfer an ungainly thought from her mind to her body. Abigail slowed their pace to the merest loitering stroll.

"Was it Shakespeare," Nora asked, "who said there's a tide in human affairs that you've got to take at the flood or not at all? Something like that. Well, I missed that tide. Perhaps I even wanted to miss it—how can we ever be sure of these things? Perhaps, when I heard of—Charity, I was just ready for a little dalliance of my own. Anyway, I lost no time at it." She laughed bitterly. "It endured one week, never mind twenty years. One week! But there was a chance it had left me in—well, in the same condition as Laon put you. And I don't need to tell you how that suddenly dominates your life and drives out everything else. How could I get your father to do—what he had to do, if I went out to St. John's Wood and turned that baggage out into the streets and made a scandal to set all London by the ears! Oh, and there were all the other, social reasons, too. What peer's wife ever made a public fuss of her husband's mistress? Isn't St. John's Wood full of carriages with all the arms in *Debrett,* from dukes to baronets, every evening of the week! I'd have been the laughingstock; John would have been the hero. I'd have lost everything. D'you want more reasons?"

"Are there more?" Abigail squeezed her mother's waist.

She wanted to say that "dalliance" was the very opposite of her own ideas about love and sexuality, but did not dare risk the rebuke it would imply; she was, indeed, somewhat overawed by her mother's confession.

"I went to see her, you know," Nora continued. "After your father went to India; when I knew he'd be away half a year. We're all animals, really. Civilization's just a veneer."

"You mean you fought?"

"Just the opposite. No." She sought for words. "You know how when you enter a new bitch into a pack, how she curls herself over and fawns to the others until they accept her? Young Miss Charity did just that. And I did what the established bitches do—I snarled and left her be. That's why I say we're all animals. I behaved just as she did when I first entered Society—when I was the new bitch in the pack. I did all the fawning then."

"Exactly what did Charity do?" Abigail asked, fascinated.

"Oh . . . she wept. Said she loved John but he didn't love her—he loved only me. She could tell it. He'd throw her over any day and come begging back to me."

"Clever thing!"

"No, I think she believed it. I even think it was true. I think John was smitten by her for a year or so—long enough to get her with child. The rest was obligation. You know what he's like with his obligations!" She pointed at an old gardener who was snipping at the fringe of lawn overhanging the ha-ha. "Old Pengilly there was one of his navvies at Summit Tunnel. He lost his foot in a rock fall. John's found him work ever since. Oh, the times his goodness has betrayed him—but he'll never change!"

Abigail, who had dared so much in raising the issue at all, dared one further question: "Do you not think that, despite all the obvious differences between you, you sensed something of a sister-under-the-skin with her—not before, but when you and she were actually face to face?"

"Who knows?" Nora shrugged, unwilling to reopen the memory.

"The one thing I still find hard to forgive is that he let her call herself Stevenson—and the children."

"I wouldn't be too worried about that," Abigail said. "They're not really Stevensons, you know—only by *charity!*"

She had waited over fifteen years to deliver this reassurance.

Nora threw back her head and roared with laughter. "Oh, darling!" she gasped, wiping her eyes. "You're a tonic!"

But a short while later she realized that the witticism was very like something from Abigail's journalism, and she grew worried. "Here," she said. "Don't go putting any of this into a book, will you. However disguised."

Abigail chuckled and gave her mother's arm a further squeeze. "No fear of that. Your behaviour is too inconsistent. In real life people are allowed to be inconsistent because, as we both know too well, they got there by *accident!* But people don't get into books by accident. They all have a Purpose. Inconsistency like yours would just destroy it."

"Forget books!" Nora said with a sudden intensity. "Forget all this unhappy past. Go back to Rome and paint—a dozen summers, if need be. Painting's such a happy art. But forget books! All painters live to be ninety. But look at the number of writers who've ended by hanging themselves."

Chapter 35

Rome gleamed in the spring—that unique rejuvenation which annually flowed through the city's arteries. Nothing Abigail had ever done felt more right than this return to the quaint atelier perched on top of the half-ruined Teatro Marcello. Even César's smugness had all the warmth of a welcome. And when he saw the Aladdin's chest of paints and pastels, of mediums, crayons, and papers, she had brought from Cornellison's of London, he hugged and waltzed her all around the studio.

"Oh"—she laughed to Celia as they swept past her—"the way to this man's heart is through his palette!"

She loved the studio smells of oil paint, which were strong enough to mask the stink of fish from the Oratory across the way. Turpentine, as clean and sharp as eucalyptus. Poppyseed oil and linseed oil, warm as cream. And all the different colours, their aromas now mingled now separate, redolent of some ancient alchemy. They were all part of the excitement of a painter's studio, just as the lack of them contributes to the sense of flatness sometimes felt even in the world's greatest galleries. Perhaps it was this intoxication, no more, that had made her heart leap up at Celia's first suggestion of a return to Rome.

Next day, the first full day of their return, they all went out painting together; they crossed the river into the Travertine district and walked down the Tiber to a spot near the Porta Portense. There was a ready-composed view of the river, with even a cluster of sailing barges moored to the right bank, and the Aventine Hill across the water, fringed with a row of medieval hospitals and convents. The viewpoint they had chosen, a nook closed off by the massive ramparts of the sixteenth-century defence wall, was a haven of tranquility in the babel of the Roman springtime.

The weather held, and they came back each day for a week. Celia could pull off a watercolour in a few hours, so it was not long before she had moved to some other vantage for a different view. But Abigail and César, working in oils, stayed at the same scene all week—though with two canvases, one for morning, one for afternoon. By the third day, Abigail was fairly pleased with both her paintings. Their composition was full of assurance, the skies airy, the hill convincingly solid, the buildings straggling picturesquely. On the sixth day both paintings were dead.

The paint lay on them like worried butter, the skies were turgid, the hill was neither flat nor round, the river was leaden. César's, by contrast, had grown lighter and fresher with every stroke. Yet he used far more paint than she had done; his shadows were as thick as his highlights.

"What did I do wrong?" she asked.

"If you wish to be Celia," he said, "you did wrong to go on after the third day. If you wish to become a painter, then you learned something. That's never wrong."

"But the painting is—all wrong. What can I do?" She was dejected. She didn't really want to know what to do. But she sat up when he took his palette knife and held it at the top of her painting. "Yes?" he asked.

Reluctantly she nodded.

He scraped off the paint in long, bold strokes from top to bottom, wiping the knife clean on the bark of a nearby cherry tree. "Perfect," he said, pleased with the result. "Look—you did some very good under-painting. Now! Tomorrow I'll finish here, so you have one more day."

It still wasn't a good painting when they finished, the following day, but it had revived a little; and she had sense enough not to want to become Titian overnight.

All that summer the three of them painted out of doors, except when the rain or the noonday sun drove them under cover. In August, when the heat (and the vile stink of the fish) became unbearable, they would go down to Ostia each day in search of seascapes and sea breezes. They ate all their meals out, and the wife of one of the artisans in the workshops below the Teatro did their washing and housekeeping—so painting became their sole reason for existence.

Abigail, who had taken to painting as a way to shut out the habits of a decade, soon became as immersed in it as if she had been born for nothing else. Her new life, at the easel and in the cafés, crowded out her old.

When groups of painters collected in the cafés, she no longer listened to their talk as an informed outsider—as a journalist seeking copy; the points they argued had become life-and-death issues to her, the corner-stones of her new universe: Is a painter bound by tradition or is each of us hurled alone against nature? Is it immoral (a violation of Truth) for us to *compose* a picture? Light is the hero of every painting—how can we capture him? Is our love affair with Nature or with paint? Is it justified to deny the flatness of a canvas—to make upon it an illusion of depth . . . should we not accept, even celebrate, that flatness? And what, when colour photography is perfected, are *we* going to do in order to make connoisseurs prefer us to the mechanics?

This last question was the nearest any of them got to the idea that art might have a social purpose, something beyond the painter's own itches and obsessions. Abigail did not notice the lack of it—not for several years. Now that painting was her obsession, too, she entered these discussions from inside. She knew what everyone was talking about, shared the same shorthand, argued with a passion that, only months earlier, she would have found either amusing or beyond comprehension. At first she spoke mainly in French; half the painters there were French, anyway. But as summer drew into autumn she found she was managing almost as well in Italian; soon she spoke French only with César.

Celia and César took little active part in these café discussions. Celia would listen intently, nod and smile when anyone said anything apt, laugh when the saying was funny—and all quite independent of the matter of the argument. Her attitude said, "I'm glad to be here. To be glad is enough." César listened warily rather than with Celia's intensity. He weighed everything and, Abigail guessed, bothered to remember very little of it. From working at his side and accepting his guidance, she knew he was far ahead of the rest of them in skill and understanding. Often the conversation would get around to some question that he had, by chance, settled for her that very afternoon; then she would turn to him, expecting him to speak. But he would smile or wink, and leave her to say it for him—and she, feeling hypocritical, would have to say it, for to leave a truth unsaid would have hurt too much. In that way she gained a reputation far beyond her skill—and she knew it. Then she grew shy of showing her work to anyone but César.

Sometimes in these discussions César would curl up and go to sleep—deliberately, not as something accidental. If Celia was there, she'd stop him and take him home, for though everyone else thought it charming, or a good joke, she could not think of it as anything but rude. Despite all that had happened to her there was still a lot of the middle-class Celia Addison there.

On those evenings someone else would escort Abigail home. Usually it was Massimo Ronzi, a tall, dark Adonis, still in his twenties. He had enormous facility with paint, which inclined him to be more of a realist, almost photographic, and entirely traditional. His great trouble was that in all Rome he could find no male model as beautiful as himself. When Abigail first heard him make this complaint, she thought he was joking. But he was quite serious. His youthful obsession with his own beauty and skill—and prowess—always amused her. It certainly lightened many journeys home.

"Celia is your friend?" he asked once.

"Naturally."

"Why don't you move out and give her a chance?"

"What nonsense now, Massimo?"

"No nonsense at all. She's in love with César. Any fool can see that."

"Then, of course, I have to take *your* word for it!"

But the shaft was lost on him. "Of course," he said complacently. "And César cannot choose between you. If you move out, he has to choose."

"Ah, youth!" she said. "It's all so easy."

"You come with me. I'm a superb lover."

She laughed and squeezed his arm. "Don't be absurd."

"And you're beautiful. With a beautiful woman I'm even more superb."

Tiring of him, she began to hum a tune.

"It's nice," he said, as calmly as if she had not snubbed him at all. "I sing too. Superbly."

And he sang *"La donna è mobile"* (what else!) from *Rigoletto*. And—she had to allow—he sang, if not superbly, at least very well. People came from their houses and out onto balconies to listen; and they clapped when he finished. Rome does not confer its accolade lightly.

"I am even more superb as a lover," he said. "Come and try."

His persistence intrigued her. "How many women do you talk to like this?" she asked.

"All. I want all women."

"And how many accept?"

He had to think. It was not a question that had concerned him before.

"Many?" she prompted. "Most?"

"One in ten," he said proudly. "Enough."

She did not want to snub him again, not outright. "I'll think about it, Massimo," she said.

"Most women say that," he told her. "And if in the end you say no, we can still be friends. I am not too proud. The loss will be more yours than mine."

"You make it very easy."

"No. It is already easy."

She often thought about what Massimo had said concerning Celia and César. And it was, she decided, possibly true. Perhaps even the pair of them did not realize it; but there was some kind of rapport between them. Strong enough to call love? No one could know that until its strength was challenged.

*   *   *

The Roman autumn was devised especially for painters, just as Travertine marble is made by nature for the Roman sun, which burnishes it with gold at the slightest touch. The autumn light is like no light ever seen in northern Europe. It sparkles. It is the light that shines from the heart of a crystal. It wakens every surface, even the dullest, with a lambent fire. That autumn it kept César and the two women painting from twilight dawn to twilit dusk. It was an intoxication that left their evenings hung over with a surfeit of visual delight. Abigail's memory of that time was of the perfect silence that reigned between them. She had, of course, seen the Roman autumn before; but not as a painter sees it. Naïve as her visual sense still was, she now knew well enough to marvel where before she had merely enjoyed.

She marvelled, too, at the vast new world painting had opened up to her. She could never be bored again. The train is three hours late? Marvellous! Out with the sketchbook and cram its pages with life, life, and more life! She could reach out and touch the world directly. As a writer she had *thought* she could do that; but now writing began to seem a monstrously stiff and roundabout way of connecting with the world. And the painter did more than merely connect. The painter loved! Every line was a line in an unending hymn of love sung to the world. In church every Sunday, while others offered up their standard prayers, she prayed especial thanks for the new eyes of childhood that had been miraculously restored to her.

In December, when winter at last fell upon them and she remembered to go and buy a little present to send to William, she said to the other two, "If Annie was to come here now, or Pepe, I think I'd worry first about which room to put them in!"

It was winter that brought home to them the reason for their astonishingly low rent. In the heady days of spring, who looks for fireplaces? Or in the torrid heat of summer? Or even during the golden hours of autumn, when the whole world clamours to be painted? But winter, rimming the tiles with frost, muting at last the stink of fish, putting clouds of breath between eyes and easel, winter revealed at once the dread fact: there were no fireplaces in the atelier.

Of necessity then they ate out in the cafés. And when the rains drove down and they had to send for meals to be brought in a pail, they also had to hire *scaldini* from the artisan's wife and sit with their feet ensconced in the warmth of them, huddled under blankets, and praying for just a touch of the heat they had cursed in summer and would curse again not six months hence.

January was worst. They said it was the hardest cold in memory. The breath froze one night in César's beard. When they arrived home he twirled the ice in fairy sherds onto their doormat. Abigail lay in bed and wondered if she could survive the night. Nothing seemed to warm her.

A voice said, "This is madness." César's.

It was all the excuse he offered for climbing beneath the sheets with her. He had brought his own blankets. He was huddled up to her while she was still deciding whether to object or not.

"Don't try anything," she warned.

"Try what, for heaven's sake!" he said.

When they were just a little warmer she asked, "Why didn't you go to Celia? She's nearer to you."

"I . . ." he began. But then he was silent.

How might he have completed the sentence, she wondered? "I respect her too much . . . I prefer you . . . I have already seen you naked, so you no longer frighten me . . . I do not love you, so you don't tempt me . . . ?"

It was strange, she thought, a token of the mystery of César, that she had no idea what he might have said.

When they were warmer still, warm enough for her to begin to feel guilty, she asked, "Will Celia be all right?"

Only by the change in his breathing did she know that the question stirred him. "People die of hypothermia," he said. Then he chuckled. "Or, to put it into medical language—they die of cold. I'll get her. It's better anyway. You smell too beautiful."

He was soon back with Celia. "D'you think it's all right, Abbie?" she asked. But she was already between them, shivering gratefully in the warmth they had created.

After the intensity of the cold they had endured separately, the warmth was all the argument needed to quell their moral doubts. In any case, having fretted awake for so long, they were soon blissfully asleep.

Their awakening was a little sheepish. The sun had taken off some of the chill, removing also the direct justification for being together—the justification their flesh could feel.

"I'll go," César said, drawing the sheets up over his head. His muffled voice added: "Soon."

Abigail laughed but Celia took action; she began to tickle him. He fled soon enough then.

"It wasn't wrong," Celia said when they were alone together. "I really thought I'd die of cold."

"It wasn't wrong—as it turned out. But it mustn't happen again."

The cold did not relent. By three that afternoon it had clamped around them once more, driving them out to the Posta, the Falcone, the Greco, the Café de Venise, the Best Society, armed with sketchbooks and constitutions that could take a dozen coffees without a flutter. On the way back they stopped in at the Osteria della Campana in the shadow of the Teatro. They had often passed it, never ventured inside.

César was delighted to find there a plaque, erected by a proud king of Bavaria, boasting the fact that "in the years 1776, 1777, and 1778 Wolfgang Goethe had amorous intercourse with Faustina, a beauteous country girl."

"The quintessence of romance and Germanic thoroughness in one sentence!" he said. "Not 'seventy-six to 'seventy-eight, as you or I would gloss it, but all three years!"

When they crossed their own threshold and sensed that especial cold which seemed to drift uniquely through the top floor of the Teatro, they did not even question that they would pass another night together. This time César slept between them, for they had discovered last night that he was the warmest-blooded of the three.

"You know," he asked as soon as the candle was snubbed, "of the German professor of aesthetics who was invited to dinner by Venus herself?"

They did not.

"Well, after the dinner, which was, of course, ambrosia and nectar, Venus dismissed her servants and, divesting herself of her raiment (which was, in any case, little more than woven air), lay back on her silken cushions and said to the German professor of aesthetics, 'You may have your will of me.' Of course, the German professor of aesthetics' eyes popped out. 'You mean it?' he gasped. 'Indeed and indeed,' replied the goddess. 'Anything?' asked the German professor of aesthetics. 'Anything, anything,' Venus said, all of a flutter. 'Only be quick!' Whereupon the German professor of aesthetics whipped out a tape measure and, approaching the goddess with trembling hands, said reverently, 'My colleagues and I have been disputing this for a long time!' "

Abigail was certain that, under the cover of darkness, César held an imaginary tape measure to some decidedly *non*imaginary points of Celia's anatomy. It annoyed Abigail.

Next morning there was some sun; and they found that by leaving the bedroom and studio doors open, enough of its heat filtered through to make the studio bearable, even though the frost persisted. But Celia came up from her room dressed for the street. She began to gather together all her watercolours from the summer and from Normandy. "I found a dealer a couple of days ago," she said. "He wants to buy. When I come back we shall be rich and I'm going to take us to the Quirinal for dinner."

When she had gone César said, "He will cheat her, this dealer."

"Why don't you go with her then?" Abigail asked.

"She must learn. It's only one season's work. She has many years to go."

"You're cool!"

"You think so?"

Abigail wondered if César was right. There was a hard streak in Celia—look how she had treated Henry after she left him. "What would you call 'cheat'?" she asked. "What ought she to get?"

"Let's say seventy-five lire per painting. She won't get it, though."

When they broke for lunch she returned obliquely to what had happened—or what she thought had happened—last night.

"Celia had a rotten marriage," she said. "Has she ever talked about it?"

He said no, but his eyes hinted at some kind of knowledge.

"Her husband was not a normal man."

"Why are you telling me this?"

She drew a deep breath and framed herself to it. "Because of what I think is going to happen."

"Which is?"

"I think you want to become her lover."

He did not betray himself by the slightest gesture, but his eyes still had not lost their omniscience.

"I would like that, César, but only if you are sincere. I know that men are promiscuous in their desires. You can separate it from love as we cannot. Celia does not need—of all people, Celia doesn't need another man who would use her like that. You may desire her . . . ?" She looked at him questioningly.

"I do," he said evenly.

"Then I beg you—do nothing about it unless you also love her. Don't make her love you, then use her, then leave her. It'd be so easy for you to do that. But it would be the end of her."

"Oh, I don't think so," he said casually.

"It would! It'd be the end of her chances of finding love and happiness."

"Those chances end only with our death."

"Please don't, César, please? I beg you!"

"What if I tell you I can't. That I desire her so much I must have her."

Horrified, she stared at him. "That's not like you," she said.

He reached across the table and took her hand. Hers was trembling but his was calm. "What's like me? You don't know. You don't care. You don't know inside me, what goes on."

Her eyes fell. "Do you want me, too, César?"

"Of course. You are beautiful, you're kind, you're intelligent, you are sympathetic. Also, most important, you are: Abigail!"

Wishing she could control her shaking hand and voice, she said, "Then have me, César. Leave Celia alone until you also love her. If it's only that pleasure you want, let me try to give it you. Nothing much can harm me now."

He raised her hand to his lips and kissed it as if each finger were due some special reverence, forcing her to look at him again. Now she saw that the look in his eyes was not the remote glint of secrets, withheld from her, but compassion. "Dear Abbie," he said. "You think it's Celia who needs such tenderness, but really it's you. Because you have a mind—because you can think about things and make a grand philosophy—you think you're no longer vulnerable. But you are. I tremble for you, not Celia. Celia can come back from hell and next day she'll be painting watercolours to show you what it was like. No man will ever harm Celia now. She never had any great passion in her. Celia will be a nice, warm, comfortable wife. But you! Why haven't I painted your portrait as I promised? Because of all I would see if I looked into your soul for three, four weeks; because of what I would put on canvas; because of what you would then discover."

"Are you trying to say you love me?" she asked, alarmed now.

"Yes. And Celia, too." He let go her hand and held up his own fingers to count upon. "First I love: painting. Second I love: painting. Third I love: painting! Fourth-equal I love: you-and-Celia—Celia-and-you." He snorted. "How unkind of Nature—to give me desire as big as a mountain but to leave my capacity for love down in the foothills. It would not harm Celia. But you—I don't know."

She was embarrassed enough to try to make a joke of it. "Poor César. You'll have me yielding out of pity next!"

Whether or not he knew she was joking, he took her at her word. "Ah! That'd be good. That'll do you no harm. Pity is a cul-de-sac of love. You will be safe for a while there."

She punched him playfully and laughed.

He stood and walked to the door. "Come on," he said without looking back.

*   *   *

It was an extraordinary experience. With Pepe she had never separated her physical from her emotional pleasure—it had never occurred to her that they could be separate. They went so completely hand in hand; when she had been emotionally out of sorts with Pepe, she had been physically unresponsive, too.

But with César there was no question of such a coalescence. Her senses and emotions, though both involved, stood a little apart. Her mind could oversee them both. Physically her senses found it as shattering as anything she had ever known. It was the same brush with intimations of death. Emotionally it was . . . comforting . . . satisfying. Her painting that afternoon went well.

Celia was late home but her face was triumphant. "Good news all the way!" she called out. "Henry is dead and I've sold all my paintings."

"Celia!" Abigail's shocked cry was simultaneous with César's "How much?"

"For the bigger ones, a hundred and fifty lire. The smaller ones a hundred. And there were three he wouldn't go above seventy-five for—but that was just to salvage the last remnants of his pride. His first offer was fifty apiece for the lot! Hoo!" She sat down, feigning an exhaustion that her face and voice belied.

"Celia, did you say Henry was dead?"

"Yes, the solicitors wrote *poste restante*. The letter's been there a week. Oh, it took me all day but I slowly beat him up and up. Fifty lire! He won't try that again."

"But how did he die? Do they say?"

"Yes." She stood up. "He hanged himself. Well, I'm going to dress for dinner. Tonight at the Quirinal we shall be *la crème de la crème*. So clean fingernails please!"

When she had gone, Abigail turned and stared at César.

With a sardonic smile he said, "What price, I wonder, for a water-colour of Hell?"

*   *   *

Next day he hired a porter with a barrow, loaded a dozen canvases on it, and sent Celia out to sell them, offering her ten percent of whatever she got. Abigail wondered if this was an elaborate ruse to get Celia out of the way again; but he made no move all afternoon. They painted on in contented silence.

Celia returned with all the paintings still on the barrow. César was aghast until she told him she'd found a dealer with a gallery, willing to offer him an exhibition in the spring. Then, of course, he was overjoyed.

That night was the last they all slept together. The cold loosed its grip on the city the following day and they resumed their solitary beds with relief, for the novelty had worn thin and only the biting cold had made Abigail's bed large enough for three. A week later, after they had retired for the night, she heard a scratching at her door. It was César.

"Obviously, you're never going to ask," he said.

"Ask what?" She felt foolish standing at the half-open door.

"So I'll just have to offer my desperation and hope the wells of pity are still yielding sweet water."

"Come in then."

At once he took her in his arms. Each could feel the other's excitement. "You do enjoy it, don't you?" he asked. "You don't regret it after?"

"It's fine. Come on."

When they were in the warmth of her sheets, he said, "Then why didn't you ask?"

Instinctively she turned her face away, though it was so dark neither of them could see the other. "I never would."

"Why not?"

"Of course I wouldn't."

For her it was as pleasurable, and as unengaged, as the time before. Afterwards he lingered a little too long and held her a little too dearly for her liking. "Don't fall in love with me, César," she warned. "Don't start to think it can ever be more than this."

"I wouldn't dare," he said.

"And forget what I said the other day. Love Celia too, if you wish."

"You mean it?"

"Why else would I say it?"

"Women sometimes say things to test men."

"I am not 'women.' And you should know it by now. I would prefer you to love Celia, even if it meant we would have to stop enjoying each other like this."

There's always Massimo, she thought. But a moment later her soul cringed at the very notion and she had to tell herself hastily that it was just a joke. A "test," in César's phrase, to see if her vision of herself was still chaste at heart.

"Shouldn't one of us take precautions?" she asked as he rose to go.

He was silent for some time. "Surely Annie told you?" he said at last. "She said I wasn't to tell you. She said she'd break it to you at the right time."

Abigail froze. Time slipped.

"Don't tell me she didn't."

"Oh . . . yes. She did. But I didn't realize it was so absolute."

"I'm sorry. It was the only time in my life when I have regretted being a painter instead of the best obstetrician in the world. Even then, I think, there could not have been much chance."

When she was alone once more, she tried to feel the sadness of this news. But she felt nothing. It seemed not even to relate to her, except in the way that a person with amnesia might relate himself to the written record of his forgotten life. It was even comforting that such a phenomenon as amnesia was abroad in the world. She remembered how Annie had once said she wasn't fit to love any more. Now Abigail said it softly, aloud, in Annie's voice. "I dunno, Abbie—I don't seem fit to love no one no more, somehow."

For a second it was like having Annie back with her, but even that memory, sharp as a pang, melted nothing within.

Chapter 36

From then on her private life ceased. And a large part of her rejoiced at it—the painter, the lover of conversation and crowds, the letter writer, the playgoer, the opera enthusiast—the public and professional Abigail, who had almost vanished from sight since the Villa Corot. Now they reoccupied her, and her time. They carried her out in triumph into Rome.

She still painted assiduously, for work was the habit of a lifetime. And César did not spare his help; everything he knew he tried to pass along to her. More than that, the very act of teaching changed him, too. As her confidence grew, she revealed a surer sense of colour than his. He was not too proud to notice it and to learn from her. And because he was a genius and she was not, he could seize on this new learning and quickly develop it to a point she could never have reached unaided. For instance, it was she who first saw how to introduce strong, even violent, colours into a painting without wrecking its unity. But it was he who turned the skill to more positive ends—he made it enhance the painting's unity.

That was the beginning of the style which was later to take him, if not to the forefront, at least to the second rank of French art (which would have outstripped the first rank in any other country). It was the style in which strong, clear colour was beautifully controlled to give light, airy canvases that looked as if they had arrived quite effortlessly.

Those were the months when he painted her incessantly—the paintings he never parted with: "Self-portrait by a Third Party," which was, in fact, his portrait of her at her easel; "A. Reading" (she was always plain *A.* in his titles), in which the light came at her from all sides—white from the page of her book, gold from the sun, green from the apple she was eating, ochre from the dry earth; "A. Asleep," where she lay in a high-backed wicker chair, dappled with the radiance of the Roman springtime; "Box at the Opera," where she sat with Celia and himself, lit from beneath with the cold limelight off the stage but engulfed in a dark, warm, fiery shadow . . . and many others.

The two best paintings of her were never exhibited—two nude studies drawn from life but painted from memory because he could not ask her to pose for the weeks they took him to finish. One showed her standing in a small footbath near an open window with the sunlight streaming in and falling over her like a caress. In the other, where she lay back upon a bed, apparently exhausted by the heat, he had painted himself, also nude, slightly intruding into the upper left corner of the picture. On the back of the first he had written, "The nakedness of woman is the work of God."

On the back of the second was an entire verse, also from Blake:

> *Love seeketh not itself to please,*
> *Nor for itself hath any care,*
> *But for another gives its ease,*
> *And builds a Heaven in Hell's despair.*

"Did I choose right?" he asked when he gave them to her. She had spoken to him often enough of Blake to make the question rhetorical. "What will you do with them?"

"Feel angry," she said. "Every time I look at them." The gift, which she had not expected, moved her deeply. She remembered the original drawings, of course, but had not even known he was at work on the paintings; he must have done them in his own room.

He laughed nervously at her answer. "Why?"

"For the fact that they can never be shown—just as *Into a Narrow Circle* can never be published."

"Never?"

"All right! Who cares for posthumous fame? I will take them, César, and I'll never part with them. One day they'll show the world that some of us at least were on the side of life. Even though we lacked the courage to stand up and say so."

Together they looked at the paintings a long time, in silence.

"Isn't it absurd," she said. "Even if these were of models—paid models—no English painter could show them. I doubt if they could even paint them. They'd have to disguise the girl in a classical setting. Or mythological."

"English painting is absurd. In France it's a joke."

"I shall never go back to England. I'm a Roman now."

*   *   *

That summer she dared at last to exhibit several paintings. All were praised—sometimes by aspiring critics who sought admission into the circle that was loosely formed around her; but established connoisseurs, too, who had no need of her patronage, admired her work, even where they recognized it as a trivialization of César's profounder and more difficult vision. And she was too conscious of her debt to mind when they pointed it out.

Her tenancy of the slummy atelier opposite the fish mart began to seem incongruous now that she was starting to move in Roman Society. At best, people thought her choice of home quaint. But to move out would have been to lose César—and what he had called the "cul-de-sac of love." He came to her still, once or twice a week, though now he was sleeping every night with Celia. How he set his visits right with her Abigail never asked. Nor did Celia ever mention it to her, except once, obliquely, when, on the anniversary of Henry's death, she cursed him for having denied her ten years of joy.

To move out would also have been to admit that painting had become the lesser half of her life, and that was something she was not willing to do. If people wanted her society, they'd have to take her for what she was. The fact that they did so was not flattering; it meant she was growing old—passing out of that young-virginal range over which Society exercises such an implacable vigil and exacts from its trespassers such cruel revenge. By the time she grew to be sixty, she reflected grimly, she could if she wished live a life of open scandal; she'd be tolerated still, even warmly, as one who could no longer make the slightest dent.

In the spring of her fourth year in Rome, César told her he and Celia would be leaving the atelier. Celia was, at last, expecting a child and they would be married. They would also be going back to France—to Paris.

Abigail decided to stay on at the atelier, even after they had gone. He smiled when she told him so. "Now I'm sure you'll go back to England," he said.

"No. I'll stay here."

"I mean one day you'll go back. The atelier has no kitchen and no fireplaces. It'll always be just rooms to sleep and work in. You'll never have roots here. That's why you cling to it—because it leaves you free to go one day."

"It leaves me free to enjoy Rome. Everyone lives in public here. Even people with homes and families still live out in their streets."

The night before they left for Paris, Abigail was astonished to hear César's familiar knock at her door; only the day before, he and Celia had been married. She did not let him in. "I want to part good friends with Celia," she said.

He laughed. "It's all right. If you don't believe me, I'll go and get her."

She let him in then.

"It's already a very French marriage," he said when they were side by side. "It would distress her only if she could not meet my mistresses socially."

"Mistresses! We are plural, then?"

"Only in the course of time. The English are confused about romantic love. They put it inside marriage and it gets swamped in bills and babies' napkins."

She laughed.

"But," he went on, "it's their only serious fault. For the rest they are all virtue. They believe in family, in lineage. They like order. They work. They put their own interests first and everyone else's nowhere—*but,* oh so politely! They know value, to the last farthing. And above all, because they know exactly what they want, they also know exactly how to compromise."

"Yes." Abigail smiled. "It's a portrait of Celia."

"Of course. Except that she has no illusions about romantic love, either."

"The perfect woman, then."

"The perfect wife. And that's all she ever really wanted to be."

"And all you ever wanted?"

He did not answer. She rose on one elbow and with her free hand began to caress his head, running her fingers through his hair and beard. For a while he did not stir, then suddenly he grasped her hand and, turning to it, planted a passionate kiss on her fingers, a kiss he seemed afraid to break.

She lowered her head on his and kissed his ear. "I'll miss you," she said, not sure what sort of comfort he wanted.

He was crying. His cheeks made wet sounds against the skin of the hand he was kissing.

"César," she said softly. "Don't leave me this memory."

"I should have married you," he said.

"I wouldn't have agreed to it. Only if you'd gone blind."

He shook his head.

"What?" She tried to joke him out of this mood. "You think you could have forced me? Against all I know of you?"

"What d'you know of me!"

At least she had managed to stop his weeping; he was trying to be heroic now. She continued: "I have it on the best authority that you love painting first, second, and third."

"I said that to make it come true."

"And succeeded."

"No!" It was a quiet howl of torment. "You've understood nothing! The struggle to remain a painter instead of devoting my whole life, my whole being, my whole soul to you. Why else did I paint you so incessantly? Why did I come to you at night?"

"I thought I knew that. But tell me."

"To keep alive the hope of you! The knowledge that you would love me if I made you my first, second, third."

She kissed him again, not wanting to say it was untrue.

"Tell me you would," he said.

She went on kissing him.

"Of course you would. Otherwise you would not have become my mistress."

She was not going to stand for that. "What then was the reason," she asked coldly, "that you became my *petit gigot?*"

He went rigid with anger. She felt suddenly the barrenness of the whole conversation. "Why have you told me all this?" she asked briskly. "Even if it's true—all right, I accept it's true, I don't want to mock your sincerity. But if you've kept it concealed so long, why come up here and spoil our last night with a confession like this?"

"I wanted you to understand."

"When the understanding could be of no possible use?"

"When I gave you those two paintings, and I asked you what you'd do with them? And you said you'd look at them and get angry, at Society and—"

"Yes, I remember."

"It was so impersonal. I gave them to you so that you could see how tenderly the sunlight caressed you. You'd remember how my eyes had feasted with the sun, and how my hand and lips had caressed you, too. I gave them to you so that you'd always know you had been *loved.*"

Oh no, you didn't, she thought. It was plausible—even plausible enough for him to believe it. *You came up here because, good and kind though you are, you wanted some power of you to linger on. You came up here to light a lamp for me to place in the cottage window of my little soul, for you, forever. You came up here because you are a man, and like all men, you think you can administer me.*

The insight had the extraordinary effect of making her want him physically more keenly than ever before. It was the only power she wanted to exercise over him, because it was so infallible. Even if he hated her, she could still wield it.

She began to caress him then, as if too deeply moved by his last words to say any of her own. She caressed him in all the places that excited him most. Her own longing made her shiver and that excited him even more, for he took it as the absolute mark of her submission. She let him think so until they had finished—the most stupendous physical love that had ever engulfed her.

Then in her afterplay she said softly, "Poor limp warrior! And poor, poor men. You think it such a marvellous weapon—and really it's your Trojan horse!"

Chapter 37

She often thought of all the marvellous times she had spent with César and Celia. The walks in the strange and beautiful landscapes of the Campana, before the season of the mosquitoes . . . the happy, silent hours side by side at their easels . . . the walks home from the cafés, arm in arm, making the streets and squares ring with their song and laughter . . . the discussions about life and love and art that had seemed so profound and wise. . . . Where was it all now? And Annie, who never answered letters? And Pepe, and all her London friends? All the grand forevers of her life—they each served their season and then she passed beyond them. Her need for them lingered awhile; then even it withered.

In her new aloneness she tried to feel lonely, and could not. No need arose within her that was not already filled. Friendship? Rome was a warren of her friends. Work? Her painting was now everything; she knew she would never be more than a footnote in the histories of art, a parenthesis in a *Life* of César Rodet, but she did not paint for such a fame. In any case she had a fame of her own—she rarely went to the theatre or opera without seeing, at the corner of her eye, someone or other pointing her out to friends. Love? Annie had said the final word on that. And sex? If César were still there, she would want it; but she was not a man.

Yet though she could identify no actual want, she knew that something was missing. Her baby? The chance of ever having babies? Unless she had found the trick of being massively dishonest with herself, it was neither of those. It was something much less tangible. Then one day, quite out of the blue and for no reason at all, she remembered a little incident from her girlhood. It was the moment she dipped her pen in its inkwell and started to write what became the Abbot's first article. She could not, after so many hundreds of thousands of words, remember what it had been about. But what she did remember was that absolute sense of certainty in the act of carrying pen to paper, a heightened awareness that what was about to happen was *right*.

And that, she realized, was the note now missing from her life. It was not dull, indeed it was exciting; nor was it profitless, nor worthless, nor stale. Yet it lacked that particular *buzz:* the certainty that what was coming next was right.

Perhaps it was the sort of signal she needed only in her youth. Certainly she could go on working and enjoying life to the full without it now.

*   *   *

In 1887 they pulled down the ghetto and turned it into a spacious square. The Jews, who had been freed from restriction at the end of papal rule, had long gone—the rich to villas amid the rich, the poor to try their luck a little apart from their history. But their tradition of cleanliness and order, despite the teeming anthill and dark labyrinthine alleys in which they had lived, remained. The ghetto had always been a friendly place, and she had often gone a little out of her way to walk through it. Now, though from the atelier she had been able to see no more than a slice of one corner of it, she missed its dark warmth intensely.

They even began to clear the rubble from the streets and excavate them down to the original level, exposing the half-buried ground floor of the Teatro. Soon, perhaps, they would close the fish mart and the whole area would become respectable. She considered moving to Venice.

It was easiest to think of such a move when she was alone in the atelier. But when she was in one of the cafés amid all her friends, arguing as if for her life about the new colour theories of Georges Seurat or the way Degas was handling pastel, then she could not even consider crossing the Tiber.

So she came to tolerate the prettification of the Vecchio, and Venice dwindled to a distant possibility.

One evening a man joined their café group with a simple, "You permit?" There was something about him that brooked no refusal. Certainly no one refused.

He had the air of an artist—perhaps a sculptor, Abigail thought. He greeted no one as he sat down, but he nodded stiffly at her as if they might once have met. He looked at least sixty, though his fair, wavy hair had only just begun to recede. His eyes were blue and challenging; even later, when she realized that one of them was glass, they did not lose their challenge. His skin was dried and wrinkled, like a peasant's; a scar ran from the corner of his left eye—the eye that proved to be glass—to his ear. The wrinkles of age crisscrossed it like a child's scribble. His mouth was set as grim as a turtle's, even when he smiled. His hands were rough; it was the sight of them that had made Abigail think he might be a sculptor.

If someone had whispered to her, "That man used to get drunk every evening of his youth . . . that man has cuckolded more husbands than Casanova . . . that man has seen the inside of every jail in Italy . . . that man used to swallow nails and fire in a circus," or any one of a dozen similar one-line biographies, she would have believed each and all of them. He looked the sort of man who might have done anything, and despite his years, he looked stocky and powerful enough—and ruthless enough—to do it all still.

Though he followed everything that was said, he contributed nothing. He drank his wine with a mechanical efficiency—up, tilt, sip, tilt, down. And never once looked at the glass. Again and again his eyes turned to her. He made her flesh crawl. She hoped he was just passing through Rome and was not set to become an habitué of their favourite cafés.

Usually their group broke up in twos and threes and drifted home, but that night someone came in and said there was a big thunderstorm descending from the Alban Hills and already it was impossible to get a cab. Everyone stood to hurry home. Massimo Ronzi walked most of the way with her; she was glad to see the glass-eyed stranger walk off up the Corso, in the opposite direction.

"I hope he doesn't come again," she said. "Who was he?"

"I never saw him before," Massimo said.

These walks home had now turned into baroque rituals of seduction and refusal; sometimes he told her of past conquests; sometimes he would court her with flowery salacity. This was such a night. He was a conquered land . . . he lay at her feet, trembling to know her will for she was his conqueror . . . he was hers to command . . . let her become his general and he would furnish her an army—all the privates she could ever want! She would see how they could stand and drill! And so on.

"One day, Massimo," she said as they parted, "you'll die of a heart attack: I will say yes to you."

"Ah—if I might lie in the count-ry of my choice, my heart would heal at once!"

He was never short of a reply. Yet it often struck her that he might, in fact, be a virgin still. It would almost be worth yielding herself to find out. With a smile she watched him go away along the Via del Portico. Then the sharp squall of wind that heralds rain swept through the streets and made her scurry for home.

A voice from behind called out her name.

She turned. It was the glass-eyed man, hurrying toward her. "I know your uncle," he said. He spoke Italian with a French accent.

"I have no uncle, signor. Signor—?"

"Your Uncle Daniel. Dan Telling? Your mother's brother."

It stirred the faintest of memories. Her mother had only once mentioned such a brother. When Abigail was a girl of about fourteen, Nora had taken them all, her brothers and sisters, to see the hovel near Manchester where she herself had grown up. She had talked of a brother then—she and her brother used to sit under their father's loom and "tie the rinks," or something. She had never mentioned his name; there was some disgrace attached to him.

"He's dying," the man said. "If he finds no safe shelter, he'll be dead before the week is out."

The first large warm raindrops fell around them. Lightning turned the man's scar into a canyon.

"We can't stand out here talking," she said. "Let's at least get under the arches over there."

They ran to the Teatro, ducking as if the rain were a fusillade of shot.

"My uncle, you say?" she asked as soon as they were under an arch. The rain now fell in stair rods. The splatters on the street, when frozen by the lightning, were like an army of miniature silver knights on chargers, each with a glistening lance.

They had to shout above the rain and between the bursts of thunder.

"Your Uncle Dan. Two years older than your mother."

"Is he a criminal?"

The man laughed. "If it's criminal to want a better world, yes! He's a criminal."

"You mean the police are after him?"

"Yes."

"What do you want of me?"

"Shelter him. Until he recovers."

"From what? Is he wounded?"

"He has malaria. We tried to hide in the Campana. He's an old man now. Harmless. But they'd still set him to hard labour."

She paced up and down beneath the arch, wishing she could simply walk away from him; but he would never let her go, not until he had an answer.

"I can't shelter him," she said at last. "He's chosen a life of risk. Why should he—or you—now try to cast it on me?"

"He is your kin."

"All of a sudden! No. I will not have him. Anyway, you can't bring him through the streets in this storm."

"He is there already."

"What d'you mean?"

"He's in your rooms. I waited until you went out and—"

She listened no further but turned to the inner portal that gave access, eventually, to her stair. He, with an agility that belied both his age and his build, overtook her.

"We'll leave," he said, hand on her door. "As soon as the storm is over, we'll go. I promise."

A woman opened the door from within. She saw Abigail and covered her face. The shawl muffled her laugh. "It was all wasted," she said. "He's dead." The laugh was not hysteria; the death meant nothing to her.

"God rest his soul," Abigail said.

"Hah!" The woman snorted and, brushing past them, fled down the stairs.

"What now?" Abigail asked, reluctant to go in. "A priest? The police?"

"I'll deal with it," the man said. "May I go in?"

She laughed at his sudden scruple and he, seeing the joke, smiled dourly and went before her.

"Who was that woman?" she asked.

"It wasn't necessary for me to know her."

He was indeed dead—already cold. "Yet he burned when I left him!" the man said. One of the dead man's eyes would not close, but it was too glazed even to hint at life. He was a shrivelled, emaciated sparrow of a man; nothing in his face reminded Abigail of her mother.

"You go on to bed," the man said. "He'll be gone by morning. We both will." He took a set of teeth from his pocket and worked them into the dead man's mouth. "In case he swallowed them in his fever," he explained. "That woman wouldn't have cared."

As he pried open the jaws she saw that the gums were badly ulcerated.

"The besetting disease of the revolutionary," the man said. "Bad teeth followed by bad dentures."

With his teeth restored, Daniel looked younger—at least, he was no longer a wizened, hundred-year-old Punchinello. There was now even a hint of a likeness with Nora and, oddly enough, with Sefton, who had passed briefly through Rome four summers ago. She had never seen a likeness between Sefton and her mother before, but Daniel bridged the gap and showed it to her.

"I'll make some drawings of him," she said. "My mother may like to see."

"And your Uncle Samuel." He saw her surprise. "Didn't you know of him? Oh yes, he and Dan corresponded often."

"Where is he?"

"He's Mr. Gladstone's valet. Your father got him that position."

She laughed in astonishment—that an utter stranger could wander into her life, here in Rome, and reveal her family's intimate secrets!

She drew Daniel's death mask from many angles, working on into the small hours. From time to time the man went out into the streets, but always found them too busy for his liking.

Toward three he came back and said, "The river has flooded the Ripetta. Every spare policeman and night idler in Rome has gone there. We won't get a better chance."

"Where will you take him?"

"Only as far as the river."

"No!"

"He expects it. His wife threw herself in the Seine, many years ago. He'll join her."

He took Daniel piggyback; in the dark he could be mistaken for a labourer carrying a gentleman through the floods.

"It's still pouring down," Abigail said. "At least come back here and dry yourself. And shelter till it stops."

He was back within twenty minutes, soaked to the skin. She fetched the dressing gown her models used when they rested a pose. While he changed she went out and got a brandy for him.

"Why did his wife throw herself in the Seine?" she asked.

He was shivering, but the brandy burned his circulation back. "She had toothache," he said. "I'd better sleep here. This rain isn't going to stop before morning."

Chapter 38

Next day he was shivering. She asked him if he, too, had caught malaria, and what should she get for it? They spoke now in French. He told her it was just a cold, and brandy and milk would cure it. She explained to the woman who did the cleaning that he was a model who had been taken ill. The woman brought up a *scaldino*, but the man said it was bad for fevers. Whenever he burned he threw the bedcovers down to his waist and asked Abigail to fan him with a towel, like a boxer.

At lunchtime she fed him hot zabaglione with a spoon. His teeth were not bad, she noticed. By four o'clock his forced cooling treatment, and the milk and brandy, seemed to have worked. His nose streamed and his eyes were red, but his fever had gone and his pulse was nearly back to normal. In the evening he accepted a *scaldino*. The evening papers had no reports that a body had been found in the Tiber.

The following morning his cold had thickened and he complained of feeling like wood; but he was obviously over the fever stage. "I'll go after lunch," he said.

But she asked him to stay. She wanted to hear all he knew of her Uncle Daniel. Curiously she no longer felt repelled by this man; nursing him had softened her aversion. It was several days before his nose and throat healed enough to allow him to converse. There was still nothing in the newspapers.

He asked her for books. She brought a selection and was astonished to see him choose one of her mother's favourites, Gérard de Nerval's *Les Filles de feu*.

"I saw them cut poor Gérard down," he said. "He hanged himself one snowy night from an iron grating outside a brothel in the Rue de la Vieille-Lanterne. He was found by a drunk, walking home with a *grisette*. The drunk said, 'Thank you,' believing Gérard had merely stepped aside to let them pass. But the girl said, 'You fool, can't you see he's hanged himself!' And the man said, 'He has his hat on. Nobody hangs himself with his hat on.' Then the girl giggled and said, 'In times like these, why not?' "

He flipped idly through the pages, reading nothing. "I was there with Arsène Houssaye soon after. Gérard had just finished a translation for the Théâtre Français and Houssaye had paid him, so it wasn't lack of money. Houssaye tried to arrange a funeral at Notre Dame but the archbishop insisted on a note from the doctor, because it was a suicide. To protect the church, you see. D'you know what the doctor wrote?"

Abigail shook her head; her eyes did not leave the man's face.

"He wrote: 'Your Grace—Gérard de Nerval hanged himself because he saw his madness face to face.' It was enough. When we buried him in Père-Lachaise there was no oration, but Houssaye turned to me and said, 'He hanged himself on Friday the twenty-sixth—twice thirteen—in the Rue de la Vieille-Lanterne at the bottom of the Rue de la Tuerie, near the ravine, and under the symbolic sign of a key. Did he think of all that? How else can we explain this inexplicable thing? This death must have its morality and its profound significance in such symbols.' "

"What did he mean?" Abigail asked.

"Houssaye was always saying things like that. But he was director of the Théâtre Français. He could make such wind sound like Socrates. Like you and your friends in the café. You think that truth drifts like gossamer in the wind."

"How do you explain it, then?"

"The doctor's note was closest. Because it told the truth by opposites. That is how it protected the Church—and the rest of us. 'He saw his madness face to face'! He saw *our* madness. He saw our whole mad world. He saw all those things you and your friends protect yourselves from seeing behind your ramparts of cleverness. Oh, you are all *very* clever!"

A fit of coughing interrupted him.

"Rue de la Tuerie," he said. "You know *tuerie* means slaughterhouse? Yes, of course. He saw the world has been one long slaughterhouse. Every day, all day, from the first day to this day, somewhere, there is pain inflicted. Someone is tortured, degraded, defiled—not for a passing instant, but for a lifetime. By *us*. Gérard could hear their cries; he saw those people face to face. And the time came when he could no longer look *us* in the face." A distant look came into his eyes. "Daniel could hear them, too—those cries. And he was stronger. You must learn to be proud of him."

"And you? What do you hear?" She just wanted him to go on talking.

"I hear so many things, so many other things." His smile mocked himself. He held up the book. "I'll read this, and its beauty will mask those cries for me."

"Are the police after you?"

"Not very seriously."

"Why not?"

"They have a nose, those bastards. They can sniff out the dangerous revolutionary lurking inside the smooth and polished cabinet minister." Again the self-mocking smile. "And they can sniff out the wet firework even in one who, like me, looks the perfect part. We have an unwritten pact, the police, my revolutionary friends, and me—live and let live."

"Yet Daniel turned to you? Not to his comrades?"

"His comrades! They take their marching orders from History, not from Humanity. Yes, Daniel turned to me because the flaw in me—the thing that failed me as a revolutionary—was by then the only thing in the world on which he could depend: humanity. Oh, I have listened for the Voice of History! No novice ever prayed for a vocation as I prayed to hear that voice. But all I hear is the babble of humanity."

" 'Pity has a human face,' " she said in English.

He looked at her with such a puzzled expression that she, thinking he did not understand, began to translate. But he waved her to silence. Then she saw that he was not puzzled but was searching his memory. "Ah!" he said at last, and went on in English:

> " 'For Mercy has a human heart,
> Pity a human face,
> And Love, the human form divine,
> And Peace, the human dress.' "

She clapped her hands and laughed in sheer delight. "You know Blake?" she asked.

"Who could hear humanity's voice and not hear his!" he said. "And now you must excuse me. *My* voice will be gone in a minute."

He began to read as if she were not there. She watched him. How could she ever have thought him repulsive! He radiated such understanding and such fellow-feeling. There was a—a *greatness* in him. Yes, it was not too strong a word. He was not great like a great painter, or a great statesman, or a great wit—great anything. He was simply a great man, whatever the world's opinion of him. She could see it.

"You mustn't leave here until you are quite well again," she said.

*   *   *

"Will your friends not miss you?" he asked her next day when once again she came and sat at his bedside.

"Friends," she said. "I'm half ashamed of them now."

To move his glass eye he had to tilt his head to one side, right or left. It gave him a kindly demeanour, even when he did not intend it. But he intended it now. "Ah, now that's my fault. I am an old man and I've lived too long—almost seventy years—in the shadow of approaching death. And too long in the company of impatient men. Everything I say is too brief and too confident. If that has made you ashamed of your friends, then—"

"Half ashamed," she corrected.

He beamed at her. "That's good. It means you were only half listening to me. Which, even so, is more than I deserve."

"Are you really getting on for seventy?" she asked.

"This," he tapped his cranium, "thinks so. But this," he thumped his chest, "doesn't agree."

Laughing, she asked him to tell her about Daniel.

He told her everything he knew, from the beginning to the end. The beginning, for Daniel, had been a strike at his mill; he had been the leader. The millowner had agreed to their demands on condition they permanently disbanded the union. "It was a terrible moment for Daniel, and he never was certain he had made the right decision. It cost him your mother's love and the lives of his little brother and sister. If he accepted those terms, the owner would see to it that they could never organize again. If he refused, the strike would be long and bitter. Children would starve. Worse still, he would be jailed—leaving your mother, who was only seventeen, to look after three even younger children. Yet he hearkened to the voice of history and refused the millowner's conditions. The last night of his freedom was spent with three Chartist gentlemen, planning his defence—all of them knowing it was futile, for he was choosing martyrdom. And all that evening your mother—that hungry, worried little seventeen-year-old—begged him to mend the door of their hovel. She would have to go out to work, you see, and leave the two infants indoors all day, alone."

"I remember!" Abigail said. "She showed us the place once. She said a boar got in and ate one of the children alive! She has never got over it, I think. She found one of the little boy's arms up in the rafters. The little girl died of rat bites soon after."

The man shut his eyes. It was some time before he resumed his tale. "Daniel never mended that door. And she never forgave him. But who was right? Who *is* right? The man who struggles for his family? Or the man who makes the oppressed of the world his family, and struggles for them?"

"My mother struggled for her family—for us."

"And she's now the Countess of Wharfedale and, some say, the richest lady in England. And her brother ends penniless in the Tiber and not a paragraph to mark his passing. The moral seems clear, does it not? But is it? Does your heart find it as clear-cut as that?"

She shook her head vehemently.

He went on to tell her of Daniel's imprisonment and transportation to Australia—the hopelessness he felt out there, the guilt at the children's deaths, his sister's rejection, the utter degradation of convict life, then the hardening of his resolve to fight all oppression and inhumanity, wherever he saw it. Then the pardon—too late, for it merely showed him that the liberal spirit is a weak spirit. The return home—the long road: night school, study, endless endless discussion. And then the turning point—the realization as he travelled through Europe of the sheer *size* of the problem that faced him.

"He often said to me, 'My brother-in-law'— He meant your father, John Stevenson as he then was—'my brother-in-law would hate to be told it, but he was the biggest revolutionary teacher in Europe. All those railways he built! Until we could travel around on them we had no idea of the size of the conspiracy ranged against us. But after that any working man who travelled through industrial England, let alone Europe, and thought he could achieve anything by combining against just one master was insane. It wasn't Karl Marx who taught me to fight a class war—it was my brother-in-law's railways!' "

During his life Daniel had been on the wanted list of every police force in Europe. He lived in a poverty more grinding than the poverty he fought to end. He was birched, flogged, jailed at hard labour, sentenced to death, reprieved, and deported more times than he could remember. Where there was a revolution—a crack in the facade that might bring the whole edifice tumbling down—Daniel was there, on the barricades, on the committees, shouting encouragement, drawing up demands, covenants, death lists. He shirked nothing. And *they* never defeated him.

"In the end it was his own class defeated him, the working class. As their lot improved, they grew less interested in the Revolution. Instead they wanted more of the same. He wanted to destroy capitalism; they wanted only to milk it. He saw it as a ravening wolf, to be shot; to them it was a goose whose eggs had recently been laid gold-plated—perhaps they might in time be all gold!" He shook his head and sighed. "It was, you see, a mature form of the argument he had had with your mother so long ago: do we settle now for what we can get, or do we fight on until we get the whole structure of things right? Like a black shadow, that question reached forward half a century and extinguished Daniel's light."

He was silent awhile, as if unsure how much she wished to hear.

"Go on," she said.

"It killed him, years ago. These last years have been like a walking death. He saw the working class settle for the gilded eggs and suddenly he realized how rare in the world are people like himself—those who will sacrifice their comfort, freedom, dignity, family, themselves, everything, for the sake of an ideal. He never expected to see the Revolution in his own lifetime. He *hoped*, of course, but he was a realist, too. He had travelled the railways! Yet it never even crossed his mind to give up the struggle on that account. Such a man *is* rare, as saints are rare. And suddenly he saw it.

"But worse—oh far, far worse!—he saw what that meant. The Revolution, you see, would never be a mass revolt. It would always be the work of a rare minority who would have to impose it by force on the mass of the people. That's the vision which killed him. When he realized he was, inevitably and necessarily, working to replace the terror and oppression of capitalism with the terror and oppression of idealism, the heart went out of him.

"Then he was a clockwork toy, running down, doing all the old tricks but ever more slowly. In the end he was so slow that even the Italian police could catch him! The rest you know, or can guess, or—like me—is unimportant."

The tears in her eyes prevented her from seeing him clearly; the lump in her throat made it hard to say, "If I had known, I'd have helped you with him to the Tiber. I would have said a prayer over him."

"He didn't go without a prayer," the man said. "Atheist as I am and as he was, if there is a God, I believe He would rather hear prayers from atheists than hypocrites. 'If I had only known . . .' is the cry of the bourgeoisie whenever its eyes are forcibly opened."

She put her hands to her face and wept silently into them, ashamed for him to see her. He made no move to comfort or touch her. When she grew calm again, she felt the need to explain to him.

"When you first asked for help," she said, "and I refused you, all I saw was a man who frightened me talking about a man my mother detested. But *you!* You knew all—all this story you've just told me, and more. And you had just sat through an evening of me and my friends—all that bright, inane chatter, while your friend, my uncle, was dying here. How is it you can still bring yourself even to talk to me? I am not worthy to do you the most menial service."

He sank his head to his hands and pushed his fingers up into the fringe of his hair, massaging his scalp violently. "I must say it again!" He looked up at her with a smile. "I am an old man. Death is too near me. I feel his breath mocking mine. It makes me impatient to speak, so I speak like a telegram. I say what is significant, but I omit what's important: I omit the truth. All you've said is true. All I've said is true. But the entire truth? No one ever says it. After every statement you must yourself supply a *but*. Your lover says, 'I love you,' and you say, *but* . . . Your mother says, 'Daniel deserted me and killed the two babies,' and you can now say, *but* . . ."

She grinned ruefully. "I say I've lived forty-two years a trivial and shallow woman."

"So you say. I don't know you. You must be able to supply many *buts* to answer that. I know only one."

"Which is . . . ?"

"But wait for the next forty-two!"

*   *   *

"Daniel's favourite phrase was, 'It's no accident that . . .' Everything to him was part of a larger structure—a conspiracy, an inevitable tide of history, something of that sort. Mere chance terrified him, because it could pull the rug out from under his feet at any moment. If he was on a train and a wheel overheated and they had to stop, he'd at once look for the secret police, or make a note to check the political loyalties of the wheelgreasers' union. There had to be a cause other than mere accident, you see."

She nodded and hung on his next sentence. Now that he knew her better and was nearly well again in himself, he was relaxed enough to speak in long detours that opened up for her the most fascinating windows into a life she could never have envisaged.

"Why did I tell you that?" he asked. "Oh, yes! I was myself about to say, 'It was no accident.' But it really was no accident that I brought him to you. He followed all your lives, your mother's and father's, of course, and also all your brothers' and sisters'. But most especially yours. He was astonished by you—and very proud. Things you wrote which he liked— little phrases or startling ways of putting things—he'd learn them by heart and work them into his speeches. Even when they weren't in the least appropriate. People laughed, of course, but when they understood, they liked him for it. He had no children of his own."

He sighed and shook his head, vanishing for a moment into a reverie.

"If he had lived, he'd be sitting here now, quoting you to yourself by the ream! You'd be really embarrassed then!"

"Yes. I'd have shattered one more of his dreams."

He smiled at her, with something of a challenge in his look. "You underestimate his powers. Even at seventy. Even burned out. He was still no ordinary man. You don't mind my going on about him?"

"Heavens no!"

"He was my lodestone. I always hoped that through him I would one day hear the Voice of History. As clearly as he heard it. He might have made you hear it, though. He often said that if you were with us, we could really have made the masters tremble!"

"What would the voice have told me, I wonder? I've never seen myself as Joan of Arc."

"No. I doubt if Joan of Arc did, either. But let's try and work it out. Tell me about yourself and your life. From inside, I mean. I know the outside."

She told him then. Everything. She thought it might take an hour. It was just after lunch when she began; she did not finish until well into the evening. He was silent for a long time, but as he appeared to be deep in thought she left him be. Eventually, though, the silence became too much to endure.

"Well?" she asked. "No voice?"

"It's too big," he said. "It can't be settled tonight. There's only one thing we can settle tonight."

"What's that?"

"I am an old man and even now I hear the men with the darkness crossing my courtyard. It makes me impatient, so forgive me if you think me brusque and unmannerly, but will you sleep with me tonight?"

There was that *buzz!* The note she had missed for so long. What was about to happen was, beyond all question, right. She began to undress.

"No questions?" he asked. "No reservations?"

"None."

*　　*　　*

Next morning when he saw she was awake he said, "There was one question you should've asked me, you know."

"Mmmmm?"

"My name."

She slipped her arms around him and tickled his ribs. "Why don't I just go on thinking of you as God?" she said.

He chuckled. "Because not even the British Embassy would have the arrogance to issue me a passport in that name."

"Passport?"

"Yes. We must go back to England."

"*Festina lente!*" She sat up. "We are not about to conduct my life at a revolutionary tempo!"

"Well, well and good. But my name—is—" He chuckled. "Look at her! She's expecting some shattering revelation. Can't you even guess?"

"You aren't—" she asked, suddenly horrified, "not Ignaz Porzelijn!"

He laughed. "There is still enough imp in me to consider that pretence. Because your relief and laughter to find that I'm not that man would be so great. But no, I'm not. You've never heard of me. I'm the man whose name is last but two or three on every police list. I am Victor Bouvier."

"And the others? The last two or three below you?"

"They were invented by informers with a conscience. So in the revolutionary dossiers I have always stood at the division between illusion and reality. It's time I found a more secure mode of existence."

When he saw the alarm in her face, he chuckled and stroked her head and neck, making her tremble.

"There's that imp," he said. "I never was a revolutionary. I hoped, of course. But I also learned to fear. Daniel was my greatest friend. Yet he was also the greatest warning anyone could have against the perils of all fanaticism. So don't worry. No one's after me."

"Why do you talk like a revolutionary then? False passports and lists and informers!"

He shrugged. "Wishful thinking. Or what a conjuror calls 'misdirection.' When you hear me at it, look around for a bourgeois. They bring it on me like a fit. I only do it *pour épater la bourgeoisie.*"

As he spoke he lowered a pointing finger onto her brow, between her eyebrows. She did not blink. Their eyes dwelled in each other's and a marvellous, rocklike certainty filled her. "I love you, Victor," she said, creeping into his embrace. "Enough for a lifetime."

"So little?" He pretended to be sad.

She clung to him. "Don't talk like that," she begged. "Don't say such things!"

Chapter 39

The biographies she had imagined for him could not have been wider of their mark. He was the son of a petty nobleman, too petty to bother even the bitterest and most ardent revolutionary—or, as Victor said, "By the time they might have worked down the list to my family, they were much too busy denouncing and slaughtering one another."

During the 1830s he had been a young man about Paris—which meant he was a poet, songwriter, tragedian, romantic, follower of fashion, revolutionary, comedian, antiphilistine, and, above all, a tireless seducer of gullible girls and older men's mistresses. It was the Paris of Henri Murger's *Scènes de la vie de bohème,* which Puccini later made famous in his opera *La Bohème.*

Victor had known them all. He had shared an apartment for a time with Gérard de Nerval, Théophile Gautier, Arsène Houssaye, and Camille Rogier. It made Abigail's Roman circle seem the very depths of tame respectability. They worked furiously all day, Gérard on *The Queen of Sheba*, Théo on *Mademoiselle de Maupin*, Arsène on *La Pécheresse*, and Camille on his famous illustrations for Byron and *The Tales of Hoffmann*.

Abigail, who knew and loved all these works, was thrilled to think of their being created cheek by jowl in one big salon. "And you?" she asked.

He laughed. "I wrote songs and ballads for street vendors. Thirty a day. All of them very good. I was the highest paid among us. For six songs we could dine at the Place de L'Odéon; for two more we could all go on to the Café Voltaire! Once a week we went to La Chaumière, where the girls were the most beautiful in Paris—and the most simpleminded. One of them told Arsène that a wise girl was one who allowed only one lover at a time! Arsène and Ourliac, who wrote *Suzanne*, had devised a fantastic quadrille depicting the complete life of Napoleon. It ended in a flourish of pistol shots and broken chairs, which was the signal for us to descend on those *horizontales* and *odalisques* like the Assyrians on the Sabine women."

He caught her eye. "It was the Assyrians?" he asked.

She shook her head. "It was the Romans, under Romulus."

He, too, shook his head, but in sadness. "Oh, Abbie, Abbie . . . you are going to be no fun! We tried to pay them in sonnets and songs, but all they said was 'Can we eat sonnets? Can we wear your songs?' What gems they refused! No one understood romanticism, even then, when it flourished in the midst of them. Mind you, I never dressed like a romantic. I was always the height of fashion. The others used to mock me and Gavarni, who was the same; but I noticed that the girls didn't repulse me and Gavarni as ardently as they fought off the others, with their dishevelled clothes and matted hair and general contempt for soap."

It was a firm tradition among them that youth ended precisely on the knell of one's twenty-fifth birthday—so much so that Théo had to start lying about his age when he wanted to go on pursuing a young *grisette* called Cydalise, who was Camille Rogier's mistress and was dying of consumption. Some of Gautier's best poetry came out of that forlorn pursuit.

"Of course, youth doesn't end at twenty-five," Victor said. "I've still got mine, even if it tastes sour at one or two of its edges—which isn't surprising after two marriages, two revolutions, and the life of a bourgeois rentier."

At that magic age of twenty-five he had won (at a game of cards where he had believed the stakes to be in mere centimes instead of thousands of francs) the Salon du Pré, a concert hall near the Tuileries in the heart of fashionable Paris. In August, when only tourists roamed the city, they used to stage human and tame-animal acts there. That was how he had lost his eye, and gained his scarred cheek—a knife thrower too drunk to take proper aim. So much for any supposed connection with revolution and romance!

After his convalescence he had become interested in the whole improbable business of presenting spectacles for the public. Soon he thought he knew enough about it to branch out into small theatres and music halls, even into *poses plastiques* and *tableaux vivants*. In the provinces he built a number of theatres for the serious drama. His feel for public entertainment made him a very rich man within ten years.

By the time Louis Napoleon came to power, after the revolution of 1848, Victor was married and lived in a large house near the Bois de Boulogne. There were no children.

"The very day he came back, I had every windowbox in the house filled with Corsican violets. In the days of the Bourbons, you know, violets were hardly ever seen in Paris. They said I was clairvoyant, but it was only the same instinct that made me a good showman and impresario. I think I

had a better sense of history than Daniel, though he made history his
god.''

Abigail and Victor went on many long walks around Rome that
autumn. He was a compulsive memory man; he had known everyone,
performed discreet services for every great lady and little cocotte, helped
grand ministers and struggling artists out of difficulties, dined every
leading singer and dancer who ever visited Paris, saved the Kaiser from
being crushed by an elephant, procured two mistresses for the emperor . . .
a rich, ordinary, useful, useless life.

"You moved in such a different world from Daniel, I wonder you ever
met," she said.

"Oh, we didn't meet then. In fact, we didn't meet until the siege of
'seventy-one. I turned my house into a hospital during the siege and all
through the days of the Commune. Daniel was brought to me wounded. I
hid him from his would-be executioners.''

"Was that what changed you?''

"Changed?''

"From the sort of man you were in your youth.''

He was unwilling to answer; he had to find a seat, as if the confession
would take all his concentration. They happened to be in the Via Veneto,
so the obvious place was a café. He waited until their cups were brought
before he continued.

"I changed, I think, in 'sixty-five, when one of my mistresses was
thrown into prison—by her husband.''

"What for?''

"For being unfaithful. Oh, it could happen. It was legal. It still is, for
all I know. The same thing happened to one of Victor Hugo's mistresses.
The worst part of it was that the husband himself was notorious; no
woman was safe. Of course, I got the wife released almost at once—knowing which ears to bend, which arms to twist. But she was ruined socially. I
gave her a job, naturally, and I think she's found a tolerable happiness.
But for me the zest of that way of life had gone. I began to look for
something else. I thought I had found it with Daniel—that was after the
death of my second wife. But—'' He shrugged. "I suppose I'm still
looking.''

"Like me.''

He smiled and took her hand. "We shall find it.'' He looked at her and
laughed. "Probably right under our very noses!''

She wrote a small memoir of Daniel, called *The Death of Daniel
Telling*. She had no thought of publication, but his death, with, as Victor

had said, not a paragraph to mark his passing, irked her, and she wanted to record all that Victor knew of him before the memory dimmed.

Victor's compulsive reminiscing was most useful. Within a month she felt she knew her uncle as well as if she had lived a large part of her life at his side. But her admiration for him was dented when she passed from Victor's judgements to the primary sources of Daniel's own inspiration—the writings of Marx and Engels.

She read *Capital* as far as chapter 3—or about two chapters further than most nonbelievers manage; it left her with nothing to admire in Daniel beyond his staying power.

"Never mind," Victor told her reassuringly, "Jules Vallès, who was one of the leaders of the Commune, always said that book was unreadable."

The *Communist Manifesto* reminded her, in a curious way, of her brother Boy. She had once heard Boy say, quite seriously, that if only everyone would obey the Ten Commandments and the commandment to love one another, all the world's problems would vanish and we would have an overnight paradise. He had been at university at the time, too—no callow schoolboy. Something of the same puerile idealism ran through every paragraph of the *Manifesto*.

"Listen to this," she said to Victor. " 'Insofar as the exploitation of one individual by another diminishes, so will the exploitation of nations by other nations also diminish. Insofar as class hatred ceases to exist within each nation, so will hostility between nations also vanish.' Really! Even forty years ago that would have been hard to swallow. But now! Did Daniel honestly believe that?"

Victor, who freely scorned Daniel's communism to her, did not like to hear her at the same game independently. He shrugged awkwardly. "You have to see it in context," he said. "What Anglican ever believed all Thirty-nine Articles—or scrupulously practised all he preached?"

She saw in this evasion a shadow of Daniel himself. It helped her understand how bitter his end must have been—the end of a life in which ideals and reality had grown steadily farther apart, tearing him apart, too, the visionary man from the everyday worker.

"All his life," she wrote in the closing pages of her memoir of him, "he cried out: 'Men are born free, yet everywhere they are in chains!' Toward the end he saw that his listeners were not actually in chains at all. They were in the pub, enjoying a beer, or at Epsom Downs, cheering on the Derby. They enjoyed his speeches, to be sure, for he was a master of rhetoric; but they enjoyed him as little more than one of the serious turns on life's unending stage. If he had dared to proclaim the Revolution for the following Saturday, they would half-promise to join in; but he knew they had already half-promised to paper the parlour, too."

Her final words were: "The streets of Rome were rivers that night, but not of blood. The Tiber burst its banks. The swirling waters carried Daniel Telling off, yet did him no other harm. By then no fire was left to quench."

Victor, when he read her draft, said, "But . . . ?"

She added an epilogue: "But Daniel Telling was right. His vision of injustice and wrong amongst us was right. His cure—that those who make wealth must share it, and thus share power and dignity, too—was right. His sacrifice of all that makes an ordinary life tolerable was right. Then what is left is left for us. And what *is* left?"

Victor chuckled. "You have a sting in your tail. An epée in your epilogue. You realize *no one* is going to like this memoir. Not of the Left nor of the Right."

She laughed. "Left and Right are, 'inevitably and necessarily,' as we say, out of step."

Chapter 40

Somehow her desire to paint began to dwindle the moment Victor came into her life. Perhaps she had been working up to this break for a long time, she thought. How else to explain her shame at the trivialities he had witnessed that very first night? The heart of the matter was that she would never be more than a competent, talented, but very minor painter. She was not even of the stature of Mary Cassatt or Berthe Morisot—and heaven knew they were minor enough. Until Victor came, the fact had not worried her in the least; but his coming had kindled something within her, an old sense of ambition.

Exactly what she wished to achieve she did not know. Painting was, for her, a cul-de-sac. A new literary ambition then? The felled oak of *Into a Narrow Circle* lay across that avenue. Yet no other suggestion offered itself—only the raw feeling that her life was meant for something more than an obscurely pleasant passage of days and nights in Rome. She had to resign herself to the hope that something would turn up.

They spent Christmas in Venice, where the slow pace, on water or on foot, exactly suited her waiting mood. She had never seen that most startling and beautiful of all cities in winter. The drift of cold, astringent mists along the canals, the black progress of rain squalls over the face of the lagoon, the forlorn and shuttered desertion of the apparatus of summer, the classical grandeur of palaces and churches, indifferent alike to the waters that were slowly drowning them and to the people who did nothing to prevent such a costly death . . . it was like a ringing down of the curtain between two acts. She hoped it was like that.

Back in springtime Rome, where the rebirth that belonged properly to the city lent a little of its colour to her life, she still found no object for the ambition whose presence and power were now undeniable. She was not unhappy for it, quite the contrary; she had never for a moment doubted the rightness of her love for Victor nor the depth of his love for her. Obituaries often spoke of couples who lived in perfect harmony through fifty years of marriage, with never a cross word or even a reproving glance. Once, a long time ago, she had written that her idea of hell was to be invited to write the biography of such a couple, for what was there to be said about them other than that they loved each other. A lot. Every day. For fifty years.

Yet that was how she and Victor lived. No one in her family would have believed it. And if his tales of his wild youth were only half true, no one who knew him would believe it either. But it was so. Every day was as tranquil and loving as every other day. They read, they slept, they walked, ate, made love, went to the theatre or opera, and talked and talked . . . and it was an eternal renewal of the first happy day of an affair. And far from thinking it dull, she found it brought her the greatest comfort—more even than that: the profoundest sense of security.

But, naturally, that very fastness of their love only heightened the feeling that her life was still fallow. What was that security *for?* Not for itself—that would be as absurd as taking out an insurance policy to insure against nothing but the failure of the policy. It had to be for something else. But what? It was a return to the same old question.

Lack of an answer did not leave her life empty, though. Apart from Roman occasions and friends, there was a steady stream of people from London and Paris. The anarchic layout of the atelier and Victor's gift for appearing to "happen by" rather than to live there preserved her reputation among casual callers.

One such visitor was Grant Allen, the novelist, nearly two years her junior. When the brilliant magazine *London* failed back in 1879, she had written her condolences to him, saying that his contributions had been among the best. She had offered what help she could through her connections, but it turned out that he needed none. She and he had since kept up an occasional correspondence, but this was the first time he had ever visited her in Rome.

He had an idea of doing a guide book based on his own notion of the unifying powers of art and history. He was the sort of man who had a dozen irons in the fire—he wrote on evolution (Spencerian, not Darwinian) and physics and falling in love; he reviewed for numerous periodicals and wrote short stories for many more. But that afternoon in Rome he was obviously withholding something. And as he left he asked if he might come back the following day.

When he returned he confessed that he was thinking of writing a novel on an entirely new theme: the Free Woman—a woman who loves and yet refuses to marry, out of respect for the dignity of her sex. Though he and his own wife were happily married, he regarded that as a lucky accident; for many women—as J. S. Mill had shown twenty years earlier—marriage was no more than servitude.

"In a legal brothel with but one client," Abigail said, testing how far he was prepared to go into this shocking business of being plain honest.

He choked and said he wasn't going that far; his heroine's objections would be more on a spiritual plane.

"Yet you must be honest, Mr. Allen," she said.

He began to look uncomfortable.

"Your heroine must still be a woman."

"Ah!" His eyes lit up. "But what is a woman, Lady Abigail? A Free Woman? We know her only as servitude has revealed her."

"I think you'll find," Abigail said, "that she's very much the same. Free Woman will still defer to that man whose manliness makes him her natural master. If she's a mother, she'll sacrifice everything of herself to the sacred ideals of motherhood."

"Then so it shall be!" he cried, delighted to find that his novel would be far easier to write than he had dared to hope.

After Allen had gone, Victor stared at her a long time, willing her to look at him. She did not.

He coughed.

She pinched her lips together, trying not to smile, but only succeeded in half smothering her laughter.

"That was wicked," he said.

"It was necessary."

"Oh? That was always Daniel's word for something he was half ashamed of doing."

"Well, I'm not at all ashamed of this. You know how you can sometimes see everything complete—a truth? All at once. You don't have to work towards it."

"You mean when the alarm bells start ringing? Or ought to, if you've learned any sense."

"Don't spoil it, now. Such moments are rare enough as it is. But that's what I felt when I heard Grant Allen talking just now. At first I was angry, because he seemed to be rewriting *Into a Narrow Circle*; but then I realized he could never do it. And that's where the whole idea came from. You'd call it an 'imp.' Grant Allen's a fine fellow—a first-rate essayist. I like him enormously. But even he, I'm sure, would admit he's only a second-rate novelist. And that's what makes him the ideal person to write the rubbish I've just poured into his ear. A first-rate writer, someone like Shaw, for instance, would see through it within a couple of paragraphs. But a second-rate writer—by definition—is someone who can take all our fashionable prejudices and make them ring like eternal truths."

"But why? Why d'you want this lie about women to 'ring like an eternal truth'?"

"Well, that's what I'm talking about—this idea I saw all at once. Grant Allen's book is going to be a shocker. That means it'll be very popular—which means a lot of men will read it (no doubt with one hand in their pocket to disguise their—ah—literary interest). And I suddenly thought to myself, what honeyed words might I whisper to them through the medium of this book? And then it came to me: *See!* the book will whisper, *the liberated woman is still a Woman! The Manly Man can still bend her to his will. Motherhood is still her destiny. So she's really no threat to you—no threat at all! Why bother to resist her? Let her clamour for liberation. Encourage her. She thinks she's found the pass through into the promised land. Let her take it. And let her discover for herself that it's just the same old box canyon.*"

"One book will do all that?"

"No, but 'every little helps,' as the soldier said on London Bridge." It was one of Annie's catch phrases; Abigail had no idea what it meant, nor did she know why it popped into her mind at this moment.

"So!" He smiled. "You've learned a trick or two from Daniel."

"Not a bit! It's an ancient Christian tradition—doing good by stealth."

"The trouble with doing good is that it becomes a habit. For a time you'll be happy enough merely hunting about for second-rate novelists to pervert; but then you'll begin to crave stronger meat—people who really can change the course of history: chefs, racing tipsters, even"—he looked aghast—"theatre impresarios! Your depravity will recognize no bounds."

She laughed, for it was a parody of the familiar argument against allowing young girls to hold hands with young men.

He joined her laughter but when it died he said, "Nevertheless, I was making a serious point: will you leave it to Grant Allen, or do something on your own account?"

She was still smiling. "It's a question that answers itself, isn't it? I can't just throw *his* hat into the ring."

"I see."

"D'you approve, darling?"

"I? Does it matter?"

She ran to where he sat and, kneeling between his thighs, hugged him fiercely. "I'm not like Daniel," she said. "I won't sacrifice the things that are dearest to me for mere principle. And dearest of all is the love I've found with you."

"Mr. Allen!" he shouted over her head at the long-departed guest. "A little demonstration for you!"

"Be serious."

Then he lifted her onto his lap and kissed her. "Oh, I'll be serious. I'll go where you go. And every day of our lives I shall renew"—he kissed her again—"my amazement."

"We'll go back to London."

He nodded.

"And we'll get married."

He nodded again. "In Paris," he said. "To show everyone how absolutely serious we are about it."

"Yes!" She was delighted. "And we can see César and Celia, too."

Later, in bed, he asked, "Exactly what shall we do in London?"

She sighed. "I don't know. Not if you want me to say 'exactly.' I want to do what I tried to do with *Into a Narrow Circle*." She pointed at César's paintings of her. "I want to find a voice like César's. Look at the physical love in those brushstrokes. You can see in them—anyone can see in them—how much we enjoyed each other. But, as pictures, they're not salacious. They're not crude. And nor, on the other hand, are they cold and clinical. They are exactly what the experience itself was—happy and natural. That's what I want to find—a happy and natural voice to talk about physical love. Not pornographic and not clinical."

He nodded but remained silent, thinking, for quite a while. "It's no small thing," he said at last. "So much else must change before people could listen to that voice without growing hysterical."

"Oh, Victor!" she said ruefully. "Who knows it better than I do!"

"You're not just asking men to change their ideas about women. You're asking women to change their notion of themselves. That's always the hardest thing."

"Well, don't talk me out of it before I've begun."

He laughed and took up her hand. "You began this long ago. Over twenty years. And so, in a way, did I—from the other side. I'd count it an honour to join in your search."

"What do you think we ought to do, darling?"

"Perhaps the first thing is to throw our weight into any movement already working for greater equality between men and women—because that's one of the changes that'll have to happen first."

"The suffragists?" She pulled a face. "Look at the number of idiotic *men* who have the vote! I'd sooner join a movement to take it away from them than one that wants to add an equal number of idiotic women to the rolls. I wouldn't even give myself the vote."

"All the same, the ideas you have to change are the ideas of your own class—the ruling class. The suffragists all belong to that same class. They're a ready-made audience. We shouldn't dismiss them too hastily."

The calculation in his words made her reconsider her objections to the suffragists; until now her aversion had been more instinctive than reasoned.

"Votes aren't important," she said, thinking aloud. "Nor money, nor power."

His eyebrows shot up.

"It's bigger than that," she said urgently. "More important. A bigger freedom. If I say it's the freedom to love, that sounds trite. But that's what it is: the freedom to love. Look at the way *we* can love—not because you're a man in your world and I'm a woman in mine, but because we're *people*. And because we're in the same world. Most men and women can't love like that. And it's wrong—they should be able to. There shouldn't be these prison walls of manliness and femininity always shutting us off. I want to tear them down. I don't know how, but I do know it's the only worthwhile job in sight. And until those barriers are gone, nothing else is worth struggling for. All the votes and power and jobs in this whole manridden world aren't worth a pinch of snuff without that."

His smile, superficially, was mocking, but she could see he was really delighted. "Marching orders?" he asked.

Chapter 41

Celia, now over forty, looked like one of Renoir's girls—firmly plump, earth-motherly, and upholstered with warm experiences. César's once black hair and beard had turned slate gray and, though not receding, it had thinned. They both looked too old to be the parents of three such lively youngsters, Hélène, Bernard, and Delfine, the youngest, who was just toddling. Cries of *"Attention, Delfine!"* punctuated Abigail's and Victor's entire visit.

They had a house on the southwestern outskirts of the city, on the fringe of the Parc de Saint Cloud, quite near César's parents' place. On the side that faced the road this house had the aspect of a prison, with high stone walls pierced by the narrowest windows, rising directly from the edge of the foot pavement. This wall continued, almost at the full height of the house, all along the roadside edge of the property. Massive oak gates, panelled solid, gave coach access to a minute drive, really no more than the length of the house.

The contrast between the public and private sides could not have been greater. Only when you were within the walls did you realize that the house was L-shaped. Here, on the garden side, all the windows were large, right down to floor level, and gave out directly to the grounds or, on the upper floors, to wide iron verandahs festooned with clematis and wistaria. The garden was magnificently planted, on a gentle slope that ran downhill and merged into the park itself. A place more private, so close to the city, would have been impossible to devise.

On the third day of their visit, Victor went in to Paris to make the final arrangements for their wedding, which was to be held the following Monday in the town hall of the eighth arrondissement, in which his own house was situated; the house itself was shuttered and empty, and they had yet to decide whether to sell or to keep it.

César and Celia took Abigail for a walk around their garden. They showed her the pond where Monet had painted the lilies, and the arbor where Rodin liked to sit and sketch the trees; but mostly they talked with laughing nostalgia of their years together in Rome. At one point Celia was called away to comfort Delfine, who, not having her parents on hand to call "*Attention!*" at every other step, had seized the chance to fall over and graze a knee.

"So, César," Abigail said as they continued their walk, "it's all turned out very well. You're famous, Celia's happy, and Victor and I are about to do stupendous things."

"What?"

"Oh, we haven't made up our minds yet. But wait and see."

He cleared his throat. "You remember the things I said our last night in Rome?"

"Oh! Dear me, César—so long ago?"

"That's good, if you've forgotten. I just wanted to tell you, I didn't mean what I said."

"Whatever that was."

"Marvellous, excellent," he answered; but she could tell from his very insistence that he was annoyed she would not remember. "I said those things because I was sorry for you."

"Oh, *those* things! Well, I knew that, César, dear. I thought it was sweet of you."

"I was never in love with you."

"Of course you weren't. I'd never have let you into my room if I'd even suspected it. The danger would've been too great. Especially as I could never have loved you back."

"Hmm." This was not quite the conversation he had hoped for.

She laughed and dug him in the ribs. "Don't be so *French!*" she chided. "Such a petulant French man-child! Celia's been spoiling you, I can see. You know we could never—never—"

"Why not? I don't see that." He was only half jolted out of his disappointed smugness.

"Because we're brother and sister. I mean we're too similar. What could I have given you? More of yourself. Or you me? More of myself. Rivers can feed anything except their own sources." It was a blatant lie, of course, but it passed his guard.

"You literary people! You were always too literary to be a good painter."

"Your first lesson . . . you remember? Tree—house—cloud! You were so kind to me, César. You may think you only taught me one or two things about painting; but really it was about art—all art. You changed my writing, too, you know. But even more than that you helped me discover so much about love and life. That's the debt I really owe you. Whatever you tried to offer on that last night in Rome—comfort or whatever it was—that wasn't important compared with the things you'd helped me to see already. That's what I'll always remember, and love you for." She smiled to stop him looking so soulful. "As sister for brother, of course!"

It satisfied him. He was jovial again. How odd, she thought, that he, so self-contained and so assured of his genius, should have craved this small eulogy from her, a comparative nobody.

*   *   *

On paper the French civil-marriage ceremony is a dull and brief affair, designed, as Victor pointed out, to offer no competition to the worldly glory of its religious counterpart. But the mayor, an old friend of his and a freethinker from Bourbon times, managed to endow it with all the ecstasy the French language could deliver, which was no small measure. Abigail would naturally have preferred an Anglican service, but she would not force Victor into the hypocrisy it would entail. When it came to their civil vows she was astonished to hear Victor addressed as "monsieur le Baron."

"What was that?" she asked afterwards.

He was embarrassed. "While we were in Venice, it seems, a distant uncle died and the title has descended on me, baroness."

"La Baronne de Bouvier . . . Baroness de Bouvier . . ." She tried it in both languages. "Either way it sounds most forbidding."

He shrugged. "We can ignore it."

"No, no. It could be useful. It's a battle-winning name if ever I heard one—I quail at the sound of it myself. Is there a château or anything?"

"Nothing."

"Madame la Baronne, eh! Well, no one can say I sound like a lower servant any more."

This visit to Paris was, in a sense, their honeymoon—at least, it was the only one they wanted; but Victor asked her if there was anywhere she particularly wanted to go, as a special mark of the occasion. She said she would like to see Gérard de Nerval's grave. Victor's story of Gérard's tragic death had been the turning point in her feelings toward him. She regretted the wish when she saw how glum a face he made, but from then on he was determined to comply. They went to the Père-Lachaise cemetery the following morning.

They walked up from the Place de la Nation, entering by the Israelite Cemetery. Gérard's grave was almost at the farther corner from there. The path led past the tomb of Abélard and Héloïse.

"Are they really both buried there?" she asked.

"All of her and most of him," Victor said.

"Oh yes, I'd forgotten. What a terrible thing to do to a man."

It was a chill spring day, the opposite of everything conjured up by the phrase "springtime in Paris." The sky was one sheet of unrelieved gray; the damp ground would never dry. Subdued birds watched sullenly from newly clad branches. Gérard's grave was unremarkable, but she was glad to have seen it—to have, in her mind's eye, a locus for the poet's memory, bequeathed to her by Victor in such graphic detail.

"We thought he'd be content enough," he said, "opposite Balzac and Bazin and so close to Nodier."

He shivered and cast his eye wildly around, like an animal seeking escape. She asked why.

"This is the very spot, between the busts of Balzac and Nodier, where the Commune was killed. Nineteen years ago this day, the twenty-seventh of May. It was a Saturday, though, not a Tuesday. And the rain fell . . . mercilessly."

"Were you here?"

"No. I was already being marched to Versailles." He looked away to the east. "You see the wall there?"

She nodded.

"That's *the* wall. They rounded up the handful who surrendered and shot them there. You know how many they shot in all? All over Paris?"

"I remember reading at the time. It was sickening."

"Twenty thousand. The stink reached Versailles. The Seine was red with blood. People think that's poetic fancy but it was literally true. The army went mad, they shot anyone, without reason. They shot all the doctors and nurses in my hospital. I'd have been shot if I'd not been on the roof, hiding Daniel. They said they'd been fired on from my house, but it was a lie. To have stayed in Paris at all—that was the crime. General Valentin said as much. He wanted to kill or transport everyone who'd stayed in Paris."

She shuddered. "Let's go home," she said.

Together they began the walk down to the main gate.

"I went out to look for food and got arrested. And because my hands were black they said I was an incendiarist. I pointed to the red cross on my armband, but the officer had never seen such a symbol. I told him it was the sign of the International Geneva Convention, which was the worst thing I could've said. All he heard was that one word 'International.' I was actually standing in a line of about three hundred people, waiting my turn to be shot, when a sergeant recognized the symbol and sent me over to join the ordinary prisoners. He'd been a medical student in the days when the world had been sane."

"Oh, Victor—why did you indulge my whim to come here? I'm so sorry."

"It's better you should know. I can't"—he gestured at the graves all around—"bury the memory. They shot anyone. If you had a watch, they said it proved you were an official of the Commune and they shot you. Even as an 'ordinary prisoner' I wasn't safe. No one was. We were marched to Versailles by the cavalry under the Marquis de Gallifet. Clemenceau calls him The Swine, but it's an insult to pigs. He stood us all in the Bois de Boulogne and the first thing he did was pick out everyone with white hair. 'You're old enough to have fought against us in the eighteen forty-eight revolution,' he said. 'Well, you shan't live to fight a third time!' There were over a hundred, and he shot them down in front of us, together with all the cripples, or even people he didn't like the look of. 'You're an ugly fellow,' he told the man next to me. 'It'll be a kindness to shoot you.' And when the man pleaded for his life, Gallifet said, 'I've been in every theatre in Paris. This acting of yours doesn't affect me.' Another prisoner told me—this was a different march; there was a march every day for weeks, all led by Gallifet: fifty thousand prisoners in all—this prisoner told me Gallifet had picked out a dozen pretty girls and told them they'd only be raped in Versailles and to spare them that he'd have them shot now. He made the soldiers strip them naked and told them to run. If they made it to the trees, they'd be safe. He held the fire until they were almost there, but—four hundred bullets! What chance had they!"

"The unspeakable—filth! Wasn't he ever punished?"

"Punished! He's in the present government."

"Oh . . . Victor." She closed her eyes tightly, but she was angry, not sick.

"I never want to live in France again. I was mad to suggest we should get married here."

"No! Oh darling, no. I was mad, to suggest coming to this place."

He smiled then and patted her hand on his arm. "No. It's better for you to know. I want you to know—if you can bear it. And it's like a purge for me. I'll tell you it all now and then I need never tell you again."

She nodded.

"More of us died on the way to Versailles. Anyone who stumbled or fainted they shot. And the soldiers relieved their tedium by tying anyone who still looked young and strong, man or woman, to a horse and then trotting, cantering, and finally galloping. No one survived that. And then in Versailles all the respectable bourgeois who had fled from Paris turned out to hit us with canes and parasols. The army tried to cram all forty thousand of us into the cellars and the riding school, and the orangery; of course it wasn't possible. I got sent with two or three hundred others to Saint-Nazaire. They sent thousands of us to islands and ports on the west coast. My party was put in open cages on pontoons in the estuary of the Loire. No regular food, of course, and no water but the river. We were kept alive for sport by ladies and gentlemen who came to throw us scraps of food and watch us fight for it like animals. Those who died were just thrown up onto the quay. I've seen respectable ladies coming down like vultures to poke at the bodies with their parasols; they tried to open the trousers and expose the corpses' genitals. Then they'd stand about laughing. I never saw gentlemen do that to the female corpses."

"It's horrible. Horrible."

"I'm sorry." He was suddenly concerned. He had been speaking in a very light, matter-of-fact way, as if about some atrocity in ancient history, and had assumed from her silence and her measured walk that she had adopted his mood.

"No," she said. "I must know. As you say: It's right I should know. When were you brought to trial?"

"Never. We were all released, those who still lived, just before Christmas. They released about half of all the prisoners without trial."

"My God! If you weren't a revolutionary before, I'd think you'd be—"

"Exactly," he interrupted. "That's what gave the socialists and republicans their great victories in the 'eighties. Even so, it's not safe to have been one of the fifty thousand. The police have long memories. And bulging dossiers."

"You mean you're not safe in Paris?"

"If I make no trouble, I probably am. Otherwise—" He shrugged. "Who knows." He laughed then. "Well, it was a lifetime ago," he said. "And it failed to break my spirit. And if I'd known that twenty years on I would be only just beginning the deepest and most wonderful experience of love, I'd have laughed my way from May to December."

She spun rapidly on one foot, throwing herself against him. They kissed tenderly. Raising his eyes, he saw an elderly lady walking nearby and looking at them somewhat askance. He broke the kiss and, smiling at the lady, said in near-flawless English, "We were married yesterday, madame."

She looked at them, at the graves all around, and, bursting into laughter, walked away. Victor followed her with his eyes.

"Did you know her?" Abigail asked.

"I thought I did, but of course it can't be. She'd be over a hundred if she were alive still. But—the resemblance! Have we just seen a ghost, I wonder?"

"Whose?"

"An actress. Mademoiselle George." He laughed at a memory. "During her last benefit, her absolutely final farewell benefit, she wasn't content to sit in her box. She went behind the scenes and begged Arsène to let her go on and sing. But he told her to be content. 'Ah,' she said, knowingly, 'if I were only ten years younger, you wouldn't give me such an answer. If I were ten years younger I could give you the sort of night no man would ever forget!' And d'you know how old she was? She was *eighty!*"

Abigail laughed and clasped his arm, marching with vigour now toward the gate. "Oh, Victor, you're invincible, aren't you? Nothing can quench your fire."

"I am an old man," he began. "And already—"

"No!" She shouted him down and would not let him continue.

But before that day was out, her question—are you safe in Paris?—was to be answered.

Chapter 42

After a light lunch they went to the Gare du Nord to arrange their journey home. Abigail, wanting to show off a little, sent in her card, which still read *Lady Abigail Stevenson*, to the stationmaster. He came out to greet her as if she were royalty—as, indeed, was any son or daughter of John Stevenson in the railway world. John had built many of the lines in Normandy and most of the line between this terminus and Le Havre; indeed, in the early 1840s he could not walk through the streets of Rouen without being pointed out a dozen times. Of course, the stationmaster assured them, he would supervise all the arrangements for their journey and there would be a special coach—the royalty coach—for them. And he would see that the best berth on the cross-channel steamer was made available. They settled their departure for a week that day.

Victor was suitably impressed; she felt highly pleased with herself as they walked over to the cab rank.

Before they were halfway across the concourse they heard a woman's scream and turned to see a gang of men attacking a young girl and dragging her toward the exit. She was now calling, in English, "Help! Stop them! Please—someone help!"

Several people nearby began to intervene, until a policeman in uniform, apparently one of the gang, though Abigail had not noticed him, stepped forward and prevented them.

"That's the morals police, you may be sure," Victor said.

The girl, seeing that no one would now come to her aid, stopped struggling; but the men grew even more violent, pushing and kicking her forward while others held her back.

"I'm going to stop that," Abigail said.

"D'you want me to take a hand?" Victor asked. "I will if you wish."

She saw the fear in his eyes. "No," she said. "Go back to César. Tell him what's happened here. His father has lots of friends in the government. It could be very useful."

"I'll stay if you wish. I mean it."

"No, darling. Don't risk it. I'll be all right. I'll go straight to the prefecture."

The men had passed through the swing doors at the head of the short stairway to the street. Moments later Abigail burst through the same doors in time to see the girl fall headlong down the stairs. One of the men, probably in the act of pushing her, fell too—but fell upon her. She screamed again, but this time in agony, not fear. The man who fell on her stood again and kicked her. "Get up, filth!" he shouted.

The girl lay whimpering.

"Stop that at once!" Abigail called out as she ran down to where the girl lay.

"If you want trouble, we're the ones to give it you," one of the men told her. He grabbed Abigail's arm and held it in a vicious grip—a grip that could have compelled any girl to follow him to the police station.

"Careful!" a more prudent colleague warned, looking at Abigail. No one could mistake her for anything but an upper-class lady of considerable wealth.

"This garbage is a common whore, madame," the observant man explained to Abigail. "She's been infecting soldiers of the army of the Republic. We are only doing our duty."

"Not true. Not true," the girl moaned in English.

"You've broken one of her legs," Abigail said.

The man lost patience with her. "She'll get treatment," he barked, and turning, signalled the others to continue. Between them they lifted the girl roughly, leaving the broken leg dangling, to crash on each step. The girl was beyond screaming; with a strangled whimper she passed out. They paid no further heed to Abigail's commands or entreaties.

They bundled the unconscious girl over the street and threw her in on the floor of the police wagon. Then, with the satisfied air of men who had already done half a good day's work, they climbed over her and lounged on the benches on each side. Abigail looked well at the face of each, horrified at the laughter in their eyes; she wanted to be sure of identifying them again. They were like hounds, grinning and panting at the fringe of a kill.

"To the prefecture," she said to the first cabman in the rank.

The prefect received her at once, the moment she sent in her card.

"I know your father, my lady. I am from Rouen. The Earl has great respect in those parts." He spoke in English.

She answered in French. "He is an old friend of Monsieur Rodet."

He nodded. He understood. She told him what she had seen at the Gare du Nord and what she expected him to do. His thin smile vanished. His voice was grim as he said, "I shall investigate. If Lady Abigail will have the goodness to return in an hour?"

She spent the hour in a parlour in his apartments. She asked for paper and pencil and passed the time drawing likenesses of the men of the morals police. Then, in ink, she wrote a statement of what she had seen, thinking that if she had spent the last twenty-five years of her life developing both talents, drawing and writing, and their only use was in this hour, it was time well spent.

The prefect returned. "There has been an error, my lady," he said. "A most unfortunate and regrettable error." He buried her statement and drawings in a pile of papers as if they would not be needed now. "The girl is not a prostitute."

"Even I could see that."

"Then perhaps I should offer you a position among our morals police?" There was a new truculence in him. She became uneasy.

"The girl," he went on, "was denounced by a jealous lover—a man she jilted here in Paris. He has just confessed."

"You've arrested him? He'll be punished?"

"No, my lady. We view it as a domestic fracas, soon forgotten. In

France we've developed a tolerance for violence in crimes of passion, as you may know."

"I know that the violence I saw, Monsieur le Préfect, had nothing of the colour of passion. But it assuredly was a crime. A cold and calculated crime. A rabid dog would have deserved less vicious handling—and this was an uncomplaining girl held by six large men."

"An understandable error, my lady. Regrettable, as I say, but understandable. The women they usually handle are worse than rabid dogs. A full apology will be made, of course."

"It will not be accepted. There must be an inquiry and discipline must be exerted."

He smiled: trump card coming. "You are travelling, I believe, with a certain—" He pretended to consult a paper, half opening the pile at random. "Ah, yes—Monsieur Bouvier. Monsieur Victor Bouvier?"

So that was it. They knew something, but not everything—not his new title, for instance. She did not want to add to their knowledge, especially as she herself knew nothing. It was pointless, and perhaps dangerous, to insist further.

"I see." She rose to leave. "I shall be staying at the Pension Boisanfray in the Rue Michel-Ange at Auteuil. You will kindly arrange for the girl to be delivered there by ambulance without delay."

She named the pension she had always used in her days as a journalist. If she was to nurse this poor English girl, she didn't wish to impose on Celia and César, nor to link them with Victor in the minds of the police.

The prefect, courteous to the last, escorted her all the way to the chief entrance. "Lady Abigail understands our language very well," he said. "It gives me immense confidence there will be no further—unfortunate occurrences during her brief stay in Paris. We must think above all of this poor young woman's reputation, mustn't we?"

*　　　*　　　*

The girl was still in pain, but a great deal less distressed in mind, when the ambulance attendants brought her into the pension. Her name was Frances Law and her father owned three butcher's shops in the Deal area of Kent. She was more worried about him than about herself. She was supposed to meet him at the train from Calais. "I was an hour early," she said. "But he must have arrived some time ago. He'll be frantic with anxiety."

Abigail sent messages by the *pneumatique* to the station and to the school where the girl had been a pupil, giving her new address. She also sent word to Victor.

The doctor, who came within minutes of her arrival, gave his opinion that the leg was fractured rather than broken. For the rest, she was badly bruised, but no internal organs seemed to be injured. He set her leg in plaster and said she might travel on a stretcher and on a calm sea within a week. He gave her opium to help her sleep. "You English ladies are tough," he said admiringly.

So, in a way, Abigail thought, were French ladies who poked at corpses with parasols. Yet there was something almost unnerving at this girl's lack of shock; still, it was preferable to hysterics or tears.

A *pneumatique* came from Victor to say that he was seeing Vauchet, a powerful minister and a long-standing enemy of the morals police. To occupy the time, Abigail rewrote her statement and repeated the drawings the prefect had casually confiscated; no doubt he'd hand the originals out for each man to frame and hang at home—all part of the well-known French "tolerance for violence in crimes of passion."

The girl's father arrived before Victor. At first he was angry and wanted to kill the entire morals police force, from the prefect down; but when he read Abigail's sober, unembroidered account, a wiser (or, at least, a more calculating) counsel insinuated itself.

"I don't know, your ladyship," he said, making implosive sucking noises at his upper front teeth. "It's a bad business. Take this charge, now—what she was charged with. That's a bad business."

"But she wasn't charged, Mr. Law. And, in any case, it was groundless."

He shook his head and went on sucking his teeth. "Mud sticks though, don't it, your ladyship. It's different for a lady of class and breeding, I daresay. No one's going to suspect—well, the likes of you, if I may make so bold. But—" He nodded at the sleeping girl. "A girl of our class don't start out with three farthings' worth of reputation anyway. There's no lean to spare, see."

Sadly, Abigail saw. She rose to go.

He handed her back the drawings and statement. "Not but what I'm not grateful, your ladyship. Mrs. Law and me, we'll never be able to repay your kindness."

"Oh, please don't think of it in that light, Mr. Law. To have done less would be despicable. I'll come back and sit with Miss Law for two or three hours tomorrow afternoon. It would be a shame for you to stay a week in Paris and see nothing of the city."

He protested. She insisted. It was arranged.

As they reached the front door, she saw Victor alighting from a fiacre. "Don't pay him off," she called. "We'll go home now."

She introduced Law to Victor.

"Vauchet's all set for a fight," Victor said in English.

She told him of Law's decision. Victor pulled a face. "That's what Vauchet said would happen. It always does. Neither the guilty nor the innocent want to stir up trouble; that's what puts these swine above the law."

"To coin a phrase!" she said, nodding at Law.

He laughed. "Above retribution, then." His English was good but not as flawless as her French. It was the first time she was more than intellectually aware of their difference in nationality. Until now she had thought of them as sharing some common but undefined citizenship.

"The main thing is," Law said as they left him, "we got our little lamb back, eh?"

On their way home Victor said, still in English, "He seems a tolerably decent sort of fellow."

His English vocabulary, unlike his French, was noticeably upper class. "Let's talk French between ourselves," she said.

He nodded. "Yet I wonder what sort of man can use as a term of endearment for his daughter the name of an animal he must slaughter and sell every day."

*   *   *

Frances was delighted to see her again. Between the lines Abigail gathered that Mr. Law was a great man for homilies.

The girl had been in Paris as part of a bargain with her father. He had wanted her to marry from school—specifically, from the finishing school, or lycée, at Gentilly where, until yesterday, she had been lodged (and where Law had now gone to collect her things and settle accounts). She agreed only if he first let her train to be a typewriter and to do simple bookkeeping, for her aim was not to marry until she had tasted something of freedom in an office. Law, seeing his best hope was to let the two ambitions, hers and his, fight it out, had reluctantly agreed. The "fiancé" who had denounced her turned out to be one of the women teachers at the school, who had made improper advances to her and other pupils and had been dismissed.

"So," Abigail said, "it's your father's half of the bargain that came unstuck."

"Yes, my lady," she answered glumly. "And he's not the man to take the loss of face lightly." Her speech was more refined than her father's; she was as middle class as Celia.

"And can you typewrite, and bookkeep?" Abigail asked.

"I came second in my class—and the girl who was top had done the course twice. I can typewrite fifty-eight words a minute on a good typer. And bookkeeping doesn't fluster me the way it does some girls."

"And shorthand?"

"I'll do some now if you want to try me."

Next afternoon Abigail asked, "Would Mr. Law consider that a position as secretary to Baroness de Bouvier, formerly Lady Abigail Stevenson, might be a better finishing school than his first choice?"

"Never mind him, my lady! If the salary is anything like fifty pounds a year, you've no need to consult wider than these four walls."

Their eyes dwelled in each other's. Abigail laughed. "You knew!"

"After your questions yesterday, my lady? After my father saw you this morning going into the lycée?"

"Ah!" Abigail became more businesslike. "Very well, young lady. Now to lesson one. You no doubt think it very much the New Woman sort of thing to leap in and talk about money like that."

"I believe a man would, my lady. New or Old."

"Not a wise man. A wise man would at least find out about the job first, don't you think?"

The girl bit her lip, worried now.

"This job, for instance, may involve a lot more than being a typewriter and keeping simple books. I may want someone who can do researches for me, meet people for me, go ahead of me in travels and make arrangements, take minutes, meet tradesmen, hire servants, deal tactfully with important nincompoops—right up to really responsible commissions, like going out and choosing me a pair of gloves of exactly the right shade. Now!" She sat back and entwined her fingers with a flourish. "Tell me, Miss Law—tell me the going rate for such a person."

Frances swallowed hard. "Er—" she faltered.

"I'll tell you. Such a person, after let us say five years of satisfactory fulfilment, would rightly expect to earn at least two hundred pounds, living in."

"A *man*—" Frances started to say.

"I would not pay a woman less. My mother will call me a fool, but principles begin at home. Now, lesson two: no one should ever get what they want—not immediately. Accordingly, I will offer you just half of what you ask, for the first six months. Then, if you look like the sort of person I need, you may expect to advance steadily to the sort of salary *I* mentioned."

She deliberately set her offer low to see if the girl was serious about working or was merely looking for a brief bit of fun and freedom with good pay as an added bonus. Frances smiled shyly. "Is there a lesson there, my lady?"

"My, my!" Abigail laughed. "Well—yes, I suppose there is: if a thing feels right, don't hesitate about it."

"Then I hope you'll find me suitable in every way," she answered.

"Good! I hope so, too. You'll live on our side of the green baize door—you know what I mean?"

Frances nodded. "And how do I address you, my lady?"

"In private you may call me 'madame,' if it's absolutely necessary. Otherwise nothing. I shall call you Frances. In public I shall always refer to you as Miss Law, and you may call me Madame la Baronne or Baroness because it's a foreign title. And if you have to ask what's private and what's public, you aren't the person I'm seeking."

She saw a hint of fear in the girl's face and was satisfied. That little injection of anxiety, if it could be regularly renewed, was going to keep this brave, confident young miss from overreaching herself until she knew her business.

*   *   *

With her anxiety for Frances settled and the girl's immediate prospects secure, Abigail found her thoughts returning again and again to the atrocity she had seen at the Gare du Nord. The look she had seen in those men's eyes came to haunt her.

How often, she wondered, are we secretly dependent on a particularly vivid image to unlock a whole train of thought? The philosopher who develops, say, an important theory of power and authority—might not the whole process have been released by his seeing nothing more apparently significant than a tree overshadowing a shrub? She remembered how, long ago, her disquiet at something Pepe had done was in part allayed when she found a satisfying image for it: the shopkeeper pinning up dead butterflies. The image had survived better than the memory of whatever Pepe had done.

Now the thing was working in reverse—the image haunted her, but the thoughts it seemed designed to encapsulate were still mere half suggestions at the fringe of her consciousness. It had something to do with her conversation with Victor after Grant Allen's visit in Rome; but it was more than that. It awoke echoes stretching back over most of her life: her conversation with Steamer, when she decided not to publish *Into a Narrow Circle*; Annie's blighted life and her hatred of men; Uncle Walter—right back to the mists of Pepe and the dead butterflies. It was the dark side of sexual love—the violence in men, the hatred, their will to dominate, and the sheer callousness of their overwhelming greed for satisfaction. She had an intuition that men, hating their bondage at the wheel of desire, hated, too, the objects of that desire. That was why Pepe had smiled like the man who transfixed butterflies. That was why Oldale had ruined Annie, why César had tried to leave her in Rome a captive to his memory, why those policemen had behaved so brutally to Frances. They could lust after a girl all week—never mind whether she was a whore or not—lie panting in her arms on Saturday, and kick her to a pulp on Sunday; and without a trace of inconsistency!

Yes, she thought wryly, it was well enough to lecture little Frances on the wisdom of finding out about a job before you undertake it—she could heed a bit of that advice herself. But how? Where do you start when your intuition is so vague? And refers to such a difficult and private area?

She had loved and slept with but three men—one of them Victor, who was like no other man in the world to her. What values could she draw from so slim an experience? Yet where could anyone turn for more general enlightenment?

At least she was aware of one danger that she might have minimized before: Her endeavour to establish happier and more natural relationships between men and women was not going to be a simple matter of moral, intellectual, and practical argument. There were dark, strong, and secret forces to contend with, too—forces that people neither recognized nor understood.

PART THREE

Bloomsbury Square, 1891

Chapter 43

They took a terrace house on the sunset side of Bloomsbury Square—her first home with a telephone. It was a spacious, elegant place with four principal floors, an attic, and a semibasement. It was also, Abigail had to admit, an upper-class version of the meanly grand houses her mother had so cynically designed (and waxed so rich upon) almost fifty years ago. It had the same pretensions to an elegance beyond its means, scaled up, it is true, but stopping just short of the actual achievement. It was a house for people who wanted to make an occasional move into Society, rather than for those who intended to "go about" a lot; in that respect it suited her and Victor ideally.

She hung César's two paintings of her at last—and in the drawing room, too.

"Is that wise?" Victor asked.

"Perhaps not," she said. "But let's not be cowards forever. Besides, I think a French baroness may do what the younger daughter of an English peer may not. Let's see, anyway."

The stationers in Drury Lane sent round a succession of typers until Frances, now convalescing on a chaise longue, found one to her liking. Abigail put her to work at once making copies of her little memoir of Daniel. Frances had not lied about her typewriting speed. From a selfish viewpoint Abigail was glad of the girl's convalescence, for the responsibility it conferred made it impossible to do what she and Victor would otherwise have been obliged to do—waste a month or more in going around and meeting the family. Instead a letter and an open invitation to "cry in, in the passing," discharged that duty much more agreeably. With each she sent a copy of the memoir; in her mother's she included her drawings of Daniel's death mask.

The first member of the family to call was, strangely enough, the one with whom she had the least contact and for whom she felt the least affinity: her brother Mather, who came with his wife, Corinna (who was Uncle Walter's and Aunt Arabella's youngest daughter). They had not met since she had been to their wedding some seventeen years earlier. Though he was less than four years her junior, they had always seemed much farther apart, in temperament, attitudes, and interests. Mather had not followed his three older brothers, Boy, Caspar, and Clement, to Fiennes School; instead, as Sefton had done later, he went to Eton. Unlike Sefton, Mather had gone on to Balliol College, Oxford, to study economics. He was now a senior lecturer in the subject at University College London, not half a mile from Bloomsbury Square; he was also a world authority on the theory of prices and wages, and a founder-member of the Fabian Society.

That was really what brought him round to see her. The Fabians, who included Shaw, H. G. Wells, and Sidney and Beatrice Webb, believed not in violent revolutions but in "the inevitability of gradualness" in the spread of socialism; they took their name from Fabius Maximus, the Roman general who thwarted Hannibal's ambitions by refusing to meet him in a set battle. Mather was fascinated at the thought that this hitherto unknown uncle should have been so ardent a revolutionary.

But as Abigail listened to him, to his careful diction, to his precise, academically tempered excitement, she could not help remembering that wasted corpse with its ulcerated gums; she could not help thinking of all the suffering and indignity Daniel had endured in the name of the same principles that Mather now enunciated with such prim engagement; and she knew that, though she felt little enough in common with Daniel, she had nothing to share with Mather. There was no point in trying to convey her own hopes and enthusiasms to him. In any case, it was not Mather's response she awaited but her mother's.

Corinna seemed a quiet, agreeable woman. She said Bloomsbury was an agreeable place to live in, university society was agreeable, the Fabians were most agreeable people. "Except when they quarrel," Mather said, "which is almost all the time."

This period of waiting was a repeat of those impotent first weeks in Rome, after she had sent *Into a Narrow Circle* to Pepe and could settle to nothing new. Now, to fill the hours, she made a short story of the Gare du Nord atrocity; the girl-victim was French, in this version, and there was no Abigail around to stir up trouble. The denouement was the same—the mistake was discovered and the girl was released, broken leg and all. The point of the story was not in its denouement but in the discoveries the girl made on her way to it, mainly in her conversations with fellow prisoners.

Perhaps because thoughts of Daniel were near the surface of Abigail's mind, perhaps because of her recent conversation with Mather, perhaps in oblique homage to Victor, or perhaps because she simply lost grip of the form of the story, she made one of those fellow prisoners a tough revolutionary woman. This forced her—for the first time, really—to look at what had happened to Frances with an impersonal eye. What, she had to ask, would a woman who had survived the ordeals Victor had described make of it? The pain and brutality would not move her greatly; she would see it in the broader terms of the class war.

Abigail remembered a passage in the *Communist Manifesto* in which the bourgeois family is presented solely as a vehicle for protecting and passing on capital—the fruit of private gain. When she first read it, she had tried to think of a single bourgeois marriage of which this was even a one-tenth part of an adequate description, except in the most trivial sense, as one might say, "The bourgeois marriage is a vehicle for keeping boot-makers or the carvers of baptismal fonts—or the writers of political pamphlets!—in employment."

But never mind, she thought now; ignore its inadequacy and concentrate on what the *Manifesto* said. Its next sentence was surely significant. "The natural counterpart to bourgeois marriage is public prostitution." The internal consistency of the argument pleased her, and, as developed by the revolutionary woman, it became quite exciting, if only because it was Abigail's first attempt at a more than personal response to the outrage.

She showed it to Victor in manuscript. He read it and passed it back with a thin smile. "Zola's safe, anyway," he said.

Frances said nothing when she handed back the typescript.

"You don't mind?" Abigail asked.

"No. Not in the least. Indeed, it makes me doubly grateful to you for rescuing me as soon as you did."

But Abigail still believed enough in the story to send it off to *Pall Mall*, whose editor, Frank Griffith, was one of the "office boys" to whom, on Caspar's joking advice, she had been kind twenty years before.

The typescript came back by return. "I was very tempted to take this," Griffith wrote, "not because I think it good (in fact, I think it dreadful), but because I know you are one of the very best, and I long to have you write regularly. A month from now you would execrate me if I accepted this. Your anger at what is obviously a real-life incident (seen by you?) is natural; and your description of the arrest had me on the edge of my seat. I thought it my luckiest day in this office that you had honoured me with so riveting a tale. Imagine, then, my disappointment when it all trickles away in that windy, shallow, platitudinous monologue by the revolutionary woman! Is she a sort of joke?

"Frankly, I don't think it makes a story. Anger is a bad muse and a worse midwife. But it would make an article; and even some of the things your dreadful woman says could actually become quite interesting in that context—because you would not then be asking us to imagine a flesh-and-blood woman mouthing such a lecture to a poor girl with a broken leg!

"What say you? We find we can print quite strong stuff if only we keep the language high. Read Acton, and Mrs. Besant, and Josephine Butler and you'll soon see the thing to do. A word of warning: Tale or article, it will, I fear, merely confirm to the average English male what he already knows about the French: that they are savages; and, thank God, they know how to keep their streets swept free of diseased girls! I was not so cynical when last you knew me. But then, nor was I editor.

"As editor I beg you to do me the honour again. And again. And again . . ."

*   *   *

Shortly after that the Earl and Countess, who had been away in Scotland, came. Both were limping, John through age (he was now eighty) and Nora (still a sprightly sixty-nine) from "a fall off a damned contrary horse." Abigail could see that her mother was in some agitation. On the one hand she was delighted that her daughter had at last married; and she and John took an instant liking to Victor—it was a meeting of three varieties of human toughness. On the other hand, she was furious at the memoir of Daniel. And somewhere between these extremes there were practical things, like the marriage settlement and the registering of Victor's foreign title, to be determined.

It was a warm day—the first really warm day of the year—and they sat out in the garden, dappled in the shade of a tulip tree. "Garden" was hardly the word. It measured but twenty yards by fifteen and was isolated from its neighbours by a twelve-foot-high brick wall on all three sides (the house, of course, making up the fourth). There was no grass; it was paved throughout in old flags of Oxford limestone. All the growth, except for the tree, was confined to tubs and urns. But, with the help of a little fountain and a couple of carefully sited statues, the effect was pleasant and relaxing. It was also extremely private.

"I gather you're displeased," Abigail said to Nora, nodding at the typescript her mother was clutching. She thought it best to dispatch the topic at once. "I'm sorry."

John shook his head vehemently at her, but the die was now cast.

"I don't mention Daniel's connection with us," Abigail went on. "It's not meant for publication but, even so, no one can trace him to us."

"D'you think I give a fig for that!" Nora said. "Though, by the way, you are wrong there, too, as you're wrong throughout. My maiden name of Telling is clear for all to see in *Burke's Peerage* and *Debrett,* and there are ten thousand people in this country who, though they may read no other book in their lives, read those two for breakfast. But I don't mind. What I object to is this glorification of Daniel. To use a phrase he would have understood, he was a class traitor. He was a traitor to the only class who should have mattered—the class of me and Sam and Wilf and Dorrie."

"He was a friend of Victor's," Abigail warned.

"A good friend?" Nora asked. "Loyal? Steadfast? True?"

To each Victor nodded assent.

"Then he learned new arts since he deserted me. Did he tell you I denounced him to the French police, after the eighteen forty-eight rebellion?"

Victor's eyes went wide with shock. Obviously Daniel had never mentioned it.

"Did she?" Abigail asked her father.

John nodded as if he, too, were still surprised.

"We had friends and interests in France ten thousand times more important than that traitor," Nora explained. As an explanation it clearly satisfied her.

"Was that the last time you met?" Victor asked.

"No, Monsieur de Bouvier. He came back once more. The next year I think it was. Or—wait! *This* was the time after 'forty-eight. The other was earlier. When the rebellion failed he asked me for sanctuary." She turned to Abigail. "I was at that inn we bought in Coutances, where Clement was born. I turned him away. He drew a gun on me, but he hadn't the courage to shoot. He hit me with it. Broke a rib. And *that's* the last I ever saw of Daniel." She looked back at Victor. "And he never told you that, either, did he!"

"No, Countess. He spoke of you—all of you—with pride and affection."

"Aye—a true communist for you. Treats history like a wife!"

Victor laughed.

"Speaking as a husband," John said, trying to lighten the occasion, "I take exception to the implications of the Right Honourable Lady's last remark. And"—he smiled all round—"talking of husbands and wives . . ." He looked at Nora.

"Yes," Nora said, speaking to Victor. "When Abigail came of age, we set aside—that is, the family trust set aside—" She came to a halt and began again. "I must go back a bit. When we started in business, back in the 'forties, the then John Stevenson had so low an opinion of our skills and prospects that he saddled us with a ten percent levy on all our profits."

John cleared his throat as a protest.

"Very well," Nora said. "Put it another way. It was a time when even fools could make fortunes. So a genius"—she waved at John—"could afford to put aside ten percent and still be keen at the job. In ten years we had a family trust worth—well, let's say one or two millions. That's the background. And when Abigail turned twenty we put aside two hundred thousand as a settlement. That's quite apart from her income, which has always stood at about two thousand a year."

"And of which I've hardly spent a penny," Abigail said.

"Things are different now."

"We shan't go about much," Abigail warned.

"Just listen!" Nora said petulantly.

Victor nodded agreement and held up a finger at Abigail.

Nora went on: "Two hundred thousand compounded at three percent over twenty-four years is—something over four hundred and ten thousand."

"Victor!" Abigail cried. "What fools we were! Oh, curses on our hasty, impetuous natures! Had we but postponed our marriage until I am seventy, we could have been millionaires! Mother, all this is so unnecessary. We don't need such money. We'll never use it. It's only a worry and an embarrassment."

"What does Monsieur de Bouvier say—or Victor? May we call you Victor?"

Smiling, he nodded and drew breath to speak.

"He's rich in his own right," Abigail answered for him. "Yet d'you know what his entire worldly goods amounted to when we moved here? Three trunks and a tea chest."

"Victor?" Nora repeated.

"Neither of you can touch the capital," John warned. "But the income is absolutely yours."

"Over twelve thousand a year," Nora added.

Abigail made an exasperated noise.

"A good marriage needs a strong cement," Victor said. "We are grateful, both Abigail and I."

Abigail stood abruptly and ran into the house.

Nora leaned forward as if to rise and follow her, but then looked at Victor. Still smiling, he asked, "You will permit me?"

He found her in the drawing room, not weeping but pounding a cushion with her fists. He watched briefly. "Ouch—ooh—ah!" he cried in apparent pain at each blow. She stopped and turned on him. "Judas!" she cried.

"No," he said evenly. "John the Baptist—if that's to be your modest metaphor." He came to her but she shrugged herself away from him.

"You could at least have discussed it with me first," she said.

"Had you any idea this settlement was in prospect?"

She waved her head vaguely, unwilling to admit it in words. But the gesture was enough for him. "Then *you* could have discussed it with *me*, for I had no idea at all."

"But what do we want with all that money? I hate the idea of it. I've already got over eighty thousand—all my unspent income over the years. I just shrivel when I think of it. And now you—"

"What does it cost to organize a petition?" he asked, still without a trace of heat. "How much to set up a clinic for working-class women? What's the price of fighting a dozen law suits, would you say? Is research free nowadays? Is the world drowning in scholarships and endowments? Even twelve thousand a year isn't going to stretch very far. So cheer up, my darling, we may yet live and die in comparative poverty!"

She laughed then and fell into his outstretched arms. "Oh, Victor—what is it about that woman? I'll always turn back into a child when she's around!"

"You must think like a politician now, which isn't as hard as you'd imagine. If you really can turn yourself back into a child, you're already halfway there. Come down and talk them into giving us twenty thousand a year."

Again she recoiled, until she saw he was laughing. They began to walk slowly back to the garden. "What was all that?" she asked. "Clinics . . . petitions . . . lawsuits . . . ?"

He shrugged. "We don't know what we're going to do yet. But it could involve all those things."

"Oh, you think so clearly, darling. I don't think at all. I just—react to things."

"Let's start by taking Frank Griffith's advice. Next stop: the Reading Room of the British Museum."

"Yes! Beginning Monday!"

"And ask them to reserve me Karl Marx's old seat. Just see if we don't put it to better use."

"Well!" Nora said, delighted at their return. "In a matter of months, Victor, you have obviously discovered some secret that has eluded our entire family for more than forty years. She not only returns, she brings a winner's smile with her."

"Is it patentable?" John asked.

"We have this marvellous, shining new thing," Victor said solemnly. "It's called The Future. It's quite new to Abigail. All I need to do is point her at it and then there's no holding her back."

Abigail pretended to kick him.

Chapter 44

"Mr. Marx?" the Reading Room attendant said dubiously. "Mr. Marx? Oh—Mr. *Marx!* Oh, yes—of course I remember. Well, fancy you knowing Mr. Marx. How's he keeping?"

"Whereabouts did he use to sit?" Abigail asked.

"Yes, he came here years and years, you know. Mr. Marx, eh!"

"Which was his favourite corner?" Victor pressed.

"Yes! Years and years. But"—he turned mournful eyes upon them—"he went away, you know. And we never heard what happened to him."

"Oh, he died," Abigail said. "Six or seven years ago."

"Well, well! Old Mr. Marx dead, eh? Dear, dear!"

He couldn't remember where Marx had sat. "We get so many in here, you know," he said.

Victor thought it the funniest little encounter of his life. "I hope the Old Karl was wrong about survival after death," he said. "I hope he overheard us. It would explain the one thing that always puzzled him—why the Revolution consistently failed to materialize in this country, despite his increasingly querulous predictions of it."

For weeks that summer they sat there, side by side, reading through Mayhew and Bracebridge, Acton, Mrs. Besant, following up all the references and footnotes, and comparing their findings at the end of each day. As yet they were looking for information rather than theories—at least, they were trying to avoid forming the sort of full-blown theory that might have led them into premature action. Nor did they confine their researches to sexual relationships. They sought any details that might form a background to those relationships: the everyday lives of the poor, their beliefs and attitudes; how news reached them; how opinions were formed among them; how their family relationships were organized; how they budgeted—anything, literally anything, that might later be useful in forming theories. Only then would they be able to think of policies and campaigns of action.

Nevertheless, there were certain facts, right from the beginning, that could not be blinked. Prostitutes were overwhelmingly drawn from the working class. Their clients were overwhelmingly married, middle-class men with families. And some female trades were so poorly paid that even eighteen hours work a day (if it could be got) yielded less than the barest subsistence; the term "lacemaker" or "shirt seamstress" was an absolutely reliable synonym for "whore."

Yet none of the (admittedly middle-class) writers they read dared to come out and say openly that poverty on the one side and surplus wealth on the other was the overwhelming cause of prostitution—or, as Abigail preferred to call it, the murder of love. They said it in one paragraph and withdrew it in the next. They spoke of "natural" lasciviousness among lower-class females and "natural" purity among ladies—as if the human race were two separate species; then they remembered they were supposed to be scientists and that such talk was nonsense, so they withdrew that, too.

"They tie themselves in knots," Abigail said.

"Yes!" Victor grinned with relish. "It must mean we're close to an important truth."

She held up her left hand. "Money," she said. She held up her right. "Poverty." She shook her left. "Lust." She shook her right. "The mechanical ability to satisfy it." She stopped.

"Go on," he said.

"I can't. There's something missing. They make a circle, but it's too small. Too neat. We need something more—something that makes the circle bigger. *Love!* We must make love fit, somehow. The circle must include love." She beat her head. "Oh, the answer's in there somewhere! It's in my life. I've *lived* this problem. But I still can't—put it together." She gave up and laughed. "I must go and see Annie."

He looked at her in surprise. "About *this?* It would be like asking a foundry worker how he explains the present demand for pig iron."

"An ex-foundry worker, I hope. No. Maybe she'll jog my memory. No, it isn't even that. I just want to see her again. I've put it off and put it off."

"Why?"

"I don't know. Perhaps because she didn't answer my letters. I don't know how much she's changed. Perhaps I'm afraid of meeting young William—knowing Annie's view of men. But I must see her. It's so easy to put it off from day to day."

A further two weeks went by before she visited Annie, and even then it was more a matter of opportunity than intention. One Sunday she went to early evensong at Westminster Abbey and then, finding herself at a loose end, she remembered that Annie's place, in Pimlico, was only a gentle walk away.

Annie was alone in the house. Beneath the superficial changes she had not altered a jot. She was greyer and more lined, but she still had that fine-boned face and those flashing dark eyes. She was overjoyed at seeing her Abbie again . . . sorry she hadn't never answered all them letters . . . and William was out kicking a ball down the old gardens . . . and wouldn't she come in, only it would soon be time to start the dinner . . . and not to mind that glass of port too much—she only took one a week, on Sunday afternoons.

It was Annie's new life in one disjointed sentence.

"Well, gel. You look bonny! How's the old Teatro? And how's Celia and Who's'sname—Julius Caesar!" She laughed at herself and clapped her hands.

A warmth Abigail had forgotten suddenly came crowding back—a special, near-Annie warmth. She was glad now that Annie had never written. Annie-in-print could never be the equal of the real Annie. Letters would have changed Abigail's memory and made this meeting harder. Instead, here was Annie, same as ever, making it the easiest thing in the world.

She told Annie of all that had happened since she and Pepe had left them in Rome, but merely said she and Victor had come back to England to write. At length she asked if Annie—or William—ever saw Pepe these days.

"He's nothing to you now, is he, me old love?" Annie asked.

Abigail shook her head.

"I wouldn't deceive you." Annie laughed. "No point—you'd find out soon enough. Pepe comes here every Sat'day night and Sunday. He's out with young William now, kicking a football. He worships that boy. You'd be proud o' them together, gel. Straight!"

"Is he happy?"

"He's still making money. Still eating, breathing, sleeping, and dancing the four-leg frolic, isn't he. You don't get no complaints out of him!" She stood to put on the kettle. "They'll be home soon."

It began to sing almost at once. While she set out the cups and a cake she said, "He carried your name a long time, but he's over it now." She stared shrewdly at Abigail. "Want to know how it started? Him and me?"

"Only—I mean, not if you—" Abigail laughed. "Oh yes, of course I do!"

"The day we came back from Italy, it was. Our first day in London. Know where? Only one place, wasn't there? Old time's sake. We was both desperate for you—and that's the top and tail of it. It wasn't me he took there, it was you. And he was the closest I'd ever known to you—I mean, he'd *been* there. You can't explain it really, except that we both kept talking about you."

"I hope you both got over it soon."

"Oh, yeah! Now? Well, you seen them old beggars under the railway arches? Huddled together when it's cold? Well, it's a bit like that." She laughed again and mock-slit her own throat. "Bleedin' liar! Tell you the truth, I quite like it again. I like old Pepe, too—he's a good 'un for a laugh and I'm fond of a good laugh myself."

"Tell me about William," Abigail said.

But suddenly there was William, glowing and breathless in the doorway. And Pepe behind him.

"Hello, Abbie," he said. "I heard you were back. I ran into Frank Griffith. He's waiting to hear from you."

"Hello, Pepe. Annie's been telling me all the news."

They kissed cheek to cheek and then he presented William—a handsome, curly-headed boy, tall for a ten-year-old. He had her chin and chiselled mouth, though not so strongly that a stranger might remark on it; but no one could fail to discern Pepe's eyes in him.

She talked with him for a while about school, where he was best at sums and composition. And art? It was not so interesting now as formerly. And outside school? He liked football best, and best of all with Daddy. Pepe threw out his chest and beamed. Also he liked reading. And what was his favourite book? With a shy smile that won her heart, he confessed it was *The Land of That'll-do.*

"Ooh, he'd keep the butter hard today!" Annie said. "Just look at them boots! They might as well be shammy leather the way he goes through them."

After tea, Abigail said she ought to go. Pepe walked her up to Victoria, where she'd be sure to get a cab.

"Daddy?" Abigail asked when they were on their way.

"Did Annie not tell you we were married? Five years ago now."

Abigail laughed. How typical of Annie that was! And how infuriating it would be if a man behaved like that!

"You only come Saturdays and Sundays, though?"

"It's easier. For us both. I love her, you know. I didn't when we married—I did that to protect my interest in, and access to, William. But I do now. I thought you'd marry César, from what Annie said."

"Me? Play fifth violinist? No, thank you. He and Celia were meant for each other. They're both very happy."

"I love her, but I couldn't live all the time with her. Put it down to my early training!"

She chuckled and took his arm, which had been tentatively on offer all the way. "I'm glad," she said. "For both of you."

"When are you going to write something for us?"

"I don't think you'd like what I want to write, Pepe."

"Frank Griffith told me. I have two quite intellectual women's mags now, you know. *Rational Woman* and *Adult Marriage*. I'll send you round some back numbers. Also books. We're just printing *The Consequences of Sexual Ignorance* by Warne. Solid university stuff. And I'm trying to get together an *Encyclopedia of Sexual Knowledge*—Ellis is doing me a prospectus for that. Things are changing in England, you see."

"Yes. I had no idea."

"Have you another book in you, Abbie?"

"Well—I still have *Into a Narrow Circle*. I hope!"

"Yes. I wasn't going to mention it unless you did. But I think you could probably look at it again. Try and rework it with just a little humour, eh? It was rather unrelentingly high-minded, don't you know."

She laughed. "Yes, Pepe dear. I do know. I know exactly what you mean."

*   *   *

"The strange thing was," she said to Victor when she came back, "I didn't want to talk about all the things that once were so important—all those feelings. I didn't even want to say things like, 'Isn't it funny how they've vanished!' I'm sure we could have talked about it without embarrassment. But I didn't even want to." Suddenly she felt forlorn.

She threw her arms around Victor and hugged him, unable to speak.

He stroked her back and her hair until she grew calm again. "And of course," he said then, "you didn't talk to Annie about—our work."

She shook her head.

"What next?"

"I think I must go and talk to Aunt Arabella. She's spent forty years rescuing girls from the streets in Bristol. She must have reached some conclusions."

"May I come too, or would it be indelicate?"

"Of course it wouldn't. No one can stay bashful for forty years. She's a hardened warrior after your own heart, I'd say. And Frances still has masses of notes to typewrite and file; we'll give her in-tray a rest and go to Bristol. Anyway, I want to show you off to everybody. I'll write to Bristol tonight."

Chapter 45

"They all think I'm mad, of course," Arabella said, indicating with a waft of her hand not only Walter, sitting white-haired and chuckling by the fire (the first of the autumn), but also the large photograph of her family on the mantelpiece: herself, Walter, and seven children, all but one reared and long gone.

"But I've had a lifetime to piece it out, and it's really very simple. The cause of it is poverty, and the answer is a fairer distribution of wages."

Victor and Abigail sat up at once.

"I've said it often to your brother, Caspar, and to the Earl. But they pretend they can't see it. I point out to them that not all their employees come through the factory gates. Half stay at home—the wives and mothers. They put the food on the table, the shirt on the back. They provide the rest and recreation. Without them, there are no well-fed, well-clothed, well-rested workers delivered to the works at every shift. Half the wage should be paid to them, not the man. More if there's children."

"Hear, hear," Walter said.

She ignored him. "They say, young Caspar and the Earl, they say they'd be paying out for work over which they had no control. But they could send round inspectors, couldn't they? Inspect the homes, look at the children, put an eye over the account books and the larder. They could fine the women who didn't do the work properly. But they won't listen. As long as the man is paid, they think justice is done."

"But if the wage is not enough, Aunt Arabella? Take lacemakers, for instance—"

"Oooh!" Arabella made a gesture that would have repelled a swarm of wasps.

"Listen to this now," Walter said.

Arabella continued to ignore him. "There's the crying injustice. Have you looked into the lacemaking trade?"

Abigail nodded.

"So have I—all the sweated trades. All that piecework, you know, is handed out and controlled by men. I've met them. They even said they hoped I'd be able to put an end to prostitution—the easy money to be got by it constantly interfered with their pool of labour! What I'd do is make those men sit down at the same piecework for a week, see how much they do, see what they need to live on, divide the one by the other, and *there's* your true rate for the job. That could be done by legislation. If the sweated trades could be properly paid, one vast swamp from which the girls are recruited would be drained. But what do men care of that! Always men, you see."

"You are a suffragist, then, madame?" Victor asked.

"The vote is only the beginning," Arabella said. "It must come, of course. But my quarrel with those ladies is that they think it's the end. Get the vote and everything else comes tumbling down. But what good is the vote to us if the men still manage the money? We're all pieceworkers for the men. Most of the women in this country."

"But, Aunt," Abigail said. "Isn't it bigger even than that? Not just money, and votes, and jobs. What about our natures? Especially men?" She succeeded in not looking at Walter.

"That's simple, too," Arabella said. "Continence! Men must simply learn to be chaste and continent. That's where we women can show them such an example."

"Hear, hear," Walter said. His voice had grown remarkably gruff lately.

"He doesn't believe a word of it," Arabella told them.

Walter looked pained.

"Oh, of course he believes in chastity and continence. He's been such a support to me there. Whenever people have told me I'm asking the impossible of men, I've always been able to point triumphantly to my own dear, darling Walter. And their opposition collapses at once and I am vindicated!" She beamed at them in yet another rehearsal of that triumph. Her fingers shot up as she counted: "*One*: Proper rewards for proper work for proper women. *Two*: Employment for people, not for sexes. *Three*: Let m-a-n spell Moral Abstinence Now!" She basked in their admiration. "Yes," she said, gently closing her eyes, "a little legal castration could do wonders."

After high tea Walter took the visitors for a walk around the garden. "You must forgive her," he said, "but if she had known the truth, it would have broken her heart and ended her work. And hundreds of rescued girls would have been the poorer for it."

Abigail did not know how to reply. Was he making a kind of round-about confession? His next words made it clear he was not. "She believes, you see, that because *I* was able to be abstinent, all men would follow suit. But I daresay you both know enough of the world to know it ain't so."

He led them through a shrubbery, walking gingerly because of his ailing heart. On the far side the lawns swept up to the Refuge. The girls were singing their evening hymns, their strong, melodious voices carrying warmth out into the gathering dusk.

"They're fond of singing," Walter said. He tried to hum a snatch with them but his voice was too gruff. "She's loved those girls," he went on. "Really loved them as every Christian should love. From the very first one—back in eighteen fifty. I don't suppose you were even born then, Abigail, were you? Never mind. Your father and I brought her here—as a joke, I'm ashamed to say. Your Aunt Arabella was set on this rescue business. So your father and I, to frighten her, went down to the docks and picked a pretty young thing who, we were sure, would break Aunt Arabella's heart. I can see her now." His eyes stared out across the decades. "Pretty thing. Name of Charity—orphanage name, of course."

Abigail did not betray herself. "Did it work? What became of her, Uncle?"

"Oh, it worked, all right. She was Mrs. Cornelius' maid for years—d'you remember poor Mrs. Cornelius? Never mind. But she ran away. They all do. But on that first night your aunt saved her—no doubting that. She went down on her knees with that girl and got her to see that in the eyes of God they were *both* sinners, with not much to choose between them. There! They prayed *together* for redemption. Never in fifty years have I heard her pray just for a girl—always for the girl and herself in the same breath. And there were girls came in there who were sunk deeper in depravity than Satan himself might dream of. And they, knowing she was a saint, saw her humble herself for them. For God and for them. She never condemned. She'd never allow a preacher here who would condemn. It was all done by example. And those girls—hundreds of them—have all worshipped the very blades of grass she touches."

He coughed awkwardly. "I just thought you ought to know that. When you heard her talking such fol-di-rol at tea, I thought you both ought to know the other side of it. The truer side. Her opinions will never get her into heaven."

Abigail, deeply moved, said, "I'm proud to have called her 'Aunt.' "

"And I to have called her wife."

This, Abigail reflected, was from the man who had debauched Annie all those years ago! She tried to relate it to him, to herself. But, like so much of her life, it was too long ago now and everyone had changed too much.

The girls began to sing their final hymn. Its stirring challenge followed the three of them back through the shrubbery:

> *"And did those feet*
> *In ancient time . . ."*

"I've passed hours with those girls," Walter said. "I've had stories from them enough for the whole of Dickens twice over."

"Really?"

"Oh, yes. I've written them all down."

"I'd love to see them," Abigail fished.

"Yes, I thought so. That's why I mentioned it. I think you ought to. If you're going into this business seriously, as you said in your letter." He smiled shyly. "I've put them all into a sort of story form. I used to take statements, but it was—like police files. It didn't seem to catch the essence. That's what you're after, what? The essence of it."

"Indeed, Uncle. I'd be most interested—and grateful."

"Unfortunately most of them are couched in the language in which they were told to me. And though the words, I'm sure, would mean nothing to you, I'd be ashamed for you to see them in my handwriting. But I'll look out a few of the milder ones to start with, and I'll make edited copies of some others, and you'll get a good idea."

"I—I'm overwhelmed, Uncle. Truly. Have you got them here?"

"Heavens, no!" He was shocked at the idea. "It would distress your aunt too much. Never mention it to her. No. I have a set of rooms in London. And in fact"—he brightened—"I shall be there next Wednesday. I shall look out a first selection and bring them to you in Bloomsbury Square."

"Excellent. And stay to dinner, too."

"Yes. I should like to talk to you some more about this."

*　　*　　*

The following Wednesday, Abigail took Victor to meet Annie. They stayed longer than they had intended. She had hoped to be back well before Uncle Walter was due in Bloomsbury; now she'd be lucky to arrive there at the same time.

Their hansom was going along Oxford Street, halfway between Regent Circus and St. Giles, when she caught sight of Uncle Walter walking on the near-side pavement, a little way ahead of the cab.

"Uncle Walter!" she called out. "Coo-ey!"

But he did not hear her above the roar of all those iron tyres. Anyway, he was far too interested in a coquettish young girl who had just flounced past him and now looked back to give him the glad eye. His pace noticeably quickened. An omnibus pulled up ahead of the girl and she, no doubt recognizing it as one she wanted, ran to board it. As soon as she was on the tailboard she turned and smirked at Walter, lifting her dress to reveal most of her leg below the knee. Then, laughing, she ran upstairs to the upper deck.

The bus began to move off. Walter, who had already been hurrying, now began to run.

"No!" Abigail cried. "Uncle Walter!"

If he heard he paid no heed. By some superhuman effort he drew level with the bus and sprang onto its tailboard. Even then he did not pause. For a man nearer eighty than seventy he positively leaped up the stairs.

At the top he fell.

The girl, no longer laughing, had backed as far down the deck as she could go. It was empty but for the two of them. Abigail waited for Walter to rise, but he made no move. Nor did the girl.

"Did you see that?" she called up to their cab driver.

"I think you, me, and that gel is the only ones what did, lady."

"I know that man. Drive ahead and let me catch that bus."

The hansom soon overtook the clodhopping dray horse pulling the bus. "Follow," Abigail shouted to the driver as she leaped out. Victor followed hard behind.

With an agility that exceeded even old Walter's, they sprang onto the bus and raced upstairs. Foremost in her mind was the thought that if Walter was ill, they would take him to hospital, search his pockets, and find the papers he was bringing her. And if he died, they would give them to Aunt Arabella. "We must get those papers he said he'd bring us," she said.

The girl was still standing as Abigail had seen her last: openmouthed and wide-eyed at the front of the bus.

Abigail stooped and searched his pockets. He was obviously deeply unconscious. The first thing she found was a key. A key! His rooms in London—full of those stories from the girls. She passed the key to Victor; he understood at once and pocketed it.

Then she found the papers, in his inside coat pocket, next to his heart. Now that he was safe from disgrace she was about to shout to the conductor when she felt his heart. Nothing. His pulse. Nothing. She opened an eyelid—and looked at death.

She stood and, for a moment, clutched at the back of the nearest seat. Victor stooped and repeated the tests. His face confirmed everything.

Uncle Walter was dead.

The girl at last began to move back up the bus, approaching them.

"Did you know this man?" Abigail asked.

She shook her head vigorously.

"You behaved as if you did," Victor said.

The girl looked down. She seemed to have difficulty catching her breath. She loosened her bonnet strings and clutched them to her, but in the instant between loosening and clutching she had afforded Abigail a glimpse of—of the impossible. The girl had an Adam's apple, shaded with the stubble of a beard. She looked guiltily at Abigail, propelling her toward the final realization.

The word that popped into her mind, after her reading at the B.M., was *transvestite!* But for that it would have been *bearded lady*.

She was incredulous that what had been written of so blandly in those books actually had physical existence out here in the streets. She looked at the "girl's" clothing. It was impeccable, to the last visible stitch. She wanted to ask "her" if it was as perfect underneath.

"Don't say," the "girl" begged (Abigail still could not think of this as a man). "Her" voice was mid-pitched, highish for a man, lowish for a young girl. "Don't tell and I won't tell."

"She" nodded and pointed at the papers, which Abigail still clutched. "All right," Abigail said. "Jump off when you can."

"She" almost fell downstairs with eagerness to be gone.

"That wasn't a woman at all," Abigail said.

"I wondered if you'd noticed," Victor answered. "Poor Uncle Walter! He chased an illusion to the very end of his days." He went down to tell the conductor there was a dead man on the bus.

Well, Abigail thought, looking down at the benign, silver-haired old gentleman, at peace finally, *at least he went out on the crest of a hope.*

*   *   *

The formalities were tedious. The body had to go to the public morgue. There had to be a post mortem. Statements had to be taken.

But Uncle Walter had not been expected back in Bristol that night. It gave them time to go home, change into mourning, and go down there on the evening train. On the way they read the papers Walter had been bringing her. They were trash—otiose, sentimental, demurely lecherous; like a painting by Greuze, they reeked of fakery.

As soon as Arabella saw them in black, she knew. "I had a premonition," she said. "Do come in. He has been so unwell lately."

Abigail, who had prepared for deep lamentations, was a little taken aback.

Arabella saw it and smiled. "You are young, my dear. But I think Monsieur de Bouvier may understand. I am old. He was even older. In a little while I shall join him. He was called before his suffering grew too deep. He lived a life of such Christian denial that he is certainly in heaven now, interceding for me and praying for my many sins to be heaped on him that we may share purgatory and eternity together as we shared our least thought here below."

It was Abigail who needed comfort, for the lies she told and the lies she let, like sleeping dogs.

There was no train back to London after half past seven unless they cared to wait for the sleeper at half past midnight. Abigail did not care to wait. Once again the Stevenson name worked its magic and, within fifteen minutes of arriving at the station, she and Victor were in the luxurious directors' coach on their way back to Paddington by "special."

"Does anyone in your family bother with train timetables?" Victor asked. "Or do you all just turn up at any old station and tell them to get you a train?"

"It's not much good having a father who's a director of fifty railways if you can't at least do that. Besides, we have to get back. We must find these rooms of Uncle Walter's and clear away anything incriminating."

"How do we do that? Those rooms could be anywhere in London."

She shrugged. "Annie may remember. She went there once. *If* they're the same rooms."

*   *   *

"He must've moved scores of times," Annie said. "They've been pulled down . . . I'd never find it . . . I'd die before I'd go back there again . . ."

In the end, by a stroke of luck and desperation, Abigail remembered

Annie's first description: "He's written them all down," she had said.

That's what those stories were, of course—his own experiences, not things culled secondhand from girls at the Refuge. It all fell into place now.

"He's got writings there about you, Annie. Don't you remember? And don't you want to save them? Suppose a housebreaker got in and found them—and started selling them in pubs all over London!"

Annie reached for her bonnet. Walter hadn't moved, they hadn't pulled it down, Annie found it first time—and she didn't drop dead on entry. But she wouldn't go into the bedroom.

"Come on, love," Abigail encouraged her. "Face it. You'll find it's all gone. I promise."

"Easy said, gel."

"Come on."

Annie edged into the room. Abigail watched her, trying to test memory against reality and finding the memory worn too smooth to rasp. "All gone? As I said?"

"I remember it, yet—it could've been—like what someone else told me once." Delighted to find no ghost to lay, she became much livelier and began opening cupboards and poking into drawers. "Bleedin' paper everywhere, isn't it!" she said.

Abigail and Victor, more methodical, found that the "bleedin' paper" comprised the galley proofs and manuscript of a vast pornographic autobiography with none of the coyness and circumlocution she might have expected to find. It was the very strongest stuff. Its author was called "Walter" but even a cursory reading showed Abigail it was not her uncle, unless he had disguised himself very heavily.

"Victor darling," she said. "If these are genuine, they'll be absolutely invaluable."

"Here they are!" Annie called out.

She had found a sheaf of the loose-leaf memoirs she had seen being written by her "Mr. Carey." It was a small sheaf and she began reading through it eagerly, looking for her own "episode."

But Abigail pulled out a trunk from the corner and it proved to be half full of almost identical memoirs, all on loose-leaf paper.

"Flaming hell! Let's burn the lot!" Annie suggested.

"I don't think so. Tell me, are these accurate, or are they all sick fantasy?"

"Search me!"

"Well, read some, Annie. Please? Just read four—pick any four at random and tell me if they at least sound plausible."

"Is it important?"

"It could be. To us."

Annie shrugged and did as she was asked. While she read she kept saying things like: "Big head! . . . Blimey, gel, you're soft! . . . He'll be lucky! . . . Oh yeah! Mr. Marvellous again!" Finally she handed them to Abigail. "Real enough," she said. "Seen from *their* point of view."

"That's what we want. I think we already know yours!"

"These seem authentic, all right," Victor murmured, reading some of the galleys. Abigail slipped out to the telephone call room in Heddon Street and rang Cattermole's in Islington and asked them to come with a covered dray and a dozen tea chests. By late afternoon every scrap of paper and every personal possession of Uncle Walter's was safely in Bloomsbury Square. On the bare table Abigail left a note asking "interested parties" to get in touch with her; she didn't want the landlord to go to Aunt Arabella for back rent.

While packing they found a recent picture of Uncle Walter in a group photo of retired engineers of the Great Western. "There he is." Abigail pointed him out. He looked so benign and avuncular, the very last sort of man you'd dream of associating with this vast outpouring of erotica.

Victor stared silently at the picture and then pointed at Walter's left foot. "It's blurred," he said.

"So it is." Walter's legs were crossed, left over right.

"You don't see much blurring in photography nowadays. His foot must have jerked."

"Oh!" Abigail said, remembering. "It did that. Weren't you there when he showed it? His foot did that whenever he crossed his legs. He couldn't control it. He said it showed how old he was—things were taking their independence. It was just a joke."

"More than a joke," Victor said. "I think that's what killed him. I think he had an aneurysm of the aorta."

Annie coughed. "Eh? What's this, gel? Do *all* your friends turn into doctors?"

Victor laughed and explained. "De Voisins died of the same thing in the Commune. And Dr. Daugny, who used to smoke the same tobacco as Louis Philippe and sent roses every day to the two little milliners in the Rue Nicolini, he diagnosed it afterward from a photograph in which the foot was also blurred."

"How Victor knows things," Abigail said to Annie, "is always very simple in the end."

Later, when they were alone, Victor added that one kind of aortic aneurysm could be caused by syphilis, perhaps contracted fifty or sixty years before.

"Somewhere here," he said, waving at the crated memoirs, "we may find it—the little sleeping death he got at twenty."

*   *   *

That evening, as soon as Frances had retired to bed, Abigail followed her up and tapped lightly on the door.

"Come in," the girl called.

"I have something to tell you," Abigail said. "It's about your work here."

"I hope it's satisfactory, madame?"

"Absolutely. Indeed, more than merely satisfactory. But I don't want to shower you with the praises you deserve, in case you imagine I'm just trying to butter you into staying when it would be distasteful to you."

"Oh, never—"

"Wait. Things have changed."

Frances was silent.

"You must know already, from the things you've been asked to typewrite and file, that the Baron and I are embarking on a study of modern-day relationships between men and women."

She nodded.

"And you must also know that we think those relationships are in a sad mess—and that someday, perhaps, he and I, and possibly others, will begin a campaign of some kind to clear up that mess."

Another nod.

"Well, some aspects of our research are distasteful in the extreme. And I'm afraid those tea chests you saw delivered today are full of papers in that category."

Her eyes went wide.

"Yes, Frances. All of them. To be explicit, they consist of the very frank memoirs of a man who, over the best part of sixty or seventy years, spent every moment he could with prostitutes; in short, it is the memoir of between seven and nine *thousand* such encounters!"

She gasped.

Abigail allowed the fact to sink before she resumed. "To us, of course, it's a gold mine of information and attitudes we could discover in no other way. But there's no denying that the task of sorting through it and reading it is going to be distasteful. It will not fall to you, or not principally; but inevitably you will come into contact with it. Now I want you to think about that, Frances, and forget any notions of obligation to me and the Baron. Think only of your future. Think of your prospects of marriage and what it might do for them if you were associated with us— Why d'you smile?"

"Bless you!" Frances said. Abigail could see the girl wanted to touch her, to reassure her. "I thought of all that weeks ago—the first day you came back from the Reading Room. I nearly handed in my notice then. But I thought better of it. I thought, no, what you're doing is good. And right. And any young man who took exception to it—well, I'd not want him to father my children. So that decision's already made, however bad these new papers are. And all you've done tonight is show me once again how kind and considerate a person you are."

To cut short the eulogy Abigail reached forward and squeezed her arm. "We'd have missed you," she said. At the door she added, "Sleep well."

She was out in the passage when Frances called, "Madame!"

She put her head back into the bedroom. "Yes?"

"Would you think it presumptuous of me if I told you what I think about all this? These things you're studying? It's made me think a lot."

"Presumptuous! Good heavens, I'd welcome it. Anything. Frankly I feel lost. D'you mean now?"

"No. Soon. When I'm ready—I mean, when it seems clear to me."

"Then I'll try to be patient. And, Frances—I've tried to wear this 'madame,' and I don't think the best tailor in the world could get it to fit. I'd be so obliged if you'd just call me Abbie when we're not in public."

"I'll try."

"There's a dear. Sleep well!"

Chapter 46

They were still wading through Uncle Walter's loose-leaf memoirs and the much more puzzling printed memoirs of what was obviously quite a different "Walter" two days later when the maid announced, "A Mr. Walter Thornton to see you, my lady." Feeling more than slightly unreal, Abigail turned his card over in her hands. *Mr. Walter Thornton* it undeniably read. He had a set of chambers in the Albany and belonged to the Garrick and National Sporting clubs. She went down to meet him.

"That public-school machine has gone berserk," Victor said as she left. "They are even coming out with the same *name* now!"

A young man in deep mourning was parading slowly back and forth admiring the two paintings of her by César, never once taking his eyes off them. The door was aslant and she paused for a while, watching him. He walked to the one in which she stood in a foot bath by the open window and he ran the tip of one gloved finger down over her back and buttocks.

She laughed in delight and stepped into the room. "Until this moment," she said, "I was inclined to disbelieve the name on your card."

He turned to her, not the least taken aback, but calm, even nonchalant. "He handles the paint like an angel, Madame la Baronne. But I see he had an angel for a model, too." He pressed her hand to his lips.

"I know all Uncle Walter's children," she said. "You must be—?"

"His grandson. You know my father, Nicholas. I have called to thank you for all you did on the day of grandfather's death, and going down to see my grandmother."

"That is kind of you. But surely we shall meet at the funeral tomorrow?"

"It was a great kindness," he said as if she had not spoken. "And greatly appreciated."

"I had nothing but kindness from them all my life," she told him as she rose. "Well, duty's done. I won't detain you. You look to me a very busy young man."

In fact he looked a dandy. She was bored with him. His mourning might have been designed by Oscar Wilde, right down to the lily which lay with his cane across his hat.

"Er—my grandfather had a set of rooms, near Langham Place."

"So I believe."

"The landlord tells me you removed a few trifling effects he kept there."

"Very little. He had some papers he had mentioned to me, papers that might distress his—your grandmother."

"Ah! Yes—I see. His correspondence, I suppose?"

"I don't know. Naturally I haven't read it."

The relief in his eyes gave him away. He knew everything. Before he could commit himself to a lie, she said, "Come on now, young fellow. You know very well what was there. You may have all the self-possession in the world, but your face is too honest to make you a good deceiver."

He slumped into a chair, but more by way of relaxation than chagrin. "You have read it, then," he said.

"In two days? Hardly! I've read enough, though. What is it? And what relation does 'Walter' in print bear to the real Uncle Walter?"

So he told her. Then she took him up to the study.

"Victor dearest, the mystery is solved. 'Walter' is both Walter *and* Walter. And this young man, by the way, is—er, Walter. The third one."

He explained it again, less hesitantly this time, now that he was sure of Abigail's attitude. He and his grandfather had on several occasions found themselves in the same night houses, music-hall galleries, cigar divans. They had passed from embarrassment to laughter and finally to close friendship. Old Walter had sealed that friendship by showing his grandson his by now vast collection of loose-leaf memoirs.

This had inspired young Walter to begin his own. Since the age of eighteen he had done nothing but live idly in London. He thought *The Picture of Dorian Gray* (which, he was careful to stress, he had read in manuscript!) divine. But old Walter's revelations had inspired him to something more realistic.

"Then one day I said to him, 'Look, old friend, your name's Walter and so's mine, and we're both writing the memoirs of our night sticks— let's combine 'em, eh? I'll outlive the old queen and you started before they popped the crown on her. We'll have the memoirs of one composite man who *was* the man of the entire reign. *Homo victoriensis* or whatever it would be—never was any good at Latin. Victorian man. Of course, the old boy took to it at once. We thought of calling the hero 'Victor' and his cousin 'Ian.' But then we thought that would give the game away—show people he was just made up. So the best disguise we could think of was 'Walter.' Vanity, I suppose."

"And the result is these proofs? It's about to be a book!"

"Fourteen books. You can say one thing for us Thorntons. When it comes to industry (and *Homo victoriensis* surely comes to that) we did our share!"

"Not your father," Abigail said. "I know him well."

Young Walter smiled. "According to Granddad, my father had his share when young, but he tired of it. Took to collecting. Books and things. He has a hundred and thirty thousand prints and photographs."

Victor laughed uproariously, beating his head with open hands. "Aie—aie—ie—ie! Humanity, humanity!"

"So," Abigail said briskly, "to get it clear, now. These loose-leaf sheets are old Walter's originals. Somewhere here—we've not come across them yet—will be yours. And—"

"No, mine are at the Albany." He looked around in dismay. "I say, here's a thing. I'll never cram all this in there. What am I to do?"

"We'll come to that," Abigail said. "What exactly do you want to do with it all?"

"Second edition," he said. "First edition was eleven volumes. But we left a lot out. D'you know"—he sighed and looked again at the crates and chests, bursting with papers—"now the old fellow's gone, I don't think I have the heart. I suppose you want to pinch them."

Suddenly she realized why he had been so frank with them: He thought they were fellow pornographers, like himself. From the moment he saw César's pictures he must have been thinking partly that way! *I'd better make this convincing*, she thought.

"We are in the middle of a study to be titled *Human Sexual Pathology*, for the University Press. You can imagine how difficult it is to collect accurate material. This is the first. I mean, that's why we were delighted to have rescued it. This is the first honest material we've come upon."

It was wasted on him. "Of course, of course," he said with a wink. "Lots of hymnbook gothic on the title page, eh? Latin footnotes. Solemn title. Just the thing! Dad has hundreds of them. Well"—he waved at the material—"I wish you luck. 'Bout time women took a hand in writing our sort of books. The dear sweet things have invaded everywhere else. I'll send you round all my stuff if you want."

Chapter 47

"Oh, Victor!" Abigail said a few days later, when they had reduced Walter's manuscript and galleys to the first semblance of order. "We must have some guardian angel above. I mean, haven't I been saying all this time that what we need is to hear the honest, authentic voice of the English *man*, the English middle-class client of the girl whose plight we know so well? And here it is—in embarrassing richness."

He nodded.

"Why so pensive?" she asked.

"Depressed," he said, waving at the piles around them. "It's so— English. So utilitarian. The Renaissance passed Russia by; that's why life is cheap there—the individual is valued at nothing. And now I see the Romantic movement passed England by; that's why women are cheap here—Walter doesn't even look for love, he values it at nothing."

"But weren't you the same once? You used to go to La Chaumière, where 'the girls were the prettiest in Paris'!"

"Good heavens, they weren't streetwalkers!" he protested. "They were *odalisques—cocodettes—lorettes—grisettes*. They lived from day to day—a dinner here, an apple there. The daughters of concièrges, apprentice dressmakers, governesses without charges, actresses between theatres, chambermaids caught bending. They walked like free, wild creatures, with bright eyes and their hair down. They knew the slightest breeze could blow them into the Seine."

"They took money for it."

"But—oh, you English!—they never *asked* it. And I never went with one I didn't also love. But Walter—he doesn't look for it, nor even want it. He'd be embarrassed by it. If I hadn't loved the girls at La Chaumière, I could've done nothing."

"Love?" She laughed.

"Oh, yes. Love! One can be in love for as little as one hour. Don't you know that?"

She shook her head. "It sounds perilously close to self-deceit."

"So? If it is? It can be only a little deceit. One hour! Forgive me, but to be in love for ten years and then to find out, after the lapse of another ten that nothing is left of that love, not even the desire to talk about it—is that a small deceit, too? Or a big one?"

She knew he was half-provokingly dealing in these paradoxes, yet there was a truth at their heart. She nodded.

"Look," he said. "Forget deceit. It's too universal. This is what I'm talking about. In my *bohème* days I'd say to myself, 'I'll go out and find a girl and pay her money to sleep with me.' But I was absolutely determined to love the girl, too." Seeing the scornful curve of Abigail's lip, he added, "Oh, yes! And often I did. Often the girl would come back and live with me for days or even weeks. Once I danced with a masked beauty—I never even slept with her—and pined for her for four weeks until she walked up to me in the street and ended my misery. Never mind! You see the point. When Walter says to himself, 'I'll go out and find a girl and pay her to sleep with me,' the very idea of love would be repugnant to him. That's what I say. It's a utilitarian act. To him a girl is a pretty kind of sewer—a gorgeous slop pail. There's no romance in it. Even at the climax of his enjoyment, his language is the language of the moneychanger. 'I spent into her,' he says. Or 'we spent together'! My God—my hair stands on end to read it!"

He smiled then and squeezed her hand, mocking his own vehemence. "But you're right. Walter's is the authentic voice we've been seeking for so long."

*   *   *

There was one of Uncle Walter's loose-leaf memoirs that she began to read with special interest. It stood out from most of the others in that it consisted of several leaves pinned together. But that was merely what attracted her attention in the first place. What held her attention—and held it riveted—was the fact that it quite obviously referred to Walter's time at Summit Tunnel, where her parents had started on the road to fortune—"Dusty," in her father's phraseology. "Loppered with blood. Bare of feet," but with sunshine in their spirit. It amused her to think that while the pair of them had been slaving eighteen hours a day, Uncle Walter had been roaming the countryside and tumbling field girls.

Devilish hot [he wrote]. I walked toward the shade of an old wall overhung by trees, amazed at the variety of grasses and plants there are in a pasture. Thought of a scheme to find the best and kill off the others. Even the birds couldn't stand the heat.

Then a stroke of luck. I thought she was a field girl, and my heart sank. I'm weary of their big, coarse bodies and gluepot stink. She was in field girl's dress, heavy blue serge, stained, torn, and muddy; but she was a tender, dark-haired little minx inside it. Been starving herself a bit, I'd say. I like to be of help when they are of use to me. Fair's fair.

She sat on the wall, dappled in the sunlight, tired of its heat, like me. "That's the best employment today," I said.

"I'd like to be the lass you were thinking of," she answered. "You looked right through me."

Her mind already leaned in the right direction. She had a grand little smile with delicious teeth that I already longed to feel about me. I sat beside her. "The stones are hot," I said.

She stood. Who said "a woman's body is the handwork of God"? Hers was. I trembled to be at her. I was melting from neck to knee, but now not with the heat—or the external heat.

"Sit here," she invited. "The stones have cooled under my skirt."

Well! She couldn't have asked for it plainer. "Oh?" says I. "Is it so cold under there?" I'd have been a fool to say anything else.

Now she played with me. Stood up . . . heavy sigh . . . stroll about . . . says wearily, "I didn't mean that."

"Wants a little warming, does it?" I asked. Always ignore their resistance; they *never* mean it, even when they believe they do. And, of course, being hungry, in all ways, she comes to it at once. Handsome girl, too. A few months' feeding and dukes would take her. "I've a belly needs meat," she said.

"Ah!" (I knew there was more to follow.)

"It'd cost thee. I canna frig with the likes of thee for naught." She haggled me up to 4*s*. 6*d*.—5*s*. being all I had (or thought I had). Of course she said the usual thing—never done it for money before!

She led me into the wood beyond the wall. I said I feared it was private property. "Private enough!" she laughed. She was eager for it, I could see. My old cracksman was sore stiff by now; he'd brook no delay, endure no finesse. When she began fiddling with the twine at her waist, I threw her down upon a smooth rock, set my folded jacket beneath her head, and leapt aboard her and spouted at once.

Of course that wasn't enough for her! And though it hurt me to do it so soon again (and she knew it hurt, sweet tyrant), she made me go on until we spent together. Then she was satisfied.

When I awoke from my slumber, she held a sovereign in her hand and looked daggers at me. "What's to be done with it?" she asked. "I thought it fell from thy keck, but thou said thou had naught."

It annoyed me, when I had hurt myself to please her, that she should accuse me of meanness. But—not to confirm her—I said, "Keep the wretched·coin! Wagered money's soon forgot, they say. And it's true, for that's how I won it—and forgot it. Now you can have it and forget it, for it cost you nothing you didn't want anyway."

She laughed and told me her name was Molly (which I later found to be a lie). What else was a lie?

I realized suddenly we were not in a grove at all but an ancient graveyard, and she and I had desecrated a grave—for our "smooth rock" was a carved stone. Tonight I pray for the repose of the soul of Nicholas Everett, who quit this life A.D. 1643.

Abigail gasped aloud. Nicholas Everett—the name Uncle Walter had given his eldest son, young Walter's father! She had stumbled here on no mere casual memoir. She read on eagerly:

I expressed my horror to her, but she was hardened, laughing at my scruple. "I don't know about thee! One minute thou art glimpsing paradise." (I may have cried out some such foolery in my ecstasy.) "Next minute it's desecration!"

Her father was recently buried nearby. She said the authorities had reopened the abandoned ground, for burying paupers. She had come to tend his grave on her way back over the hills to Leeds. And suddenly, as if to shock me on purpose, she said her father and she had frigged for years, ever since her mother had died. She had borne him children, too, "meagre wrecklings, born dead and soon cold."

I had been defiled by her. But she continued her scorn. She told me I "knew nothing." My sort "knew nothing." She meant nothing of poverty, of course. But why should we? We are not poor. She knew nothing of railway engineering, but I did not taunt her for it. Instead I asked what of the rest of her family?

Abigail laughed. "Old Walter's a dedicated researcher!" she said. Victor, deep in another section, nodded. Abigail sighed and returned to the memoir:

She had one brother transported, another in service, and of the two "bairns" one had died of rat bites and the other had strayed "right into the jaws of Tom o' Jones's boar as weren't penned. There were naught left but one arm to bury."

Abigail shut her eyes and stopped breathing; her hand flew to her mouth.

Victor saw the change in her at once. "What?" he asked.

She shook her head. Gently he tugged at the paper in her hand. She clutched it to her. "What?" he repeated.

"I'm going to be sick, I think."

Her heart, having stopped, now hammered like a pile-driving engine. Everything blurred and swam. She heard the window sash screech as Victor threw it open. She attempted to rise but staggered and sat again.

"Don't," Victor said. "I'll get a bowl."

She shook her head; the nausea was dwindling. Now she was weak; her muscles had jellified.

"Water?"

She nodded but he had already gone for it. The relief was astounding. The flying miasma before her eyes drained itself down and settled. Her mind was cleared. She sipped again and managed a weak smile.

"What was that?" he asked.

She tapped the paper.

"Just something you read?"

Still holding the paper, she stood and began to pace about. At last she said, "There's no one else in the world I'd ever reveal this to. But you, I know, will understand." She gave him the paper. "The girl he is writing about here, the girl who gives her name as 'Molly,' is my mother. You will recognize the point at which that became clear to me. Will you, my dearest, read to the end and tell me if I should go on? Please?"

He did as she asked. He was stolid; little showed in his face. But she saw when he reached the bit about the boar. Then she ran to him and kissed his face and head over and over again. "Darling, darling Victor! Don't if you don't want. I don't mind—we'll go for a walk and I'll calm down and read it myself."

But he merely patted her hand and read on.

"You must read it," he said when he'd finished. "Read it and pity these poor people." He passed the paper back to her, and she, standing now, read on. He at once began to search for something through the pile of printed proofs.

I marvelled at the force that drives these people to survive [she read]; they live in degradation that would kill me in a week, yet they face the world with the beauty and scorn of this young tigress, who defers only to my money (all of which she now has, save 5s.). I looked at her body, which I had enjoyed so bounteously, and thought, perhaps a new life, half mine, is already kindling in her—to be born, to survive plague and disease, to worm its way up through the gauntlet of human cruelty and indifference, to eat its meagre fill, get drunk, frig, beget, and die. The futility of it—of our whole existence—it was all there in the stone and the air, in my limp prick and her charged body. Vanity! Even the vanity of the cypher in the stone: Nicholas Everett—it took me minutes to make out your name!

Victor handed her a page of proof. "In case you worry how much has survived in print, I came across it last week. You'll see how I recognized it."

It was a passage describing how composite-Walter watches two agricultural women go into a churchyard "for a piss." And he, "dying for it" as usual, follows them. A lot of banter, some of it quite amusing. One woman agrees. He rolls his coat for a pillow and has her on a tombstone—"and there we were laying [sic] in copulation, with the dead all around us; another living creature might that moment have been begotten, in its turn to eat, drink, fuck, die, be buried, and rot." Then he turns over and has the other woman.

"He keeps the elements, you see," Victor said. "The churchyard, rolled-up jacket, tombstone, intimations of mortality, and two women to stand for two acts. But the rest is gone. Young Walter said they left out a lot. They surely did! They left out their own humanity and understanding. *But!*" He brightened and, wagging a finger, added, "As a great man once said: *That is no accident!* 'Walter' is how old Walter and young Walter want to reveal themselves to the world. He may not be real Victorian man, but he is authentic—as Ulysses is authentic ancient Greek. How d'you feel, my darling?"

"Go on talking. Say anything. I feel like a walk."

They walked aimlessly, threading through the maze of narrow streets between the house and Lincoln's Inn Fields. "They're going to pull all this down," she said, "and drive a great *boulevard* through the rubble."

"You're a romantic."

"I used to come and hunt for books here." A parallel memory of the demolished Vecchio ghetto passed through her mind and a rare mood of nostalgia suddenly depressed her. The past. The past! She must not let it hamper her. The past had nothing to offer but the secrets it still concealed.

They walked the Fields in easeful silence and turned again for home; but a sharp image of those pinned-together memoirs—now safely locked away—halted her. "No," she said. "I can't go back yet."

"Shall we walk up to St. Paul's?"

Nothing in her responded to the suggestion. Then suddenly she knew what she wanted. "Let's take a cab out to Highgate Cemetery and look for old Karl's grave."

He laughed. "Why on earth? A cemetery? After what we've just read?"

She had not made that connection. "It'll take two or three hours," she explained. "It'll demand no effort of us. It's something you wanted to do. If we don't do it now, we never will. Oh, come on! I just can't go back home yet."

It took an hour to locate the grave, with its modest headstone, tucked away on a ridge near the eastern edge of the grounds. Victor stood above it, head on one side; his glass eye seemed to stare down at the grave, his good eye looked absently at her.

She laughed. "Listening still?"

He collected himself and looked at the grave. "Not to this one." He shook his head. "He wasn't a *good* man even. He wrote insulting letters to his friends about Lafargue, who was his son-in-law and who founded the French Communist Party. And he treated Charles Longuet the same way, who married his other daughter, Jenny. They were both refugees from the Commune. 'The Devil take the pair of them,' he wrote to Engels. He was prejudiced against us Latins."

Still looking at the earth, he fell back into silence; but his mouth went on working.

"What?" she asked, knowing the signs.

He chuckled. "I was thinking of a poet of my youth, Olivier Roux. No one reads him now. He was the generation before ours—you know, the generation that believed it did all the hard work while we skimmed off the rewards."

"What generation doesn't believe that!"

Victor smiled at the truth of it. "Olivier was a lifelong atheist. Yet he called us all to his deathbed 'to see how a good Christian can die.' He even had a priest there." Victor laughed. "It must have put the fear of God into God, because Olivier recovered and died of drink in the arms of a *grisette* a year later to the very day."

She joined his laughter. "Why think of that just now?"

"So that you won't misunderstand me when I say . . ." He paused and looked about them. "This would be a good place for us when our time comes."

"Here?" She was looking at the nearby ground.

"No!" He gave a theatrical shiver. "Cleaner earth. Over there." He pointed at the unbroken turf several dozen yards away. Then he stooped to pick up a stone and threw it to mark the spot.

"Robin Hood!" She laughed again.

He was sucking the back of his wrist, just above the hem of his glove. "Stinging nettle," he said. "The old bastard."

"Wait," she told him. "There'll be a dockleaf somewhere. There always is." She found one and pressed its juice to the pale blisters of the sting.

"In nature," he said, smiling down at the concentration on her face, "where the poison lies, the antidote is never far to seek."

She raised her eyes to dwell in his and smiled back. "D'you really think she did it, Victor?" she asked. "Or was it just bravado, to shock Walter? My God—think of those two going on meeting all their lives! Our families have been so close! D'you think she did it? With her own father?"

"Over fifty years ago," he answered. "Is it the kind of truth that need concern you now?"

"I've seen that dress, that blue serge dress she wore. She showed it to me. And a sovereign she kept—I'll bet it's the same one. She said she kept the dress because it's the one she was wearing when my father proposed to her. And the sovereign was her savings—her contribution to the firm's beginnings. But now look at the clouds of double meaning surrounding them. Has she forgotten all that half of it? Or am I being too fastidious?"

He bent at the knees to kiss her. "Home?" he asked.

They began the downhill walk to their waiting cab. "And she threw Annie out into the street!" Abigail continued. "Just for telling me the simplest, most elementary fact about men and women. She threw her out. Yet she knew *exactly*—I mean, personally, from her own life's experience;

it wasn't a vague something in a book, it had actually happened to her!—she *knew* what would happen to Annie."

"And yet, one would say she is a kindly woman. No monster."

"And even Annie said my mother was right to throw her out." She laughed a humourless laugh. "It isn't just me that's confused. Everyone is."

At the gate he turned and looked back up the hill.

"Shall I stay?" he asked.

She laughed in bewilderment. "What d'you mean?"

"I'm an old man. And already I'm wondering if the cab fare home isn't an extravagance."

She hugged him fiercely and stopped his mouth with a kiss. "Don't," she pleaded. "Never talk like that. I can't imagine this world without you. Oh, my darling, my darling!"

Chapter 48

It was two days before she dared to look again at Walter's Summit memoir. Victor complained of having drunk too much wine at lunch and was taking a nap on a divan in the corner of their study. Feeling private yet not alone, she unlocked the drawer and pulled out the papers.

They lay face down, and she saw there was writing on the back of the last sheet, something she had not seen the first time. It ran:

Oh, Nora, Nora, what a blind fool am I, and how I curse this fiend-prick that reduces all women to a simple harbour for him to anchor and toss in but never rest. You are a jewel among women, the most perfect who ever lived. John Stevenson will be a great man but *you* will make him so; without you he'd just be one of two dozen clever, jumped-up navvies. But I saw you before he did. I talked with you before he did. Why then did I not understand you as you are? I know why—because my old one-eyed Polyphemus was looking at you. Not I. Oh, my love, I love you, my love, my love. Nora, Nora Nora.

How, she wondered, could one ever judge such a man? He was a monster hypocrite and he was sincere; he thought himself marvellous and he disgusted himself; he loved his wife and fought like one possessed to undo her life's work; he felt contempt for women, reduced them to a single commodity, pursued them relentlessly until they yielded it—and then wanted to know all about them as fellow human beings!

You could make sense of him only by ignoring one half or the other. She wondered what Victor would think of it. Anyway, it was time for him to get up or he'd not sleep tonight.

"Darling?" she said.

He did not stir. Smiling she walked over to shake him, but when she stood above him the smile vanished and she froze.

"Victor!"

A light sweat beaded his face. He stirred feebly. She heard no breathing.

"Oh, my God! Victor!"

With fevered hands she loosened his collar. She plucked out his hand-kerchief to mop his face. She felt stupidly incompetent. What else should she do? Fetch a doctor! She ran to the landing and screamed for anyone to come. Frances was there, on the landing below, immediately.

"Run and get a doctor," Abigail shouted down. "The Baron's not well."

"Shall I telephone?" Frances asked.

The telephone! Oh, the habits of a lifetime! She must calm down and think. "Yes, Frances. Ring my brother Clement. His number's in our own book. Tell him it could be life and death. Tell him to come at once."

She ran back to Victor. He was stirring slightly, muttering something. ". . . doctor."

"He's coming. The doctor's coming, darling. Oh, stay . . . stay, Victor. Don't leave me."

He smiled and fumbled for her hand. "No . . . doctor," he whispered.

"Of course we'll get a doctor. He's already coming. My brother Clement's coming."

"Pills . . . potions . . ."

"Are you in pain?"

"Listen! Pills . . . potions . . . poking about . . . fiddle-faddle. Don't want it. Time's up."

"Victor! Please! Oh, God, where is Clement? Frances!"

"Calm! Be . . . calm. Let it . . . be calm."

"Victor?" She climbed on the divan beside him.

"Love," he said.

She fought with herself not to cry.

"Sing."

She raised her head and hummed, a formless tune at first but it soon resolved itself into the humming part in the "Habañera" from *Carmen*; they had recently heard Emma Calvé sing it at a recital.

A smile settled on his face. Looking at the creases in his flesh, ravaged by more than time, she felt a sudden hatred of it—for failing him and giving up like this. Then, still humming, she leaned forward to kiss it, with some half-clear notion of coaxing it to stay by him and see him through.

Clement came within twenty minutes, though it seemed like twenty hours. He was a quiet, observant man, sparing of gestures and superfluous words. He worked at Victor's body with an efficiency that did much to calm Abigail.

"It was undoubtedly a heart attack," he said at length.

"Will he live?" Abigail asked.

"Oh, yes." He smiled down at Victor, who was watching him with heavy eyes. "A year from now, Victor, you'll probably be healthier than you have been for the last five years. I'll give you a minute dose of—" He hesitated and smiled at both of them. "I never know whether to tell this to patients or not. The treatment is arsenic and strychnine! But I stress: the dose is minute. It will stimulate your heart."

"You mean flog it at hard labour," Victor said in a near whisper.

Clement laughed. "It's used to that," he said. "The heart is a mere hewer of wood and drawer of water. Don't heed the poets. But, to make the hard labour somewhat less hard, I'm also going to give you something that'll open up all your arteries so they'll offer less resistance."

"What?" Abigail asked.

"Oh, the usual nitrites. Nothing exciting."

He gave Victor several small pills of different colours and wrote a prescription for a regular supply.

"You look pretty comfortable there," he said.

Victor nodded.

"Might as well stay there tonight." He turned to Abigail. "Just take off the outer garments and cover him lightly. Keep a fire in. I'll be back tomorrow and we'll move him to bed."

Abigail saw her brother to the door. "We'll do some tests," he said, "when he's over this."

"I want to know the truth, Clement."

He looked at her, assessing how deeply she meant it. "I'll tell you the worst I suspect. I think he's had high blood pressure for rather a long time."

"Which means?"

"It means I can invite you to dinner in two months' time with fair confidence—but two years? The tests will tell. Some hearts adapt amazingly."

Chapter 49

"Compensatory hypertrophy will fail," Victor said complacently. "Dilatation will increase and lead to mitral incompetence with regurgitation, leading to pulmonary congestion and all the usual signs of failure of compensation."

"You are looking well this morning," Abigail said, drawing the curtains.

"Attacks of angina and syncope will be common, accompanied by dyspnea and hyperventilation."

"I told Frances to burn those books."

"I know them by heart. Pathologically the cardiac muscle evinces brown atrophy and fatty and fibroid degenerative lesions."

She kissed him lightly. "It sounds dreadful, but I must say you look as if you thrive on it."

"It's a just punishment—kiss me again—a just punishment for turning myself into a *petit bourgeois*."

"In what way?"

"This regime—three light meals, light exercise, fresh air, no worry, watered whisky, free purgation, sleep!"

"It's what old Karl wanted for everyone. The chance to write poetry. You're going to get up today and walk around."

He was delighted, really, once he discovered he wasn't going to be a helpless invalid but could even recover completely—if only for a time. She contained her anxiety by badgering him, and he teased her, to make the badgering easier to sustain. That was his true regime. And under it he made remarkable progress. By Christmas he was his old self again and they both allowed themselves to hope, against all medical opinion, that his attack had been a mere episode.

*   *   *

One evening in the following spring, the spring of 1891, Frances asked Abigail if they might have a word.

"You remember I said I'd been thinking about this work you're doing?"

"Yes." Abigail poured herself a Madeira. "For you?" she asked.

"Please. Goodness, I should be doing that." She rose again.

"You sit where you are. I'm much more interested in your ideas." She handed her a glass. "To health."

"Indeed." She sipped. Abigail noticed that her hand trembled; it was the first sign of nervousness she had ever seen in the girl. She left the gaslight deliberately low. Bare branches stirred outside; their shadows bobbed in stately dances up and down the walls.

"I'd imagine you're pretty well unshockable by now," Abigail said.

Frances snorted. "It doesn't *mean* anything to me. I mean I've never—well—I've never—"

"Of course not. But I imagine you knew something of the facts?"

"Yes," she admitted grudgingly. "But—well, for instance, you can know that chocolate's for putting in your mouth, can't you. I mean that's a *fact*. But it doesn't tell you anything about the taste, does it. Nor about how you can get a craving for chocolate."

"Very good! Is that what has surprised you?"

"Well—I mean: Walter! Craving isn't the word, is it. Are they all like that? Men?"

"To a degree they are. Not so exaggerated, perhaps."

"Another thing, Abbie. What's that blood we get each month?"

"I'm not sure. My brother Clement, who ought to know about these things, says it's because girls outgrow boys until they're about fourteen or fifteen, then we slow down and they catch up. But meanwhile our bodies have got used to making fresh blood at the faster rate—and anyway we have to keep it up for when we have babies. Because it stops then, as I suppose you know. In between, well, it's just our bodies keeping in practice. And when we reach my age it begins to stop because"—she smiled—"we're past having babies. Tell me, has this anything to do with—you know?"

"Not really. Except that it's strange, isn't it, all this ignorance. Anyway, I was talking about Walter and how strong all their desires are. And going on all the time."

"Yes."

"Well now, that's point number one: you can't stop them. No one can stop them. All right?"

Abigail grinned. "All right."

"Now, point number two. What was point number two? Oh yes! All those notes you and the Baron made on different civilizations, where you found they all of them said that intercourse was only to be inside marriage?"

"Yes?"

"That's point number two. Now, if you put one and two together—well, it's like a law against breathing, isn't it? I'm sorry I can't say this in a very literary and proper way, but—"

"Go on, Frances. It's splendid."

"Well. That leads to point three, which is that all those civilizations had some form of prostitution. They said 'don't do it'—officially—and then they tolerated it unofficially. But only for the men. They don't tolerate it for the women."

"That's because of inheritance. A husband's illegitimate children stay outside the family; but a wife's—"

"I know. I know. That was point number four: you're bound to get two standards. Because of that. A loose one for men and strict one for women. Funny, isn't it!" She laughed. "We're brought up thinking all this is just Holy Writ and keep-your-mouth-shut, and really there's a lot of good reasons for it and it's quite interesting to think about and talk about."

Abigail was now torn between two reactions. On the one hand, she was delighted that Frances had reached this freedom of thought on her own; but, on the other, if this trivial conclusion was the *result*, the thought itself wasn't worth much. "Is there a point number five, Frances?" she asked.

"Five, six, seven, eight . . . hundred!" Frances smiled proudly. "For a long time I was stuck there. At point four. Then I read Mrs. Besant's book, you know the one, *The Law of Population*, and *The Malthusian*, and *The Wife's Handbook*. How good are they, Abbie? Those things they talk about—those Malthusian devices?"

"Well, they're not perfect."

"Oh." Frances pulled a face. "Pity."

"Why?"

"Well, that'd be the answer, wouldn't it? If a woman could be sure of not having a baby, that would do away with point number four, wouldn't it? There needn't be two standards. It could be the same standards for us as for them."

"Frances!" Abigail began to feel excited.

"But wait!" the girl said. "It's a lot more than that. It's everything. You'll see! You know where Walter says he prefers working-class women to his own class? He can talk to them more easily and so on? Well, now we can see why. Upper-class men can never be natural and easy with girls of their own class, can they—because we know what natural and easy leads to. But suppose it didn't! You can't stop the men wanting it, we know that. But suppose you didn't have to!"

"Yes! That's it, Frances: suppose we didn't have to!"

"They wouldn't go running after working-class girls then, would they. It would put a stop to all that."

"Of course—and the men who didn't develop that habit when young wouldn't retain it into later years. Frances, you—you genius! You may not have it all yet but there was a—there was a *log jam* of thoughts in my head, and you've broken it up. Bless you! Is there more?"

"Well, then I started thinking, that's all very well for the upper classes—all the fun and frolic as usual. What about the ninety percent of us, right down to the working-class girl brought up ten in a room? From what you've been writing, I think it's them you want to help more than your own kind."

"They are my kind, Frances. My dearest, warmest friend, apart from the Baron, grew up ten in a room and lived half her life in the workhouse orphanage. But you're right, yes. I don't really give a pinch of snuff for 'my' kind. What follows?"

"What follows is that a girl can't love as we'd like her to love unless she has a sense of her own dignity. And she can't develop dignity ten in a room. She needs a room of her own. Dignity is privacy, really, isn't it."

Abigail was silent a while. "You shame me, Frances," she said. "You cut through everything so exactly. But what you're saying is that the task I've set myself is impossible. To go from ten-in-a-room to a situation in which everyone has privacy—it's centuries away."

"Yes, Abbie!" Frances grinned broadly. "That's the whole point."

"Well, it doesn't delight me as it seems to delight you."

"It ought to. Don't you see—it frees you from trying to do *everything*. That was your Uncle Daniel's real mistake, you know. He tried to do everything, upset the whole arrangement of things, and he succeeded in absolutely nothing. But we can pick our area and concentrate on it with a good conscience, even though we know we're neglecting lots of other important things. You could write a book about these ideas, and that would be right. Or you could set up a Malthusian clinic in the East End, and that would be right, too. Or you could promote better housing and health, and *that* would be right. Even assist the struggle for better female wages and more secure jobs, because that would also be going our way. You see? Anything, almost, because you're not just saying that *love* ought to be different—even though you are. I mean—" She choked in exasperation at the vastness of it all. *"Love can't be different until everything else is different."*

Chapter 50

Their first venture, they decided, would be a clinic and dispensary for the poor, somewhere down in the East End. As part of its general medical service it would offer Malthusian devices and counsel. Clement began to take a side-lines interest in his sister's ideas, and Abigail asked him to help her find a good woman doctor to operate the clinic. Then she went to see Annie.

"I don't know the East End these days, me old love," she said. "Time was when Whitechapel was all Scotch and Irish; now it's all Jews. Everything's changed. It's still poor, but it's changed. I can't help you, gel."

"Where was the poorest area—that can't have changed. The toughest, roughest part?"

Annie laughed at this show of spirit. "They pulled it down—what didn't fall of its own accord. All round Liverpool Street station—*my* area. But you could try Shadwell or Wapping. Or up Hackney way. Just stick a pin in the map, love—there's a thousand miles of poverty over there. What you going to call these places of yours?"

"We haven't decided. I want to call them Bouvier Clinics, but that depends on Victor."

Annie tested the word and began to laugh. Abigail asked why. "You got to think how they'll say it, love. None of your Boo-vee-eh. *Bovver-yer!* That's what they'll say. Bovver-yer!"

"Meaning 'bother you.' Oh, dear!"

"No," Annie laughed. "You still don't get it. Like, a woman'll say, 'Does your old man bovver yer much?' or 'Her old man's a right cater-wauler—he bovvers her every bleeding night.' See! The Bovver-yer Clinic. That'll catch on fast."

"Well, that puts an end to that."

"No!" Annie was vehement. "It's perfect. They'll all have a good laugh. And who isn't fond of a good laugh, eh! Only I don't like that 'Clinic'—there's a mortal fear of doctors and hospitals and messing about with your insides down in those streets."

Abigail blessed the instinct that had led her to start with Annie. "What would be a better name?"

"I dunno. Words isn't my lark. What's a place where everyone goes? Palais? Emporium? Club?"

"Institute?"

"Yes! That'll do. Like, there's working men's institutes, evening institutes, polytechnic institutes—why not a bovver-yer institute!" She cackled richly at the comedy of it.

Abigail did not find it quite so funny. "The Bouvier Institute for Healthy Girls. What about that? It should remove all doubts."

*   *   *

"Not 'Girls,' " Dr. Stubbins said, clenching her gloved hands even more firmly together. " 'Wives.' The Bouvier Institute for Healthy Wives. I couldn't consent to treat unmarried females with Malthusian devices."

"Not *treat*, Dr. Stubbins," Abigail said. "*Advise*. Perhaps you aren't aware of the scourge of illegitimacy? Some even consider it to be worse than the scourge of indiscriminate breeding within marriage."

"It may be, Baroness," the doctor said primly. "Indeed, I believe it is. But I cannot regard its cure as falling within the medical sphere. If you wish to deal with illegitimacy as well, then the Institute should employ a minister of religion. As I see it, my task—on the Malthusian side—is to assist married people to ascend from the trap of excessive childbearing and the resultant poverty and infant and maternal mortality. I'm quite prepared to treat unmarried females who have medical complaints and on separate premises. But I wouldn't want confusion to enter anybody's mind on this matter."

Abigail drew a sharp breath but Victor laid a gentle hand on her arm. "Dr. Stubbins has made an excellent point," he said. "We must obviously discuss this further. Meanwhile, I suggest we try to decide on one of the three buildings available to us."

Abigail pinched her lips together; the rims of her nostrils went white, but she did as Victor suggested.

"This woman, Dr. Stubbins," Victor said later, "is our barometer. She's a Modern, a Progressive."

"She's a bigot," Abigail complained.

"Yes—a modern, progressive bigot. If she's *for* something, you may be sure it's on the very fringe of what society and the law will permit; but if she's against . . ." He mimed a policeman putting handcuffs on her wrists.

"I'm not afraid of a fight."

"Ah, yes! A fight—what a lovely word! What a *Daniel* word! Fight—smash—crush. He used them like small change. Shall we, instead, talk about a means to victory? We *are* interested in victories, aren't we? Not in mere fighting?"

Warily she nodded.

"I say make haste slowly. Let Dr. Stubbins treat only the ladies with the marriage lines. The first thing she's going to find is that a lot of them don't have marriage lines—yet in every other way they are respectable 'married' women; sober, faithful, excellent mothers and housekeepers. The good doctor won't be the first missionary to adapt high-flown ideals to uncomfortable local ways. I'm thinking that'll be the crack in her facade. But even more than all this, we mustn't forget that the local police will be watching us like cat and mouse. When they see we are absolutely firm in treating only married women, and when they see what an impeccably moral person our doctor is, they'll think twice about taking action against us. But if we began to give advice and safeguards to unmarried women—"

"But we must, Victor. At some stage we must—that's the whole point."

He held up a finger. "How can we do that without a fight? Smash nothing? Crush no one? Eh? How can we get even the police to say, 'Yes, that's all right, too'?"

She laughed grimly, thinking these questions to be rhetorical.

But he went on. "What's the English saying? 'Hard cases make bad law'? No one likes to administer or enforce bad law. Not even the toughest of your English police. So we must find a good hard case."

"For example."

He shrugged. "One will turn up."

Her face brightened. "I know one," she said. "A perfect case. And there must be dozens of them, everywhere."

"What?"

"In the village where I used to teach at Sunday school there was an imbecile girl. Not a mongol, you understand, just very simple. And she was always either expecting or having babies. The village youths used to line up in wait for her. Out in the fields every night."

"Excellent," he said. "That'll be our first. Then we'll find a case just a bit softer, and then softer, until in the end—"

"—the law is 'more honoured in the breach than . . .' Oh, but honestly, Victor, doesn't it make you *sick!* When you think of the official tolerance that is daily extended to the debauching and seduction of those same unmarried girls, and how widespread—"

"Debauchery and Seduction, Unlimited, is an old established firm, my precious—mankind's family business, you could say." He laughed. "But what can we say of Advise and Consent, Universal, eh? It's still looking for share capital!"

"Talking of which," she said, "we must take our begging bowl to Steamer."

Chapter 51

"Forget the East End," Steamer said. "Come and open your institute in Stevenstown. You're welcome to treat unmarried females, too, if you want."

"Really?" Abigail could hardly believe her ears.

"I won't say bastardy is a big expense to us, but it's not small, either."

"To you?" Victor asked in surprise.

"Haven't you told him about Stevenstown?" Caspar asked her. Then, without waiting for an answer, he went on, "It's our own company town, up near Stockton, in Durham. Everyone who works in our steel mills there, even the managers, has to live in it. We built it in eighteen forty-six, forty-seven. Neither the Earl nor I ever understood why the working man wants a lot of cash to jingle. They only drink it, or gamble. So we have the lowest-paid steelworkers in the land—and the best housed, best educated, healthiest, and best fed. And I daresay the happiest. There's a hospital, nurseries, libraries, foot baths, swimming bath, concert hall, evening institutes, museum. So a 'Bouvier Institute' wouldn't be too out of the way." He turned to Abigail. "You know our latest? This'll please you. We pay the wives half the wage—Aunt Arabella's been badgering us for years to do it."

"Does it work?"

"I think it's a disaster. The wives hate it. In the bad old days most of them got *all* the wages! But we'll let it run for three months. Damn!"

They had been standing in the dark, on the terrace at Falconwood, soaked by a light autumnal drizzle and admiring the effect of the electrical arc lighting on the great southern facade and clock tower. The drizzle had just extinguished one of the arc lights in a spectacular burst of sparks and crackles. Moments later the three other arc lights put on a similar display of pyrotechnics and left the world to darkness—and profanity.

"Well, at least you saw it," Caspar said.

"Very impressive," Victor assured him.

"It smells like a photographer's studio," Abigail said.

"It's the smell of progress," Caspar answered testily. "Why do you women always complain so bitterly about anything that smells of progress! The Conservatives are mad not to give you the vote—they'd double their representation by it."

They walked back across the terrace to the warmth and low-wattage lighting of the house.

"Talking of complaints—you're sure we'd have no trouble with the police?" Abigail asked.

Caspar laughed. "Who d'you think put the chief constable where he is, eh? Who provides the quietest, soberest, most trouble-free streets in all England? Who pays for the annual police ball? I could open a casino there if I wanted."

"Then I don't see," Abigail said, "why we shouldn't open two Bouvier Institutes. One for 'Healthy Wives' in the East End and one for 'Healthy Women' at Stevenstown. What about that? Of course, we'll need the most generous support from the present owner of Stevenstown."

*   *   *

Annie was a marvellous recruiting sergeant; she knew exactly the right mixture of comedy, bullying, and straight talking to use. She also knew that if she harped on the medical services offered by the Bouvier Institute, she would frighten off as many as she might attract, so she concentrated her recruiting speeches on the one aspect that would prick their curiosity and allay their fears.

Her target for each "drive" was an entire street and all the little yards and courts leading off it. She and a couple of helpers would run up and down knocking on all the doors; as soon as a woman answered they'd say, " 'Ere—come out and have a cuppa tea, love. Come and listen to this." They wouldn't stay and argue, but ran straight to the next door as if breaking the news of the century. The woman would look up and down the street in bewilderment, see the mobile tea stall, and curiosity would do the rest. It wasn't every day you were given a free cuppa by someone who looked like the queen's own cousin—for it was, of course, Abigail who poured and served the tea.

"They'll never forget it, love," Annie said. "That's what you want, isn't it—for them never to forget. Also they'll know it's respectable—which is important."

As soon as the crowd was gathered, Annie would mount up on an orange box and say, "You know who's just given you that cuppa tea, with her own hands? Well, it's not everyone here who could say—until today—they've taken tea with the daughter of an earl in the English peerage, is it! Yes! Baroness Bouvier, daughter of the Earl of Wharfedale. What? I should say! And it's not the only thing she wants to give you—no, it's only a start. What else, d'you say? I'll tell you what else. The chance of a rest, that's what. A rest from having one bleeding nipper after another. What you going away for, gel? Going home, are you? Is your old man home already?"

Even if no one made to leave, Annie still looked vaguely at the back of the crowd and followed this line of patter.

"Well, you can still feed him, my love—if you take my meaning. You can still give him his greens. What? I should say! He can have them on the kitchen table if he's that eager. The Baroness don't want to stop none of that. That's not her game. Only you needn't do a kitten as the other part of a bad bargain. What's that, my love?" And here she would look at any woman near the front. "Not possible? 'Course it's possible! All the nibs and nobby persons—they're doing it all the time, aren't they! They have their conjugals any time they like. And they don't have no nippers unless they want them. Now here's *our* chance—and about time, too, I say."

Here she would look back at the woman who had apparently said it was impossible. "Look at her—she still don't believe me." She began darting her finger over the crowd. "D'you believe me, love? D'you believe me? Do you?" She didn't wait for an answer from any of them. "It don't matter. You don't have to believe me. I'm not asking you to believe me. All I'm saying is come and see for yourselves. 'Cause seeing's believing, ain't it? Come up the Bouvier Institute any afternoon, any evening. What's that, me old love? Where's the Bouvier Institute? Blimey! Where've you ladies been living? Where's the Bouvier Institute? What? The Bouvier Institute for Healthy Wives? Where is it? Well, here's a shilling for anyone who can tell me."

Here there was a dramatic pause while dozens of uplifted eyes fixed on the shining silver. Dozens of brains were racked and dozens of lips licked in forlorn hope. "The Bouvier Institute for Healthy Wives?" Annie repeated slowly, fixing the name—and the simultaneous sight of the silver—in their memories. "No? Pity." She put the silver away amid gasps of disappointment. "Well!" Her eyes begged for fair play. "I can't give a shilling for nothing, can I! But I'll tell you what I can give you. I can give you sixpence! Yes—each and every one of you, I can give sixpence. What about that, then!" She fished out an impressive-looking voucher. "There! You take that up the co-op in Dalston Lane and Mr.

Watts there, he'll give you six penn'orth of groceries for it. I s'pose you do all know where the co-op is!"

Of course they all nodded and murmured yes. "Well, that's a mercy because the Bouvier Institute's right next door, on the corner of Mare Street! One other thing—see this white space here, on the bottom? That's for Mrs. Fletcher, very nice lady up the Institute, to put her stamp and sign her monnicker. Mr. Watts won't give you nothing till that's filled in proper. Is that all right? Any other questions? What's that, love? Me? No, I won't be there meself—I'll be up the Throat Hospital, 'cause I'm losing me voice, see!"

Annie must have delivered the speech forty times over the two months during which the clinic was put into operation. Toward the end when everybody knew where the Bouvier Institute was, she changed "the shilling question," offering the coin to anyone who could spell it properly or give its exact title. And since the cockney genius had, just as she predicted, already transmuted Bouvier into Bovver-yer, her coin was usually safe. The sixpenny vouchers were her idea, though she intended it only as a come-all-you. Abigail decided to make it permanent: every woman who visited the clinic got one, every time. In the end they cost nothing, for the co-op was willing to drop threepence on their value for the sake of the extra trade it brought, and the manufacturers of the various medicines and devices they dispensed made up the other threepence.

Abigail carried home to Victor and Frances all the tales of these recruiting drives, doing so perfect an imitation of Annie that, as Frances said, "it makes the hair rise on the back of my neck to watch it."

Abigail took the precaution of writing personally to the Home Secretary, asking his advice and seeking to know whether his ministry was aware of any unwitting contravention of the law by the Bouvier Institute. She explained their procedure in the fullest detail, making it clear that their Malthusian work was confined to married females and was, in any case, only a small part of their charitable work. Henry Matthews did not reply in person, but the writer drew their attention to Section III (Protection of Women and Girls) of the Criminal Law Amendment Act of 1885. She sought counsel's opinion at once.

"It would be very English," Victor said, "if we were to be prosecuted under an Act for the *protection* of women and girls."

But counsel's opinion was that the reply was bluff. The only paragraph of the Act with any conceivable relevance read: "Any person who procures or attempts to procure any girl or woman under 21 years of age, not being a common prostitute, or of known immoral character, to have unlawful carnal connexion, either within or without the Queen's dominions, with any other person or persons . . . shall be guilty of a misdemeanor, etc."

Since, in English law, he continued, carnal connexion was unlawful only with girls under sixteen, or girls who were imbeciles, or in the case of rape and incest, and, furthermore, since the offence of procuration required the procurer to receive some reward or consideration from the person on whose behalf the female is procured, no prosecution could be sustained. Writing to the Home Secretary was a shrewd move, he added. "Make copies of the reply and keep several on the premises so that, if you are raided, they will know at once what the Home Office view is—and will, moreover, be directed up the blind alley of the C.L.A.A., 1885, Part III."

Counsel added: "As to literature, keep as little as possible on the premises. With your clientele I imagine word-of-mouth instruction would be in any case more effective. Books already on open sale are safe enough, such as *Law of Population* and *The Wife's Handbook*; also journals like *The Malthusian*. Since the utter collapse of the Bradlaugh and Besant prosecution in 1878, the authorities have been shy of a second humiliation."

When the Gladstone government came in that August, Abigail took the chance to write to Asquith, the new Home Secretary, and ask if his opinion and advice differed from that of the previous administration. He replied that it did not. Copies of that letter, too, were kept at the Institute.

It was very much to Abigail's chagrin that, after taking such elaborate counterprecautions, they were never once raided—not even by cat burglars or pruriently curious small boys.

Chapter 52

Once the Institutes at Hackney and Stevenstown were established, Abigail found herself with less to do than she had expected. The day-to-day running was a matter for Dr. Stubbins and the secretary, Mrs. Fletcher, in London and their counterparts in the north country. Abigail was eager then to plan the opening of more institutes, but Victor was adamant: They needed at least a year—preferably two years—before they would know if the problem could be tackled this way at all.

Suddenly what had promised to be a life rich in work and fulfillment became flat. There was no other word for it. She did not love Victor the

less; indeed, if more were possible, she loved him more. And he felt the
same about her. The problem was not there. It was something to do with
the Institutes. Somehow—and quite reasonably, she now realized—she
had expected more of a relationship to grow between herself and the
women who attended. Not the full richness of her rapport with Annie, of
course, but *something* of it nevertheless. Instead, she felt nothing.

William Morris had once told her how keenly he resented his inability
to get on cordial terms with working-class people, despite their evident
(and his own undoubted) goodwill. She wondered if she was now to suffer
that same disappointment. Was Annie just a special case in her life?

Or (she wondered guiltily) had Annie herself made it impossible for
any of those women to befriend her? The recruiting speech certainly
spelled out the enormous social gulf that separated them, and Annie had
given her good reasons for stressing it. But Annie had behaved in strange,
jealous ways in the past, so it wouldn't be out of character now. What a
funny, complicated person she was. She claimed to be so simple—and
probably even believed it. All she wanted was "a good laugh." But
underneath it all she was a boxful of Chinese puzzles, and not a simple bit
of grain in her.

Abigail began to look for other outlets for her energies. She attended a
number of suffragist meetings that autumn, though she valued the vote so
little. There were two kinds of suffragists. On the one hand were those
who campaigned for woman suffrage—that is, they wanted the present
franchise (which, being restricted more or less to property owners, was
middle and upper class) extended to women property owners and the
wives of men of property. By and large these campaigners were upper-
class, Conservative women who would no more think of campaigning on
behalf of all women than they would support the cause of democracy; the
very word was as hateful to them as to their husbands.

On the other hand, there were the campaigners for full adult suffrage for both sexes—a small, powerless group compared with the woman
suffragists.

The aims of both were so far removed from hers, or, at best, were so
small a part of hers, that she decided to quit their meetings, though she
continued to send donations to the adult suffragists. In any case, Victor
was now beginning the series of tests that Clement had promised, which
took her mind off any public involvement for a time.

The results were not encouraging, though they pretended otherwise
to Victor. His high blood pressure did not respond to treatment. "He
must have arteries like clay pipestems," Clement said. His heart, respond-

ing to the extra work, was steadily enlarging, and the roots of its valves were thus being stretched. Inevitably the day would come when they were stretched too far. Then, with each heartbeat, some of the blood that ought to be pumped out into the body would instead leak back through an incompetent valve into the blood vessels of his lungs. This would increase the strain on his heart many times over, and from then on his decline would be rapid.

They told Victor none of this but, of course, he knew it anyway.

"I have travelled the railways," he said with a smile.

Until that fatal overstretching of the valve occurred, there would be no sudden change in his general fitness; life could go on very much as it always had.

"Shall we go back to Venice this winter?" she asked. "We had such a marvellous time there."

"And leave Walter?" he joked. "No—London's the place for us now."

The inevitability of death did not move her, but its nearness seemed, at first, intolerable. She thought of taking him to Heidelberg, where the world's best doctors lived, or to Marienbad, where the regime and diet had prolonged thousands of lives, or to the Alps—perhaps the mountain air and clean sunlight would do wonders for him.

But, as one possibility succeeded another, they merged into a composite vision of precious months squandered in the fruitless cosseting of a body whose failure no external agency or regime could postpone. And with that realization came a sudden calm. It was almost an exhilaration—at least it turned each normal, uneventful day into something special. What had someone once said to her—to survive one day is a mercy! It was no exaggeration.

*   *   *

One afternoon a Mrs. Elkington-Laud came to call. Abigail remembered her as the madam chairman of the woman-suffragist meetings she had attended; she asked the maid to show this visitor into the drawing room.

Mrs. Elkington-Laud was visibly taken aback by César's paintings; she looked from them to Abigail and back, and so far forgot herself as to say, "Good heavens."

"By Rodet," Abigail said. "I shared an atelier in Rome with him and his wife for many years." She laughed. "Of course in those days he alone knew what a great painter he was!" Her speech was long enough—and inconsequential enough—to allow Mrs. Elkington-Laud to recover herself. Abigail's composure was helped by the fact that she didn't give a rap for the woman's opinions, nor for her talents as a tale bearer.

"No doubt, no doubt," Mrs. Elkington-Laud said in a conciliatory tone. And then, pricked by a genuine curiosity, she asked, "Tell me, why do you hang them so publicly, Madame la Baronne?"

"I find it invaluable, Mrs. Elkington-Laud. Those pictures infallibly divide the world into people who believe it matters and those who know it doesn't."

"Yes?" she said dubiously, neither agreeing nor seeing the point.

"Well, since I know I should find the former tedious . . ." She smiled sweetly. "But do sit down, I'm sure you didn't call on me to discuss paintings! I fear I'm in for a wigging for not attending your meetings?"

"A wigging! Dear me, Madame la Baronne, certainly not. The very idea. No, but, since you are good enough to mention it, I'm sure I'd be most interested to know why we have not seen you recently. Nothing is amiss, I hope?"

"To be candid, Mrs. Elkington-Laud, I find I am not enough in sympathy with your particular aims."

The visitor made a tight-lipped smile. "Perhaps you feel, like Lady Ashburton, Lady Londonderry, Lady Jeune"—she listed more than half a dozen eminent political hostesses—"you feel you do not want to dilute your family's influence?"

The maid brought in some tea.

"Not in the least, Mrs. Elkington-Laud. But does it not strike you as extraordinary, the number of prominent women who have made their own way in life and their own mark on the world who are antisuffragists? Ouida, Marie Corelli, John Oliver Hobbes, Violet Markham, Mary Kingsley, Gertrude Bell—even Beatrice Webb. And you know I could name dozens of other talented women, all opposed to you suffragists. And we are all very far from matching your hobble-di-hoy picture of a downtrodden, simpering, semi-invalid, know-nothing, half-child female. I'm sure there are more women of achievement and sense against woman suffrage than for it." Abigail poured the tea as she spoke.

Mrs. Elkington-Laud was crestfallen. She sipped abstractedly, as if the arguments going on in her mind were by now too tired to muster. "You are probably correct," she said at last. "I cannot understand it. It's the most discouraging thing of all, Madame la Baronne."

"Oh, please call me something less formal, Mrs. Elkington-Laud. As to our reasons for opposing suffragism, I'm sure we each have our own.

For my part, I have no deep-rooted objection to our getting the vote. I simply put it very far down the list of things that cry out for attention. If the men in Parliament had tried to block higher education for women, or the new laws on women's property, on the age of consent . . . the Contagious Diseases Acts . . . factory legislation—all the causes where women were the leading campaigners—I'm sure I'd think differently. But Parliament has proved highly responsive to our aims. If women had had the vote, I doubt if any of those measures would have gone through the quicker for it."

Mrs. Elkington-Laud became livelier. "But that's where they're so clever, Madame de Bouvier. They give way to us on these lesser issues so that they may stand fast on the main issue of the vote."

"*Lesser* issues, Mrs. Elkington-Laud?" Abigail's patience was growing thin. "To raise the age of consent for girls from twelve to sixteen? Lesser? To end the degrading harassment of respectable women by a notoriously corrupt branch of our police? Lesser? I'm afraid this shows how different our notions are. And so much remains to be done that only we women can do."

"For my part I see nothing more important than the vote."

Abigail sighed. "How would one describe the sky to people who had lived a lifetime in a cave? And yet," she went on quickly, seeing the offence begin to grow in her visitor's eyes, "there is among you suffragists an inkling of my own views. I was in conversation with Olive Schreiner at one of your meetings." Interest began to replace that look of offence. "She told me that the parasite woman is very little different from the prostitute. 'They shade off by degrees,' she said, 'the one into the other.' Now, that—"

"Indeed!" Mrs. Elkington-Laud broke in, eager to seize on a point of agreement, however small. "I firmly believe it. But I'm sorry—I interrupted you."

"I was saying that that is so profoundly true. The vote, you see, is only one small aspect (small to *me*) of the entire set of relationships between men and women. I believe those relationships are wrong at their very heart. On the one hand men idolize us, on the other they belittle us, patronize us. To be blunt, they degrade us. That's where Miss Schreiner was so exactly right—the parasite woman is the epitome of their idealization of us, and the prostitute is the very image of their degradation of us. I want in some way to help make our ideas about each other—men and women—less extreme. Why is courage a 'manly' virtue? I want it to become a human virtue. Why is compassion so necessarily 'feminine'? I want us to think of it as human. I want men and women to develop a more equal view of one another, you see. That's the *equality* I shall campaign for. All the other equalities—the vote, political power, employment, rewards—they follow. Or, to put it another way, as long as men believe we are so utterly different from them, then each one of those lesser equalities will have to be fought for piecemeal.''

Mrs. Elkington-Laud caught her first glimpse of the sweep and power of Abigail's vision. Her eyes shone as she drew breath to speak. But Abigail had one more thought to implant. "Even worse," she said, "such a piecemeal fight would be, at heart, irrational. The only rational basis for granting those lesser equalities would be a general acceptance of our equality as 'humans first, male and female second.' And I fear the irrational in us, Mrs. Elkington-Laud. I fear the violence and the passions it brews.''

Mrs. Elkington-Laud could contain her excitement no longer. "Oh, Madame de Bouvier. What a truly inspirational leader you would make. Our critics say we're interested only in feathering our own nests—but so, I think, are they, even the women among them. And I came here believing you to be one of them! Yet you soar above us in the grandeur of your views and put us all to shame. If you cannot join us, would you at least consent to speak to us? Not even the men among us have developed a philosophy so profound. Will you? Please?''

Abigail thought for a moment, not about her acceptance—that was never in doubt—but about ways of using the occasion to the best advantage. "I'm going to suggest something that may be disagreeable to you, Mrs. Elkington-Laud," she said at length. "I shall have to ask you to trust me. For myself, I'm honoured at what you say and I'm delighted to accept. But I would like to bring along a fellow speaker, a friend of mine, a very dear friend, who was once, long ago—a prostitute.''

Mrs. Elkington-Laud's eyes went wide with shock.

Abigail went on. "Before you speak, let me tell you about her and say why I think you ought also to invite Mrs.—ah—'Flanders,' let us call her. Mrs. Flanders is a highly respectable woman who owns a small haberdashery and milliner's in one of London's western suburbs. She has a husband, a good and kindly man—I would say a great man—with a responsible job in the City. He knows all about her past. They have a son of school age who is everything most parents desire in a boy. Yet when I first met Mrs. Flanders, long before she *was* Mrs. Flanders, so let's call her 'Moll,' when I first met Moll, she was just about to embark on her brief career as a prostitute—not that I knew it then, of course, or I'd have prevented her. The point is that I know this woman's entire life story. I know that what she has to tell would be enlightening. You talk of the 'grandeur' of my views. The grandest building in the world would look thin and flat without its shadows. Mrs. Flanders' story forms, if you like, the shadows that throw my ideas into the strongest relief."

"Well . . ." Mrs. Elkington-Laud was still dubious.

"There will be nothing—ah—incandescent in her tale, I assure you. She is a most fastidious and correct woman."

And so it was agreed, though with no great eagerness on the part of Mrs. Elkington-Laud.

Chapter 53

For two weeks Annie held out. She'd die of fright, she said. She'd forgotten it all. What was the point of raking over those dead ashes? Respectable ladies gave her the terrors, always had done. People would find out who this "Mrs. Flanders" was; she'd never be able to hold her head up again. Anyway, she'd never made a public speech in her life.

Abigail was on the point of giving up when Pepe said to her, privately, that underneath it all Annie was quite keen. He was walking her, as usual, up to the cab rank at Victoria.

"The only thing I'm afraid of is that her hatred of men will start bubbling out," Abigail said. "A hint of it would be fine. But stark hatred does put people off so."

Pepe laughed. "Good heavens, there's none of that left in her. That was all years ago. My fear is the opposite—I'm afraid that this speech will bring it all back. She was dreadful with it when we were first married. It kept coming out in all sorts of ways she couldn't help. I wouldn't like to live through that again."

"It's *you*, Pepe," Abigail said suddenly. "You've done that for her—with your goodness and understanding."

"You could say," he answered with a laugh, "that I know what it's like to be her. An ambition achieved!" He became serious again. "But you persist with her, Abbie. She'll agree, I'm sure. And don't be afraid of her getting cold feet at the last minute. I'll make sure to deliver her to the stage door in plenty of time."

"You're a good man, Pepe. I never deserved you," she said. "Nor did you deserve the terrible way I treated you."

"But it's all turned out for the best," he told her cheerfully. "You're happy with Victor—but I doubt you're as happy as Annie, William, and I. She and I have a strange Saturday-and-Sunday marriage, I know. But we're the happiest people alive. So don't talk of 'deserve.' None of us deserves it. Let's just be content we've got it."

*　　*　　*

The day of Abigail's and Annie's speech finally drew round. Annie had been in an agony of indecision—or, to be exact, an agony of multiple decisions—over what to wear. In the end she had agreed to Abigail's suggestion to put on full mourning. "The veil will obscure your face," Abigail pointed out. "Even the people beside you on the platform won't recognize you again. And black is so respectable and so penitent. And besides it always evokes such sympathy!" When Annie said she had no full set of mourning, Abigail brushed the objection aside. "I'll bring mine to the hall. Then anyone who waits to follow out a woman in black will have a long wait indeed!"

It was not a large meeting, by suffragist standards; only a hundred or so women were there. But the press had remembered that the Baronne de Bouvier was once Lady Abigail Stevenson, alias the Abbot, Drucilla Getz, and others who had joined the minor pantheon of journalistic legend, and who had always been good for a quote; the press was there in some strength.

"All set?" Mrs. Elkington-Laud said for the fortieth time, and for the fortieth time she dry-soaped her gloved hands in the air.

Abigail, who had given up replying, nodded and smiled all the little reassurance she could muster. Why did the buzz of a hall full of women sound so angry? The deeper-throated hum of muttering men would, she was sure, be much more soothing. And where was Annie?

Yet again she sent Frances out to the stage door to see if there was any sign of Annie and Pepe. It would be so like Annie to change her mind; but surely Pepe would keep his word. Meanwhile she began to think of things to add to her own speech, to give Annie more time. Frances returned and shook her head.

"I think we'd better begin," Mrs. Elkington-Laud said with a smile. Annie's nonappearance was a matter more of relief to her than of concern.

Abigail agreed; she could do nothing now but hope that Pepe would deliver Annie sometime before her speech was finished. She followed the madam chairman onto the stage.

The sight of a hundred pairs of sharp, bright eyes—all upon her, her clothes, her hair, her walk, her face—was something for which not all her nervousness had prepared her. It was terrifying. There wasn't a woman present with whom she would not gladly have changed lives—and thrown in ten thousand pounds for the inducement. She was their prisoner, the prisoner of their expectations. She sat there hating them, shivering, while Mrs. Elkington-Laud, all calm and confidence, breezed through an introduction that would have flattered Socrates himself.

When Abigail stood to speak she was as curious as anyone there to know what her voice sounded like; and to her astonishment it sounded calm and assured. To be sure, there were little tremblings and catchings of breath at unintended pauses, now and then, but its ringing clarity in no way mirrored the turmoil that still seethed within.

"From Mrs. Elkington-Laud's most flattering introduction," she said, "you must imagine I make it a daily exercise to address large crowds. I assure you this is the first such occasion in my life. And I must tell you, it is a chastening experience to live for—well, I shall admit to thirty-nine years in the closest intimacy with the English language, and then to stand here and to see the entire dictionary and syntax departing quietly by one of the side doors. It is both novel and humiliating!"

There was a laugh at that. Her heart began to slow its manic hammering. She could breathe more deeply. *Come*, she thought, *this isn't so bad.* She continued:

"I fear, madam chairman, that you may inadvertently have given the impression that I am in some ways opposed to suffragism. Far from it, as I hope to show this evening. Indeed, I must begin by confessing a profound gratitude to the movement. Why, only today it has helped me to elucidate a puzzle that has tormented me for—well, thirty-nine years at least."

The laugh again. It relaxed her still further.

"A letter in this morning's papers from a worthy gentleman points out that if women are ever called upon to vote, the exercise of so grave a responsibility will unhinge many delicate minds."

They laughed scornfully.

"Oh, yes. He confidently predicts a doubling or even a trebling of the incidence of neurasthenia." There was laughter again, for "neurasthenia," an imaginary disease attributed to tight lacing and too little exercise, was often imputed to suffragists by their opponents. She added: "I believe he quoted as his authority the late Sir Henry James!"

The laughter rose to a roar. James had been the archenemy of all suffragists in the 1870s; he occupied a special seat of loathing in the demonology of the movement. She had picked well (for, of course, the letter was her own invention).

"Now, all my life I have wondered why such an unearthly hush settles upon the country at every election. Why do groups of silent men stand about the streets with such drawn faces, their brows so pale? Why do our husbands and fathers and brothers refuse their food, preferring to stand long hours at the window, tugging at their beards and muttering strange formulae?"

A titter grew through the hall as the more astute of her listeners began to anticipate her drift.

"Why do they start up in the night, uttering harsh cries of pain, and fall back upon the pillow, wild-eyed and sleepless? I had no idea. Until I read that letter this morning, I was not aware that this demented behaviour was but the merest outward, flickering show of a titanic inner struggle. A struggle so valiantly and uncomplainingly endured by our menfolk out of their deep-seated instinct to protect us. A struggle that only their rugged and manly constitutions can survive. A struggle, in short, with the dreaded toils of . . . forgive me—in this company I must whisper the word: *neurasthenia!*"

It was a very stage whisper. And it was a platform from which her listeners launched a delighted and prolonged roar of laughter.

"And, as I say," she shouted over their laughter, forcing them to stop, "but for the suffragist movement, such a revealing letter would never have been written. But for the suffragist movement, our menfolk would have kept forever secret from us what a hellish torment it is"—she paused and smiled in apparent wonder—"to mark an *X* upon a slip of paper"—she held aloft the first page of her speech—"and drop it . . . in a box!" She let go the paper and, wide-eyed, watched it fall.

From that moment on, they were hers. She let loose several more barbs, all pointed as sharply, at the "antis." Each time her listeners' delight and laughter rose to a new height; and each time she let the laughter draw out a bit longer before she interrupted with her next dart. Finally she let the laughter and applause work itself out entirely. She looked at Frances in the wings; Frances shook her head—still no Annie.

She let the last titters die, the last sighs, the last little clearings of the throat. She looked around with a smile more wistful than satisfied. She waited for a small rustle of bewilderment to begin. Only then did she continue.

"Yes. It's a sad movement that can find no cause for laughter—and a sad world, indeed, that yields none. Yet it *is* a sad world, and it is upon one aspect of that sadness that I wish—no! that I *fear*—I must dwell tonight. Please bear with me."

Now that her wit had won them, she could say the things she could otherwise never have said. "It's a sad world in which people build entirely false pictures of one another—and sadder still when they live their lives in the shadow of that falsehood, never once experiencing the golden radiance of truth. One of the saddest falsehoods of all is the view of womanhood now common, if not universal, among men."

"Hear, hear," came from several parts of the hall.

Abigail held up a finger. "For this let me say I blame womankind every bit as much as I blame the men. We have connived at a falsehood, because it was flattering to us. And now our connivance is proving to be our undoing. We have allowed to go forth a picture of ourselves—a picture, do I say? An *icon*, in which the humanity is barely present while the spirituality is all pervasive. Woman is tender, gentle, and modest. Woman is shy and retiring. Woman is emotional and intuitive. Woman is rudderless without a man. Her natural environment is domestic. Her natural mood is sympathy. Her natural inclination is to sacrifice herself.

"No one can deny that most of these statements are true—they may be true for as long a time as five minutes each week. For the rest of the time we are reassuringly human. Or would be, if we had not made the fatal error of conniving at this iconography. For now when we lapse, we do not lapse into our common humanity; we fall from grace—into the very pit we helped to dig!

"We are not united with men by our and their humanity; we are divided from them by a false—and cruelly false—iconography.

"Yes, cruel. For we are judged, and we judge ourselves, by an impossibly superhuman standard. And when we lapse from it, as lapse we must, into mere humanity, we are called fickle . . . feather-brained . . . selfish . . . petty . . . frivolous . . . *female!* I wish we could adopt a view of ourselves at once more humble and more honest. We are tender, gentle, *and* brusque. We are retiring *and* aggressive. Shy and brash. Emotional and calm. Intuitive in this, logical in that. We love and like, dislike and loathe, men and other women, *and*, for heaven's sake, our own selves! We can be callous. We can feel sympathy. We can be yielding. We can be implacable.

"What man—what honest man—could put his hand on his heart and say that none of those statements also applies to men in general? Is tenderness unknown among them? Is the 'gentle' to be struck from gentle-man? Is modesty no longer on the curriculum at our sons' schools? You may continue the list at your leisure. But you see my point.

"We have this vast and endlessly fascinating reservoir of human strengths and failings. It continually irrigates our characters, men and women alike. Yet we have become so obsessed with the minor variations which separate us that—to judge by the utterances of the more virulent antis *and*, I have to say it, of the more extreme suffragists—you would think we were two different species.

"You may ask the relevance of this to your struggle. It is this: I do not believe we will win the vote as long as the false and cruel icon of woman hangs, as it were, in the hearts and minds of our menfolk. How we may change that icon, I (who have but lately, though after half a lifetime's thought, come to hold these ideas) cannot presume to say. Certainly we must not do it by acting out the opposite, for that would be to replace the spiritual by the devilish—one icon for another. Then indeed we would justify that least worthy of all the sayings of the great and wise Doctor Johnson. We should be like dogs walking on their hind legs, and men would marvel, not that we did it well, but that we did it at all!' "

She deliberately pitched this sentence like an ending, to force their applause. Mrs. Elkington-Laud drew breath to thank her. But Abigail raised a hand for silence. In the corner of her eye she could see Frances, frantically shaking her head. Still no Annie. But she was committed now—emotionally, if not in practice. One way or another she was going to proclaim the point that was her sole reason for coming here tonight.

"You applaud," she said, when they were silent again. "I'm glad. Though it was an easy point to applaud. I told you of truths you already knew well. I showed you how we suffer because men have developed an entirely false and hopelessly idealized picture of us—but you already knew that. I showed you how the counterpart to that idealization by men is a subtle kind of degradation—but you already knew that, too.

"Now I'm going to ask you to do something you will find much more difficult. I have said that somehow we must induce our menfolk to do us the courtesy of seeing us as human beings. Now I am going to suggest that *you* should extend that same courtesy to another group in our society, a group that has also suffered, and suffered cruelly, from false views, generally held—and from a denial of its humanity. I am going to introduce you to one member of that group, though the introduction is superfluous: you already know her well.

"She has brought you tea in your drawing rooms. She has scrubbed your scullery floors. She has served you ribbons at your haberdashers. When you bought your last dress, you did not see her, but hers were the deft fingers that made it so inexpensive. And, in all honesty I must tell you, you have looked briefly into her shame-filled eyes (and looked long away) when you have seen her in all her tawdry finery on the pavements of Piccadilly."

Here there was a sharp, indrawn gasp. But the earlier half of her speech, combined with her blazing sincerity now, gave her enough authority to hold up a hand and say, "In her later years you failed to recognize her, for she was not the human wreck you expected, but a respectable small shopkeeper, happily married, a devoted wife, a fond mother, and a pillar of her local church.

"I asked men to see the humanity in us, and you applauded me. Now I ask you to see the humanity in this person, and I shall applaud you. I said that the vote, and other measures of equality, will not come until men have acquired a truer and more honest picture of womankind. You agreed with that notion. When you have heard this woman's story, ask yourselves if men will *ever* form that honest picture while some women—not you, not me, but some women, some tens of thousands of women—can undergo the sort of life you are about to hear unfolded? Can we achieve recognition of our humanity and still withhold it from such as these? If we can, then what sort of humanity *is* ours—and is it worth the achievement?"

The applause was greater than she had expected. Clearly it did much to ease Mrs. Elkington-Laud's mind, too. Now surely Annie had arrived—she'd had over half an hour of grace. She turned to Frances. But Frances was not there.

What on earth to do now?

As an afterthought—and as a last, desperate play for time—she turned back to the audience and added, "For your peace of mind I should tell you that you will hear nothing tonight that you could not repeat in mixed company to an unmarried grown-up daughter." She looked to one side of the hall. "I'm sorry if that disappoints the gentlemen of the press." She hoped Annie would make it true.

The little joke did much to ease their mood.

"Where is she?" Mrs. Elkington-Laud hissed.

"She must be there by now," Abigail said. "I'll run and see."

She walked off the stage and dashed toward the street door. Frances was there, looking wildly up and down. "Not a sign of her," she said bitterly. "Oh, to let you down like this, Abbie. It's too bad."

"I'm afraid it's rather like her, though," Abigail said. "She has the greatest heart in the world, but . . ."

"What'll you do?"

"Go back and apologize, I suppose."

"Couldn't you at least tell them what she would have said?"

Abigail stared at the girl, openmouthed. "Genius!" she cried. Then, wringing her hands and beginning to pace up and down, she said, "But dare I! Dare I!"

"What?"

Her heart beating like a flail, Abigail said, "Find a cloak. I haven't time to change everything but I'll put on the boots, the skirt, and the veil. I'll put on your navy-blue cloak."

"No!" Frances said, half-fearful, half-delighted. "You'd never be able to do it."

"Just watch!" Abigail said. And she ran back to the stage. An expectant hush fell. "I'm sorry, everyone," she called out. "Your next speaker feels no relish for the story she has to tell. You will understand that she tells it with no sense of pride. Indeed, she is, it seems, terrified—not of telling it to you, but of telling it to you in my presence. So—by your leave." She bowed her head.

While the applause rained down, Abigail said to Mrs. Elkington-Laud, "Have you any news or administrative matters to announce?"

"Always!"

"Now would be a convenient moment for them."

She walked off stage again and then dashed to the cloakroom.

"Please don't," Frances said, though she had everything ready. "If you fail, if they find out, it'll be such a humiliation for you."

"I can't draw back now, Frances. I'm on fire, I tell you. I shan't fail. Have no fear. Oops! Me beads!" She slipped into character as swiftly as she slipped into her black skirt and boots. "Blimey, gel," she said to Frances, "what's that long face for then? Let's have a bit of a laugh, eh! How do I look?"

Frances inspected her minutely. "Well—I don't recognize you."

"I can't hardly see through this veil."

Frances put her hand to her mouth. "I must go outside," she said, shivering with fear, "or I'll be sick."

"Suit yourself, me old love. Just point me the right way."

She felt not the least bit afraid. Not the veil, not her disguise, but Annie's accent and personality made the perfect mask; she understood how an actress who might be terrified of addressing a crowd as herself could go on stage as a character and feel only the faintest stirrings of the butterflies in her stomach. She was a little drunk with the power of her concealment.

She edged onto the stage and stood irresolute. A deathly hush fell. Then a sibilant whispering. Mrs. Elkington-Laud, all brave smiles, beckoned her to the table with encouraging dips of her head. Abigail stood beside her and forced her own hands to tremble. Silence returned.

"I'm not proud of what I'm going to tell you," she began. "I'm not proud of what I had to do. But if any lady here can tell me what I might of done different, then—like Lady Bouvier says, there's ten thousand girls and more want telling."

The veil was a perfect ambush. Through it she could look *at* people. She realized that when she had spoken earlier, as herself, she had not actually looked at any single member of the audience but rather had let her eyes flit over them as over a sea of small waves. Now she looked to see if recognition lighted any eye. None did.

"It's hard to believe I had a happy childhood, but I did. There was ten of us shared one room. My dad was a billposter, which pays about a farthing above portering—and portering often don't pay nothing at all."

Someone giggled and corrected her English. A small, uncomfortable laugh spread among them.

"Yeah," she answered. "Another thing was me governess. She was often away drinking when she should've been teaching me grammar." The laugh that followed this was much more wholehearted.

A movement, about the fifth or sixth row back, caught her eye. It was the sort of movement she was on the lookout for—an excited dart of the body and a whisper in a neighbour's ear as the discovery was made and communicated.

But a moment later it was not fear that moved her. It was terror—stark, numbing terror. The woman who had moved was her sister Winifred. Beside her sat Steamer. And beside him sat their mother.

Abigail's knees jellified. Her innards fell into the perpetual vacuum of her midriff. Her throat went as dry as a ship's biscuit. A violent ague of shivering paralyzed her.

"Have a drink, my dear," Mrs. Elkington-Laud advised.

She raised the tumbler like an alcoholic at his breakfast; water slopped and spilled over the table and all down her cape.

"Take it off, there's a good woman," Mrs. Elkington-Laud advised, standing to assist. "I'm sure it's too cumbersome anyway."

"No!" Abigail said, still in Annie's precise tones. She clutched the cape to her. This real threat to her imposture did more to calm her than the psychic terrors induced by the presence of her family.

"Yeah. Ten in a room," she said. "And often we'd have to take in a lodger to help with the rent. . . ."

And she told them Annie's tale, in Annie's bright words, with Annie's surprise in her voice that it should have happened to her and that she should have survived it. She told it just as she had heard it in those whispered, giggling memories as they had lain in bed in the dark, in Buckingham Street, at the Villa Corot, and in Italy.

She told them of the workhouse and orphanage, of the joy when their father got into work. She made them understand that hers had, indeed, been a happy childhood.

In a curious way she found she soon ceased to be Abigail; that is, she began to think of "Abigail" as another person. She did not become Annie, though, but hovered some undetermined way between the two. Or perhaps she became an amalgam of them—a nameless person inhabited by both. Her story was no longer being assembled in her mind and then passed down to her throat; it welled up from unsuspected sources within. The talk was no longer an intellectual and dramatic exercise; it had become a compulsion.

She told them of her training for domestic service and of her first jobs, of the marvel of eating every day and always having boots on her feet, of the ambition that led her from scullery to upstairs maid in five hard but satisfying years.

And they're still listening, she thought. It was amazing and exhilarating. An audience of rich ladies listening in respectful silence, some visibly moved—and she nothing but an orphanage scullery maid! Of course, it was because of what that Baroness had said first.

She described the many kindnesses she'd been shown, and then—the beginning of her shame. How, in the last great house, she had repaid her employers' generosity. How the young daughter of the house had asked her to tell secrets that no decent young girl should be told. And she had told those secrets.

She gave herself all the excuses: the girl had made her take drink . . . she was commanded to tell . . . it flattered her to think she knew more than the young lady with all her Latin and Greek . . . she was showing off. And then it came to her—the real reason, the one she had forgotten and buried all these years.

"No," she said in a hushed voice that compelled attention. "No excuses. I'll tell you—I wanted to spoil her innocence, as mine had been spoiled. I loved her. I loved my mistress. There's nothing I wouldn't of done for her. But I hated her innocence. I wanted her to know of life what I had always known.

"It was wrong. But I paid for it. Oh, I paid as I believe no woman should be asked to pay for so brief a slip."

Her eyes found the Countess and a hatred inflamed her. Others did wrong too, but they had not been asked to pay.

She told of her dismissal without a character and the impossibility of finding honest and honourable work, of the rotten food she begged in the markets, of sleeping rough and feeling herself hourly slipping from the respectability she had known as an upstairs maid down to the lowest depths. She described her spell as a shirt seamstress and remembered for them the dingy garret, the numb fingers, the smarting eyes, the body that would never leave off aching—and the few shillings a week it brought in. The starvation. The sickness that followed.

Again and again her eyes returned to the Countess; *that woman should pay*, she thought.

"Then they said me dad had died. They said he was buried in the pauper cemetery out in Highgate. It could of been—well, it could of been halfway to Leeds to a starving, sick gel. But somehow I got there. Somehow I gave his grave a last tending before the cross rotted. But it was my undoing, that cemetery. Or was it? That's what I want to ask you. That's what I want to know.

"The only honest work I could get was killing me. In two more months I'd of been dead of honest work. Then here was this gentleman. A kindly, youngish gentleman—a railway engineer, he said he was, soon to be married. He told me what he'd like, and he showed me four and six-pence. I said no, but he said gels like me always say no and we never mean it. That was the first time in me life when I realized I was a 'gel like me.' Afterwards, when he found out I'd never been 'a gel like me' before, he took me back to his rooms in London, and when I left next day I had food inside me and a sovereign in my pocket. A month's earnings for a shirt seamstress."

The Countess was weeping. Other women were dabbing their eyes, too, but the only one who mattered was the Countess; her tears discharged a debt. The woman on the stage was satisfied.

"You may imagine I gave up sewing shirts at once, but I didn't. I was brought back to sickness and starvation again before I took, once more, to being 'a gel like me.' And then it was only the once—until I was starving again. And so I went on, four or five times, only taking to my shame when I could bear the hunger no further.

"But there was no future in it. I could see that. The day would come when I'd be too old to escape starvation in that way. I nearly said 'in that easy way,' but it's not easy. I won't dwell on it, but I'll say this: Walk along any street and pick any dozen gentlemen who look as if they might have a loose guinea about them and then imagine how 'easy' it might be for a woman brought up respectable and religious to come between that man and his gold.

"But I won't pretend it was all disgust, either, though after four years I was glad to hang up all me finery and buy a decent, honest little shop and settle to a respectable life. In those four years I knew the first companionship with refined people. You'd scarce credit the number of gentlemen who paid me—paid me five or ten pounds—to do nothing more than listen to them talk. They'd kick off their boots, lay on the bed, and *talk*. Talk about their work, their wives, their homes, their families. All their fears and disappointments. All their lost hopes. All their dreams. That's all they wanted me for—to listen. And to say I understood.

"The funny thing was, I *did*. I did understand. I used to cry for them at times it was so sad. Sad they couldn't be laying by their own wives, telling them. Confessing where they failed instead of hiding it and then coming and telling the likes of me. But many and many's the man who's said to me, 'You're the only person in the world I can really talk to.' If you ask me, being a man—*having* to be a man—is a terrible burden at times.

"Times was I'd feel guilty at all the affection they gave me when they should of given it their wives. And I didn't want it—what could I do with it? Other times I'd be angry. Why couldn't they get that understanding back home!

"If you want to know, I quit after four years because I'd saved two thousand pounds."

There was a concerted gasp.

"Yeah! 'Course, I'd lived meanwhile, and lived well. I daresay I took three thousand in them four years. Yes—*took*. Not from men, but from their homes and their wives and their families. That's who I really took it from. And what did I give? I thought I gave nothing. To the men as talked, I gave an understanding that was useless. To the rest I gave an imitation that was worse. A nothing—and a nothing. That's what I thought I gave. But I was wrong.

"I gave the most precious thing what I had. I never even knew I had it, and no one knew they'd tooken it off of me. What is it—you tell me—what is it as lets us love? 'Cos that's what I gave in those four years. I didn't miss it—I never knew it was there. But after that I could no more love a man than I could save Margate beach from the tides. I hated them—men.

I could of killed them all. If there'd been a legal day for murder, I'd of worked all twenty-four hours at it.

"So what did I escape from?—one prison to another. It served me right. I should of done the decent, respectable thing and died of starvation like a good, quiet needlewoman. Instead I was set to die in mortal hate. Even if I lived to be a hundred, I'd die in hatred. That's how strong it was. But then I met a man. . . ."

She paused and looked far away. His name was Pepe. She remembered Pepe. . . .

"A man who was as rare . . ."

His infinite tenderness to her. Their gentle, marvellous unity.

"A man who . . ."

Their love!

She broke down and wept, for suddenly she remembered everything.

There was a commotion in the hall. Someone was striding down the centre gangway, but Abigail could see nothing through her tears and through the veil. The person came up onto the stage. An arm went round her. A voice spoke. "All right, me old love?"

It was Annie. Bewilderment stirred her mind. *That* was Annie. Then . . .

"All right, gel?" Annie repeated, concern beginning to edge out the warmth in her voice.

She nodded. Annie drew breath and faced the audience. "I am this gel's sister," she said. Then she laughed—a strained laugh. "You'd never believe it to hear us speak, would you!"

Among the audience it brought the slightest relaxation to a tension that had become intolerable.

"I'll tell you what she was going to say. She was going to say she met a man who *was* a man. A gentleman and a gentle man. You may think it was important that he'd been to Cambridge University, but it wasn't. You may think it important that he owned property and businesses into hundreds of thousands, but it wasn't."

Annie stood with her arm still about Abigail's shoulder. She gave another hug. "Not to her it wasn't. To this day she lives in a house most of you would consider mean. Mean? I tell you that house is her paradise. That's where he courted her—through five, long, patient years. That's where he endured her hate and all the mean tricks it served him. That's where he humiliated himself to teach her to . . . to *love*. Not again. Not to love again. Just to love. For five years he waited, never giving up, always tender, waiting for her to—like—fish inside herself, fish through all that—filth—and find what was still there. 'Cos he knew, see! He knew it was still there.

"The old songs are true: Love is golden. It don't tarnish. And so she found it in the end. No—in the *beginning* . . . the beginning of these last seven years. And she's found it every day since—for seven years. With him. And with their son. Who is, and will be, another man of that same kind.

"What she never told you is this. That man—her life—the marvel and wonder of her life—died. Two days ago. Or yesterday. Yesterday morning. I don't know. It don't hardly matter no more." Her voice trembled. She paused, gave Abigail another hug, half for the support she gained herself, and then, rallying, spoke on into the profound silence that now reigned. "Of *nothing!*" she said. "He just—died. Just died. Of nothing. You may think it cold for her to come out tonight and talk to you like what she did. But *he* wouldn't. He wouldn't have thought so. And nor don't I. It was her . . ." She was not going to be able to finish. ". . . memorial, like. To him." She was crying and speaking at once now. "And we . . . my sister and I . . . beg you . . . to take it as such!"

They stood forlorn upon the stage, clasped together, weeping in a bereavement that was far, far beyond the reach even of the infinite sympathy that welled up toward them.

Chapter 54

It was a large funeral. All his publishing and business friends were there, as were most of his employees and contributors. It took Annie and Abigail the best part of four days to organize, even with the help of an excellent general manager (whom Pepe had appointed in his will to run things until William was of age).

The two women sat dry-eyed through the funeral service, thinking every tear they had was already shed. But at the interment, at that dreadful moment when the dark of the pit engulfs the coffin, and again when the first symbolic shot of earth thunders on its resonant lid, they broke down once more and held each other for comfort.

Afterwards, as they walked slowly back to the carriages, Nora joined them. They were the last to leave. It was a bright winter's day, cold, but full of sunshine. They paused and lingered often, without looking back, both feeling a reluctance to leave Pepe for the last time.

Nora had joined them because she could contain her bewilderment no longer. "How did you know?" she asked Abigail.

"I found some papers of Uncle Walter's, after he died." Then, seeing the pain and fear in her mother's eyes, she added, "But I've destroyed them."

Annie was too inward with herself to care what they were talking about. But Abigail said, "Tell Annie, Mama. Explain it to her."

"Not explain," Nora said. "Apologize." She laughed without humour. "A dusty, rusty word in this mouth, I fear. I must apologize, Annie, and ask you to forgive what was unforgiveable and what no words can adequately make atonement for."

"What are you on about?" Annie asked angrily. Her anger was really fear. Annie always grew afraid when people stepped out of their expected roles. For the Countess to apologize and eat humble pie was as frightening as an earthquake.

"Many years ago—but not so many that I had forgotten it—I, too, was starving and penniless. And I, too . . ." She could not say it. "You heard Abigail tell of a visit to a cemetery and a young gentleman there? Did you hear that part?"

Annie, wide-eyed, nodded.

"That was part of my life. Not yours. She wanted me to acknowledge it and so to acknowledge the wrong I did to you. And she is right."

But Annie did not hear these last words. She had already turned to Abigail and was saying, "You never!"

"I did."

"Well, I call that wicked," Annie said, dropping Abigail's arm and linking instantly with Nora's. "A wicked thing! You done right, my lady."

"I wouldn't do it again, not now, Annie."

"No? Well? Times have changed, eh? Anyway, if you hadn't have done it, I'd never have turned into her sister, would I! And that's all about it."

She linked arms again with Abigail and together they walked out to the coach, where Victor was waiting for them.

Chapter 55

That suffragist meeting was the last of Abigail's public involvements for many months. All that spring and the ensuing summer she devoted to Victor. There could be no pretence between them; he was dying, day by day.

They spent as much time as possible out of doors, for the sun and the fresh air relaxed him more than anything—and there was nothing so good for his heart as that relaxation. She read to him. She listened to his reminiscences. She held his hand. She soothed his pains. And she kept back her grief at his diminishing tenure.

At weekends Annie and William came round and they would all get into the carriage, Frances too, and take a picnic up to the Vale of Health in Hampstead. William was an avid admirer of H. G. Wells and read the whole of *The Time Machine* to them, stretching it as a serial over four picnics. Abigail could never thereafter contemplate the End of the World without seeing the Time Traveller, sitting in his frail craft of brass and ivory, marooned forever on the shores of the deserted ladies-only swimming pool in the Vale of Health. The image carried a pleasing sense of finality.

And when William went off to look for rats or frogs, Annie would match Victor, memory for memory. He loved her stories and borrowed the fire of her vitality on those last sunlit afternoons of his life.

Then, with a golden autumn already upon them, his decline accelerated. With his lungs "waterlogged," even breathing was difficult. To cross the room from bed to chair became a major exercise, and a cause of searing pains that radiated from his chest sometimes to his toes.

One evening she was pouring his draught of digitalis, the only medicine now that could keep his exhausted, overextended heart going. He raised his eyes to hers and said, "None of that tonight, eh?"

She undressed and lay beside him, cradling his failing body without adding the burdens of weight or constriction to its last struggle.

"You know where I want to go," he said.

She nodded, afraid that if she tried to speak the tears would betray her and pass out of her control.

"Did we ever quarrel?" he asked. His voice was little more than a slow, watery whisper. "Or even think one harsh thought?"

She shook her head vigorously.

"Yet we lived for conflict all our lives!"

"Darling!" She whispered it; her throat was too tight for her voice.

"I have loved you."

"Oh, darling!" The tears flowed now. What point was there in stopping them? She rose on an elbow and began kissing his face.

"You will go on with our work."

"Yes . . . yes . . . yes. For you."

"For everyone."

A silence fell. Children's voices rose from the square below. A bee, dying too, buzzed on the window sill. The clock on the landing chimed some half hour.

"You are a rare . . . revolutionary," he whispered, failing fast. "You have done things in the proper order. First practice. Then theory."

Another silence. His feeble fingers tapped her hand.

"I am an old man . . ." he began. A faint but regular tremor—the laughter he could not, or dared not, make—shook him.

She kissed him again and again, then lay whispering into his ear, knowing that while she spoke the last of life slipped from him.

"Goodbye, my darling, and thank you and thank you and thank you for being you and caring so much for me and saving me from the waste and emptiness and . . . and . . . oh, Victor! My love . . . my most precious, my darling, my everlasting love . . ."

An eternity later the clock on the landing chimed the hour.

Chapter 56

She buried him near the spot he had chosen, in the empty quarter of Highgate Cemetery. She, Annie, Frances, and William were the sole mourners, at her request.

She kept reminding herself of the pain from which death had delivered him. She told herself that all the wonder of him still lived in her, and would live there until she joined him in this very place. She remembered the work they had conceived and begun together—and would finish together. He would be there, in every moment of it.

She knew all these things to be true, but her dumbfounded body would give her no peace. Already her eyes pleaded with the sunlit air to part, to enclose and reveal that all-precious shape of him. They searched among the golden, weeping trees for the merest passing shadow that might turn into him. As Frances and William walked quietly away, leaving the two ladies for their moment there alone, she discovered how cruelly the gravel could mimic that most beloved footfall.

Annie touched her arm. She looked around, astonished to see the other two already so far away, almost at the cemetery gate.

But as she turned and began to walk, an amazing lightness, almost a piercing joy, filled her. It was as if his spirit had leaped from the earth and joined her. No longer did she feel so desolately alone. She heaved an enormous sigh, ventilating her whole body, bracing every corner of her.

"He was the most wonderful man who ever lived, Annie," she said. No tears pressed behind her eyelids now. She even managed a smile.

"That's better, gel," Annie said. "We can't none of us weep forever. I bet old Pepe, wherever he is, couldn't never believe the gallons I wept for him."

"I think I'm over the worst already. As long as I have our work . . ."

"That's right. Keep smiling, eh?"

Abigail slipped her arm into Annie's. She was all warmth and reassurance.

"We're both alone, now, Annie," she said. "Two rich widows, who'd give it all just to—" She almost broke down again.

"Now, now. Come along then. We're bound to be alone, love. We're made of tougher stuff than what they are. I always thought that."

"Annie? Come and live with me now. We've got so much to share. Do say yes!"

It was quite unpremeditated. But it was heartfelt. And she knew it was absolutely right. For both of them it was right.

Annie stopped dead and turned, delight and disbelief all over her face. "Straight?" she gasped.

"Straight!"

"You don't know what you're saying, gel."

"I do."

"I got a shocking temper."

"Don't I know it! You've got all your spirit. You'll never lose that, I know."

"What's it to you?"

"I need it, Annie. I'm being selfish."

"Blimey! Who'd ever have thought it'd come to this!" She looked shrewdly at Abigail. "It'll be forever, won't it?"

"It'll be forever, Annie."

"Not afraid?"

"Not afraid."

Annie gave one vast sigh of satisfaction. Her dark eyes sparkled. "All right, gel! Give it a go, eh?"

She took Abigail's arm and together they walked with springing steps down to the waiting carriage.

Then Annie said, "Anyway, I daresay we could all do with a good laugh now and then, me old love."